The Chasm

Book 2.0 of the Finding Humanity Series

Branwen OShea

Sigma Orionis Publishing

First published by Sigma Orionis Publishing 2022.
Copyright © 2022 by Branwen OShea
Cover Art and Illustration by Rai Fiondella

This novel is entirely a work or fiction. The names, characters and incidents portrayed in it are the work of the author's imagination. Any semblence to actual persons, living or dead, events or localities is entirely coincidental.

Identifiers: LCCN 2022905202 (print) | ISBN 978-1-7359159-4-4 (paperback) | ISBN 978-1-7359159-3-7 (ebook)

Publisher's Cataloging-in-Publication Data is available.

First Edition

Sigma Orionis Publishing 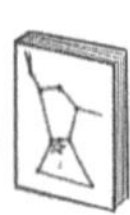

To Bahujnana, Kalakanya, and Vadin for always answering my endless questions.
To Hakan and Mican for endlessly explaining ways that humanity could improve, lol.
And to Nur and Samina for being the best possible people to be stuck in lockdown with.
Without all of you, this book never would have happened.

THE CHASM

Finding Humanity Book 2.0

Branwen OShea

Glossary of Names and Key Terms

(And a bit of fun trivia)

Abdul Zinnas: Northern Havener and Medic for the second expedition to the Surface. Prior to training as a medic, he worked in the eyeless fish farm, and despised the smell of fish. Killed in a cave-in. The first human to be honored with a star being ceremony for the dead.

Ameya: Star being girl killed when Commander Savas attacked Peleguin-Rookery-By-The-Lake.

Awareness: One of the three areas of consciousness all beings possess, and that star beings must develop to Crown: sentience, capability, and awareness. Awareness is the ability to understand your effect on the whole of existence and how to utilize that interconnectedness. Trees rate high in awareness, since they share nutrients with others through their roots and change their growth based on their surroundings to benefit all.

Atsushi Collins: Northern Havener, son of Councilman Seth Collins and Sarabella, brother to Liam. The last frozen embryo from the Surface to be born in Northern Haven. Hobby: spends his free time in the records room investigating ancient Japan and listening to ancient music, especially dance music.

Ayanna Reinier: Northern Havener, daughter to Dr. Cassandra Reinier and Tadwell, younger sister to Bleu. Hobby: Drawing and naming the characters in Northern Haven's murals after famous artists from before the Great Change.

Bahujnana: Star being healer at Peleguin Rookery. Odd fact: He's the only Crowned One in Peleguin Rookery who's bald.

Balavati: One of Rana's best friends. Extremely talkative, and has gotten Rana into trouble more times than either of them can count.

Beam: (see star beam)

Belt: The star being word for the equator, which they avoid. The Crowned Ones sometimes star beam south of the Belt to meet with other star beings.

Bleu Reinier: Northern Havener, son of Dr. Cassandra Reinier and Tadwell, older brother to Ayanna. Bleu is a bit of a social chameleon-he's quite extroverted when with his friend Stamf in the gaming arena, but is truly more of a daydreaming introvert.

Call (Called, Calling): A star being method for telepathically contacting another star being or animal. Sometimes it also designates specific ceremonies used when the contact would be too difficult for an individual to achieve on their own.

Capability: One of the three areas of consciousness all beings possess, and that star beings must develop to Crown: sentience, capability, and awareness. Capability involves all inherent and learned skills. Inherent as in using your body's natural skills, which is different for each body. Learned skills include mind talking, shielding, emotional wellness, and so on.

Cassandra Reinier, Dr.: Northern Havener. Both mother and Mater to Bleu and Ayanna, and married to Tadwell. She runs Northern Haven's Sickness Unit and has no tolerance for politics. Her kids and patients come first.

Cave digger: A bear-sized mammal that resembles a wolverine in shape, but has the markings of an American Badger. Their legendary claws can slice through any known substance. Only known creature that is always hostile to star beings and refuses to have anything to do with them. This behavior is a great mystery to the star beings.

Crowned One: A star being who has reached the final ascendent stage of a star being's life cycle. Crowned ones change physically (white hair, stop aging unless they choose to continue to do so, need less food and sleep) and mentally (more awareness and wisdom, they can Call and mind talk over longer distances, they can star beam to different known locations, and shielding is much stronger.)

Crowning: The nearly instantaneous metamorphosis into a Crowned One that occurs after years of preparation and training.

Dala: Younger brother of Rana, and biological son of Desna and Gandhapalin. He was born after Rana was adopted by his parents, and he's quite close to her and her friends.

Descension Day: Also known as the Descent. This is the day that the chosen people were taken to the secret Haven locations and descended into their new life. This day was marked with world-wide riots that ironically caused so much chaos that it kept attention away from where the chosen were going.

Desna: A star being Crowned One. Maha to Rana and Dala, partner of Gandhapalin. Her special capability is talking to furred ones.

Digga: Cave digger pup rescued by Rana. She's trouble dressed in a fur.

Diggory Girak: Northern Havener Educator married to the love of his life, Josefina. Declared a Deplorable after being blamed for Josefina's death. Member of the third expedition to the Surface and the expedition to

Western Haven. Hobbies include reading horror stories and creating extra science fun for his students in Northern Haven.

Eastern Haven: One of the four subterranean sanctuaries created by SHAST at the start of the new ice age. Exact location classified.

EMF detector: Northern Haven technology. Detects the electromagnetic fields created by electronic technology.

Eka: Star being from Conifers-Greet-Mountain's-Shadow and friend of Tejas, Rana and Kahali. Brother to twin Crowned Ones, Jagrav and Asav, and son of Sara. Haunted by his cousin Gian's strange death (see novella *The Cords That Bind* for the full story). Eka is a talented wood carver and loves to carve stories into useful wooden objects. His special capability seems to be shielding, as he can do it at the level of the Crowned Ones.

Falling stars: Star being expletive.

Feathered one: Star being phrase for bird.

Finned one: Star being phrase for fish.

Furred one: Star being phrase for mammal.

Gandhapalin: Star being Crowned One from Peleguin Rookery. Rana's adopted father, partner of Desna. Generally, he's a quiet guy with a quiet sense of humor.

Gian: Star being from Conifers-Greet-Mountain's-Shadow. Cousin of Eka, and killed under mysterious circumstances (see novella: *The Cords That Bind*).

Girak: (See Diggory Girak)

Great Change: The apocalyptic time period of a few years where the Earth unexpectedly and rapidly entered the new ice age.

Hakan: No information known at this time.

James Bergstrom: A northern Havener who is classmates with Atsushi, Ayanna, and Sera. Son of Councilman Bergstrom.

Josefina Girak: Northern Havener who served as a Science Officer for the second expedition on which she died from an ectopic pregnancy. Married to Diggory Girak. She was known for her fire and wit. During her graduate studies and prior to her marriage to Diggory, she was smitten with younger Savas' passion for going to the Surface and finding the other Havens. She loved children and couldn't wait to start a family with Girak.

Kagni: Star being from Peleguin-Rookery-By-The-Lake. Father to Kahali and partner to Luminary Vadin. Kagni loves to work with leather, cloth, and embroidery, and enjoys making extra colorful clothing for Kahali and anyone else who will enjoy it.

Kahali: Star being from Peleguin-Rookery-By-The-Lake and Rana's best friend. In love with Rana. Fathers are Luminary Vadin and Kagni, and sister is Sohana. Cousin to Kalakanya. Kahali loves everything to do with music and dancing, though his specialty before losing his arm was playing the drums. His special capability is unknown when he embarks on the expedition.

Kalakanya: Star being from Peleguin-Rookery-By-The-Lake and known as the Daughter of Time for her unique capability to read the threads of time.

Kern Savas, Commander: Northern Havener and Council's strategist. Commander and sole survivor of the first expedition to the Surface. Has since led multiple expeditions to the Surface. Pater to Stamf Herrick, but despite knowing this, Savas kept the secret from Stamf and the public until

Stamf's death. He did this to protect Stamf from ever being associated with Savas' mother. Despite his personal vow never to marry and endanger a family as his mother had, Savas fell in love with Josefina during their intense friendship, and never forgave Diggory for marrying her.

Lee Thanh: Northern Havener who runs the holographic Gaming Arena. He is mater and father to Neviah.

Lion Circle: A sacred circle of boulders built near each star being village for ceremonies. Rana often hangs out at the Lion Circle near her village when it's not in use.

Magellan: The flight management computer aboard the helicopters nicknamed Magellan by Neviah. It's computerized global positioning system is based on maps, distances traveled, and speed. This allows the expedition to navigate without satellites.

Maha: Traditional star being title for mother.

Malakut: A grumpy male sea bear that often assists the star beings of Rana's village when they Call for a sea bear.

Mater: Biological mother. Usually one's biological mother raises them, but this is not always the case. *Mother* simply means the woman who raises you in Northern Haven.

Medicci's device: Wrist-worn device designed by Dr. Medicci of Northern Haven.

Mind talk: The star being word for telepathic communication.

ML's (Morning Lights): The system of lighting in Northern Haven. ML's mimic a twenty-four-hour day with a gradual sunrise, a fourteen-hour long bright cycle, and a decrease leading to an eight-hour night. Residents are expected to be quiet and stay in their modules during the eight-hour night, except during holidays.

Nest (The Nest): A large boulder outside Peleguin Rookery that is shaped vaguely like a peleguin nest. It is used as a special meeting place by Rana and Kahali, but known by all the village.

Neviah Thanh: Northern Havener. Team member for the third expedition to the Surface, one of three trained helicopter pilots, and daughter of Lee Thanh. Brilliant, she has always spent much more time engineering gadgets than socializing.

Northern Haven: One of the four subterranean havens established by SHAST at the dawn of the new ice age. Exact location classified.

One In All: The star being concept of an underlying force that connects all life.

Oneness: Star being expletive.

Paternus: Biological father/sperm donor. One's paternus is usually unknown in Northern Haven, unless one has medical access. The man that raises a child is known as their *father*.

Peleguin: A large gray and white bird that gathers annually to raise young. They have a large noisy rookery near Rana's village. Also, a favorite prey of the white lions.

Peleguin-Rookery-By-The-Lake: The closest star being village to Northern Haven. Home of Rana, Kahali, and Kalakanya.

Prime Minister Pridbor: The elected Prime Minister of Northern Haven and Commander Savas' mentor.

Rana: Star being teen who lives in Peleguin Rookery. Adopted by Desna and Gandhapalin and lives with them and their biological son, Dala. Rana's budding capability, evidenced by her connection with Digga, seems to be communicating with animals.

Samasti, Luminary: One of the two elected officials of Peleguin Rookery. The position holds no real power, but rather the responsibility to help the Uncrowned participate fully in the telepathic discussions the Crowned during meetings. They explain and summarize what happened during the telepathic joinings.

Sandor: A full grown male white lion. Lion Master Sandor is the father of Sukti, Rana's friend. Sandor and his family assist the Crowned Ones.

Savas: (See Kern Savas, Commander)

Sentience: One of the three areas of consciousness all beings possess, and that star beings must develop to Crown: sentience, capability, and awareness. Sentience is the ability to differentiate oneself from others. Most of life has this ability, though sometimes star beings lose all sense of themselves in deep meditation.

Sera: One of Ayanna's close friends before she got the Sickness. Also, a classmate of Atsushi and James.

SHAST:
1.Subterranean Haven for the Advancement of Science and Technology. When interventions for global warming went awry creating the new ice age, the world governments came together to create SHAST to save as many people and as much technology as possible. SHAST strove to accept equal numbers of people from all areas of the world, so that each United Peoples' Haven held as near perfect balance of races, ethnicities, religions, and genders as possible. People with inheritable and untreatable health concerns were excluded unless they were a specialist and well past the age of having children. Competition for inclusion was fierce for the limited

spots, and the four massive subterranean havens' locations were highly classified to avoid later plunder by the Undescended left to die on the Surface. The fate of the individual builders and technicians that built the havens is unknown-either they gained admittance to the havens to prevent leaking the location, or they met an untimely end.

2. In Northern Haven, as people dealt with their own survivors' guilt, SHAST evolved into the swear word, *shast*.

Sickness: An illness that starts during adolescence and was unknown to humans before the Descent. It started several generations before Bleu, Ayanna, and their friends were born. Symptoms include confusion, hallucinations, violent outbursts, and eventually death. No known cause or cure. Often occurs in families, but no specific genes have been found to cause it, leaving scientists baffled as the population dwindles.

Sinhika: A full grown white lioness Lion Master. Mother to Sukti and partnered to Lion Master Sandor. She and her family assist the Crowned Ones of Peleguin-Rookery-By-The-Lake.

Sohana: The first star being to Crown that Rana can remember knowing before she Crowned. Sohana is Kahali's older sister, and is the daughter of Luminary Vadin and Kagni. She's also Kalakanya's cousin.

Southern Haven: One of the four subterranean havens established by SHAST at the dawn of the new ice age. Exact location classified.

Spatial Anxiety: Anxiety experienced by Northern Haveners when they first leave the enclosed tunnels of Northern Haven and experience the vast open Surface and endless sky.

Spiral Ceremony: Ceremony held when a star being Crowns. The newly Crowned star being often receives a message from the One In All during the ceremony. During Sohana's Spiral Ceremony she received the Prophecy of the Three Blue's that included the need to contact the humans.

Stamf Herrick: A Northern Havener teen. Bleu's best friend and gaming partner, team member of the second and third expeditions to the Surface, and trained as a helicopter pilot. He was killed when forced off a cliff by attacking cave diggers, though Savas blames Kalakanya for his death. Savas was his paternus, but never told him or others until after his death. Has no siblings. His uncle is Prime Minister Pridbor.

Star beam: Star beings get their name from their ability to instantaneously star beam from one location to another known location. When they travel this way, they disappear in a star-shaped flash of light and reappear in the new location in the same flash of star-shaped light. Only Crowned Ones can do this, and it's fatal for the Uncrowned to do. Eka has nearly died on several occasions from unconsciously attempting to star beam when Rana is in danger. *The Cords That Bind* covers this in more detail.

Star Beings: Mystical humanoid beings that exist on the Surface of the Earth. They evolved from humans, but are a separate species.

Sukti: A young white lioness that is friends with Rana. Daughter of Lion Masters Sandor and Sinhika.

Sunrise sit: Daily pre-dawn meditation of the star beings.

Surface: Northern Haven name for the glacial surface of the Earth after living below ground for centuries.

Tadwell Reinier: Northern Havener engineer who is father to Bleu and Ayanna, paternus to Ayanna, and married to Dr. Cassandra Reinier. Tadwell manages the upkeep of the ventilation shafts and air flow in Northern Haven. He also organized the other parents of teens with the Sickness to demand the Council allow the star beings to treat their kids.

Tejas: Star being from Conifers-Greet-Mountain's-Shadow. Best friend of Eka, and like Eka he is also a wood carver. Tejas is obsessed with feathered ones, and once rescued and raised a bunch of hatchling birds.

Transtemporal scan: A special capability of Kalakanya where she can read the past and future of a particular person. When she reads a person's past or future, that person experiences a strange tickle or tingle on the back of their neck.

Uncrowned: Star beings who have not yet Crowned.

Undescended: The vast portion of humans not chosen by SHAST to descend into one of the four Havens. Before Descension Day, a worldwide group of terrorists took on this name and rallied the world to stop SHAST. This terrorist group vowed to discover the secret SHAST Havens and destroy them.

Vadin, Luminary: One of the two elected officials of Peleguin Rookery. The position holds no real power, but rather the responsibility to help the Uncrowned participate fully in the decisions made by the Crowned. Father to Kahali and Sohana and partner to Kagni.

Valley of Ice: The long, wide valley that runs between two cliffs immediately outside Northern Haven's Surface door. It was named by Commander Savas.

Vincent: Northern Haven agriculturalist who was to be Bleu's new boss before he joined the expedition team. He got drafted into helping Commander Savas guard Rana when she was captured by Northern Haven.

Web of Life: Star being term for all life connected by the One in All. Humans are viewed as part of the Web of Life, but mentally disconnected from it. Cave Diggers are also disconnected from it. All other known beings are connected.

Wedding ink: Matching tattoos married couples in Northern Haven receive on their wedding day. This custom started because of the limited resources. Most couples get tattoos of rings. Diggory and Josefina got matching spirals on their palms because Josefina wanted something different.

Western Haven: One of the four subterranean havens established by SHAST at the dawn of the new ice age. Exact location classified.

Zachary Adelstein: Northern Havener who was one of two Science Officers for the second expedition, after which he wanted nothing more to do with the Surface. His hero, Commander Savas, convinced him to continue to assist with Surface dealings. Zach agreed to go on the expedition to Western Haven.

Epigraph

Dearest Josefina,

I have waited
Forever, it seems,
For the surging waves
To crest me over
Into the tomorrow of myself.

Missing you terribly,
Dig

From the private journal of Diggory Girak

Chapter 1

Peleguin-Rookery-By-The-Lake: Rana of Peleguin Rookery

Rana itched to jump up and leave, but first the sun needed to break the horizon so she could excuse herself from sunrise sit. Every moment she waited, the odds increased that Savas or Zach would be released to participate in the big meeting before she could leave the village. *Come on, sun...*

She didn't want to live with this fear of those humans. It permeated her mind, messing with her ability to meditate. She'd never Crown with this fear. She glanced around at the others, sitting peacefully, eyes closed, chanting. *How can they still do this?*

Finally, the apathetic sun edged over the horizon, and she sprang to her feet.

Digga, her cave digger pup, scratched the ice and growled, eager to romp after being still for so long.

"I agree," Rana replied to her furred friend. "Let's get out of here before the humans wake up."

Rushing through the blissed-out crowd, she swept along like a lone storm cloud in a clear blue sky. She couldn't deal with her elders' reassurances that all was well and as it should be.

Not today. Today felt all wrong. As she wove through the still seated, placid star beings, a wave of concerned looks followed her hasty retreat.

"Rana." A gentle hand grasped her own.

She turned, ready to growl like Digga, but Kahali's mischievous grin did her in.

Never one to let her remain in a bad mood, he spun her in a circle and bowed. "A morning dance, my love—ly friend?" His black hair was tied back neatly as ever despite the dark circles under his twinkling eyes.

Despite herself, she smiled. "Maybe later."

"Want some company? Other than Digga, that is?" His grin failed to completely mask his own unease at today's negotiation between their village and Northern Haven. He was trying, but they'd both experienced how badly humans could mess things up.

She shook her head. When she got this anxious, all she wanted was alone time at the Lion Circle.

"Okay." Disappointment added to the worry etching his face—another thing she blamed on the humans. He glanced toward the guest hut, where the human guests probably still slept. "No finding trouble without me, okay?"

She snorted. "I don't have to. It finds me."

"You and me both." Kahali squeezed her hand. His touch, warm springs and starlit nights, made her reconsider her need to be alone this morning. "Be careful out there. Savas and Zach are being allowed free range today."

She involuntarily shivered. "I know, but they'll still be watching them," she said as much to reassure herself as to reassure him. Savas and Zach had been under constant supervision by the Crowned Ones since their violent attacks, but they'd been limited to separate huts and had been kept away from the Uncrowned.

Kahali frowned. "Yes, but that Savas is a slippery one."

Digga had raced ahead and now turned back to grumble her impatience.

"Don't worry. Without his hunting stick, Savas won't come near Digga, and she's always with me." She gave Kahali a reassuring hug and realized she didn't quite want to let go. She melted into him, inhaling the scent of warm leather that had seeped into his skin by suns of caring for the drumskins.

At her inhale, he gave a slight chuckle. "I'm still available if you want company. No amazing plans have appeared in the last few moments, so I can fit a walk into my morning's schedule."

She laughed and let go. "No, I'm good. I need some time alone. You be careful, too, okay?"

He nodded, his gaze lingering on her.

"Okay, then." She yearned to stay with him, but she didn't need distractions. Clear thinking was required if she were to Crown. Also, she wanted to be out of here before Savas and Zach were escorted out of the village and triumphantly strolled back to Northern Haven. She turned and hurried off through the remaining crowd.

Rana strode eastward over the thawing ground toward the Lion Circle, their sacred stone ring. It was her safe place, her sanctuary when life became a swirling storm cloud of chaos. And if anything made her feel chaotic, humans did. She yearned for the return to normalcy, to the assumption of her people's safety.

"At least we still have these early mornings to ourselves," she grumbled, stomping across the frosted field toward the Lion Circle.

Digga trotted along beside her and grumbled in agreement. Rana sucked in the cold air scented with melting snow and lichen and blew out a long breath. If only her tension over today's negotiation with the Northern Haveners could be blown away that easily.

To be fair, it wasn't just the humans. She hadn't heard from Eka in several suns. His village's Crowned Ones had insisted he return home to address his attempt to star beam, and he'd gotten no word to her since then. She had told him they had to be friends, but friends stay in touch. Kahali would never just disappear on her.

Breathe. Be in the moment. These chaotic emotions are exactly why you're not dating either of them.

The salmon-colored sunrise bestowed a glorious pink glow to the icefield. As she strode farther from the village, she extended her arms, savoring the delightful quiet. With each step across the thawing plain, the Lion Circle's familiar pulse of energy increased as if pulling her in for an embrace.

Arriving at the circle, she sighed and rested her hand on the closest towering stone. The nondescript grayness gave no indication of the massive amount of energy coursing through it. The energy flowed into her fingertips. This land always supported her, always provided a safe, human-free zone. Her tension drained away as she sank down beside the rock. Its icy touch cut right through her cloak and seeped into her spine, lending her strength.

To her left, Digga rumbled in satisfaction as her shoulders and then hips disappeared into her newest tunnel. Someone was having fun.

The sun climbed higher while Rana sat in reverie. To Crown, she'd need to hold this tranquility inside her no matter what the humans did. Once, before they had Called the humans, her village had always been this peaceful.

She closed her eyes, soothed by the distant, rhythmic squawks of the peleguins and the cool morning air. At moments like this, when the visiting humans still slumbered, it was as if the Earth children had never emerged from their deep den.

Above her, a hawk screeched. Her eyes snapped open, alert for intruders. As she scanned the horizon, a sudden prickle hit her spine. She spun, alerted to the nearby shift in energy. Within the circle, a shimmering spirit materialized—a small, raven-haired female. The woman turned about in the middle of the Circle as if searching for something.

"Impossible," Rana whispered.

Heart racing, she stepped backward and glanced around. She couldn't be alone—someone must have activated the Lion Circle. Except for the spirit, she was alone. Her heart quickened. Spirits could use the Lion Circle like a portal, but only after Crowned Ones had opened it for that ceremony. And this female spirit was human.

Rana groaned in frustration. As if their village hadn't been overrun with humans from Northern Haven, now their spirits were entering the Lion Circle? Were these chaotic beings determined to haunt her every waking moment?

The shimmering spirit glided toward a boulder on the far side and pointed at the ground beyond as if she wanted Rana to see something. Knowing Digga could be happily underground for a while, Rana dashed from stone to stone, circling the perimeter, staying as silent as a salt deer. She wasn't about to enter the sacred space when she had no grasp of why it had been activated. Or by whom.

Just to be safe, she stopped one rock away and peered around at the spot the flickering woman was still gesturing toward. At the boulder's base, a slumped figure lay curled up. A solid, real figure. From the size and clothing, it was one of the human men.

Rana inhaled sharply. How *dare* he be in their sacred circle without permission? Fists clenched, she crept forward for a closer inspection.

The ghostly woman waved an arm at Rana, encouraging her to hurry, but the spirit appeared bound by the circle's edge and unable to reach the man herself. Was she warning Rana of his presence or asking Rana to help her contact him?

Rana's mind raced. The man could be asleep or injured. There were only five human guys staying in the village—Atsushi, Girak, Bleu, Zach, and...Commander Savas. That last possibility sent shivers through her, and so she remained where she was, debating this man's identity.

The unconscious figure sat on the ground, curled against the rock, and wore the same orange parka all the humans wore. His hood covered his head and face, leaving no clues as to which male lay before her. The puffy parka and pants camouflaged body shape differences, but this prone figure was too broad to be Atsushi or Bleu.

The spirit's gesticulations for Rana to rouse the man sped up, becoming more desperate. The woman's lips moved as if shouting, but no sound emerged. Then, with a silent sigh, the raven-haired beauty grew still, imploring Rana with dark, soulful eyes. Her eyes reminded Rana of the human girl Ayanna, who had saved her life. The distraught spirit needed her.

Humans always needed her.

Grimacing, Rana tip-toed closer to the recumbent figure. How long could a human be outside at night before they froze to death? On the other side of the rock, the spirit waved her arms and flickered as if she was having trouble staying visible.

It can't be Commander Savas...he's still being watched by Ameya's family. And Zach should be with Sukti's family. Rana took a deep breath to calm her racing heart and leaned over to tap his shoulder, but a shiver trickled down her spine. The memory of Savas' ice blue eyes blazing with hatred made her pause, her hand hovering just shy of making contact.

Beside her, the spirit fell to her knees, begging Rana.

Just then, the man shifted, rolling in his sleep. His hood loosened and revealed his pale white skin, reddened by the cold. Of all the humans she'd met, only Girak had light skin.

Rana sighed with relief. Girak was one of the three humans who'd helped her. He'd been withdrawn since helping Rana reach the safety of her village, but when she'd learned of his wife's recent death, his reclusive behavior had made sense.

She narrowed her gaze at the young spirit woman. Was this the spirit of Girak's wife? And if so, how had the portal opened?

Girak. Girak, wake up. Rana mind talked so he'd understand her and gingerly shook his shoulder. Knowing how reactive humans could be, she had no desire to startle him.

Girak mumbled something incomprehensible and opened puffy, red-rimmed eyes. She reeled backward from the waves of sadness radiating off him.

When he saw Rana, he sat up groggily.

"Where? Oh..." He rubbed his forehead with his palm as if his head pained him, and then he examined his fingers. "They've lost most of their feeling. I could have frozen to death. I'm sorry." He strained to keep his eyes open with one hand still clasped to his forehead. He did not look well. "I couldn't sleep and went for a walk..."

It's not safe to wander around at night. Something hit Rana's chest. A small pebble tumbled to her feet. She glanced up at the desperate spirit. Had she thrown it?

"I'm sorry. I was so upset I didn't even consider my safety. I ended up here, so I sat—"

Rana pointed over his shoulder.

"What?" He looked over his shoulder and gasped.

"Josefina!" He fell over his own boots, landing sprawled, his hand lifted toward the spirit. She grinned and touched his trembling gloved hand. "How? Jos, are you...what?" He made no sense as he clambered to his feet and rushed at her. His arms passed through her as he tried in vain to grasp her. Jos likewise tried to touch Girak, but her hand passed right through his red hair and halfway into his face before she yanked her hand away in confusion.

Girak, she's a spirit. You can't touch each other.

Girak stood, smiling as tears tumbled into his beard. "Jos, I've missed you so much. Can you talk? Are you alright? How is this possible?" The last question gushed out of him as he turned to Rana.

Girak, you're in the Lion Circle. That's not safe for you. She stepped forward and pulled him back as he continued gaping at the spirit.

"No, please. Jos—"

Come outside the circle. She had heard from her friend, Balavati, how Bleu and Neviah had collapsed from standing in the activated Lion Circle. Rana tugged him beyond the circle of boulders. *Stay outside. Otherwise, you might get hurt.*

Girak nodded, his gaze never straying from the spirit's face.

Who is she?

"Josefina." Girak had begun trembling all over. "My wife."

Rana wasn't sure how much his trembling was from exposure and how much was from emotion. She looked over her shoulder, but no one else was nearby. They were probably all at the Gathering Hall. *Girak, did the Crowned Ones activate the Circle?*

"No. Can she leave it?" His breath came in ragged gasps.

Take deep breaths. If you pass out, you won't be able to see her, right?

He nodded, eyes still fixated on his wife as his breathing slowed. "Rana, is she alive again?" The desperation in his voice tore at Rana's chest, reminding her of the first time she had seen her parents' spirits.

Their silent presence had acted more as a knife than a comforting balm. Dead loved ones spoke to you when they appeared at the Lion Circle, but her Uncrowned parents had been mute. The memory still cut deep. She swallowed the lump of grief in her throat and put her hand on Girak's shoulder. *No, she's not alive again. It's her spirit, which never died. She's like...visiting.* How could she explain to a human who didn't even know who the One In All was?

"A ghost? Her soul?" Girak reached past the boulder, trying to interlace his fingers in Josefina's. They both had the same spiral tattoo inked onto their palms.

I think her soul. Not a ghost. If she were lost, she wouldn't come through the Lion Circle. Can you hear her? Sometimes they talk. Rana's eyes stung. *But not always. My parents never did.*

Girak tore his gaze from his wife to stare at Rana. "I thought Desna was your mom and Gandhapalin..."

They adopted me when I was eight.

"Oh, I'm sorry." He sniffed as his gaze bounced from her to the spirit. "They showed up but never talked? What does that mean? I can't hear Jos..."

Desna told me they wanted me to see that they were okay. I still wonder, though, why they wouldn't communicate. Or, more likely couldn't communicate because they'd never Crowned. Rana wiped her eyes. *They don't come anymore.*

"She could fade any minute and I'd never see her again? Can she hear me?"

The spirit nodded, her eyes showering him with their warmth.

"She nodded! Jos, I love you! The baby? Are you both okay?"

You had a baby?

The spirit nodded again and moved her mouth. The love that flowed between them was incredible. So much so, it made Rana reconsider human capabilities.

"I can't hear you. Are you both okay? Is there something I can do? I'm so sorry..."

You let me be me, Josefina responded. *You let me go to the Surface. I will always love you for that.*

"I hear you!"

Rana stiffened. Josefina had mind spoken. A deep anguish inside Rana reawakened and uncurled its darkness. She had consoled herself that her parents hadn't been able to speak because they weren't Crowned.

But this *human* spirit could talk. Which must mean...

They hadn't loved her this much.

The spirit shot a concerned look toward Rana as if she'd overheard the horrendous conclusion she had just reached. *I'm sure they love you tremendously.*

Rana's eyes narrowed. Familiar, hot anger surged through her body all the way to her fingertips. *I just needed them to talk to me.*

Josefina's presence flickered as if she were having trouble remaining present, and she turned to Girak, her brow furrowed in concentration. *My love, our goal...saving the kids of Northern Haven...* Wavering, she reached toward Girak. *You can still save them. Our child will still come to you, in another body, but you must stay alive to receive her. Never go back to Northern Haven. Don't wander around alone like this. And don't let our doctors—*

She faded. The Circle's hum decreased as if it had been deactivated.

"No!" Girak rushed into the Circle.

But she was gone.

"Jos..." He spun, arms outstretched. Seeing the emptiness around him, he fell to the ground, forehead to the ground as he sobbed.

Rana's heart went out to him. The spirits never stayed long enough, and every parting tore at a loved one's already shredded heart.

I'm sorry. She won't come back now. She entered the deactivated Circle and touched his arm.

Girak wept, and each sob reverberated and echoed in the deep, empty caverns of her own heart. Finally, as if wrung dry from his loss, he sat up, wiped his face, and struggled to his feet. Eyes closed, he wobbled as if the ground shifted beneath him.

It's too much energy for you. Come on. She can't come back. The Circle's not activated. She extended her hand, but he remained teetering with his eyes shut. She took his hand and was shocked by the icy coldness seeping through his glove. Holding on, she pulled him outside the Circle.

After a moment, he opened his eyes, stunned.

The energy in the Circle made your friends pass out before. It's too strong for you, I think. We need to get you back and warmed up. I didn't even see you by the stone. If Josefina hadn't shown you to me, you might have frozen to death.

He nodded as his gaze scanned the circle for another miracle. It remained desolate. "It's incredible. What a gift."

After a moment's consideration, Rana nodded. She had never imagined life without the Lion Circle. He still didn't seem to grasp how close he'd been to dying. If he had slept a few more hours, he may have been too cold to walk back. "We need to get you back to your hut."

Girak tilted his head at where Josefina had stood moments before. "What did she mean about our child coming back in another body?"

I don't know. Maybe the soul can be born into another baby?

His blue eyes widened. "That can happen?"

Rana shrugged. *Why not? Nature recycles everything else.*

"Huh." His face scrunched up in thought. "She said not to go back..." He stared longingly in the direction of Northern Haven. "I knew it was a bad idea to leave, but how can I not go back? Where else would I go?"

Rana shrugged. *This is because you helped me escape, isn't it?*

"That was the clincher. They also blame me for Josefina's death. The Council felt I should have forbidden her from going to the Surface because she was pregnant."

Forbid her? Were you the leader of Northern Haven?

Girak laughed. "Far from it. No, they expected me to control her because..." Girak's pale, exhausted face reddened. "Well, this will be another thing about us you don't like: they expected me to control her because I'm her husband."

Rana's lips curled in disgust. *That's—you're right; I don't understand why you humans are so mean to each other.* Rana tilted her head and studied her friend. *So, why did you let her go if you knew you'd get in trouble?*

"It was the right thing...like helping you escape."

Thank the One In All you're different, Girak. She grinned, but it faded as she considered what she would do if she couldn't return home. If Girak hadn't helped her escape, she wouldn't have survived Northern Haven to be able to return home. She owed him her life. *You could stay with us...but you'd want other humans sooner or later. Maybe the other Havens? Let's go ask Desna if we can attend the meeting. You got me back to my village. I can help you find another Haven to live in.* She stiffened. What was she thinking? She had just committed herself to helping him, meaning more time with humans.

More time with Savas. Guns. Chaos.

"What?" He had noticed her panic.

I just committed myself to spending more time around the same people who wanted to cut me open to study me. She tried to laugh it off so he wouldn't feel bad. She wanted to help him. Just not be forced into a long journey with...them.

"Digga," she yelled. "Time to go."

The pup remained out of sight.

She turned back to Girak. *Are you okay to walk back? You're not too chilled?*

He took a few stiff steps. "I seem to be fine," he said, shrugging as if not really sure.

Are your feet frostbitten? Does it hurt to walk?

He stomped his feet. "They're a bit numb, but I'll survive."

"You're really lucky," she said, striding back toward the gathering hall for breakfast, knowing Digga would follow.

"I'm sorry you got stuck in the middle of our mess, Rana." Girak huffed to keep up with her brisk pace.

So am I. But it wasn't his fault. She slowed her stride.

"I won't hold you to your offer. I'll figure something out."

I'm not going to desert you after you risked everything to save my life. I'll survive. She gave a rueful chuckle. *Hopefully.*

Girak glanced over, the slightest hint of humor on his exhausted face. "We're really that bad?"

She bit her lip. *Not you or Atsushi and Ayanna. Ayanna says her brother Bleu is okay, but he's killed so many of us that it's hard to believe her. You're all so reactive, so incomprehensible, that I'm always a bit...careful.*

"Yes, that probably sums us up accurately. But as a past educator, I always like to think we humans can learn." He turned back to the Circle. "Is there a way I can reach Josefina again?"

Maybe if you Crown...

Girak's face fell. Crestfallen, he looked over his shoulder at the empty Lion Circle one last time. "I said we can learn. But we can't become something we're not."

Maybe. You know, back in Northern Haven, before I knew your name, I gave you one. Meeting him had been the one good thing that happened to her in Northern Haven, and between his unexpected kindness and bright hair color, the naming had been a spontaneous act. She grinned, waiting for him to ask what she had named him.

"Really?" He rubbed his beard and made a sour face. "Given how much we annoy you"—he chuckled—"do I dare ask what it was?"

Yes. I named you Pleasantly Surprising. At the shock on his face, her smile grew. *So, Pleasantly Surprising, perhaps you will one day surprise yourself.*

He laughed. "Humans don't Crown. I don't stand a chance."

Neither did either of my parents. So, let's hope I can be pleasantly surprising as well. She'd need all her strength to gain the capabilities she'd need to Crown and survive helping Girak find the other Havens. *Come on, the meeting is going to start soon, and I'm hungry.*

Chapter 2

Peleguin-Rookery-By-The-Lake: Commander Kern Savas

The early morning light filtered through the ice hut's walls, illuminating Savas' prison. He lay in the furs the star beings had provided for him, feigning sleep. Despite his attempted ruse, he was keenly aware that the two nearby murmuring mind readers probably knew he was awake. They had watched his every move since capturing him, always doing so with the insistence that they cared about him. Their "concern" made him want to vomit.

However, as much as he hated their righteous act, their ability to consistently maintain it impressed him. It took a lot to keep that sort of act up for weeks. He of all people knew that. After his mother's murder when he was seven, he'd survived by deceiving the adults around him that he had no memory of what they'd done to her.

The star beings had been so consistent that at times he wondered if he had finally met his match—a whole society of deceivers. He'd been staying with these two star being parents in their cramped ice hut for almost two weeks. Despite the fact that he'd killed their daughter in his attempt to rescue his missing team members, they acted like they wanted to forgive him. As if anyone was *that* forgiving. He still had regular nightmares about the star being Kalakanya dropping his son Stamf to his death off the cliff. He'd never forgive that bitch.

As if in response to his anger, the mother turned to him. *Luminary Vadin will be here shortly to speak with you. Would you like some breakfast first?*

If he had Kalakanya as prisoner, he'd never serve Stamf's murderer breakfast. But since accepting their food was the only way to keep up his strength, he nodded.

"Yes, thank you." He could play the polite game as well.

They'd agreed to release him today to participate in the meeting between the Crowned Ones and Northern Haven officials, but he wasn't going to risk messing up his release by being rude. Instead, he studied her hands. She'd star beam away to get his breakfast, and he hoped this would be the time he figured out the technology.

She chuckled, held out her empty hands, wiggled them, and then disappeared in a flash of light. Moments later, she reappeared with a steaming bowl of some sort of meat and some sort of plant material. Whatever it was, it tasted way better than anything he'd eaten at home. When they'd first fed him, he'd been unsure if the exquisite flavors were an illusion created with their mind control. That unknowing still rankled him.

He ate slowly, partly to fend off the upcoming boredom and partly because he wanted to somehow hide a sample of the food. If he brought a sample back to Northern Haven, they could study it and see if the layers of flavor were real or an illusion of some sort. He needed to know how much of the past two weeks was reality.

The problem was these damn clothes they'd given him that had nowhere to hide the food. They'd said his clothing lacked pockets to prevent him from hiding a weapon. What the hell did they expect him to use as a weapon? Since his capture, nothing remotely useful as a weapon—metal, hard objects, or even sticks—were allowed near him. So why the lack of pockets? Did they fear he'd bludgeon them to death with the small wooden spoon he ate with? Even he wasn't that talented.

A male-sounding star being voice came from outside. The father stood and lifted the woven mat covering the door to let in Luminary Vadin. He held Savas' original expedition clothing in his arms.

As Vadin exchanged a few words and laughter with the parents, Savas stopped eating. He set his bowl beside him, saving the rest of his food to hide later in his parka pocket, hoping they were too distracted by their conversation to read his mind.

Vadin turned to him and smiled as if they were old friends. *I brought these*—he held up the stack of clothing—*in case you'd prefer to return in your own clothes. But you can keep the ones you're wearing. My guess is that you might want to take them back and study them?*

Vadin grinned knowingly, making it clear they all knew he'd been gathering intel the whole time.

Savas chuckled as if he were fine with Vadin's knowing, stood, and grabbed his clothing. He hadn't been trying to particularly hide the fact. Only a fool wouldn't learn as much as possible about their enemy if given the chance. He tossed his clothes on the floor, knelt beside them, and riffled through his belongings. Parka, layers, snow pants, boots, undergarments, socks...he sucked in a quick breath and checked through them again, heart racing.

It wasn't there.

"Something's missing."

Luminary Vadin frowned. *Your weapons were destroyed.*

Savas froze. No. Not his mother's compass. That compass was the only thing he had cared about, other than Stamf. His hands fisted at his side as he stood. "The compass wasn't a weapon." He took a step closer to the tall, white-haired freak. "I told you it was important to me. *Why* would you destroy it?"

Vadin stood his ground. *We destroyed your long and short hunting sticks. Your dagger will be returned outside the village.*

His guns were nothing compared to the compass. That he needed to fulfill...he stopped mid-thought, fearful of Vadin and the parents overhearing. "My compass? Where's my compass? The round, metallic thing on a chain?"

Luminary Vadin nodded. *We could not decipher what that was. When we captured you and removed it, you called it a directional device, but we sense there is more to it. We will not return weapons.*

"It's not a weapon. It was my mo—" He snapped his mouth shut, realizing he'd almost revealed the compass had belonged to his mother.

He began a mental recitation of prime numbers to confuse their mind reading. *One, two, three, five, seven...* If Northern Haven knew he remembered anything about her, he was as good as dead. How had he been so careless? Had these star beings weakened him this much? *...eleven...thirteen...*

Luminary Vadin furrowed his brow. *We don't destroy things we don't understand. Sit with me and explain what the compass is.* The tall man sat in front of him and motioned for Savas to join him.

"Why should I?" He sounded like a petulant child even to himself. Savas hated them for reducing him to this.

Because despite what you think, I am not your enemy.

Luminary Vadin looked over his shoulder to the observing parents. *I know this is your home, but I suspect Kahali is resting at our hut. Could you please lend me your hut so Savas and I may converse in private?*

The parents nodded and left.

Kahali. Savas had heard that name before. It was significant. He'd met the humans or something.

Luminary Vadin gave Savas a pained look. *Kahali is my son, whom your people shot. He lost his arm in the attack. I know you lost your son. Both sides have losses that are too great. Sit down, please. Let me explain.*

Vadin, on a woven mat across from Savas, looked up and waited.

Savas grunted in annoyance and sat opposite Vadin. Stamf's death was *not* the equivalent to Kahali's losing an arm.

I realize it is very hard for you to trust us, but I am only trying to keep our people safe. You came in and hunted our children. You will not get your hunting sticks back. I hope you have learned something, but it is not clear to me that you've taken anything from this experience except the information you've gathered to use against us.

Vadin's amber eyes with their freaky black horizontal pupils stared deeply into Savas' eyes in a way no human could. He felt naked when the Crowned Ones peered into him like this.

Doing his best to ignore the intrusion, he glared back. "I never asked for you to fix me. You took my teammates, and I was attempting to get them back. If you don't like my methods, that's on you. At least I don't try to manipulate others by messing with their minds. That's despicable."

We don't manipulate minds.

"No one that does would admit it." He knew that firsthand.

The Council had completely hidden all evidence of his mother's murder. If he hadn't only been seven, they would have murdered him as well.

Damn it, he'd thought of her again. Nausea swept through Savas, and he swallowed hard against the acid rising in his throat. He continued his ongoing recitation of prime numbers, hoping it confused their attempts to read his thoughts. *Twenty-three, twenty-nine, thirty-one...*

It seems we still have a wide chasm of distrust and misunderstanding to cross between our peoples. Luminary Vadin gave him a sad, concerned look as if Savas were an ignorant fool.

Savas itched to smack that pitying look off his face. Instead, his fists grew so tight that his nails dug into his palms. Still focused on the prime numbers, he began not just reciting them but picturing them in his mind's eye, giving himself something to focus on other than the emotions roiling through him.

The Crowned One remained quiet. Too quiet. His eyes looked strange, and Savas assumed he must be mentally connecting with the others.

After a long while, Luminary Vadin blinked and mind spoke. *You have an exceptionally strong mind, Savas. You would do well to consider expanding it rather than building protective walls around it. You're the only human I've met so far who seems focused on developing such capabilities. It gives me hope, though you seem confused as to the best way to use these skills you've developed.*

"Everyone deserves privacy."

Luminary Vadin tilted his head and considered him with his strange amber eyes. After a moment, he cleared his throat. *Our goal has always been to increase understanding between you and our people, not to create more distress. The other Crowned Ones have just agreed that if the compass is not a weapon, you may have it back. They are bringing it now. You must demonstrate how it works. If I agree it's safe, then you may keep it.*

"It's still intact?" He pressed his hands against his thighs to hide their trembling.

Vadin nodded, still pinning him with that creepy, perceptive look.

He ignored Vadin's intrusive stare. His compass was safe and on its way back to him.

Heaving a massive sigh of relief, he said, "It's not a weapon. I know you don't believe me, but it's a directional device."

A feminine voice from outside called in what Savas suspected was a greeting. Vadin responded from where he still sat cross-legged before Savas.

A moment later another white-haired Crowned One entered with her hand clasped around Savas' compass, its metallic luster sparkling between her fingers. Before Savas was captured, no one other than his mother had ever touched it, and the wrongness of her carrying it infuriated him.

With a nod, she handed Vadin the compass and ducked under the woven door hanging. Savas winced at Vadin's long fingers encircling the compass. How many other star beings had handled and prodded its secrets in the last two weeks?

It took all his willpower not to snatch the glittery golden compass from Vadin. It wasn't true gold, as that would be too soft for something designed to last eons, but the metallic sparkle was beautifully out of place in this damn village of ice, rock, and leather.

Vadin slid closer so they were facing each other, knee to knee. He held the compass in his huge palm. *Don't touch it. Explain to me, so I can use it. If it's safe, you may have it back. No tricks, okay?*

Savas wasn't sure if Vadin meant he'd return the compass without trickery or if Vadin was reminding Savas to not trick him. Either way, Savas would do whatever it took.

"Fine, but I'm going to point." He pointed to the button. "Press that and the front opens."

Vadin gave him a long assessing look, then pressed the button and opened the compass. *We've gotten this far ourselves.*

Savas nodded. He'd be surprised if they hadn't figured out how to use it. In fact, this whole thing felt like a test of some sort, but he was willing to play along.

"Okay, if you turn it until the needle lines up with the symbol for north, then you can read the directions." He shrugged. "That's the only use it has."

That was the truth, at least up here. It had other uses in Northern Haven and symbolic meaning meant to keep SHAST Agents like himself focused.

That's it?

Savas gave a curt nod, but panic roiled inside him. "I told you when you captured me that it has sentimental value. It's a key, connecting me to my family."

"Hmm." Vadin stared deeply into him again. *This isn't connected to operating a weapon?*

"Not unless you consider me a weapon." His laughter rang hollow.

Vadin remained serious, still assessing him. *You are not a weapon, Savas, though you have chosen to act as one in the past. I'm hoping you've learned to see us as fellow beings on this planet, beings that you may someday appreciate.* Vadin snapped the compass closed and handed it back to him.

Savas' hand closed around the familiar shape, his fingers molding to every curve and knick. His whole body relaxed. He'd been so lost without it these past weeks.

"Thank you," he mumbled, and flicked the compass open.

His thumb rubbed the glass above the symbol for north. The center line of the "N" had been dropped a bit on the left to resemble an "H" for Humanity, reminding all SHAST Agents that their first and foremost goal was to ensure that humanity survived by whatever means were necessary.

Savas startled, coming to his senses, and looked up at Luminary Vadin, instinctively restarting his internal chant on prime numbers. After decades of maintaining perfect secrecy, had he just undone everything and undone his oath to humanity?

Perhaps, Vadin said, his mental tone serious, *the real issue is that you're not remembering that we're your descendants. We're human, too.*

The *nerve* to claim being more evolved than humans one day and then conveniently fellow humans the next day blew his mind. It was the same technique the abusive adults had used with him—telling him how wrong his mother's beliefs had been one day and then the next day telling him he'd never had a mother.

He'd never fall for it.

Struggling to regain control of his roiling emotions, he shouted, "You're nothing like humans. You're too tall, your heads are too long, your pupils are horizontal, and you've apparently lost the ability to experience anger."

Why did their damned presence make him feel like a child?

"You're no longer human. This"—he held up the compass—"has nothing to do with you!"

The jerk had no visual reaction at all to his outburst. *I hope your beliefs on that change as you come to see that we are not your enemy.* He had the gall to look saddened. *Don't worry, I wish you no harm. Your secrets about your mother are safe with me.*

Fury electrified him, but terror gripped him as well. Despite his rage, he couldn't move. He'd be killed if Vadin told anyone. If the Council realized he remembered his mother's mission, he'd be promptly executed. Erased.

Savas, I do not understand. Why would your own people kill you?

"You misunderstood."

No, you're panicked because I understand your thoughts correctly. I don't want you to die. I have no reason to take an action that would result in your death.

Savas glared at him. "So, you're going to blackmail me."

Vadin grimaced. *I have no intention of controlling you. Is this compass dangerous to us star beings or the other humans?*

"No." That was completely true.

Then you'll need to trust me to keep your secret.

No, this couldn't be happening. He'd never trust him. The star beings' mind control was even more dangerous than the mind control techniques he'd fought off as a child.

His mind raced, searching for options to trusting Vadin other than killing him—an impossibility without his weapons. His only option was to cooperate and get out of here. With his compass.

Since the damned creature was probably reading his mind now, he went with the truth. "I don't trust anyone."

Vadin gave a soft sigh. *Savas, I'm about to release you to meet up with Zach and return home. We have never shown you any reason to not trust us. I hope you will return and cooperate in the meeting so our people can co-exist in peace.*

"And if I don't, you'll tell them, and I die."

I won't tell them. As long as your past doesn't endanger anyone, it stays private between you and me. You have my word.

Savas scoffed. But if they wanted him dead, they could have killed him anytime during the past two weeks. What was the guy angling for? What motivated these creatures?

If Vadin wanted to blackmail him into cooperation, today's meeting would be the time to do it. But he hadn't made a direct threat about today's meeting. No, this was about something else, a long game, but Savas had no idea what. He'd need to stay alert and prepared for whatever they were planning.

"I suppose your word is as good as it gets," Savas said. "If you want my cooperation in negotiations with Northern Haven, you'll need me alive."

He could do this. He'd played the long con with the Council. He could do it with the star beings as well. He'd do whatever it took to protect humanity.

Pocketing his compass, he forced a smile. "When can I see Zach?"

Chapter 3

Peleguin-Rookery-By-The-Lake: Bleu Reinier

Weaving his way around the star being ice huts, Bleu slipped in the slushy path and had to flail out his arms to stay upright. The movement quickened the throbbing pain from his healing bullet wound. "*Shast,*" he cursed, hoping the star beings beginning their morning activities nearby didn't yet recognize it as a swear.

Despite Northern Haven's recent celebration of the Spring Reigns Festival marking the vernal equinox, the snow melting underfoot surprised him. He'd always imagined the ice age that ravaged the Surface as an endless frozen hell. He'd never expected seasonal changes. As he slipped again, a dark billowing movement to his left caught his eye. It resembled a star being cape caught up in the spring breeze but quickly pulled under control.

Suddenly alert, he ducked around the nearest ice hut and waited for the approaching footsteps, audible only because of the wetness of the slushy path. Someone was shadowing him.

A moment later, the always suspicious Kahali rounded the path and nearly smashed into him. Gasping and holding up his hand in shock, Kahali lurched a few steps backward and then glared at him. *Where are you going?* The guy grimaced, as if annoyed at either Bleu or himself, and then added a half-hearted, *Do you need assistance?*

Bleu heaved an annoyed sigh. The jerk had been following him everywhere lately, just waiting for him to commit some horrible act against the star beings. "I'm not sneaking around plotting nefarious crimes, I'm on my way to see your healer for the bullet I took two weeks ago trying to protect one of the kids."

"Hmm." Kahali glared at him but didn't leave.

"Look, I need to be in good shape for today's meeting, because I'm one of the few humans that can speak in your defense."

We did nothing wrong. We Called you to help you.

Bleu sighed in exasperation. "I know that now, but our Council doesn't. I need this to go well too for my sister and the others with the Sickness. And I don't think either of us wants a war. We need to establish some ground rules, or at least basic communication."

"Hmm," Kahali said, as if not wanting to speak anymore, but then continued to stare him down.

"See you around." Bleu turned, wincing at the pain in his chest, and hurried down the path. The nearly silent footfalls of Kahali followed him through the village all the way to Bahujnana's hut.

Remembering his manners, Bleu paused at the entrance and loudly called, "The One In All brings love," their traditional greeting before entering another's hut. Without turning, he knew Kahali was still behind him. Maybe the fact that Bleu had learned their greeting and was doing his best to follow their customs would earn him some points?

The One In All receives love, came the healer's reply as he pushed aside the woven mat covering his door. His warm smile faded as he eyed Bleu up and down. *I'm glad you came. Come in and lie down on the furs.*

"Thanks," Bleu said and ducked under the mat still held up by Bahujnana. The healer had the same light brown skin as Bleu, a quick smile, and, unlike the other white-haired Crowned Ones, a bald head. Today it was covered with a thin fur hat. His hut smelled of medicines, but not the stringent, acrid smells of Northern Haven's pharmacy. This was a warm scent of oils and plants that reminded him of the agricultural floors of home. Comforted, Bleu lay down on the soft animal skins as Bahujnana knelt beside him with radiant hands.

At the Crowned One's touch, the pain of Bleu's still-healing chest wound melted away, making him gasp in relief and sink deeper into the furs. The glow of Bahujnana's healing hands shone through his closed eyelids. Even though the bullet wound was mostly mended, his chest had been stiff and throbbing with pain since he'd awoken. "I really appreciate you seeing me without an appointment."

Bahujnana laughed a full belly laugh. *I don't make appointments. You need me, you come by, okay?*

The pulsing, healing energy soaked into Bleu's chest and spread throughout his body. His pain evaporated, and his shoulders drooped against the furs he lay on. If only Kahali, who hovered near him, would evaporate like the pain. The guy's lack of trust irritated Bleu to no end.

Kahali, rubbing his shoulder above his new wooden prosthetic arm as if it pained him, took a step closer to Bleu. *So, let me get this straight. In the past moon, you've been attacked by a wolf pack, knocked unconscious when your commander shot the shield enclosing you, shot by your Commander Savas when you saved Shams, run through poisonous gas, and then shot by one of your own hunters when we were stopping the missile? Is that amount of violence normal for you humans?* Kahali glared at him with a combination of horror and awe.

Bleu snorted. "Normal? No. I can't believe I'm still alive." He sat up and stretched his arms, testing his torso's flexibility. The stiffness from the last few days was gone. "Thank you, Bahujnana. That's much better."

We need you to be ready for the meeting, Bleu. You must help your humans understand us. Bahujnana smiled. *Kahali, do you need some healing? How's the arm? The anger? I know you want to attend, but you can't go and remind our new neighbors of all the mistakes they've made.*

Kahali tensed, the muscles of his jaw clenching and unclenching rapid-fire. *Like hunting me? Yeah, wouldn't want to remind them of that.*

Kahali stormed out of Bahujnana's ice hut.

"If he hates me so much, why does he follow me around?"

The healer tilted his head as if impressed with Bleu's skills of observation. *You intrigue him. He wants to hate you, but he is a star being.*

"At the risk of appearing a stupid human, what exactly are you saying?" Defensiveness at being an outdated species flared inside him. Was he insinuating that only lowly humans were capable of hate?

Bahujnana chuckled. *He wants to hate you because hate is easy. But he also, I suspect, sees the greatness in you.*

Bleu scoffed. "Greatness?"

Or maybe he follows to make sure you don't trick us. Bahujnana, apparently amused with himself, laughed wholeheartedly.

Unsure whether he should join in the laughter or was being made fun of, Bleu managed a weak smile. Sometimes, all he wanted was to be back in his own module with his family, where everything made sense. He was sick of trying to figure out when the star beings were serious or joking. Especially the Crowned Ones.

"Well, thanks. I gotta go." Bleu stood and turned, overcome with loneliness. As fascinating as the star beings were, he needed someone he understood. Someone who understood him. Not just another human, but a friend.

He needed Stamf.

Stamf, his best friend who had fallen to his death while Bleu attacked star beings like an idiot. If only he had realized his mistake soon enough, maybe he could have stopped Savas from attacking Kalakanya, and she could have saved Stamf. His best friend, who had never killed anyone, was dead. Now, Bleu had to deal on his own with what he'd done. A horrible spew of guilt and desperate sadness clawed its way up his throat. His eyes stung.

But he was in Bahujnana's hut, a lone human among a sea of star beings. He couldn't lose it. He swallowed hard and forced the pain back into the void deep within him.

As he lifted the woven mat to pass through the Crowned One's door, Bahujnana touched his shoulder. *Bleu, wait. This meeting may put you in a difficult predicament. Commander Savas has not shifted in his attitude as much as we had hoped for, and getting the outcome we all want may demand that your role may be larger than you expect.*

"Huh?" He dropped the flap and turned to face the healer. "I'm sorry, but I'm really tired. What exactly are you saying?"

Your sister, Ayanna, is symptom-free now. I believe she's cured, but I want to keep an eye on her and make sure the symptoms don't return. We need your leaders to cooperate so all of your mother's patients can receive treatment.

"I understand the stakes." If the diplomacy today failed, Ayanna's and the others' lives were at risk. "But your leaders need to address Prime Minister Pridbor and Commander Savas, not me."

You're underestimating yourself. We've noticed how much you've changed. A few weeks ago, you were hunting us, and now I believe you consider us...friends? Bahujnana tilted his head in silent question.

He nodded.

The healer's face broke into a warm grin, and he clasped Bleu's arm. *This brings me joy, my friend.* Bahujnana released his arm and again grew serious. *We need your help getting your leaders to consider such changes. Northern Haven's destructive urges put all star beings at risk, as well as the planet. I know you can help us get along, but you don't seem to believe yourself capable.*

Bleu sighed, exhaustion wearing his patience thin. "Can we just focus on this meeting and coming up with a basic plan to maybe avoid war? Then we can figure out how we can possibly change to become a more harmonious society."

Of course. I'm not expecting us to solve everything at this meeting. But you need to know that we aren't asking the impossible. According to Kalakanya's reading of the time threads, some human societies achieved it in your deep past.

Bleu stifled his groan with a cough to avoid sounding like Commander Savas.

Not missing it, Bahujnana shook his head and gave a soft laugh.

"I already told Kalakanya we'd try. I just don't see how it's possible or how I have any power to create that sort of change. As I said before, you need to talk to Prime Minister Pridbor and the Council." Bleu managed a polite nod and hustled out before Bahujnana put more pressure on him. It wasn't like he had any real power to control the outcome of the meeting. Why did the star beings seem to think he played an important role? He'd say everything he could to defend his new friends, but he'd be an eighteen-year-old nothing arguing against Commander Savas, the Council's strategist. With clenched fists, he strode through the serene star being village. He had no authority, no way to protect Ayanna's access to the star beings and their treatment. Ayanna's health and safety was what mattered to him, not changing a whole society.

"I can't even keep myself safe," he muttered. His own people had tried to kill him multiple times over the last few days. And since he'd helped

Kalakanya and Kahali destroy Northern Haven's nuclear weapons, he certainly wasn't on the Council's good side. If he returned home, he'd probably be declared a Deplorable like Girak.

He had reached the Surface and seen the sky, but now he was stuck up here, away from all he knew. *Stuck up here, away from all...* A strange, prickly electric feeling rose up his spine and smashed into his lower skull. *I'm stuck up here...stuck up here...stuck up here.* The words echoed with increasing vibration, pounding inside his brain like they were knocking open some door that should remain shut.

I'm stuck up here...without her. Bleu had no idea who his mind was talking about, but he began to sweat as he recognized the familiarity of this odd sensation. Another vision. In a desperate attempt to gain control, he searched his memory for when he had heard the words, "I'm stuck up here without her." As he searched, the words thrummed louder and louder. The door exploded, and human faces appeared in his mind, screaming, reaching for each other and being forcibly separated. There was no longer snow or ice around him, only an ancient city from before the Great Change. Unsure who or where he was, he was swallowed by the people's anguish as they were torn from each other. Grasping his head and unable to see anything except the awful images in his head, Bleu stumbled forward, plowing into someone.

"Bleu? What's wrong?" Atsushi, despite being three years younger, protectively led him to a boulder and guided him to sit down.

His heart thumped wildly, and salty sweat dripped down his brow into his eyes. The horrific screams faded, and he blinked in the bright daylight, unable to focus his vision or form words. What was wrong with him?

"Did someone hurt you?" Atsushi said, wrapping his arm around Bleu to keep him from wobbling off the boulder.

Bleu shook his head but immediately realized his mistake. The movement worsened his head's pounding tenfold, and only Atsushi's strength kept him from falling off the rock. "No. I just...I don't know."

Atsushi waited, his dark eyes filled with concern and his arm still on Bleu's back.

Bleu was mortified to be seen in this emotional state. As he lowered his hand from his brow, he was relieved that the dizziness was gone. From his expectant head tilt, Atsushi still anticipated an answer, but Bleu didn't even want to admit to himself that he may have had another vision. He took his time catching his breath, seeking an acceptable explanation.

"Bahujnana, who is like their doctor...he told me he needs more time with Ayanna and the others with the Sickness. If the meeting doesn't go well, the Council will want her and the others to return immediately, and he won't be able to keep helping them. And if the meeting goes *really* badly and the truce doesn't stand, well..." He wasn't willing to voice that possibility. If Northern Haven pushed the star beings to war, the star beings would either remain nonviolent and eventually exhaust their shields and be slaughtered, or they'd turn to violence and destroy Northern Haven. "And then my head got weird, and I bumped into you."

"Stress attack, I bet. It's not like we've been under any pressure, right?" Atsushi grinned. "And don't worry about Ayanna—she's cured." He crossed his arms and nodded confidently.

"I hope so, but what about all the others with the Sickness? And we still need to find the other Havens to enlarge our gene pool and keep from going extinct. We're lost up here. We need the star beings' help."

"Kalakanya said we'd all go to find the Havens. Remember? I'm sure she'll convince them. She's Super Star Being or something, right?"

Bleu grinned at Atsushi's comparison of Kalakanya to a superhero, but Atsushi made a good point. Kalakanya had appeared like a superhero when he and Kahali had accompanied her to stop the nuclear weapon. "Maybe. We should probably find Neviah, Girak, and my mom and get going to the meeting." Northern Haven had agreed to meet the Crowned Ones in the Valley of Ice, probably because it was near the door but not immediately outside it.

"No hurry. Luminary Vadin said if we want, he can star beam us there. That sounds a lot more exciting to me."

"Ugh." Bleu shook his head in distaste. The sensation of evaporating into nothingness and then reappearing, even though instantaneous, freaked him out. "I'm walking. Girak will walk with me."

"You're wrong," Atsushi teased. "When Rana's friends brought us here, Girak *loved* the star beaming. You should have heard him try to explain it scientifically. I'll bet you whatever the dessert is tonight that he'd rather star beam."

Bleu couldn't imagine Girak choosing star beaming over walking. Science or not, Girak wasn't the wild type.

"Okay, it's a bet. Where are the others?" Bleu stood and scanned the pathways between huts for Ayanna, his mom, Girak, and Neviah. Instead, his gaze found Commander Savas and his minion, Zach, lounging under a distant evergreen as if they had every right to wander the village.

Chapter 4

Peleguin-Rookery-By-The-Lake: Bleu Reinier

"Oh, *shast.*" The last people Bleu wanted to see after having a vision were Commander Savas and Zach. How were they out under a tree, free as birds?

"What?" Atsushi sprang up from the boulder and followed Bleu's gaze.

Savas had casually flipped his headpiece back in the day's warmth but still wore his goggles as if trying to look cool. Zach, as always, mimicked his hero, but his goggle strap made his brown curly hair poke out at strange angles. Sandor, the massive white lion with similar powers to the Crowned Ones, sat nearby watching the two men, flicking his tail in amusement.

"Why are they out in the open? I thought they were still under guard, and the Crowned Ones would do a prisoner return or something. Please tell me they're not released and coming with the rest of us." Bleu's stomach knotted as Commander Savas turned, spotted him and Atsushi, and gave them a congenial wave. He bit back a grimace and nodded back.

Atsushi shivered. "Ew. That was quite the friendly wave from someone who tried to kill us only a few days ago." His lips curled upward in sudden mirth. "Maybe Mr. Lion will need a two-course lunch on his way to the meeting?"

Bleu snorted. "If only we could be that lucky. Let's find the others."

They hurried out of Commander Savas' sight toward the hut the star beings had constructed for the visiting humans. As they approached, a mixed crowd—both human and star being—came down the path toward them.

"Bleu!" Ayanna, his kid sister, burst from the group and raced toward him, and then purposely slid on the half-frozen muddy path to stop in front of him.

Laughing, he caught her arm to steady her. "Nice entrance. What's up?" Her enthusiasm for everything new on the Surface matched his own.

"I'm going with you to the meeting to show I'm still doing well. Kalakanya said it would be a good idea. You're stuck with me again." She grinned proudly at Bleu and then flashed Atsushi a flirtatious smile.

"Great..." He attempted a grin, but worry over Ayanna's safety at the meeting won out. Did she still need to avoid over-stimulation to prevent Sickness episodes like she did before? When could he relax and assume she was fully cured? He blew out a deep breath to calm himself. Hopefully, Kalakanya had fully thought through having Ayanna participate.

"Where is Kalakanya, anyways?" he asked. When she was around, everything went smoothly. Plus, she was, well, around.

As Bleu scanned the crowd for his favorite Crowned One, Luminary Vadin approached, his lips curled upward in amused warmth. *She's not coming. She had to go take care of something.*

"Take care of something?" What the *shast* was more important than this?

Luminary Vadin furrowed his brow. *She left us a list of things we need for the journey's success.*

Realizing the luminary had heard his thoughts, Bleu felt his face flush.

"But I—" Bleu winced at his slip, and then fumbled on, "I mean, *we'll* need her there."

Of course, his mom and Neviah had just joined their group, and he looked away, hoping they hadn't noticed his verbal slip. It was embarrassing enough that he liked Kalakanya, he certainly didn't need others noticing his hopeless wish that she'd notice him as well. She probably thought of him like a Neanderthal.

Luminary Vadin's smile deepened. *She also said you would be upset and to tell you to trust her.*

Kalakanya had thought of him specifically and had asked their leader to give him a personal message. His face warmed at that, and he wanted to ask more about why she couldn't make it, but that probably wasn't appropriate. But he really didn't want to face the meeting with Northern Haven without her. *She* had been the one to destroy the weapons, but *he* would be seen as the betrayer. "I don't have a good feeling about this meeting."

Luminary Vadin nodded. *Things often don't go exactly as we envision or wish them to. You might need to compromise on something.*

"Huh? I can't compromise on getting help for my sister and the others with the Sickness." Weren't Crowned Ones supposed to be comforting?

Luminary Vadin chuckled. *The only way to know what will truly happen, Bleu, is to experience the moment. Or in this case, the meeting.* He held out his hand. *Hold on, and we'll all star beam.*

Bleu stayed put. "Don't we have time to walk?" He flipped on his head piece to check the time. Today's warmth allowed him to breathe the air directly. "It's still early. Can't some of us hike there?"

Luminary Vadin glanced at the sun. *If you prefer, but a Crowned One should accompany you. Does anyone else care to walk?* He had turned to address the crowd, which now also included Girak.

No one raised their hand, and Atsushi grinned at having won their bet. "Can't wait till dessert, Bleu. Yum."

"I'll walk with him." Commander Savas strode up, his head held proudly, like he had never done anything wrong.

Bleu's heart raced as he fought to keep his neutral expression.

Luminary Vadin's glance twitched between Bleu and Savas. *Fine. Master Sandor, would you care to join me in walking with them?*

The lion's intense blue eyes seemed lit with amusement as he gazed at Commander Savas and bowed his maned head in agreement. Could lions be amused?

Good. Luminary Vadin, seemingly satisfied, arranged for Desna to star beam the humans to the meeting site.

Ayanna's eyes narrowed at Savas, and her hands fisted at her sides, but Atsushi whispered something to her. A moment later they were both quietly giggling.

If the others are walking, we can wait a bit before star beaming, Desna said to the group gathered around her. *All of you have done it before, right?*

As the others talked with Desna, Bleu stood alone with Luminary Vadin, the massive lion, and the man who had suggested euthanizing the kids with the Sickness.

Queasiness filled Bleu. If only he had agreed to star beam. *Anything* was preferable to walking with Commander Savas.

"Come on, Bleu. It's this way, right?" Commander Savas smiled pleasantly as he motioned with his chin that Bleu should follow him.

Bleu froze, his heart pounding. Commander Savas was taking control, and he wasn't going to have any part of it. *But I have to make this meeting work. Will Northern Haven still see him as the team Commander? Shast, half these people are listening to me think!* His feet refused to follow Savas.

Walk with me, Bleu. Lion Master Sandor had silently approached him and now walked off after Savas.

Bleu blinked, confused momentarily. Hearing the lion mind talk was just too odd, but he recovered and lurched forward to walk alongside the huge beast.

Thank you, Lion Master Sandor. Bleu thought it, hoping the lion master could read his thoughts like Kalakanya had when he was shot and too weak to speak.

The lion, without turning his gaze from Commander Savas, nodded slightly.

Luminary Vadin caught up with them, and they continued strolling through the village in silence. As they passed star beings cleaning skins, carving, and playing about, they all motioned the same blessing Rana had once taught Bleu. Savas only nodded, but Bleu paused and did his best to return the blessing. With both palms to his heart, he simultaneously bowed and swept his open palms from his heart toward the others. The star beings grinned at his attempt, but Savas grunted in annoyance.

They hiked past the playing fields where Savas had shot and nearly killed Bleu. The man who had pulled the trigger on him now casually strolled in front of him. Bleu shivered.

Luminary Vadin stepped closer and put a warm hand on Bleu's shoulder. *Trust your gut. But also, consider forgiveness.*

Bleu felt like a germ under a light scope, studied by the two powerful beings walking on either side of him. Even knowing they supported him,

Bleu still felt his gut squirm. Yet Commander Savas seemed to not care that he was surrounded by such eminence. As much as Bleu despised the man, a sense of awe filled him at the jerk's composed demeanor.

Savas was an untrustworthy, murdering control freak. And yet somehow, he led the way to the meeting, while Bleu trailed behind like a docile child. He had to get it together, or he'd be no help to Ayanna or anyone else.

With each step closer to the arranged meeting location, the tension in his body grew. This meeting would be a disaster. Northern Haven would follow whatever lead Savas took, because he was the Council's strategist. Zach idealized the ass and would never go against his commander. Neviah would work to undermine Savas, but she was too shy to openly challenge him in a meeting. Girak was a Deplorable and had no say. Atsushi and Ayanna were fifteen-year-old kids, and his mother needed to stay on the Council's good side to protect her patients. That left only Bleu.

Commander Savas outranked and outskilled him, but he had to think of something quickly. He couldn't allow Savas to lead his friends into disaster again.

Chapter 5

Between Peleguin-Rookery and Northern Haven: Commander Kern Savas

Commander Savas strode confidently toward the meeting spot with Bleu, Luminary Vadin, and the giant lion freak surrounding him. He knew he was under observation on all levels and anticipated putting on a good show so that Luminary Vadin wouldn't know how thrown he'd been by their earlier interaction. Despite the day's dreary start, it was now warm and sunny, and he sucked in a deep breath of the thousand-scented air.

The wild air invigorated his every step. What a relief to be free from those incessantly grieving star being parents. They had tried to retrain him to be a proper, compassionate human. If they wanted to *pretend* to forgive him for shooting their offspring, then he would *pretend* to accept it. But he would never forgive the beings that had murdered his son. That would be a betrayal to Stamf.

He checked the lion and luminary walking on each side to make sure they focused their concern on Bleu before allowing himself the luxury of his rage.

The memory of Stamf's body, limp at the bottom of the cliff with Kalakanya standing over it, made his fingers twitch with fury inside his gloves. No more humans would die on his watch. He had taken the secret SHAST Agent oath to protect them, even if they hated him and his methods for ensuring human survival. He was a man of his word, and he *would* finish the task SHAST and his mother had set before him.

As he walked, he puzzled over how to make this meeting achieve his goal of installing an armed fort on the Surface, manned with his own men. He would need to find the other Havens and get more humans. Fresh blood to spice up Northern Haven's limited gene pool and give him more able bodies to man his fort. The star beings seemed willing to help them find the other havens. He wasn't clear on their motives yet, but if he could gain some leverage over them and figure out how to keep them from constantly reading his mind, he might be able to use them as allies. He tucked that snippet of a thought deep in his mind and began humming to himself, hoping to block his thoughts from his watchers.

"Bleu, get up here. We humans must confer before the meeting." As always, he spoke to his man without as much as a turn of his head. Bleu would come. He was ultimately a peacekeeper. And a star being lover.

"Confer, sir?"

Commander Savas grinned at Bleu's use of "sir." He had him. "Yes, *confer*. Get up here now!" *What have they already told him in mind speak?*

Bleu sighed and jogged up. "You realize they know everything you say, right?"

"Of course, Bleu. I've lived with them, remember? By the way, that bullet was not meant for you."

"Is that an apology?" Bleu looked at him dubiously.

"You jumped in the way. I was not meaning to hit you."

"Okay...but you meant to shoot a kid."

He tried not to wince. That had not been one of his finer moments, but how was he to know from a distance that it was only a kid? "This is a peace negotiation, Bleu. Let bygones be bygones."

Bleu stopped in his tracks. "You shot me."

"You need to forgive. Our lovely hosts have been teaching me a lot about the power of forgiveness. Haven't they forgiven you? How many of them have you killed?"

Bleu paled and looked down.

"Exactly. Now if this meeting has any chance of working, we all need to forgive." Even speaking of forgiveness curdled his stomach, but he maintained his smile. He needed Bleu on his side. The kid's ability to kill as many star beings as he had managed to during their first confrontation demonstrated his potential. "The star beings clearly have the ability to help us reach the other Havens, and you and I are two of the better trained individuals, and we should work together to help Northern Haven, agreed?"

"I guess..."

"Good, we're going to this meeting in agreement. Thank you, Bleu. You're a good team member. I'm sorry I ever doubted you." With Bleu, Zach, and Neviah, he still had three trained team members for the mission. Now he just needed to gain some leverage over the star beings.

Chapter 6

On the Surface: Bleu Reinier

Bleu bit his inner cheek in frustration at how completely Savas had dominated their conversation, and dropped back a few steps to keep pace with Luminary Vadin and Sandor. His lack of ability in standing up to the jerk left his stomach queasy. *Did I just agree to work with him?* He'd meant he wanted to help Northern Haven, but judging by Savas' gloating grin, he thought Bleu was now another minion like Zach.

He shuddered and avoided his companions' gazes by pretending to be interested in the upcoming nests of the large, threatening gray-and-white birds. As they neared the rookery, a slightly sour smell curled Bleu's nose hairs, making him grimace.

Avoid stepping too near the nests, Luminary Vadin said, encircling them in a shield. *Peleguins are not forgiving.*

Bleu remained inside the shield but as far from Commander Savas as he could. How dare Savas expect Bleu simply to forgive him? He'd be dead if Kalakanya hadn't been there and done her wild healing thing. His emotions whirled like a tornado, whipping themselves into a frenzy. To top it all, Luminary Vadin and Sandor the Lion flanked him, probably observing his mental chaos.

Passing the rookery, they began descending the steep, boulder-strewn hill to the vast ice field beyond. A few scraggly trees stood like bent, weary soldiers battling the wintry forces. As he passed a particularly bowed one, he grimaced. Would he end up like that, bent to Commander Savas' will?

Halfway down the last steep hill, Bleu stopped and scanned the ice field. The meeting space lay just beyond the small rise at the end of the field. He could just make out the reflective glare of sunlight off metal as a snow rover approached. The representatives from Northern Haven awaited them. He yearned for friendly human allies, and a wave of grief for Stamf threatened to overwhelm him. Again, he squelched it.

The sun's glare off the flat field nearly blinded him. Savas pulled on his goggles, and Bleu reached for his, but then reconsidered. Would that look like he was following Savas' example?

Savas turned and grinned at him. "Put on your goggles, Bleu. We're not like them." He motioned to Luminary Vadin and Lion Master Sander.

Now he's giving me orders? Bleu fumed, torn between taking care of his eyes and appearing weak.

"Look, Bleu, I know I offended you, but you were my son's best friend. I'm looking out for you. Wouldn't Stamf want that?"

Bleu glared at Savas, unsure whether or not the man spoke truthfully. It had been a shock to learn his best friend was Savas' son, but they did both love hunting and women, and sort of had the same jawline. When Girak had shared Savas' revelation, Bleu had somehow known Savas hadn't lied.

But the jerk had never cut Bleu any breaks before, and Savas certainly hadn't interceded when Stamf had begged to have Bleu released from quarantine and returned to the expedition team.

Bleu's eyes started to tear from the brightness of the sun on the ice. With a growl, he retrieved his goggles from his pocket and continued following the tireless Savas. Even though Savas walked in front of him, Bleu had no doubt the ass was grinning at his complying to wear goggles.

Sandor huffed. *He's testing you, Bleu, like a predator tests a herd of salt deer, pressing them to find their weak spots. So far, he's gotten you to agree to help Northern Haven and put on your goggles, simple things that make sense, but by establishing himself as the speaker of the obvious, he hopes to reel you in and establish dominance. It's a game. You will need to learn to recognize his manipulations to protect yourself and your friends.*

Bleu gave a tight nod. Standing up to the Council's strategist seemed way beyond his agriculturist-wannabe skill set.

As they topped a slight hill, he made out a shiny snow rover and three separate orange-clad men, who stood surrounding a brown-clad individual. If they were making different parkas than the standard issue orange, who wore the special brown one? His stomach churned. Surely the prime minister hadn't come?

As they paced closer, he strained to identify the four individuals, but despite the day's warmth, all four Northern Haveners wore their hoods. Realistically, it didn't matter who stood there. He couldn't imagine anyone left inside Northern Haven would have an open mind for today's meeting, except his father. But his father's crucial engineering skills kept Northern Haven's air shafts functioning. He'd never be allowed to leave.

They stopped ten meters from the Northern Haveners. Bleu nodded and smiled at the hooded humans, but they gave no response. He squirmed inside, unsure if he should further greet his fellow humans or continue standing with the star beings. Who, exactly, was he representing?

A bright flash occurred to his right, and he lurched aside before recognizing the others star beaming in. Luminary Vadin caught his arm, steadying him on the icy ground. The clicks of readying guns echoed across the frozen field. Bleu froze, expecting the worst. Luminary Vadin still held onto Bleu's arm, and the powerful crackle of the quiet Luminary's withheld energy prickled against Bleu's forearm.

He and the star beings stood still, facing the raised guns. Northern Haven's new recruits couldn't have received much training, but at this close range, Bleu and the others were easy targets. His insides quivered.

Savas, standing on his left, only chuckled. "Okay, men. Let's not waste the ammunition."

The Northern Haveners glanced at the brown-clad figure in the middle of their cluster but didn't lower their guns.

Bleu marveled at their restraint. It was too easy to blast away at star beings and ask questions later. He of all people knew that.

Each side sized up the other. Northern Haven held all the weapons, and three more people had climbed out of the snow rover, making a total of seven guns now pointed at Bleu and his friends. Three Crowned Ones—Luminary Samasti, Desna, and Bahujnana—stepped out in front, assumedly to shield if necessary. The only sounds were the shifting of feet on ice and the distant screeches of peleguins.

Commander Savas broke the stillness by waving and striding over to the four Northern Haveners. "We've returned safely." He made it sound like his life had been in mortal danger, not that he had attacked a bunch of unarmed children. "Let's get started."

The man in brown greeted him with a nod and then clasped his shoulder. Bleu's eyes narrowed. So, he was still a Commander. As the two men turned their backs to the others in a momentary private conference, the brown-clad individual handed Savas a small gun. Not a good sign. As if on cue, the other armed Northern Haveners stepped around Savas and the man in the brown parka, completely concealing them from sight. That couldn't be good.

Bleu quickly turned to see how his fellow humans from the village would react. His mom, Ayanna, Neviah, and Girak stood their ground beside Rana and Kahali. No one moved to follow Savas except Zach, who held out his hands as if surrendering and stepped around the star beings and into the open field.

"Don't shoot, guys. I'm on your side," Zach said, scurrying across the icy middle of the field to the Northern Haveners.

Bleu growled and strained to see around the man-made shield, his suspicion growing.

It's to be expected, Bleu. It's his home. We half expected you all to hurry back, Vadin said.

"Nope," Bleu whispered, surprised himself that his remaining human friends still stayed put. Why were they all staying on this side? They were standing with the star beings, the Undescended, the sworn enemies of SHAST.

Moments passed with the guns still aimed at the star beings, and the Crowned Ones nearly bursting with energy. Commander Savas' laughter rang out, and the guards parted for him and the brown-clad leader as they moved to the front of the group. Despite the leader's goggles, his light brown skin, aquiline nose, and thin-lipped sneer were immediately recognizable.

"Greetings, star beings! I am Seth Collins, representative for Prime Minister Pridbor. And these four are my security detail to make sure I return safely."

"Dad?" Atsushi's shocked whisper carried across the open field to Bleu's ears.

Luminary Vadin furrowed his brow. *You are in no danger from us. I thought Bleu and Kalakanya had clarified that. Please, put your hunting sticks away.*

"Forgive my human insecurities, but I feel freer to talk knowing I am protected from any further *accidents.*"

Bleu! What are they doing? Their thoughts are completely blocked. I can't understand what he is saying. Luminary Vadin mind spoke privately to him.

Bleu widened his eyes. He studied the Northern Haveners for anything different, wondering what had happened since he left. It had only been a few weeks... *I don't know. Want me to translate?*

Tell them we cannot understand their language. Ask them why, please.

Heart racing, Bleu stepped forward and cleared his throat. "Luminary Vadin can't understand you. He would like to know why."

Commander Savas smirked as Atsushi's father declared, "Good, now the playing fields are equal. No more mind reading. It is extremely poor manners and bad form for establishing diplomacy. Where is Neviah?" He took a step sideways, looking for her.

"Sir?" Neviah raised her hand but remained where she stood. Atsushi leaned over to whisper to her, his eyes never leaving his father.

"Neviah, come here and translate. Repeat what I say. He will understand you."

"Um, okay. Sir." Her tone gave no indication that she was okay being used as a translator.

With an apologetic glance toward Crowned Ones, she stepped past them. She stomped over the cold, empty ice field toward Seth. As she walked, she unhooked her headpiece completely and tossed it back over her shoulder, where it hung like an unnecessary appendage.

If she had meant it to spurn the men hiding behind their hoods, it had the opposite effect. She looked shorter and unprotected. Vulnerable.

Her uneasy glance traveled between the two groups. Bleu shot her what he hoped was an encouraging smile. Wringing her gloved hands, she repeated loudly what Collins had stated.

Luminaries Vadin and Samasti both took simultaneous inhalations of horror, though their expressions remained neutral. Too neutral. Bleu watched them, suspecting they were communing privately. Were all the Crowned Ones connecting?

I am sorry you feel it is necessary to block yourself from the One In All. It was our understanding that you have requested our help healing your children and finding the other Havens. Is that not true? Neviah, can he understand me? Luminary Vadin tilted his head toward Neviah.

Neviah turned toward Seth, who grinned wickedly and nodded to the gathered crowd. "Yes, he can."

The four Crowned Ones seemed baffled by this and did not hide it well. Bleu knew star beings understood the thoughts behind human words, not actual human language. Not yet, though he'd seen signs that they were learning it. But now suddenly Savas' and Seth's thoughts were blocked, while the two guys could still receive the star beings' mind speak? How could that be possible? Bleu inwardly groaned. If this meeting didn't go well, Ayanna and the others were screwed.

"We would like your help but refuse your attempts to control us. We are not star beings. We will carry weapons, and you cannot abuse your psychic gifts, or we will respond with our own *gifts*." He lifted his own rifle at the last word. "This is, ultimately *our* planet." Seth spoke, and a mortified Neviah translated.

The planet belongs to all of its beings, not just humans. We want to help you be safe and heal and find your friends. Luminary Vadin glowed slightly as he spoke.

His glow was oddly familiar. Bleu smiled, both from the peaceful energy wafting off him and the memory of when he had first met Kalakanya. She had done a similar thing when Neviah and he were first captured and had panicked. His heart swelled for his new friends and their boundless compassion that extended even now to the humans pointing guns at them. Sudden clarity of where he stood in this meeting flooded over him.

Had his fellow Northern Haveners noticed what Luminary Vadin was doing? Savas stood stiffly, eyes narrowed as he studied the glowing Luminary Vadin. Seth Collins softened his shoulders but then suddenly stood erect. He barked something to his armed guard. Despite his command, the armed men wilted and lowered their weapons.

"Neviah, tell them to cease their pathetic attempts to manipulate us. We are here to communicate openly, not to suffer being brainwashed."

Neviah grimaced as she repeated Seth's words.

He can see you glowing. Bleu attempted to mind talk just to Luminary Vadin.

Vadin glanced at Bleu. *Can't be helped.*

Desna stepped forward. *We never control; we cooperate.* She smiled. *Perhaps your doctor, Cass, could clarify that we have been working nonstop to determine the cause of the Sickness your youth suffer. Cass?*

"Of course." Bleu's mother donned the steely professional smile she reserved for politicians as she stepped around him and took her place beside the front Crowned Ones. "Their healing is unlike anything I've ever seen. They believe that the cause is related to the polar shift that occurred, as verified by Zach and Josefina on the Second Expedition. Both the magnetic North and South Poles have moved dramatically, affecting everything on the planet.

"We were always just searching the body for a cause, not the electromagnetic field that each of our bodies generates. Our individual magnetic fields exist within the Earth's fields, and when the poles shifted, it affected us all in some way. Some of us have more sensitive fields. That part may be genetic, but that needs continued research. But during the hormonal changes of puberty, individuals with sensitive magnetic fields are greatly thrown off, and various systems begin malfunctioning. In a few days, the star beings have surpassed decades of our research." Her eyes glittered with excitement. Bleu grinned at her endless, bubbling passion, despite the life-threatening rifles pointed at them.

"Are they teaching you how to heal it, as Kalakanya promised? Or are they creating a dependency? We need to be able to treat our own youth, as I'm sure you are aware, Dr. Reinier." Seth Collins seemed to have studied with Prime Minister Pridbor, for he too managed to look down at the star beings who towered above him.

Bleu's fists clenched. They expected too much too soon. Bahujnana had worked ceaselessly beside his mother. In just two weeks, the star beings had found the issue, healed many of the teens with the Sickness, and managed to translate what they had discovered into terms his mother could now work with.

"I do not know if I can learn their methods. But as they explain their theories, I can see the possibilities for medical interventions." His mother's voice remained strong, unaffected by Councilman Collins' attitude.

"Good. You must return with us and record your observations with Dr. Medicci."

"I am the lead investigator on the Sickness, and as such"—her eyes flashed with ferocity—"of course I will share my findings."

"Good. I'm glad that's settled. You will return with us now."

"Now? No, there's too much more to learn."

"The Council ordered you to return immediately. Are you going to ignore their direct order?"

"Of course not," she retorted.

Bleu almost pitied the Councilmen. They would get an earful from her.

"Good." Councilman Collins turned toward Neviah. "Commander Savas will be leading the next expedition to the lost Havens, and we need to know if the Luminaries would lend us star beings with pertinent information or skills to assist him."

Lend us? As if the star beings were things, not individuals?

At Neviah's translation, all the star beings stiffened in unison, as if an electric current had rippled through them. Kahali let out a sharp hiss that carried across the field like a whip.

Luminary Samasti recovered first. *We can certainly provide assistance, but we will not accompany you under the command of Savas. We believe he has more learning to do before he is capable of making wise decisions. Please understand, Savas, that we do not mean this as a personal insult.*

Savas chuckled, a sardonic smile curling his lips. "There was never a need or expectation for you to accompany us. You can simply share your elevated wisdom, and we will be on our way."

Luminary Vadin seemed unmoved as Savas' words were translated. *As you may or may not be aware, one of our Crowned Ones has the ability to see future events. If you proceed on your own, your mission will fail, resulting in the deaths of all going and the loss of the helicopters you so value.* He paused as if to let that sink in. *We want you to be successful and are willing to accompany you, which does make your safe return more likely. But we will not go under any command. We are free beings. Furthermore, if you insist on going alone, we advise our human friends*—here he turned and looked at Bleu, Ayanna, Neviah, Atsushi, Girak, Cass, and then across to Zach—*not to shorten their lives by going with you.*

Bleu inhaled sharply, his heart racing. *Resulting in the deaths of all going? Kalakanya saw us die?* He had no doubt of her power, but how then could they fulfil their desperate mission to find the other havens?

He didn't need to be a star being to feel the crackle of fear this fatalistic statement created in himself and the others. Everyone stood in silence, considering Vadin's words.

Savas stepped forward, his fingers tapping his rifle as he approached. "Why should we believe your Crowned One? This could be an attempt to gain the location of the other human havens."

At Neviah's translation, Luminary Samasti chuckled. *I am not sure why you believe we would seek their location. We have enough trouble communicating with one group of you.*

Savas grunted loudly enough for it to carry across the field. "How do we know she is accurate?"

Because she foresaw your doubt of that, and said when you questioned her abilities, I should tell you that she also foresaw your new wrist band. Did you during this meeting somehow receive a gift of a new wrist band? Luminary Samasti's tone remained warm, but her confident motion toward his wrist left no doubt that she already knew his answer.

As Luminary Samasti spoke, Savas' right hand had moved to protectively cover where his left glove met his parka sleeve. *Busted,* Bleu thought.

"My actions are of no matter to you." Savas shifted his lower jaw side to side as if chewing this new information. "What advantage would your presence bring? Other than not all supposedly perishing a terrible death." Savas smirked.

We can begin teaching you how to survive in alignment with the environment. Bleu shared that you have lost many humans since emerging from Northern Haven.

"I wonder how much else Bleu has shared. I assume you have picked all their brains about us the last few days?" Seth didn't bother to hide the disgust in his voice.

We have done nothing that was not in your best interest. We want you to be successful.

Savas snorted and yanked off his goggles. "If you come, you will need to share your knowledge and healing, fly in our helicopters, and listen to the commander, which will be me. *Those* are the conditions." He glared at Luminary Vadin.

This was not going well. Luminary Samasti had already made it clear they would not go under Savas' control. Bleu's heart pounded out a warning. He had to keep this truce in place. If the last few days had taught him anything, it was how much they needed the star beings for their healing and knowledge of survival on the Surface.

Bleu took a step forward. "Excuse, me, sir. But I'm confused. Who will you command? I for one do not want to go if it is certain death. Have more been trained for an expedition in the last few weeks, or am I the only one of us from the last expedition that's concerned by this warning?"

Bleu turned and looked at Girak, Atsushi, and Neviah and then back across the open space that lay like a chasm between the two groups. As his gaze focused questioningly on Zach, the guy looked frantically between the Crowned One who had verbalized his doom and his beloved Savas. His indecision sickened Bleu.

Bleu turned back to his human friends. "Am I the only one who's concerned about going without the star beings' help?"

His closest of friends squirmed under his gaze, shifting from foot to foot on the crunchy ice and glancing at each other. His heart sank. Were they second-guessing themselves for believing and trusting the Undescended? Bleu held his breath, waiting for them to traipse across the snow to join Savas.

Girak suddenly stood taller and shook his head at Bleu, indicating Bleu was not the only one concerned. Neviah took a hesitant step closer to the star beings, as if expecting backlash from Savas. Ayanna and his mother stayed put next to Rana and Kahali.

Luminary Vadin said, *Perhaps there is a compromise? Our people are loathe to fly in your machines. Perhaps we could beam to where you will be landing?*

Bleu gave Vadin a sidelong glance. Why was he sidestepping the leadership issue? The Luminary's stern expression yielded no clues to his game plan. If he had one.

"I am not willing to give you the locations. You will fly with us or not come." Savas seemed okay with avoiding the leadership crisis for the moment.

A compromise then. We will risk your machines, but we will require a more neutral leader. You seem to trust Neviah. We will follow her lead.

Neviah's eyebrows shot up. Seth barked in laughter, and Savas smirked and shook his head.

"A woman? Please, be real." Seth's cruel voice rang out.

Neviah looked down so that her dark hair hid her face as the men continued laughing. Then she looked up, face flushed with anger and eyes flashing. She spun to face her attackers. "I nominate Bleu."

Chapter 7

On the Surface: Bleu Reinier

"What?" Bleu recoiled at Neviah's suggestion that he lead the expedition. Surely, she was joking. He couldn't lead; he was only eighteen and had no experience that remotely qualified him as a leader.

What we expected. The two Luminaries glanced at him, smiles tugging at their lips. Bleu sensed no one else had heard them.

You planned this? His mind raced over the last few days. The Crowned Ones had come to him several times with their concerns. He sucked in the frigid air, trying to calm the panic building in his chest.

"Bleu is only eighteen. He's not old enough to lead." Savas regarded him with a hunger that sent a shiver up Bleu's spine.

"He is the only human to have completed a solo mission to the Surface, and he successfully brought back the Second Expedition." Atsushi flashed Bleu a quick grin and then turned to Savas. "I'd follow him."

"Atsushi!" Councilman Collins glared at his son. "Don't you *dare* further betray us. You're lucky you're too young to have been declared a Deplorable for kidnapping the prime minister. Stay out of matters that don't concern you."

Atsushi's expression crumpled, and he looked down.

Actually, our Crowned One who sees the future specifically stated that Atsushi must come.

"Of course, she did," Savas quipped.

She also stated you must come, Savas. That the safety of the team requires you as well.

"Obviously. Just not as the leader." Commander Savas scoffed. Then he leaned in toward Seth, and they turned their backs to the group.

This was Bleu's chance. He had to correct this. He shuffled closer to the clustered Crowned Ones.

I can't lead. Bleu tried to reach the Luminaries. They had to stop this. How could he command Crowned Ones? It was a ridiculous notion.

You don't know that, Bleu. It is just your current belief. And an incorrect one, in our opinion. Desna gave him an encouraging nod.

Councilor Collins and Savas faced the group. Savas wore a steely-grim expression.

Collins cleared his throat. "We will leave in a week with Bleu leading and Commander Savas as his second. If my son wishes to go, I will give him my blessing as long as he returns to Northern Haven for vaccinations, medical deposits, and to arrange continuing his studies. However, for safety's sake, only Commander Savas will know the final location. This will protect the other Havens from any possible treachery on your part, as you clearly can no longer read his thoughts. Since Bleu does not have this strength, only the commander will know."

You mean, the second, not the commander, I presume? Luminary Vadin seemed to have grown bigger, more commanding himself.

"Savas will always be a commander to Northern Haven. We are not demoting him just because he will not lead this particular mission."

As long as it is clear that Bleu leads this mission.

"I believe I just said that. Is Neviah not translating correctly?"

Neviah reddened as she translated Seth's words.

One more piece. It has come to our attention that Girak may not be welcomed back into his home. Therefore, we request that he also come on the mission, so that he may either stay with another haven or, if he does not choose that, that he may return and be welcomed at our village.

Bleu glanced at Girak but couldn't catch his eye. Never return? Had Savas threatened him again?

"Do with him what you will. We don't want him." Councilor Collins didn't even look at Girak.

"Jerk." Atsushi's sharp whisper carried in the windless air.

Bleu winced at Councilor Collins' biting words and glanced toward his past science educator. Girak's face was set in stone, but his blue eyes glimmered. He had been on the verge of tears since Josefina's death.

Girak? Do you need time to decide? Luminary Samasti turned to Girak.

Girak looked Bleu in the eye. "I'll follow Commander Reinier."

Bleu wasn't sure whether to laugh or scream. This was insane. He shook his head slightly, warning Girak that he would suck as a leader. Girak would be better off staying in Rana's village.

Bleu, act like a leader. Don't make me go under Savas' command. Please! Rana had somehow managed to add a screaming quality to her mind talk.

Her desperation clicked something inside him. A finality.

This leadership issue wasn't about him at all. It was about all of them.

Bleu cleared his throat. "Thank you, Educator Girak." He purposely reinstated Girak's title.

Girak slowly cracked a half smile.

Good, it's decided. Luminary Vadin smiled broadly and then raised an eyebrow to Bleu and Commander Savas. *Do you need star being assistance deciding any other aspect of the journey?*

"We—" Bleu began.

"*I* will return to Northern Haven today, and then Bleu and I can meet with you tomorrow. Acceptable, Bleu?" Commander Savas gave Bleu a sickeningly sweet smile as if they were best friends planning a party.

"Fine. But the star beings want no weapons in the village, so you'll need to come unarmed."

"As Seth Collins said, we humans must protect ourselves. You were attacked by wolves just outside our door. I will not put myself in jeopardy. They'll just have to trust that their pacifist influences the last few days have changed me for the better." He held out his arms, palms up to demonstrate his newly refined qualities. "I am, after all, a reasonable man. Surely you agree the wolves are a threat?"

"Yes, but so is your weapon a threat. I'm sure a Crowned One can meet you outside the door and escort you safely to the village."

"Whatever works." Commander Savas shrugged and gave another maddening smile. "Come along, Dr. Reinier. You must update us on the details of your findings." He pivoted and left with the other Northern Haveners.

Bleu watched them through narrowed eyes. *Whatever works. Did he think I am so stupid to not notice he didn't agree?* Bleu watched the pompous commander stride to the rover.

"Bleu, I'm proud of you."

His mother startled him. She must have approached while he glared at Savas' back like a fool. *So Commander-like of me.*

"Savas is impossible. Just hold your own." She grabbed his gloved hand. "I never thought I'd say this, but don't let our medical staff touch you. Commander Savas holds too much sway." She swallowed as if trying to avoid the words rising up her throat. "Bleu, for your own safety, I don't think you should ever..." She paused to swallow again, tears welling in her eyes. "Don't come home, Bleu. Not even if they do something to me. Promise, please?" Her dark eyes shone fiercely.

"What? No. I'm not promising that, Mom. They touch you, and I'll get Kalakanya to beam me in with a rescue team."

"Bleu, always the hero." She placed her palm on his chest. "You're a mission commander now. If you get hurt rescuing me, all humanity has left is Commander Savas. What kind of future is that? You and Ayanna are safe here with the star beings. I love you both beyond words, but I also have a duty to my kid patients dying of the Sickness down there. I can't desert them. I gave them my word." She paused, waiting for a sign that he understood.

He did. He just didn't want to. Swallowing the lump in his throat, he gave a slight nod.

"Of course, you understand. That's why the star beings would let you lead. You have honor." She smiled. "But you"—she patted his chest for emphasis—"you watch your back. I saw the look Savas gave you. He wants you out of his way. Permanently. Never trust him, no matter what he tells you, okay?" She locked her gaze on his. "I mean that. No matter *what* he says." She patted his chest, and before he could ask what she meant, she spun and left.

Never trust him, no matter what he tells you. What did that mean? What could Savas possibly say that would make him seem trustworthy?

Bleu raked his fingers through his hair in frustration. This whole day had been too much. Everything was happening too quickly, and everyone assumed he would somehow handle it. Biting his lip, he watched his mom climb into the snow rover behind Savas. The rover started up and became a distant dark dot on the endless gray and white horizon. Someone touched his arm.

"Bleu?"

Ayanna. She was still with him. For another week, at least.

"I'm okay."

"Liar." She gave a hollow laugh. "How's it feel to be a leader?"

"I haven't led yet. There's still time to stop it." He chuckled, but it held no mirth. "Yanna, it's a set-up. Once we're out there, Commander Savas will take over one way or the other. If only Commander Savas has the final location, how can I even begin to lead the team there?"

"My first suggestion is to stop calling him *commander*."

"My buddy Kern, then."

Ayanna's barking laughter soon had everyone looking at them. "It's a start. 'Hey, Kern, get that helicopter started.' That would really piss him off." Her face grew serious and scrunched. "Maybe disarm him first."

Bleu frowned. "Now you see my point."

Chapter 8

Peleguin-Rookery-By-The-Lake: Atsushi Collins

After returning from the meeting to the village, Atsushi's fellow humans dispersed as if they were native villagers. Ayanna and Bleu went to have a sibling planning session in the guest hut. Neviah went to help Bahujnana check on the Sickness patients. Rana and Girak were meeting with some Crowned One. His friends all had purposes and missions. He had nothing except the lasting sting of his father's words.

Alone and not needed, Atsushi wandered the length of the path until he'd passed the laughing children and last ice hut. He stomped up the rising path that led to the gathering hall, huffing in fury. Even though he'd saved Rana's life and helped prevent a war, his father blamed him for making him look bad. The trail ended at the gathering hall, but he continued onward, hiking down the little hill to a secluded, sheltered space under tall evergreens.

Panting, he leaned against a tree, shaking with fury. His own father not only had judged him nearly a Deplorable, but he'd also shamed Atsushi in front of all his new, hard-earned friends. He yearned for invisibility. Or maybe fading into nonexistence. He belonged nowhere. So, he just sat.

Atsushi shivered on a flat boulder, keeping his back to the village above him on the hill. The last thing he needed was some Crowned One finding him to ask about his dad. Below his perch, trees with long green boughs broke up the endless white and gray. But nothing could break up the bleakness of his brooding.

The clanking of cooking pots and acrid wood smoke drifted down from the large tent-like gathering hall behind him. But even these usually comforting signs of dinner prep only served to remind him that he'd been discarded. The rock's cold seeped into his legs. He welcomed the coming numbness. It wasn't like he had anywhere to go. Anywhere to be.

He'd left Northern Haven because he couldn't let them kill Rana, and Educator Girak's idea seemed the best way to prevent war. But now he was like the wood smoke, adrift on the Surface with no family and no purpose.

Why did they have to pick my father to represent Prime Minister Pridbor? He preferred his anger over that to facing the other bit he kept pushing away. It pierced his chest like a slow bullet, weaving its way through his ribs until it ruptured his heart.

His father had dismissed him like an old, used piece of clothing.

He had long suspected his father of not truly caring, but today's evidence at the meeting smacked him in the face. Instead of asking Atsushi why he'd made the choice to save Rana, his father only thought of how it might impact his own career on the Council. *He never loved me. He never even cared enough to get to know me.* Atsushi's eyes stung, but he blinked ferociously, unwilling to deal with the added discomfort of frozen-tear-streaked cheeks. *If I had a Sensei, this is when he would tell me to do some meditation thing to keep my cool.* Instead, the only thing keeping him cool was that he was nearly frozen stiff.

Singsong warbles of star being chatter carried across the village to his high seat, but he didn't understand any of it. They were probably discussing how rude his father had been, how ungrateful for their help, how accusing of their intentions.

How Atsushi was the jerk's adopted son.

They don't even miss me. I'm nothing to them. He meant his parents, but now the horrible thought occurred to him that no star beings had come looking for him, either. Maybe he could just fade away...

Before him, the tree boughs lifted in the breeze, the movement a mesmerizing distraction. He swayed in rhythm with the tree boughs, nostrils flared to catch the trees' bright tang. Scents were endless on the Surface.

The boughs lifted and fell. Lifted and fell. The trees were sighing with him.

Rana had explained that trees were all different. Each species had a name, different smell, and individual gifts that contributed to other beings. Even trees belonged in groups and had a purpose.

This cluster, right now, called him to touch their feathery branches. He slid off the boulder, his legs stiff from having rested too long against his frosted perch. He stumbled down the rocky hill. It wasn't far, but steep. Giving in to gravity, he raced to the trees and dove under their swaying branches. The enticing aroma engulfed him, holding him in its embrace.

Inhaling deeply, he turned, taking in the wonder. Strange brown pointy things covered the ground beneath the boughs. He removed his gloves and touched them. They snapped, releasing more of that smell. He unzipped his parka pocket and shoved handfuls of the sharp, needle-like things into it for later.

To his left, several large branches had fallen. A fun idea formed in his mind, and his heart raced in anticipation of trying it. He broke off pieces and swished them through the air.

No, not right. He tried again, stepping on the branches and snapping them under his own weight. He moved deeper into the jumble of trees. Snap. *No, that won't work.* Snap. *Yes, that's perfect.*

Grinning with excitement, he raised his two sword-like weapons and twirled them about. Their weight was pretty good, almost equal to each other. So was the length. He imagined them as extensions of his arms, fighting off imaginary beasts. An efficient warrior, he quickly slashed through the roaring creatures.

He imagined his nasty brother, Liam, riding a slathering monster and carrying off Ayanna. In a clean sweep, Atsushi knocked Liam to the ground, beheaded the monster, and saved Ayanna. Liam begged for mercy.

Something crunched the crusty snow behind him. Something real. Atsushi spun, whipping his swords around and extending the left-handed one forward in a thrust.

Whoosh! Golden light slammed into him, knocking him backward. He lost a branch as he tried to break his fall. Scurrying into a crouched position, he gripped his remaining sword, suddenly very aware of its branchlike qualities.

Don't you ever *attack me again!*

The mind talk blast vibrated Atsushi's skull. Facing him was a furious, impossibly tall male star being surrounded by a golden shield. Atsushi's heart raced as he glowered into the fierce face.

Above him towered Kahali, Rana's friend who had been attacked by the second expedition and lost his arm. The one who hated humans. *Great. I'm alone in the forest with the only star being who hates us.* Careful not to startle him, Atsushi climbed to his feet.

Kahali's only hand trembled palm outward, as if prepared to blast Atsushi. Could star beings even do that? The impact of his shield knocking him backward had been bad enough. He tightened his grip on the remaining branch and remained still. The other was too far to reach.

"You snuck up on me," Atsushi muttered. "What did you expect?"

Do you attack everything first and ask questions later? Kahali shook his long ponytail behind his shoulder as his upper lip arched in revulsion.

"No." It sounded defensive even to Atsushi's own ears. "I thought you were a wild animal."

So, it's okay to attack a furred one for no reason? I was being loud on purpose, so you'd know I was coming. If I were a predator, you would have heard nothing.

Atsushi considered the safety of lowering his branch, but Kahali still held his shield and shook, eyes wild. "What do you want?"

To converse in safety. Kahali's eyes flashed, but he seemed to be wilting.

Perhaps it was difficult for him to maintain his shield? "Look, I'll lower my branch if you calm down. That shield's scary. Clearly, you can kick my ass if you want to."

Kahali raised an eyebrow. *Cleary? Does this*—he motioned to his shoulder that extended to a stump—*look like I can keep myself safe?*

"I don't have a gun. I've never even held a weapon." Atsushi lowered his gaze. "You scared me. I'm sorry. I'm lost up here…" Why was he blabbering to this guy? Why did being around star beings make him feel so exposed, like he was naked? He dropped the branch.

Kahali stood stone-faced, his dark piercing gaze boring into Atsushi's core. A shiver rippled up his spine.

Your emotions control you. It's what makes you humans so dangerous. Kahali's shield faded away.

Atsushi looked down at his own body, the one he had one minute willed to disappear, then ferociously used to attack an imaginary Liam. He had never considered emotions dangerous, but he *had* almost accidentally struck Kahali.

Still panting with exertion, he looked up to see the star being studying him. Kahali's disapproving glance swept him head to foot, and then he grunted at the stick by Atsushi's feet.

In an attempt to prove he didn't want to fight, Atsushi gently kicked the stick farther away from himself, but that only made Kahali tense even more. They glared at each other. From the hill above, conversations and laughter of star being families drifted down as they walked to the gathering hall for dinner.

"Why did you follow me down here? Don't expect me to explain my father. He's always a jerk like that."

Kahali furrowed his brow. *I have no idea what you're going on about.* He shook his head in annoyance. *Coming here wasn't my idea. The Luminaries and your Educator Girak just met to discuss your education. I've been assigned.*

"You?" Atsushi laughed silently, his shoulders heaving at the irony. He wanted a Sensei, and he'd got assigned the only star being with anger management issues. "Sorry." His hand covered his mouth too late to hide his laughter. "I thought I'd be learning from a computer or Girak. You're a teacher?"

No, Kahali sent as he rubbed his arm stump and scowled at him, annoyance dripping off him like water. *And my anger problems are only with humans.*

Oops. He'd have to better watch his thoughts. "So, why you?" Atsushi considered the bristling star being before him. He made the most unlikely teacher—angry, paranoid, and only a bit older than his would-be student. Kahali didn't appear any more enthused with the assignment than Atsushi.

Kahali shrugged.

"Are you teaching me everything?"

Kahali snorted, and a hint of a grin replaced his annoyance. *You have high expectations. For everything, you need a Crowned One.*

Atsushi's jaw dropped in awe. "They know...everything?"

Kahali gave a strange, barking laugh. The tension electrifying the air between them evaporated.

"Everything?" Atsushi repeated.

They are one with the Web of Oneness. They can communicate with all beings and feel their experiences. They can beam to any location and heal. And most stop aging. So, after an eternity of living with that, yeah, they pretty much know everything.

"Wow. Can you teach me to Crown?"

Kahali passed his hand over his tied-back hair. *Haven't made it there myself.*

He had to be referring to his lack of white hair.

"Right." His assigned teacher's rating dropped a few pegs. He struggled to keep his face from showing it. "So what *do* you teach?"

How to connect with the One In All, and how to use your energy. Girak said you were trying to learn this in your den.

"Oh. You can teach that? *All* of that? Wow!"

You say that word a lot. What does it mean? "Wow," Kahali said, trying it out with his mouth.

At the spoken word, he froze and then chuckled. He'd grown so accustomed to their mind speak that he'd forgotten they were capable of vocalizations. "It's cool to hear you speak Standard. It's a word that shows the speaker is both surprised and impressed."

Interesting.

"Wow." Kahali tried it again, and a glimmer of playfulness crossed his face.

We should go. It's dinnertime.

Atsushi looked longingly at his two precise branches. He didn't want to leave them, but Kahali viewed them as weapons.

Kahali followed his gaze. *Weapons are not allowed in our village. Bleu told you all that at the meeting.*

"I know. I don't see them as weapons, though. Not really. They felt like extensions of my arms, like they made my arms longer so I could better protect myself." He grinned. "And they were fun to twirl."

Kahali had stopped walking away and turned slowly, a thoughtful expression on his face. *Extensions of your arms?*

Atsushi followed his thoughts immediately. "Yes. Like something was flowing down my arms into them and they were a part of me. It sounds crazy, but it felt really powerful."

Kahali tilted his head, examining the branches. *I'll keep them as tools, and maybe we'll experiment with them tonight after dinner.* He scooped them both up in his hand and smirked. "Wow."

Chapter 9

Peleguin-Rookery-By-The-Lake: Rana of Peleguin Rookery

After that stressful meeting with the humans, Rana aimlessly wandered with Digga through her village, hoping to slow her racing mind. She couldn't understand the connection, but something about seeing the humans today with their unnatural guns and technology reminded her of her parents' untimely deaths. Their deaths by avalanche, something their shields should have protected them against, had always seemed unnatural to her, and humans specialized in creating unnatural things. Though small in stature, they created huge disruptions.

Even now, a group of young kids that should be practicing their capabilities for Crowning were instead gathered around Girak, examining his noisy, metal contraption that emanated voices. Girak meant no harm, but try as she might, she couldn't release her suspicion that the humans had brought disaster to her life long before Savas had stolen her. Atsushi and Girak said they had only recently emerged for the first time, but so many of their devices—like the one Girak was showing to the kids, and their snowmobiles that Savas had driven to the village in—created unnatural vibrations. The kind of vibrations that might cause a sudden avalanche.

She had only been eight summers but had overheard strange things about that avalanche. Things that no one had ever explained properly. And while her parents weren't Crowned, they could shield and weren't fools.

Her need for the truth battled her fear that knowing might rekindle that old anger she'd worked so hard to douse.

Spotting her adopted maha Desna at the base of the hill with the salt deer, Rana wandered that way. She needed the truth about her birth parents. Acceptance of truth led to greater awareness, which led to Crowning.

Stepping off the path to reach Desna, she sneezed as loose salt deer fur wafted up from where Desna worked. Every spring softening, the salt deer craved grooming, and the star beings desired the loose fur to weave into clothing. It was a win-win relationship, and the full collection bag at Desna's side promised Rana new socks or a scarf.

She dashed down the last few steps between them, reveling in the squishing sensation of thawing ground under her boots. Several skittish deer bounded off at Digga's excited approach. The nearest buck strode toward Digga, head erect and snorting.

Digga froze, one clawed paw still raised mid-stride.

Digga's not going to hurt you, Rana soothed, but the buck seemed undeterred. In his defense, an adult cave digger was well equipped to kill and eat a buck, but Digga was no threat. The buck's shaggy chest expanded, and he bellowed a loud threat.

Rana looked back at Digga. Her pup had already completely submerged herself in a newly dug hole, only her flared black nose protruding.

"Well, that's a new one." Rana laughed and turned back to the buck. After a few sniffs at the hole he returned to Desna, allowing himself to be groomed again.

Rana peered down the hole. "It's safe to come out. You can't hide from your fears forever, you know."

Digga put her head down on her huge claws and stared up at Rana with her big, brown eyes.

She laughed. "You're supposed to be the fiercest predator around, not the cutest, but if you prefer to stay in hiding, I'll be with the salt deer and Desna for a bit."

Digga gave a contented rumble and began chewing a root she'd dug up. "Okay, have fun."

She joined her maha and the buck, holding her hand out to greet the creature. He gently nibbled her hand with his soft lips and turned his shoulder to her in welcome of a grooming.

Rana chuckled at his lack of shyness and scratched his neck. "Maha, do you think I handled myself well with the humans?"

"Of course. You showed great courage and compassion." Desna arched an eyebrow toward Rana. "But we've already discussed this."

"I have a question. I've wanted to ask you this for ages, but I sensed you didn't think I was mature enough to handle it before." Rana bit her lip. "Since we found the humans, the question seems even more important."

Desna's other eyebrow joined the arch. "Go ahead."

The warmth emanating from Desna's eyes encouraged Rana despite the clenching of her stomach. She continued to knead the young buck's fur. Her birth family's weaving, still hanging about her sleeping mat today, featured a salt deer and a lion. The presence of the salt deer encouraged her to press on.

"After my parents died, I overhead you and Gandhapalin. He said there was something unusual found with them. When I asked what, you said it didn't change anything. But I remember there were extra meetings of the Crowned Ones, and then you and Kalakanya had an argument about my parents." Rana looked up from the deer and into her maha's similar doe-brown eyes. Her throat tightened with tears, making it hard to talk. "What really happened?"

"Oh, Rana. You've been wondering all these years?" Desna pulled her close into a hug. "We found something we couldn't explain, but given recent events—"

Rana stiffened and pulled away. "Did the humans kill them?"

"No. Yes. Well, not on purpose." Desna's eyes filled with sadness.

Rana's mouth flapped open, but she couldn't form her jumbled thoughts into words. She took in a shuddering breath. "They...I knew it couldn't be natural...not both at the same time."

"No, they were too well trained, Rana. They would have sensed a natural avalanche coming. Under normal circumstances, the energy shifts beforehand. But none of us were watching for danger. There weren't any humans around then. There never were any until recently."

"But you found...something?"

"We found an odd metal thing near them. Like their snow rovers, but much smaller. We think it may have flown. Whatever it was, we suspect it created a vibration that started the avalanche. They had no warning. Even if they had thrown up a shield, they were still buried under a mountain of snow. It took days to get to them, you remember."

Rana's insides seethed. Humans ruined everything.

She wished they'd never emerged from their den. They disrupted everything and were only capable of ruinous behavior. No, that wasn't fair. Ayanna, Atsushi, and Girak had risked being hunted to save her. She rubbed her temples to clear the violent images. "Humans...killed...my parents."

"I'm sorry. But I don't think they had any way of knowing the effect of their machinery. They seem quite oblivious to their effects on others. Our agreement to help them find the other human havens not only assists them, but it also protects other beings from their blunders while they search."

"Ironic role for me." Rana kicked the ground.

The buck jerked his head up in alarm.

Sorry, she mind spoke.

He leapt away to the cover of evergreens. The remaining deer eyed her nervously.

Desna watched her through narrowed eyes. "Yes, it is ironic. But they would be incredibly proud of your willingness to help."

Rana grunted.

"You know, I knew your parents well. You have your father's stubbornness. You're too stubborn to consider you've been wrong about them."

"About what?"

"Your parents. I told you they had their reasons—"

"What reason is there for getting pregnant before Crowning?" Rana's raised voice rippled across the salt deer, who tensed and snorted.

Desna's gaze met Rana's glare. "Crowning is about raising and expanding your consciousness. There are many obstacles to mind development—getting caught up in one's new abilities, becoming intoxicated by the power rush, or…" Desna sighed. "Or staying too attached to a belief, or more commonly, another star being."

Rana stiffened. "I know you all say that, but I still don't fully understand it. You love Gandhapalin, and Dala, and me. How can being attached to another star being be so bad?"

Desna chuckled softly. "Stop seeing things as good or bad. Connection is never wrong. But sometimes, the connection is so *personal* a love that it blocks the lovers from seeing the larger Love."

"Falling stars! Are you talking about Eka and Kahali? I told them Crowning is my priority!"

"We're talking about your parents, Rana."

Rana clamped her mouth shut to stifle the urge to scream in frustration. *Too attached?*

"It's not my place to say for sure. But I suspect that's what held them back from Crowning. Since you brought him up, it's also what almost killed Eka."

She groaned in frustration. "You said this was about my parents. No one knows what made him try to beam when I was attacked by the humans."

"Eka and the Crowned Ones from his village have been exploring his experience. We know. He's bonded—*attached*—to you energetically in a way that puts him in danger. It's why his Crowned Ones are working with him."

"That's why he had to go back to his village and stay this whole time?"

"Rana, if something happens to you, it appears that Eka may die. He can't safely star beam, and yet has no way to prevent himself from doing so."

Her mind whirled, trying to make sense of that. She began to feel dizzy. Vibrant, healthy Eka dying needlessly for something as nebulous as his attachment to her? "Wait. Are you saying it's somehow my fault?"

"Falling stars! Of course not. But given your worries about your parents' lack of Crowning, I thought you should know so that you don't repeat their pattern." She patted Rana's arm. "Unless you choose to. It's okay to choose not to Crown, Rana. But do it consciously."

She scowled. "I'd never choose that."

"No." Desna sighed. "But Eka might."

Chapter 10

Northern Haven: Commander Kern Savas

As the nano cleaning spray hit Savas, the nostalgia of returning home washed over him. He'd heard of homesickness and nostalgia in ancient stories, but having never had anywhere to go other than Northern Haven, this was a new feeling.

The elevator held all the people who had gone to the meeting. He leaned back against the elevator wall next to Zach and basked in the familiar hums of technology.

Dr. Cassandra Reinier sneezed. "Ugh. Did they have to make this nanowash smell like bathroom cleaners?"

He chuckled, thinking he probably needed something as strong as a bathroom cleaner to cleanse him after two weeks on the Surface. How much harder did the nanotech have to work disinfecting Zach and him of foreign pathogens after their extended time with the star beings? "Ahh, it's nice to be home," he said, elbowing Zach. "Right?"

Zach laughed. "Definitely. I've never wanted a shower so badly."

Cassandra scowled at the two of them. "You seem clean enough. Didn't they give you access to the bathing hut?"

Savas chuckled. "It was *cold*, Cass, and—"

The elevator door clanged open, and Savas froze at the armed men greeting them.

"What's this?" he demanded.

The men stepped backward and looked uncomfortable. "Sorry, sir, but Prime Minister Pridbor insisted this was your own protocol."

"What protocol?"

All three of you"—the man nodded at him, Zach, and Cass—"need to be fully checked by medical and psych staff before you can return to normal status."

He groaned. "This better not take long. I have a lot to do before I go back up there tomorrow. And are the guns necessary? I'm wearing this." He held up the wrist device Dr. Medicci had made to block the star beings from reading his mind and shook it in front of him.

"The other two don't have that. Follow me. The medical team is waiting."

❋ ❋ ❋ ❋ ❋ ❋

Two hours later, Savas strode from the medical suite toward the prime minister's office. He'd much prefer a real shower and normal food, not a lengthy talk, but the needs of Northern Haven always came first.

He pressed his newly re-created identification card to the security device at the door. It opened with Prime Minister Pridbor about to walk into him.

"Ah, you beat me. I thought the medical staff would take longer." Pridbor gave him a rare, genuine smile and motioned for Savas to follow him. "I'm sure you're anxious to get home. We can talk there, and I've asked someone bring some food."

The prime minister stopped walking and looked him up and down. "At least they didn't starve you. And somehow, your medical stats are better than ever."

"What?" His heart sped up. "I was very careful to watch everything they did. They barely touched me."

"Eh." Pridbor gave a dismissive wave of his hand. "Perhaps they don't need to touch. In any case, it appears they did you a favor."

"I don't want any favors from them."

"No, I suppose you don't. Open it." Pridbor motioned to the door of Savas' module.

Savas pressed his card to the door and sighed as the door opened. He was fully home.

"Have a seat," he said, motioning to his couch.

After scanning his module for signs of intrusion while he was gone, he dropped his expedition outerwear on the bed. He promised himself a delightful sleep in a real bed soon and returned to the seating area. Fortunately, he'd left the place clean. He'd known Pridbor his whole life, but a dirty module would have been unfortunate.

"So, has anything changed here other than this amazing tech?" He held up his wrist.

"We've been very busy. Even now, the scientists are working on some simple tests for you to run on the star beings during your trip together."

Savas snorted. "They'll never cooperate."

"They won't need to know." Pridbor gave him a smug look. "And neither will the rest of your team. You're the only one with the new device. It's a long process to make the special chip in it. Hopefully, by the time you return, we'll have more. But in the meantime, you need to keep the tests to yourself." Pridbor's lips curled into a half smirk. "You've always been good at secrets."

The prime minister referred to their secret strategy meetings, but after this morning's accidental reveal to Luminary Vadin, Savas' stomach turned. At some point, the star being would hold his secret status as the last SHAST agent against him, but the star being had no reason to contact Pridbor already. Even Savas couldn't see a strategic value to that. Not at this point, at least.

"Keeping the tests secret shouldn't be a problem."

Pridbor's gaze narrowed with paternal concern. "Are you truly okay?"

"Yes, just hungry for some familiar food."

Pridbor leaned forward and touched his forearm. "It's me, Kern. If you need to talk about what they did to you—"

"I'm fine, sir." Damn, the "sir" proved he wasn't fine at all.

They never spoke formally in private. Pridbor was the one adult who had been there for him as a kid, practically adopting him as an understudy. He'd grown up understanding that power motivated Pridbor, and that the prime minister saw Savas as his right-hand man and his legacy.

When in private, Pridbor insisted on relinquishing all formalities and speaking as family. If only the star beings were as obvious in their motivations.

Savas cleared his throat. "It's an adjustment being back underground after all that constant exposure to the elements, but I'm fine."

"Hmm." His old friend nodded. "You probably want a shower. And I'm sure all your girlfriends want to see you before you go on your next expedition."

Savas chuckled. As if he had time for that. "You don't need to leave."

"It's fine. We can talk early tomorrow before you go back up for your meeting. I know you have things to do." He stood.

Savas stood as well.

"But if you need to chat, you know how to reach me," Pridbor added.

"Thank you." He extended his hand.

But when Pridbor clasped his hand, he pulled him in for a quick hug. The guy gave dreadfully stiff hugs.

"The star beings don't know who they're messing with, Kern. Enjoy the food when it comes, and make sure you get some rest."

"I will. Thank you, sir." He winced at his second slip into formality, but the prime minister was halfway out the door.

As soon as the door closed, Savas scheduled a session in one of the holographic entertainment rooms, saying he had a date and they would want privacy. He reserved it for three hours, and then pulled out his communicator and messaged Corissa. Of all his girlfriends, she would question him the least. Seconds later, he grinned at her immediate acceptance to meet that evening. Perfect. He arranged to meet her ninety minutes after the reservation started. If anyone wondered why he wasn't in his module resting, she would be his alibi.

With that settled, he could finally get the shower he desperately needed. As the hot, steaming water hit his skin, he sighed in relief. The village's wood smoke stench that had clung to him faded, and his tense muscles began to relax. Here, no Crowned Ones could analyze his every thought.

Too soon, the timer chimed five minutes and the water shut itself off. He'd assumed his rationed shower water credits had built up during his imprisonment and would still be available to him. Cursing at his lost shower time, he dried and hurriedly threw on his black tunic and pants. Black clothing would allow him to avoid being seen in the dark tunnels.

Now for the tricky part. Patting the compass hidden under his tunic, he whispered, "Our time to shine."

From under his bed, he grabbed a small flashlight and a random fake ID stashed in a box, snagged the sandwich that had been delivered, and hurried out. At this time of the evening, most people were home, and the halls were mostly empty.

After logging in to the entertainment room and activating it, he left it running. He left and used a fake ID to access the Agricultural floor, careful to avoid being seen. As he walked, he checked the location of all the hidden cameras, ensuring they were scanning another area as he hurried by. As he ducked past another hidden camera, memories of sneaking here with his mother lapped at his mind.

Tucking him against her shadow as an agricultural worker passed by, his mother whispered, "Stay quiet, or the nasty Undescended will catch us. Now, see that camera over there?" She pointed at a barely perceptible shadow that moved. "That's the next thing to avoid. Do exactly what I do..." She hurried across the hall and into an alcove.

In both the past and today, his steps followed her path precisely. Back then, it had been a game they played against the evil Undescended—humans left above on the icy Surface, who had sworn vengeance on the founders of the four SHAST havens. He hadn't realized she'd been teaching him skills that would later save his life.

Still tracing the echoes of her guiding footsteps, he reached the particular grain room he needed. The familiar waft of damp soil greeted him. The grain had been harvested before he had led the ill-fated second expedition, and the dark, rich soil was in its rehabilitation period before replanting.

The cavernous room was nearly pitch black. He pulled out the small flashlight, and careful to disguise his steps, he strode to the far end. As he crept deeper into the darkness, he could almost feel his mother's hand guiding him forward.

The back wall of this room had been their special spot. She'd bring him here at night for secret picnics and games. He'd been good at keeping secrets then but never understood why she wanted him to know how to access this area until years after her death.

Checking that he was alone, he pulled out her compass and pressed it near the wall where he and his mother had always sat. The first time he'd done this, he had come here hoping to connect with the mother he wasn't even supposed to remember had existed.

As he sat alone near the wall, the compass had vibrated, and he had pulled it out of his tunic to see if he had somehow broken it. As he clicked open the casing, a door opened in the wall, revealing a hidden room.

He'd been amazed by the depth his mother's genius and commitment to her work. He had been too young for her to risk telling the whole truth, but she had suspected she was in danger. *That* she had told him even though he'd only been seven. And by their shared experiences and her leaving him the compass, she had given him the knowledge of how to find this room without telling him of its existence.

He strode inside, and the door silently closed, the light inside clicking on. The far wall, about five meters from the door, had the same SHAST insignia that covered the door to the Surface. Below it were two computing workstations, constantly reminding him that he should have had a fellow agent.

Each of the four SHAST havens had a lineage of two agents supporting each other. Years ago, he'd unearthed evidence that another adult was killed the day his mom died. The two SHAST agents of Northern Haven, tasked with making the hard decisions to protect humanity that no one wanted to make, were both murdered.

His appreciative gaze travelled along the familiar floor-to-ceiling data file storage that covered the left and right walls and stopped to admire the small munitions cabinet beside the door. He'd survived the star beings and made it back here. Home at last.

Sighing with relief, he took the familiar dozen steps past the shelves of computer files and sank into the left desk's chair. His desk. For the first time in weeks, he allowed himself the luxury of relaxing.

When he'd finally figured out how the compass worked as a key, he'd found the note left for him by his mom at this desk. The note that had explained all this.

Sighing as he leaned back against the fake leather, he eyed the computer. "Please, tell me there's a way to identify agents at the other havens. It would make my job so much easier."

When he'd proposed to the Council that they needed to be tougher in conserving vital resources, he hadn't *wanted* to suggest killing the teens already ill with the incurable Sickness. But that was the type of tough policy choices his ancestors had been tasked to propose and carry out—preserving humanity by any means necessary.

Even so, he wasn't meant to be doing this alone. There should be two agents, to keep each other in balance. If he could find Western Haven, they might still have their agents. He'd have others to consult with when needed. However, even if he found the other havens, SHAST agents' identities were known only to those who held the position. He had no idea how to identify them.

"Tell me there's a way to signal them," he mumbled, typing in his search for agent codes or signals to the secret database.

If he could identify them, he would never again be alone making these decisions. He checked the time on his communicator. Only an hour left before he had to meet his date. He needed Corissa to say he was with her tonight.

He began another search. This one yielded all the codes he already knew, but he found nothing about how to identify other havens' agents. By the time he'd read all the resulting files, he was out of time. If only he hadn't been captured, he could have researched this at his leisure before the mission left.

"Damn it. Can't things for once be easy?" Smashing his fist against the desk in frustration, he flipped off the computer and stormed out.

Chapter 11

Peleguin-Rookery-By-The-Lake: Atsushi Collins

At dinner, Atsushi sat with his human friends, but even Ayanna's presence couldn't stop him from worrying about what Girak and the Luminaries had gotten him into by assigning Kahali as his mentor. He forced down another bite of stew and managed a smile at Ayanna's joke. He had wanted a Sensei for so long, and life had given him Kahali. The idea of a star being instructor intrigued him, but Kahali seemed anything but the calm, self-assured guide he'd dreamed of.

Every time Atsushi's attention travelled across the hall to where Kahali sat with Rana and their other friends, his grumpy mentor somehow knew. He looked up from their conversation and narrowed his eyes at Atsushi. It was downright unnerving. If just his glances angered the guy, Atsushi had no idea how he'd study with him and not get blasted with an energy field.

"Not hungry?" Ayanna asked, motioning with her spoon at his still-full bowl.

"I can't stop wondering what he'll teach me."

Ayanna laughed. "You'll know soon enough, since he's motioning for you to come over."

"What?" Atsushi turned toward where Kahali had been seated. He was gone.

"By the doorway," Ayanna said, pointing.

Kahali already stood by the exit, waving for Atsushi to follow him outside.

"*Shast*, wish me luck," he said, jumping to his feet.

"I've got something better," she teased, blowing him a kiss.

Blushing, he had no idea how to respond, especially with Bleu giving him the side-eye and Girak quietly chuckling.

"Okay, I'll find you afterward." He flashed her a grin and then rushed after Kahali, who had already ducked under the mat and was holding it raised for him.

As Atsushi reached the door, Kahali frowned and pointed back to where Atsushi had been eating. *Lesson one: clean up after yourself.*

Atsushi wanted to face palm. "Right. Sorry. I got nervous that you'd leave without me."

Kahali's frown deepened. *That would be an odd way to start our lessons. You're not expecting your girlfriend to clean up after you, are you? Everyone is equal here.*

"No, I just spaced on it. Hold on." Atsushi hurried back and put his plate and utensils away. Kahali watched him every step of the way. By the time he made it back to the exit, his heart raced. "Okay, I'm ready."

Kahali snickered, shaking his head. *One In All, help us. Come on.*

They hurried down the path, Kahali immediately outpacing him.

"Where are we going?" Atsushi asked, panting to keep up with Kahali's much longer stride. Atsushi was average height, but star beings stood at least a head taller than the tallest humans.

I want to show you where I live. You'll need to meet me at my hut tomorrow morning, and I'll take you to sunrise sit.

"What's that?" Atsushi jogged to stay beside him.

It's our morning meditation. Have you ever meditated?

Did his pathetic attempts to learn from the Records Room database count? "I've tried, but I don't really understand it."

Trying counts. Kahali stopped abruptly in front of an ice hut. Two Crowned Ones stood outside it, talking animatedly. *This is my hut, and these are my fathers, Luminary Vadin and Kagni.*

The two men turned, bowed, and grinned down at Atsushi.

Welcome, said the one with a more pointed nose that matched Kahali's. *I'm not big on formalities, so you may simply call me Vadin. If you need anything, let me know.*

"Thank you. I saw you at the meeting, but it's nice to meet you directly," Atsushi said, attempting the bow of greeting Rana had shown him.

Ah yes, I was there, Vadin said with a chuckle. *I hope your father can learn to be as open-minded as I've heard you to be, Atsushi.*

Atsushi froze, unsure how to take that. Had he just been complimented by one of their leaders?

Vadin, having heard his thoughts, nodded. *Your openness helped save Rana's life.*

For which all of us, especially Kahali, are grateful for, the second father said, grinning at his son.

Kahali mumbled something in their language, sounding embarrassed.

Sorry, I'm Kagni, the second father said. His smile was a bit shyer, but none less warm. *Are you two meeting in here? Should we leave?* He motioned to their home.

Kahali spoke rapidly in their language, and his fathers frowned and answered in a somewhat stern tone.

"If now isn't a good time..." Atsushi took a step back.

Kahali turned back to him, looking a bit embarrassed as if he'd just been admonished. *Sorry, I didn't mean to be rude. Now is fine. I was just explaining that I had told you to meet me here, but they said I should meet you at your hut until you get to know your way around in the dark.*

"The dark?" Atsushi grimaced. Kahali had expected him to maneuver their village in the dark without even a flashlight?

Don't worry, I'll come to your guest hut tomorrow morning. Come on, we can walk while we talk. He plodded onward, but this time in a much slower pace.

Maybe his fathers had noticed Atsushi's panting and had also told him to walk at human speeds. What would it be like to have two fathers involved in his life?

As they passed the last ice huts on this end of the village, a curious thought popped into his head. "Your fathers seem nice. Do all star beings have two fathers and two mothers?"

Kahali choked with laughter. *No, do humans?*

"No. I just don't know how different you are from..." *Shast.* What had he gotten himself into?

Our first lesson is to be on reproduction, then? Kahali struggled to keep from laughing.

"No! I just wanted to make sure I understood. I'm sorry, I didn't mean anything. I just know you do amazing things with energy. I mean, maybe you reproduce with balls of light or something."

Kahali doubled over with laughter. *Balls of light?* He was struggling for breath.

Atsushi wanted to crawl in a hole. "Okay, so you have sexual reproduction that resembles human reproduction."

Kahali, still chortling, managed to stand upright. *Not if you do it with balls of light!*

"Okay, I'm a fool. Forget I said anything."

Not likely. Kahali grinned as if looking forward to telling all his friends of Atsushi's ridiculous question.

"Sorry." Atsushi glanced about, suddenly grateful no one else seemed to be in earshot.

No need to apologize. I haven't laughed that hard since before... He grimaced and shifted his residual arm as if it pained him. The awkwardness returned.

"I'm sorry," Atsushi said, hoping he could somehow overcome Kahali's distrust of humans.

Stop apologizing. You didn't cut my arm off.

"No," he said, and they both stood on the path in the growing darkness.

After a long silence, Kahali heaved a huge sigh and started walking again, this time very slowly. Atsushi followed, worried when Kahali started massaging his arm stump. How much pain was he in?

Let me try to accomplish teaching you something tonight, okay?

"I'm—"

Stop apologizing.

Atsushi nodded.

Only apologize to me if you're mean or you hurt someone. Mistakes are okay. And questions about star beings are okay. You're okay with my dads loving each other, right?

"Of course. Humans sometimes do that, too. It's normal."

Good, because I've had relationships with all genders. Wouldn't want you freaking out on me about that. Kahali side-eyed him.

"Love whoever you want." Then a horrible thought occurred to him. Kahali was a good-looking guy and Ayanna seemed quite comfortable with the star beings. "Just...please don't fall for Ayanna."

Kahali snorted. *I said I've had relationships with all genders. Humans, however, are of no interest to me.*

"Good." His shoulders sagged with relief.

Hope that didn't come off as offensive.

"Not at all."

Okay, let's accomplish something tonight, so I don't have to report to my fathers that we discussed balls of light.

His face heated. He'd never live that down. "Please. Teach me something completely unrelated."

Okay, good. Kahali grew serious. *Normally, our lessons will focus on three different things. First, how to be safe up here without being violent. You said you never held a weapon. I don't want you to ever hold one.* He stopped walking and turned to glare at him. *No violence, do you understand?*

Atsushi nodded, but he *didn't* understand. How was he supposed to keep himself safe up here when he couldn't shield like them?

Trust me. Kahali gave a tense smile.

Kahali had been roped into being his teacher, and now, he was going to have to protect him. Atsushi couldn't help but think of his father this afternoon, so readily allowing Atsushi to leave on a dangerous mission. If his own father wouldn't protect him, why would this guy?

Look, this isn't easy for me, either, he said. *We'll just have to figure it out.*

"Figure out how to keep me alive up here?"

That shouldn't be too hard for me to do. Unless you do something really foolish, which might not be too hard for you to do. Kahali grinned.

"Thanks for the vote of confidence," Atsushi said.

It was only a joke. I do hope you humans joke?

"Yes, of course."

Good. What I meant before is that we both need to figure out this trust thing. I won't hurt you, Atsushi. Star beings aren't violent. Kahali winced and bit his lip as if the pain had grown.

Should he suggest they go back? Maybe the walk was too much for him. Then again, if he suggested that, would Kahali only be insulted? After a moment, he decided to trust Kahali knew what he could handle.

"I'm sorry about that." Atsushi nodded toward his stump. "I'm not at all like Zach or Commander Savas."

He gave an unconvinced grunt. *We'll also work on your being more mindful of your emotions, how to feel energy and connect with the One In All. Does that sound agreeable to you?*

Atsushi nodded. "It sounds pretty amazing. I hope you don't mind teaching me that much."

He released a huge sigh. *I'll deal with it.*

Atsushi nodded and looked away, mortified that his teacher didn't even want to deal with him.

"Wow."

Atsushi looked up at the tall star being, who was grinning.

That was a joke.

"You sure? I mean, I'd understand. If a star being had cut off my arm and shot me...well, I'd be pretty wary of hanging out with you." Had that come out right?

I'm starting to like you, Atsushi. Kahali grinned, then tilted his head toward the drifting tune of a flute-like instrument. *Any chance you like music?*

"Yes!" Atsushi nodded. "When I go back to get the computer stuff for school, I'm hoping to get all my music."

Get your music? You mean your musical instruments?

"No, my music. It's music that's been recorded over thousands of years. If you like, I can teach you about our music. I mean, if star beings evolved from us, then it's kinda your music, too, right?"

Kahali's eyes grew wide. *You can play it without instruments?* He glanced at where his other hand would have been. *Yes, I'd be very interested in learning that.*

Chapter 12

Peleguin-Rookery-By-The-Lake: Bleu Reinier

After surrendering to discomfort on the hopelessly hard floor of the guest hut and tuning out Girak's snuffling snores, Bleu had finally fallen asleep.

Movement awoke him. What the hell was Atsushi doing up now? Bleu had moved his bedding next to the kid's when his mom had returned to Northern Haven. After all, Ayanna was in the same hut, and Bleu wasn't taking any chances.

The thump of Atsushi's footsteps and the shuffle of clothing continued. "Oh, man, Att. Keep it down," Bleu groused.

"Sorry. I have to go to sunrise sit." Atsushi yawned and stumbled over something in the dark.

"It's not sunrise."

"It ends with the sunrise. Kahali just woke me. Part of my school on the Surface." Atsushi groaned at the torturous nature of his studies.

"Woke you? He came in?" Bleu sat up, suddenly alert.

"I wish. It was a nightmare...an insistent voice in my head telling me it's time. Apparently, that mind talk works as an alarm clock, but there's no off button." Atsushi snorted in disgust.

Bleu gasped at the invasion of privacy. "That's not right. Wait, school? I'll get Ayanna, then." Bleu groggily sat up and tried to decipher Ayanna's pelt-covered lump from Neviah's in the darkness.

"Just me, Bleu," Atsushi replied.

"No way." Ayanna's shape shifted and rose. "No special, boys-only training. If you learn it, so do I." She yawned. "What are we learning?"

Typical Ayanna. Beside Bleu, Atsushi's dark form chuckled. The kid shouldn't know his sister's silliness when she was half asleep. The lack of privacy in this place made keeping an eye on his sister a living nightmare. Girak's snores had stopped. Every pelt-covered lump probably lay awake and listening.

"Just go and let us graduates sleep." Neviah sounded cross, but Bleu knew that under her furs she was probably smirking at their new excuse.

"Everyone back to sleep. School later." Educator Girak sounded rather unenthusiastic about his chosen profession.

"I'm going. Ayanna, you can sleep." Atsushi shuffled toward the door.

"No. Rana said everything's equal here. I'm coming." She jumped up and, in her effort to pull on her parka as she approached the door, kicked Bleu. "Sorry." She giggled as she and Atsushi struggled under the woven door into the darkness beyond. "Which way?"

Another set of footsteps approached the outside of their hut.

"Oh, good, see him? Follow Kahali..." Atsushi's voice trailed off as their footsteps receded.

Bleu wished he could still hear them. He didn't like them traipsing around in the dark together. *It's not just that he likes her. It's dangerous out there.* He silently cursed the situation, though a part of him knew he was worrying too much. Kahali would keep them safe. He sighed, now wide awake.

"Bleu, go to sleep, or I'll create some post-graduate assignments for you." Apparently Girak had not gone back to sleep, either.

"Is that any way to talk to our new *Commander?*" Neviah quipped, giggling.

"Arghh! Stop it!" Bleu playfully smacked Neviah's pile of furs.

"They'll be fine, Bleu," Girak reassured him. "Get some sleep before that madman Savas returns today."

❋ ❋ ❋ ❋ ❋ ❋

Too soon, the bright sun intruded through the edges of the door flap. Bleu could deny the new day no longer. *I have to meet with Savas. Stamf's dead. Savas. Stamf.* The weight of his new responsibilities pressed him into the ground, making it hard to breathe.

"You can do it. Come on."

Bleu blinked. Educator Girak stood over him, offering a hand. Neviah must have risen earlier and snuck out while they still slept. Bleu clambered out from under his furs and forced a grin.

"That's right. Fake it till you make it." Girak smiled ruefully. "You don't have to do everything alone, Bleu. I'm not Stamf, but if you want to talk…" He turned and grabbed his parka and goggles. "Well, I'm around. Breakfast?"

Bleu nodded and slipped on his coat and boots. He'd deal with bathing after breakfast.

Girak pushed open the mat, and the morning sunlight poured in. Bleu stumbled backward from the door, eyes smarting, and yanked his goggles from his parka's pocket.

Girak chuckled. "Blue eyes are more sensitive to the brightness than brown. But Rana doesn't cover her eyes, so maybe there's hope for us?" Girak turned onto the path winding through the huts toward the gathering hall.

"She's a more evolved being. I'll hold on to my goggles." Bleu wondered if Kalakanya's green eyes were sensitive to light.

Since the ice huts housed even the tallest star beings, Bleu couldn't see over the sparkling structures, but he turned about on the path, hoping to catch a glimpse of her. From all directions came calls and gentle laughter as star beings strolled about, greeting each other. Their lilting language resembled a singer sweeping up and down the musical scale. Bleu paused, enjoying the morning symphony of their conversation, the light breeze, and the endless sky arching over it all. Stamf would have loved this new world.

"Bleu, come on." Girak laughed and motioned for him to keep walking. "I need food before I face Savas."

"Man, I need more than food."

Bleu hurried up the frozen, mud-covered rock path behind Girak. Higher up, a star being family exited the gathering hall and headed toward them. Their spirited daughter scampered ahead, then froze, her eyes wide as she took in their goggles. When the parents caught up to her, they offered the traditional greeting of touching their hearts, bowing, and extending their hands toward Bleu and Girak.

Bleu and Girak attempted to return the greeting, and the couple barely concealed their mirth. As the young girl giggled and hid behind her mother's cloak, Bleu laughed. "Guess we need to practice that pronunciation, eh?"

Perhaps, the mother replied, a mischievous twinkle in her eye, *unless you want others to think you're spontaneously squawking like a peleguin.*

Bleu laughed. "No, I wasn't going for that." As commander, he should probably ask Kalakanya or Rana to teach the team the proper greeting and other key phrases.

Bleu turned to suggest this, but Girak had knelt to allow the girl to examine his goggles. Her slender finger poked at his eye. Always the educator, he tapped on the lens, allowing her to do the same. Her eyes widened. Girak pulled off his goggles, wincing in the brightness but smiling. The girl grabbed his goggles and trilled in joy as she ran to her father, taking them with her. The father responded in his deep singsong voice, and the suddenly shy girl returned and handed the goggles to Girak.

"Thank you." Girak put them back on, and his whole face relaxed.

You may want to get breakfast before your friend Atsushi finishes everything. The father barked that strange star being laugh, and they continued down the path.

"You're a natural with them," Bleu said. "You should be the commander of our joint mission. Not me."

Girak waved his gloved hand in dismissal of the idea. "Not my thing. Consider me your ambassador, Commander Reinier." He laughed. "As such, I now lead you toward a delightful sampling of the local breakfast fare." Still beaming from his interaction with the family, Girak hurried up the hill.

Bleu followed him, tripping in his exhaustion the whole way. He was almost two decades younger and less qualified than Girak. He'd never led anything. Even in the holographic games, Stamf always took the role of leader. Bleu would make a royal mess of commanding.

I'm glad I found you two.

Startled out of his grouching, Bleu spun. Kalakanya approached from a crisscrossing path. Bleu's mood stopped mid-plummet and soared skyward.

"You're back." He couldn't stop the silly grin that overtook him.

Her smile deepened. She bowed low in the traditional greeting, revealing the intricate braided spiral of hair on the nape of her neck. Her whole body flowed through the greeting with elegant ease, the words flowing like music from her lips.

Shast. It was their turn to return it. "Don't laugh."

As Bleu shifted through the gesture and attempted the phrase, Kalakanya bit her lip to hold back her amusement.

"I was planning to ask you to help us all with the pronunciation," he added as he straightened.

Probably a good idea. Her jade eyes sparkled with mischief. *We found you all some clean clothing and left it at your hut. However, you should eat first. Savas will be here shortly, and we must prepare. May I join you both for breakfast?*

"Of course. Right, Girak?" If his ambassador said no, he'd fire him.

Girak raised an eyebrow at the two of them. "Actually, we're walking there together, but I'm looking for Atsushi. I promised to check in after his sunrise sit. Did you need to speak with me specifically?"

His ambassador was setting him up. In a good way.

No, not specifically. Was that amusement crossing her face? *If Atsushi had any issues with the morning meditation, Kahali should also be able to address them. If not, send him my way.*

"Thank you." Girak turned and looked Bleu in the eye. "Make sure you eat. We're out of protein bars until we get more."

"Understood."

Girak hurried up the path, away from them. Suddenly, being alone with Kalakanya seemed a ridiculous notion. Trivial in comparison with the weight of leading humanity's mission to save itself. All his previous concerns rose with a vengeance, swirling into a tornado of troubling threats.

"You said we need to prepare for meeting with Savas?" He looked hopefully at her. "You have a plan?"

I have suggestions. She smiled and motioned for them to continue toward the hall. *First of all, always keep yourself emotionally balanced so that you can act, not react. Savas will try to throw you off balance to gain the upper hand. For you to feel balanced, you need to learn to trust the One In All. But also, you must never forget the basics, like regular meals. You need food.*

"Okay." He hesitated. "Not to sound ungrateful, but I was hoping for something a little more specific to today's meeting."

I know. She continued in silence.

Bleu bit back his frustration and followed her into the hall. Kalakanya said something in her native tongue to one of the cooks. As soon as Bleu sat at an empty mat, a large platter of food appeared before him. In the corner to his left, Girak stood with two older star beings, chatting away. On his other side, Rana and her friends sat with Atsushi and Ayanna, surrounded by an enormous pile of empty platters.

Ayanna beamed with health. Just a few weeks ago, he had feared she would die. Now, she and Rana joked about how much Atsushi had eaten. Given all the scraped-clean dishes, they had good reason to tease him.

Your turn. Kalakanya sent. *Eat.*

"Thank you." Bleu pushed the plate between them, indicating Kalakanya should eat first.

I don't eat.

Bleu smirked. "Okay." Clearly, she was still in a cryptic mood. "Not hungry?"

That, too. She motioned toward the steaming food. *You eat. I'll talk.*

Bleu dug in. Truth was, he probably could eat it all. He had been starving ever since he reached the Surface. She must have eaten earlier, because no one could abstain from such delicious-smelling and colorful food. He scooped up a mound of orange mush, adding in a bit of what he hoped was berries. His taste buds practically danced at the exotic flavors. The sweet tang of the berries complimented the savory mush with perfection. *I'll need to make sure we pack plenty of food for the expedition. Stuff like this.*

Yes. The Furred Ones may not want to provide all our needs.

Bleu looked up puzzled. He'd been thinking, not conversing.

Sorry. Her face scrunched up apologetically. *Your thoughts weren't private, so I responded.*

"They were private. We've already established that I can't block you." Bleu studied her face for secrets. Her jade eyes never shifted, remaining always unguarded and true. Beyond the two of them, the others chatted and laughed. How did they focus if they heard all everyone's thoughts? "Is that normal, me not being able to block you?"

It doesn't seem unusual for you humans, but I'm not sure if its permanent or simply that you need to learn how to do it. She tilted her head as she watched him eat.

He took another bite, keenly aware of her gaze upon him while he chewed. Well, this was awkward. He quickly swallowed and then had to cough. "What? Am I doing something wrong?"

She smiled and shook her head. *No, I just get a different sense from you than the others.*

He chuckled. "Different? Like in a good way?"

He so wanted her to see him as different in a good way, but the odds of her being interested romantically in him were ridiculously low. She was another species. A more advanced species. And she still hadn't responded to his question, so it must be different in a bad way. He shoved in another mouthful of berries and wished Girak would come save him.

She raised an eyebrow playfully, as if she had heard that as well. Bleu turned away to pretend cough and recover himself. When he managed to face her again, she appeared thoroughly amused.

Different in a prophecy sort of way, she said, answering his earlier question. *You were mentioned in the prophecy I received, and I'm still trying to unravel what it means for the two of us.*

Bleu paused, his next spoonful halfway to his mouth, then lowered it. "The meaning is specific to you and me?"

She nodded. *I believe so, but with both of us in the middle of it, I'm not sure what to tell you.*

"The truth."

It's not that simple. She remained silent, staring at his chest where the heirloom pendant from Ayanna lay tucked under his clothing. Could she see through his layers to the pendant's blue lapis and silver design, cracked by the bullet Savas had shot at him?

Her gaze narrowed, and then she sighed, apparently making some sort of decision. *Before I Crowned, I had unusual visions. At first, they made no sense. Gradually, we figured out they were a mixture of past and future events. They connected to whoever I was staring at when the vision started. I call them transtemporal scans, because I can scan someone and see into their past and future.* Kalakanya's thought tone had grown soft, almost wistful. She focused her mesmerizing jade eyes on him. *It's not appropriate or helpful for me to share everything. But I still have to deal with what I see.*

Bleu nodded and looked away. He had trouble understanding his mom's visions, but compared to Kalakanya's, they were child's play. He stared at a berry stain on the mat by his bowl, feeling her gaze on him.

Blood pounded in his ears. Her power overwhelmed him. How had he even considered that she may think he was different in a good way? He was an amoeba to her.

Bleu. Her hand gently clasped his.

At her unexpected touch, he looked up.

You already knew most of this, didn't you? I'm the same star being you've known for fifteen suns.

"I know." He slowly shook his head trying to comprehend what it must be like to live with her abilities. He took a steadying breath, but it accomplished nothing. "Sorry, it's not you. It's that the more I learn about what you deal with, the more I feel like I'm a useless friend. How do you deal with knowing all that? Isn't it a huge burden?"

Surprise rippled across her face. *Sometimes. I thought I'd scared you.*

He met her gaze. "No." He flipped his hand so that his hand clasped hers back. "I just can't imagine living with that much information that no one else knows. It must be so...tricky?"

Her eyes widened. *Yes!* She nodded in excitement at his understanding. *Everyone assumes I can give them information like it's no big deal. But I must live with the responsibility of whatever I suggest. It's why I couldn't come to the meeting. I needed a break to clear my head after figuring all that out. I'm sorry you felt like I deserted you.*

"I never said that." He grinned. Had she been reading his thoughts even though she hadn't been at the meeting?

She shrugged, a slight smile tugging at the corner of her mouth.

Bleu chuckled. This was the weirdest conversation ever, but he was thoroughly enjoying it. "So, if I'm different somehow, why haven't you just read me? Make my neck prickle as you do the scan. That's what happens, right? What's the big secret? Do I die today or something?"

At his words, several nearby Crowned Ones turned toward the two of them. Bleu's face burned, and he gave the couple an embarrassed grin. "I'd rather know than not know," he explained to them.

They gave him and Kalakanya concerned looks before turning back to their meals.

Bleu, that's just it. When we first met, I could read you, though not as well as I usually read. But ever since I saw your pendant and realized that it was one of the blues in Sohana's Prophecy of the Three Blues, *I've had trouble reading you.* She frowned and looked down. *I've tried not to be intrusive, but I've never not been able to read someone before. I kept trying because I'm worried about what Savas is planning. I want to make sure you're safe.*

"Thanks, I appreciate it," he said, biting his lip to conceal his grin. She wanted to protect him. Maybe just because she was kind, or maybe because of something else. Either way, it was something.

His fingers traced out the smooth silver edge of the pendant under his shirt. Its warmth tingled against his skin. As his gaze rose to hers, a strange prickle travelled up his spine and knocked the base of his skull. It wasn't the subtle tickle of one of her transtemporal scans, but the blunt force of another vision barging into his mind.

No, not now, he begged. But visions don't listen to reason.

Everything fell away. The room, the mat, everything. He tumbled helplessly through empty darkness, wind whipping his hair and leaving his lungs unable to inhale. His arms clawed for something to hold on to.

Hands forcibly grabbed him, stopping his fall through the black nothingness. The violence of the fingers digging into him only increased his panic. What held him suspended? A strangely familiar blonde woman and her children reached for him as they were shoved past him, screaming. Desperately, they reached their arms toward him, trying to hold on, but they fell past him into the void below, crying in terror. The angry hands holding him yanked Bleu away while the woman and children continued to plummet into depths as deep as Northern Haven's elevator shaft.

Suddenly, he smashed onto the hard ground. Cold sweat covered his shaking body. He flung out his arms, grasping for something to prevent another fall. He grabbed with both hands, yanking something, no, *someone*, on top of him.

"Bleu!" It was Kalakanya's voice, too close to his ear. His eyes jerked open. A blurry Kalakanya pulled herself free and slid onto the floor beside him.

As she moved away, the world tilted, and he grasped at the mat, desperate not to fall forward onto the ceiling. Then, with a sickening lurch, the world righted itself, and he found himself panting on the floor.

He blinked, horrified at his own behavior. "What? I'm...I'm sorry."

"Try sitting up slowly," Kalakanya said, extending her hand.

He released his sweaty grip on the mat and accepted her hand. She pulled him upright.

Shast, every human and star being in the gathering hall stared at him. The echo of his screams mingled with those of the family, lacing around the pounding of his own heart.

From the hall's entrance came a sickening, almost embarrassed laugh. Bleu's gaze jerked toward the sound. *Shast*. Savas stood in the doorway, fiddling with the cuff of his orange parka. Bleu's stomach twisted. Why did that jerk have to show up right now?

"You'll have to excuse Bleu, everyone. He's had a lot of responsibility thrown at him the last few days. Come on, Bleu." He motioned for Bleu to get up and follow him. "Let's go talk about this expedition." Savas smiled broadly and again adjusted his parka cuff.

Struggling to contain his shaking, Bleu refused to respond to Savas' demand. Instead, he turned toward Kalakanya, hoping she'd explain his strange experience. But her face showed his own wide-eyed shock.

What happened? She took his hand in both of hers. Warm healing energy emanated from her palms into his still trembling hands. *The others cannot hear you if you mind talk to just me. Tell me what happened.*

Bleu stood straighter and swallowed. If she hadn't witnessed his weird mental spasm, he certainly wasn't going to tell her. *Nothing. Nothing happened, except I was...choking. I choked and fell.*

Her hands stiffened around his. *That's your explanation?* She waited, the hurt clear in those endless jade eyes.

He nodded and pulled his hands away.

Bleu, please don't shut me out. You can tell me—

"I'm sorry I made such a mess," he said loudly enough to be heard by all. He forced himself to focus on the fallen food rather than the dying screams. He had to concentrate on being a commander, not a fool.

"I'm fine." He cleared his throat to get rid of the hollow tone in his voice. Then, gaining his wits, he added a theatrical cough. "I just choked. The fall must have dislodged it." He grabbed the fallen food and stood. "Savas, why don't you eat something while I go clean myself up? I'll meet you back here."

Bleu strode past Kalakanya and Savas, avoiding eye contact. He rushed outside and downhill toward their guest hut. He'd inherited his mother's cursed visions, but his were even more frequent and dramatic. He'd made a fool of himself in front of everyone. With each thump of his feet, the horrible reality pounded deeper into his very bones. No matter how far he walked from the others, it wasn't far enough to ease his shame.

He hurried inside his hut and away from prying eyes. The promised clean clothes sat waiting. He grabbed them and ran to the bathhouse, hoping a bath would settle him.

Chapter 13

Peleguin-Rookery-By-The-Lake: Commander Kern Savas

Clearly, Savas's timing had been perfect, pushing open the entrance mat to find Bleu thrashing about on the floor. As Bleu rushed past him, Savas' nostrils were overcome by the salty brine of the kid's sweat. *Panicked. What did these* shast *creatures do to him while I was gone?*

Commander Savas stood completely still, baffled by his strong urge to protect the annoyingly virtuous Bleu. *Are these creatures affecting me, too?* He glanced at his wrist, stroking the new band with his fingertips. Its internal workings purred in perfect working order shown by the small green dot in the corner; the star beings couldn't reach his mind.

He stepped back outside and watched Bleu's hunched form hurry down the hill. The kid had always been odd and certainly didn't deserve to lead the expedition, but he *had* been Stamf's best friend. If the star beings were messing with Bleu, it was still his sworn duty to SHAST to protect the upstart. Running his fingers through his freshly cut and lightened hair—the one luxury he'd allowed himself on his return—he sighed and re-entered the gathering hall.

He scanned the gathered crowd, strategizing the best way to gather intel on what had happened to Bleu. Everyone had reseated themselves after Bleu's hasty exit. Ayanna. Atsushi. Girak. But Neviah wasn't present. He sighed at her dared absence when he needed her. She'd done a good job parroting his words at the meeting. Perhaps she was running late? Since he wasn't about to turn off his protective wristband to converse with Kalakanya on his own, he decided to start with the kids and hope Neviah showed up to interpret.

He strode through the diners, aware of the star beings' gasps as they experienced his unreadability. Grinning, he approached the kids, nestled near the warmth of the cooking fires. He nodded to a startled Crowned One, full of pride at the scientists' ingenuity that produced his protective wrist device. He paused within hearing range of Ayanna and Atsushi to eavesdrop while pretending to warm himself by the fire.

"I can't believe you're eating more," Ayanna teased. "You're a bottomless pit."

Atsushi grinned. "Atsushi lesson number four—if I'm hungry, all is well. If I ever say I don't have an appetite, be very, very concerned." He grimaced as if dying and faked falling onto the mat.

"Fine. Ayanna lesson four—if I'm hungry, you better share." She grabbed a pastry from his plate and tossed it into her mouth. They both erupted into laughter on each other's shoulders.

Savas stifled a chuckle at their behavior, stepped around the Crowned Ones' mat, and squatted on the floor near the pair. "Hello!"

Ayanna startled, and her stew-filled spoon lurched in her hand, dumping its contents onto Atsushi's knee. Atsushi wiped his pants clean, while Ayanna apologized for the dumped stew and then glared at Savas.

"Sorry, kids. Didn't mean to scare you. Everyone here's on edge. What did they do to Bleu after the meeting?" Savas glanced over to make sure Kalakanya had not left. He wanted to speak to her. Interrogate her, really.

"He choked on some strange food." Ayanna had her mother's dark eyes. Eyes that shot daggers with incredible precision.

Someone needed to teach the little darling some manners. But he kept his cool. He was trying to protect Bleu, and if she couldn't recognize that, then he shouldn't waste his time with her.

"I was here. Didn't look like choking to me." Savas leaned in toward Atsushi. "Do you think they were trying to control him?"

Atsushi scrunched his face. Both kids remained silent. Beyond them, Savas noticed Kahali glowering at him as if he'd actually hurt the kids.

That brooding teen was the only star being who openly admitted to hating humans. Did that make him more or less dangerous? He'd need to keep a close eye on that one.

Savas waved to the scowling fool, who broke his glare to glance at the kids and then back at Savas.

"Look, he didn't choke. I'd bet my life on that," Savas continued. "Either his mind is being messed with, or he's getting the Sickness. Neither one is good, but we can help him in either situation if we stay a team."

"He's. Not. Ill." Ayanna's steely voice rang clear. "You just want an excuse to replace him as commander."

"I'm still a commander, Ayanna, so you'd do well to watch your tone. I can't replace him. The star beings made that clear. Without him, we fail. So, like I said, we need to be a team even if you don't like me. Has anything odd happened while I was away?"

"No. They are wonderful people." Atsushi put down his spoon and turned his shoulders, squaring himself between Savas and Ayanna.

"They're the Undescended. Remember that, Atsushi. We don't know their intentions for humanity."

"Aghh!" Ayanna rolled her eyes. "They are not the Reapers you imagined, Savas."

"*Commander* Savas. So, if it's not the Sickness or mind control, what are your theories?"

"A chunk of elk. He choked, *Commander* of Northern Haven." Ayanna glared. "Just remember, Northern Haven ends at the door."

"Someone slept through her history classes. Northern Haven was founded by SHAST, The Subterranean Human Advancement of Science and Technology Project, formed by a coalition of all the world's nations. Its authority extends over the entire planet."

Ayanna looked away, mumbling something under her breath.

Fury rushed through him, but Savas squashed his anger. As annoying as she was, humanity needed strong-willed individuals to survive up here. However, she needed to wise up and realize her anger should be directed at the star beings, not him.

"I don't know what happened, but it's not the Sickness or the star beings." Atsushi put his arm protectively around Ayanna.

She didn't shrug it off, and Savas wondered what else had developed during his imprisonment. He nodded to Atsushi, smiled, and stood. "If you think of anything, anything at all related to this, let me know. We need to all work as a team for the common good."

Ayanna spun on him like a snake. "You know, maybe you should consider that the star beings *are* already acting for the common good, that Bleu's *not* sick, and that the *real problem* is that you see everyone as a potential threat."

Savas chuckled. She had no idea how close to the truth she was. "That, my dear, is what a strategist does. Who else is going to keep humanity safe? Someone has to be willing to ask the tough questions." The Council believed he did it as their strategist, but he knew otherwise. He was his mother's son and the last living Agent of SHAST.

"Arghhh!" Ayanna groaned and buried her face in her hands.

"The problem with that philosophy is that is that you're attacking our new allies," Atsushi said.

"If I'm wrong, yes. But if they're really as great as you claim, they'll tolerate it. However, if I'm right and this is all an act, I'll have saved your lives. So, consider me horrid if you must, but I'm not going to let Northern Haven be caught off guard."

He turned and realized Kalakanya had disappeared. *Of course she had. She knew he was on to them.*

"Just be careful, Atsushi. That's all I'm asking." With a nod he turned to leave.

The remaining star beings eyed him with concern as if he were a preternatural creature. Perhaps he was—a newly evolved human, impenetrable to their mental prowess. He gave his best smile and strode from the building.

Chapter 14

Peleguin-Rookery-By-The-Lake: Bleu Reinier

Bleu's frigid wash in the drafty bath hut did nothing to improve his day. But if he couldn't return to Northern Haven, he'd have to bathe the star being way. He rubbed himself dry with the wafer-like wood chips. Their chafing against his skin made him yearn for even the coarsest of towels. But when he was done, the wood's wonderful astringent tang clung to his goose-bumped skin.

Shivering, he struggled into the new leather shirt, pants, and long, furred vest. They slid over him, softer and more flexible than he had imagined. Once on, they were more form-fitting than his usual loose tunics and pants. He glanced downward and heaved a disgusted sigh. Years of Ayanna's constant commentary on his lack of fashion haunted him. He tucked the too long pants into his boots and shrugged hopelessly.

The clothing was not nearly as bad as his spectacle at breakfast. On his first day as commander, a vision had made him flail about at breakfast like a fool. In front of Kalakanya. In front of everyone. A deep inner chill swept through him, making his shivering even worse.

His mother's affliction had sowed havoc in her life. And here he was, already lying like she had to cover his visions up. His mom's visions had seemed sporadic. His own always involved Kalakanya in some way. His first one had been her giving him the dagger the day Ayanna got sick. Then he'd had another one after he'd been shot and Kalakanya had her strange reaction to seeing his pendant. Then today again in the gathering hall with her.

The disappointment in Kalakanya's eyes when he had lied to her haunted him. But he couldn't explain it to her in front of Savas. Even if the jerk hadn't been able to hear their conversation, Bleu would have had to relive that experience, and the family's screams had nearly done him in the first time. He shook out his tight arms and legs. He needed to move but couldn't get himself to leave the safety of this enclosed space and face the others.

Rap. Rap. Rap.

Bleu's stomach lurched. Knocking meant a human stood outside. Star beings cleansed freely in front of each other regardless of gender.

"Hold on. Be out in a minute." The events of the last week and the upcoming responsibilities cascaded down, smothering him. His breath came in unsteady rasps. *Stamf, I need you, man.* He paced back and forth, ever faster.

"Bleu? I'm coming in." Educator Girak's voice sounded unsure. The door swung out, and Girak stepped inside, looking down. "Sorry to crash in." He glanced up, and relief flooded his face at Bleu being fully clothed. "Savas is strutting around out there, inquiring about you and feigning concern."

Bleu continued pacing.

"You know we're all watching him, right? We all have your back."

"I know. Thanks. Just not having a good day." Bleu couldn't even make eye contact with Girak. He needed to keep moving, to keep convincing himself he was free and in control of something. He could walk. He could control his body. His mind was in his body. Maybe he could keep from spinning off in another vision if he kept his body busy.

"I saw your...whatever in the hall. What happened?" Girak stepped into Bleu's path, but he sidestepped around Girak and continued his pacing.

"I don't know. Nothing. I choked."

"Are you trying to convince me or yourself?" Chuckling, Girak put an arm out and clasped his shoulder. "Listen, strange things are happening to all of us, not just you. Rana and I saw Josefina in the Lion Circle."

He stopped in his tracks and stared over his shoulder at the older man.

Girak nodded, tears glistening in his eyes. "I know it sounds crazy, but ask Rana. I don't think you're crazy. And neither am I. Around these star beings, impossible things happen."

Bleu shook his head. His brain couldn't accept them seeing Josefina. "Was she real? Or are we just hallucinating from their exuded energy or something?"

"I don't know about your experience; you should ask them. Rana said sometimes the dead can communicate at the Lion Circle." Girak rubbed his forehead. "I know it makes no scientific sense, but that's where Jos appeared."

"Was she okay? Did she seem...mad?" Grief at his inability to rescue her in time flooded him.

"Angry? Whatever for? No. We talked, and she gave me information. Look, I'll tell you about it later, but right now, you need to be a commander."

He snorted at the ridiculousness of his situation. "Bleu Reinier, Commander of the Bath Hut."

"Commander *in* the bath house getting dressed for work. A commander who needs to deal with Savas. Don't let him know you were thrown by whatever happened. Act like it meant nothing. Keep up the choking story if it's the best you have, but don't let him see your fear."

"Hmm." He stopped pacing. Kalakanya had said something similar about staying balanced.

"You can do this. Stamf would tell you to go kick butt, right?" Girak said.

"Yeah." He sighed.

"So, go kick butt."

Bleu snorted. "Sure, nothing to it." He had to laugh at Girak's verbalization of one of Stamf's sayings. He took an odd comfort in knowing others remembered him. It kept his friend alive. "Thanks."

Girak nodded. "Get out there, Commander Reinier."

"Right." He rolled back his shoulders and pushed open the door and grinned over his shoulder at Girak. "Here goes nothing."

Girak grinned and waved him on, allowing the bath hut door to swing closed between them.

Commander Bleu Reinier did have a nice sound to it. The crisp air flooded his lungs, but its cold assault no longer made him wheeze. The sparkling light, though, was another thing. He fished in his parka's pocket for his tinted goggles.

Bleu. Kalakanya hurried around the corner of the bath hut and nearly sped into him. *Are you okay?*

"I wish everyone would stop asking that. I'm *fine.*"

But when hurt flashed in her eyes, he wasn't fine. He couldn't crack his facade. Not yet. If he shared his vision of the screaming people, he might not get himself put back together before Savas found him. Better to remain nonchalant and shut off from her.

Kalakanya sighed. *You and I have much to discuss at a later time, but right now, we need to meet with Savas.*

She turned and wove through the village's hive of activity. Crowned Ones gathered on logs serving as benches and engaged in woodworking, weaving, and teaching children. Adults tossed rocks at grinning adolescents who attempted to create an energetic shield and block them. Still others waved their arms in the air and created beautiful pictures that glinted like rainbows in the bright sunlight.

As they passed, the villagers smiled and paused in their activities as if mind speaking with Kalakanya. They'd then grin at Bleu and return to their work. Despite living in the village for over a week, he still marveled at their daily happiness.

As they approached the outskirts of the huts, they passed several groups cleaning large animal skins. Despite the horrid smell, the star beings sang bright melodies as they scrubbed the stretched pelts.

Suddenly, Kalakanya waved like a human. Bleu followed her gaze and resisted cringing. Savas approached with Neviah in his wake, fiddling with her communicator. Savas strode toward them, waving back as if greeting long lost friends. Of course, no one ever misplaced a friend in Northern Haven. There was only so far to go.

Bleu nodded and forced a smile. It seemed rude not to, given the facade of comradery and goodwill bearing down on him.

"Feeling better, Bleu?" Savas raised his eyebrows playfully, but Bleu only saw a cat waiting for the perfect moment to pounce on its prey. Neviah stood behind Savas, an unwilling witness to the feline antics.

"Yes. A bath and clean clothing will do that." Bleu managed a smile in Neviah's direction. "Is he going to drag you everywhere to translate for him?"

"Apparently." Neviah, still behind Savas' back, rolled her eyes. "Not sure what your plan is while I'm piloting another helicopter, Savas. Guess you'll survive by miming?" She looked very unconcerned for his survival.

Savas snorted with laughter. "I'll manage. I always do."

Come in. This is my home. Kalakanya took two steps to her left and motioned to the smallest hut in the village.

Given her elevated powers, Bleu had expected the grandest of homes. But star beings didn't equate power with status. *This must confuse the hell out of Savas.*

As Kalakanya lifted and held up the door flap for Bleu, he noticed her lips had curled into a mischievous smile. He grinned back, this time not caring that she'd listened in on his thoughts. Maybe if he stopped thinking the term "commander" and "Savas" as synonyms, he *could* do this commander thing.

Chapter 15

Peleguin-Rookery-By-The-Lake: Bleu Reinier

Ducking under Kalakanya's arm, Bleu entered a hut as sparsely appointed as their guest hut but smaller. Mats covered the floor, and a pile of neatly folded furs designated where she slept. He pictured her beautiful jade eyes closing in sleep and immediately stopped his mind. No privacy. His face crimsoned.

"What a cozy home." Savas' voice jerked Bleu back to the present. Neviah translated.

Thank you, Savas. Let's sit and get started. Kalakanya motioned to the floor mats.

As Bleu sat, the comfort of his new clothing surprised him, the leather conforming to his every move. He carefully sat erect, his shoulders rolled back, hoping he at least appeared confident. Beside him, Savas sat awkwardly in his bulky snow pants.

"Our helicopters will be ready for flight by this evening," Savas said, suddenly all business. "Neviah will need to return for the test flights. We should be able to leave in a few days. By my count, we have seven humans coming—myself and Neviah as the pilots, Bleu as Commander, Zach, Atsushi, and Girak. And the star beings will be?" Savas asked Kalakanya, leaving Bleu out of the discussion.

Rana, Kahali, Eka, and myself. I'm not sure if you've both met Eka, but he'll be returning to our village soon. I have also considered bringing

Bahujnana, our healer, but I think he will be needed here with the Sickness patients. Are any of your people that are coming healers?

"No, but we've all been trained in basic first aid. Our medic was killed during the atta—"—Savas' lips twitched upward—"unfortunate encounter where we shot Kahali. No one else has volunteered."

Neviah translated, leaving out his fumble.

Bleu leaned forward. "Kahali wants to come? Doesn't he prefer to avoid us?"

He has been assigned by his teachers to instruct Atsushi. We have found that avoiding those you disagree with only increases the chances for continued conflict.

Savas cleared his throat. "Look, this will be a difficult journey. We don't need the added complication of dealing with a trigger-happy star being."

"Trigger-happy? *We're* the ones who shot him." Fury coursed through Bleu.

He looked to Kalakanya for backup, but she sat completely composed. Savas glared at her, jaw muscle twitching.

Silence.

"I'm the commander," Bleu said, "and if Kahali is teaching Atsushi, then he's necessary."

"I still don't see why we're taking up seats with Atsushi and Girak," Savas said. "We could use those seats to bring back more people."

If we keep quarreling over things we have already decided, you will never find any humans.

"Each helicopter fits twenty-five people." Bleu said. "We can bring back thirty-nine, more if there are small children who can sit in their parents' laps. That would be a great boost, uhm...like thirteen percent of our population."

Savas raised an eyebrow. "Thirteen percent? You just calculated that in your head? I thought you applied to work with plants. You should be an engineer."

"*Commander* seems acceptable." Bleu grinned. "They're coming. We'll assess everyone's strengths and divvy up the jobs."

Savas' eyebrow stayed raised but his lip curled into a wolf-like grin. "I see. And I was concerned that you weren't feeling well. Have you seen

Bahujnana since breakfast? You know, to make sure everything is okay after your *choking*?"

I agree.

Bleu nearly did choke. "What? I'm fine."

Savas shrugged. "Then it will be a quick checkup. Unless you prefer to return with me this evening and have a full workup?"

Bleu clenched his jaw to avoid saying something he'd regret. "No, Bahujnana will be easier. He's right here, and I've grown quite fond of the fresh air."

"Great! Now food and gear. How much do you star beings eat? Would it be better if each species brings their own? We're planning on hunting along the way. To reduce the amount of food we need to bring."

That is not acceptable. You do not have the permission of the local furred ones.

Savas slapped his knee and threw his head back in deep laughter. Neviah's eyes widened, and Bleu realized the depth of the chasm between his expedition team's species.

I am serious.

"I know you are. That's what makes it so damn funny!" Savas shook his head, still guffawing. "Ask them for permission..."

"Savas. If we expect the star beings to assist us, we must respect their beliefs." Bleu turned to Kalakanya. "How much food will you need?"

Rana, Eka, and Kahali are still growing, so about what you would eat, Bleu. Don't worry about me.

Savas sobered, a suspicious look on his face. Before he could say anything rude, Bleu interjected, "What do you mean? You must eat."

Crowned Ones don't need to eat. Or rather, we eat extremely little.

"Like the vampire myths." Savas narrowed his eyes. "So how do you sustain yourselves?" His hand slid along his thigh toward his pocket.

Kalakanya, he has a weapon. Bleu hoped she got his attempt at mind talk.

We draw energy from the air. She gave Savas an amused smile. *We are no danger to you.*

"Let's talk on the level here. All life requires energy, and I've seen you manipulate large fields of energy. You must refuel yourself."

Kalakanya smiled. *As I said, once we are Crowned, we gain most of our energy from the One In All.* She waved her hand at the room. *Energy surrounds us.*

A shiver passed down Bleu's spine. He wasn't sure he wanted to know the answer to the question, but it burst from his lips. "You pull it from other living things?"

Kalakanya snorted and let out the disconcerting gurgling noise. Their laughter still unnerved him. Bleu glanced at Savas' hand, now inside his pocket.

Savas, I can shield faster than that bullet can pass through your parka and into the air. Maybe let me answer your question? She raised her eyebrows in a questioning manner.

"All the same, my hand is comfortable where it is." Savas' expression had gone cold, his jaw clenched. "Where. Do. You. Get. Your. Energy?"

Her lips curled in disgust. *We don't suck it from other things. That would be vile. We simply utilize the life force that surrounds and nourishes the planet.*

Savas face was a frozen, unreadable mask. "Prove it."

"That's wild!" Neviah seemed unfazed.

"Neviah, shut it." Savas snapped. "You're here to translate."

Neviah did not translate. She glared at Savas, then turned to Bleu. "This could change science as we know it."

Savas repeated, "Prove it. Prove you get it in a way that's not dangerous to us."

Neviah translated.

Kalakanya sputtered. *I— How? You would not see anything. If I'm tired, I enter a special meditative state, and the energy enters me. Perhaps your equipment might pick up something, but there is no way to prove it at this moment.*

"You don't need to prove it," Bleu said, shaking his head at Savas.

"What if we get halfway around the world and she sucks the batteries dry? We won't have a way home!"

Kalakanya snickered. *I assure you I will not suck your technology dry. We have been living up here quite fine without technology.*

"Unless you stopped using technology because it gets drained around you." Savas wouldn't drop it. "Why else would humanity's descendants stop using tech?"

As annoying as he was, Savas asked excellent questions. They waited.

Kalakanya took a deep breath as if to pull patience from the air. *I suspect our ancestors' technology didn't survive the harsh elements. Have you ever noticed that your technology allows you to do what we can do naturally? I believe technology served humanity to expand our minds to possibilities. You have many devices to communicate over distances, but you became dependent on them. Our ancestors lost that tech but instead of settling for no communication, found another way to achieve the same thing—mind talk.*

"You're saying humans created tech to experience possibilities that we can achieve without it?" Neviah's face glowed with excitement.

That is my theory from reading the time threads, but there's no way to prove it.

"If humans still exist on other parts of the planet, can you talk to them? Mind speak to them?" Bleu asked.

I can only search for and communicate with humans or star beings that I know. If you survived, it would seem likely there are others. I could Call them, like we Called you, but that would be futile and cruel as they'd have no way to answer.

"You're saying maybe not everyone on the Surface evolved into star beings?" Savas had rejoined the conversation, but Neviah remained silent.

Kalakanya raised an eyebrow and looked at Neviah, then Bleu.

Bleu turned to Savas. "Turn off your device. You must be able to, because they understood you in the gathering hall this morning."

"No."

"Why?" Bleu studied Savas' immovable face.

"I am protecting classified information."

"Ugh." Bleu rolled his eyes. "What? Our secret military of five thousand hiding behind the hill? What secrets could we possibly have?"

"The location of the other Havens. SHAST went to great lengths to protect that from those left on the Surface." Savas sneered at Kalakanya.

"Kalakanya, are you saying all humans on the Surface evolved?" Bleu asked.

Savas smirked at Bleu's restatement of his earlier question, making Bleu's stomach turn. But he had to know.

Kalakanya silently watched them. She seemed in no hurry to respond.

You are the first humans I have met.

Savas growled. "Not a direct answer."

"He's right. You seem to be avoiding the question." Bleu's stomach sank.

You are the first humans I have met. I cannot search for humans I have not met.

"But you are in contact with other star being villages. Someone must have seen humans," Neviah insisted with annoyance.

Kalakanya closed her eyes and was silent a long time. Her breathing became slow and deep. Bleu and the others exchanged concerned glances.

Finally, she opened her eyes. *I cannot give you the information you seek. There are some things beyond even our abilities. Can we not focus on finding your Havens?*

Bleu studied her face for the openness he had always found there. It was gone—like the humans left on the Surface centuries ago.

He became very still. Outside, the star being children continued with their games. On his one side sat the secretive Kalakanya, who apparently played games as well. On his other side sat Savas, hand in his pocket, probably aiming his gun at Kalakanya. Neviah was studying Kalakanya's features with fascination, probably mentally deciphering the evolutionary process for humans to become star beings. No one cared to patch this up.

If this alliance didn't stick, Ayanna wouldn't get treatment, and they'd have nowhere to live. *Has everything I've done been a mistake?* Bleu's heart beat out the seconds. The air around them was electrified, ready to ignite at any moment.

It was not a mistake. She had sent it only to him.

But as commander, he needed answers. Bleu studied her eyes for the openness he'd always known. "Trust goes both ways. What are you hiding?"

Bleu, it is not an option. I will not forfeit your lives. You know me.

"I thought I did." It was as if the ground had opened up and he was falling, unsure of anything. His heat raced as he searched for what he had known of her before. What he had trusted. It was gone. He was a fool.

"Then there's nothing for us here. See you around." Savas stood and walked toward the door.

Neviah blurted out a translation.

The answers you seek lead to death. You will die, Savas.

"That's your standard response whenever I disagree with you, sweetie." Savas shook his head in apparent disgust. "We all die sometime." He glared at her. "At least, those of us still human do."

But there is no reason to die young for a lost cause. We have a chance to successfully find your humans at the Havens. I will not participate in your deaths.

Savas narrowed his eyes. "Okay, Kalakanya. Tell me this. At which Havens do you see us finding humans—the Southern, Western, or Eastern? And Neviah, restate that exactly."

Neviah did.

Silence reigned as Kalakanya's pupils dilated. Her eyes moved rapidly left and right. They watched in silence until her pupils returned to their elongated normal state and focused on Savas.

Not the Eastern.

A muscle in Savas' jaw twitched as he glared at her in silence. Bleu was missing something. What had just happened? He glanced at Neviah, but she shrugged, clearly baffled as well.

Savas sighed and returned to his mat. "How did you know? Is my device not working?"

"What's going on?" Bleu felt like a child watching his parents talk circles around him in adult code.

Savas wants to know how I know that we should avoid the Eastern Haven. I know because I scanned the future of us going. We would find no humans there.

Bleu's fists clenched with rage. "Savas, what are you not sharing? How can this work with all these secrets?" Of course, Savas didn't want this expedition to work. At least, not with Bleu leading it.

Savas sat back and condescended to answer. "The Eastern Haven was destroyed years ago." His steely gaze never left Kalakanya's face. "We received an encoded message as they were attacked."

"What?" Neviah stiffened. "Why wasn't I told? I've been working on that for years!"

"We thought maybe they survived. But their last message was an SOS. They were being overrun."

Bleu's mind worked furiously. Savas had intel Bleu needed. And Kalakanya had just proven her skills. Again.

It would be so easy to trust her avoidance of his earlier question, but Bleu couldn't shake the fact that she had purposely avoided sharing important information. Her betrayal of their friendship was a knife in his back. Why had the Crowned Ones set him up as commander? Were they only pretending to help him? For the moment, he turned back to Savas. "Who overran them?"

"Humans. At least we assume so. The attack they reported sounded human, not something these"—he waved at the village beyond the walls—"would do."

We do not attack.

"Whatever." Savas casually studied the details of Kalakanya's hut. Except Bleu knew nothing he did was truly casual.

"Anything from the other Havens that we need to know, Savas?" Bleu wanted to smack the guy for setting him up to look the fool.

"No, Bleu, I believe that's it." He smirked. "But maybe you should ask your new girlfriend."

Neviah raised a questioning eyebrow at Bleu but remained silent on that one.

Kalakanya looked to Bleu, expecting him to translate when Neviah didn't. Bleu ground his teeth.

"Anything else we need to know, Kalakanya?" He tried to sound reasonable. But really, why bother? She must feel the anger pulsing through him ready to blow.

No. Luminary Vadin presented the rest at the meeting.

So, he had all the information he was going to get. They could search for Western Haven or Southern Haven. Savas probably had more intel on both of them, but he was done dealing with that egomaniac. He might as well choose at random. If he chose horribly wrong, Savas would no doubt inform Bleu of his foolish mistake to save the helicopters. "Good. We'll check out the Western Haven first. Savas, have the food arranged so that we carry it all. Kalakanya, bring what you all want to take to the helicopters before we leave in—how many days?"

"Three days," Savas answered.

"Good. I need some fresh air. See you in three, Savas." Bleu strode out, mindless of the others, the cold, and the blinding sunlight.

Chapter 16

Outskirts of Peleguin-Rookery-By-The-Lake: Kahali of Peleguin Rookery

Kahali's breath came out in steady huffs as he strode toward the lake, swinging one of Atsushi's sticks. He had to get stronger and healthier. Quickly. The mere idea of leaving with the humans in a few suns terrified him.

How could he keep himself and the others safe when short walks still exhausted him? Yesterday, he'd made it to the lake's edge and back, and he was determined to do it again today. And soon, he could switch to a heavier stick to build his arm muscles.

Yesterday, Atsushi had shyly suggested Kahali attach something to his stump to build his other shoulder's muscles as well. The idea had intrigued Kahali, but he hadn't let on to the kid. That human was an odd one, and Kahali had no idea how he was supposed to teach him survival stuff. The kid couldn't even walk properly in the slush without slipping all over.

Thrump.

Kahali scanned his surroundings for the source of the odd sound. Ahead, along the edge of the lake, a human tossed rocks out onto the ice. Anger radiated off him. Kahali froze and then ducked behind a nearby boulder. He was still a safe distance away, assuming the unidentified human hadn't snuck a hunting stick into their village.

Thrump. Thrump. Two more rocks skittered across the ice.

The last thing Kahali wanted was to be around a crazed human. But what if he was up to no good? The lake provided the village's water, and if that human was Savas, he might be up to something. Ignoring the masking hood and goggles, Kahali zeroed in on identifying the human's energy.

Bleu. Not the worst by far, but still, being far from the village with only a human in sight... Kahali shivered. Bahujnana had warned him that he'd have to mentally talk himself down in situations like this.

Bleu wasn't all bad. He'd hunted Kahali's people, but then jumped in front of Shams to save the child. He'd gone back into the poisonous gas at his own risk to get Kahali when they entered Northern Haven to stop the missile.

Bleu saved me. Kahali released his pent-up breath. Like all humans, Bleu could be violent, but even Kahali doubted he'd shoot him outright.

Kahali straightened up from behind his hiding spot. He had a walk to finish, and apparently now a lake to save from being stoned by Bleu. Kahali crunched a fallen branch, purposely alerting the human to his presence.

Bleu spun, a rock gripped over his shoulder like a weapon. Kahali raised a hand in the human greeting, and Bleu's hand dropped to his side. Bleu's face was covered, but his energy prickled. He wanted to be left alone.

"How long have you been watching me?" Bleu demanded.

The accusation riled Kahali, but he continued to walk forward. He stopped swinging his stick. Humans were reactive. *If you insist on staying at my village, you should realize that you will see us, and we will see you.*

"Nice avoidance of my question. I've noticed you all do that quite well." Bleu's thoughts, clear as his spoken words to Kahali, continued griping... *You answer indirectly. Don't tell the whole story. I thought you were better than that.*

Bleu turned toward the lake, raised his arm—

Panicked, Kahali threw up his shield.

Bleu hurled the rock as far as he could toward the center of the lake. *Thrump.* He turned to glimpse Kahali's shield before he could drop it.

For a moment, they just stared at each other. Kahali had overreacted. Made himself look like a reactive fool in an almost human response. Heat flushed his face.

"Sorry. I forgot..." Bleu took off his goggles as if to remind Kahali who he was. He winced at the bright light. "Kahali, I'd never—"

You're angry. Kahali couldn't resist the urge to defend his cowardice. *At us.*

"You're right. But that doesn't mean I'd whip a rock at your face." Bleu sighed, clearly frustrated. "I know you don't like anger, so I'll just stay away, okay?" Bleu stomped off down the shore.

Kahali let him go. What was the reckless human doing out here alone anyway? He couldn't walk any better than Atsushi, lacked a walking stick to test the edge of the lake, and couldn't shield against predators. He was going to get himself killed.

A ridiculous protective instinct rose within him. Bleu had kept him safe in his territory of Northern Haven. Shouldn't he do the same? But he froze, letting Bleu stride farther away from the village with each step.

He yearned to do nothing and ignore the human's predicament. Continue his walk in peace. Let the stupid human die. It was only fair.

No. He was a star being, not a violent human. He was better than that. Bleu had saved him that day in Northern Haven. Responsibility churned within him until it rose from his innards and erupted through his lips.

"Bleu." Kahali tried the strange word, heavy and clumsy in his mouth like lumpy porridge.

Bleu continued on. He hadn't heard. Or he was ignoring him.

"Bleu!"

Bleu stopped midstride and turned around. He had donned the goggles again that made him resemble a walking finned one. "Did I just *hear* you?"

"Wow." Kahali smirked. *You can hear.*

Bleu laughed. "You're... Who taught you that?"

"At-su-shi." And that was as much as he could do in human tongue. *You're right. I don't want to deal with angry humans. But I'm not going to let you do something reckless and get killed, either. And I have to finish my walk, which includes swinging my stick around as if I want to—*Kahali waggled his eyebrows in jest—*kill you.* He hoped the human recognized the joke for what it was.

"I don't need a babysitter." Bleu turned and continued walking away.

Kahali stood there a moment, grasping for the gist of "babysitter" from the mental image it sparked in Bleu's mind. The problem was, these Earth Children *did* need babysitters. And Kahali was the only star being around.

He jogged to catch up with Bleu, wincing as each impactful step stabbed into his shoulder. Panting and a bit lightheaded, he finally reached the human. As he teetered, he risked grabbing Bleu's shoulder to stop him.

Bleu shook off his hand and looked over his shoulder. His mouth frowned. "*Shast*, you look awful, Kahali. Go home. I'm fine."

No. Kahali plopped down on the snow to rest. The weird pain started again in his missing arm as if it were still there. Grinding his teeth, he glanced up at Bleu. *You're stuck with me, and I'm stuck with your anger. What are you so angry about?*

Bleu groaned in annoyance and looked around.

Kahali already knew no one else was in sight. He had stated the obvious—unless Bleu deserted him, they were stuck together for the moment. But if Bleu insisted on continuing onward, Kahali would be unable to follow.

"Did she send you to watch me?"

Who? No one sent me.

Bleu narrowed his eyes, and he bit his lip as he again turned and scanned the icy shore.

As he awaited Bleu's response, Kahali began massaging the end of his stump. Sometimes it helped with the pain. He had all day, though he was already swaying a bit with exhaustion.

Bleu hissed through his teeth. "Damn it, Kahali! Can you even make it home from here?"

Kahali snorted. Foolish human—even his concern was laced with anger. *Yes, and now who's avoiding answering questions?*

"Did Kalakanya send you to watch me?"

No. Why in the world would his cousin care what Bleu was doing?

Bleu's energy tangled itself in knots—relieved, disbelieving, angry at himself, and disappointed. Kahali observed it like a swirling flock of feathered ones, shifting and moving, never settling. No center.

Either he helped the human with his anger, or the guy was going to explode. *This anger. It's aimed at Kalakanya?*

"I've been thrown in charge of this expedition, which apparently she and the other Crowned Ones planned behind my back. And then instead of answering my questions so I can plan, she's withholding information. I'm responsible for lives. And Savas wants me dead. And all she can do is play games?" Bleu hurled another rock onto the lake. "She said she wanted to help. How is that helpful? I have no idea what crucial information she's withholding. But apparently"—his lip sneered—"I'm too *stupid* to handle it."

Kahali's laughter exploded out like a bark, and he fell back, striking the snow with his hand at the comic cluelessness of the human.

"How is that even remotely funny?"

Tears streaming down his face, and gasping for breath, Kahali sat up. The clueless human scowled at him. Kahali covered his mouth. *Sorry, but that's how the Crowned Ones operate. They do that to me and Rana and Balavati all the time. You do realize they're Crowned Ones, right?*

"The white hair kinda gives it away."

Ah! You do have a sense of humor. Another set of chuckles escaped him. Stifling his glee on this was harder than he expected. *They operate on a totally different level of consciousness than us.* Kahali grinned and waited for Bleu to see his error.

Bleu's deepening glare sobered him.

Kahali sucked in a deep breath and tried to make Bleu see reason. *When we Crown, we are forever changed. They don't think like we do, so I guess since you clearly think I'm weird, they must seem incomprehensible. And my poor cousin, Kalakanya, has it worse than most of them. You know about her transtemporal scan, right?*

Bleu furrowed his brow and gave a slight nod. "She explained it. I didn't know she was related to you."

Yeah, that's how she ended up in our village. Her parents lived way south, but she insisted they let her move up here to be "closer" to some future thing when she started her weird transtemporal scans. Her parents stayed up here with her until she Crowned, and then went back.

Bleu nodded, but still dripped anger. "Not to be rude, but she still has no reason to treat me like that. Like I'm a child." *Or a lesser species.*

Again, Bleu's thoughts were as readable as the sky, and Kahali fought back his annoyance. Humans thought everything came in levels of importance and that they should be on top. *You said she'd explained her transtemporal scans to you. Doesn't that explain why she's even harder to get a straight answer out of than the other Crowned Ones?*

Bleu shook his head and hurled another rock at the lake. "Seems to me she should be better at answering questions because she has more information."

He snorted. *No, it's the exact opposite. She usually won't answer anything because if she sees things and what she says doesn't make people happy, she has to live with it. She tries to help us pick the right path, but she often can't tell us much because telling the future sometimes changes it. It's a huge burden.* Kahali tilted his head and waited.

Bleu tapped the log at his feet with the tip of his boot while he mulled it over, and then nodded that he understood.

It probably was a lot to grasp for a human that hadn't grown up surrounded by Crowned Ones. *When she is refusing to answer something, that's why. She can't. It would hurt you or others. It would mess up the best possible path. It's why she spends so much time avoiding the rest of us.*

Understanding dawned in Bleu's eyes. His anger dropped from him like a clump of snow from a pine tree. "So, you just do whatever they say? That doesn't seem like much of a life for you." Shaking his head in disbelief, Bleu plopped down on a log beside him. "Or for us."

Kahali shrugged. *It works. It always has. When they share information, you know it's best to listen...* Except when they'd said not to do anything to help Rana escape from Northern Haven.

"I thought Kalakanya and I had a connection. Now I can't trust her." Bleu sighed and put his head in his hands. "Not anymore. Not now."

You trusted her enough to take her into Northern Haven to disable your weapons. What's changed?

"She's hiding something..." Bleu's voice dropped to a murmur. "She's become someone else."

No. She's the same. If anyone has changed, it's you. You're living with us and trying to understand our ways. But in the past, you hunted us.

Bleu's face crumpled. "I don't know what I was thinking that day."

You weren't thinking. Kahali snorted. *Humans lack that ability.*

Bleu grunted. "How do you stand us? How do you stand *me*?"

To not stand you would be to live in denial of your existence. And—Kahali poked him with his stick—*you pretty clearly exist. I'm stuck with you.*

Bleu chuckled, and they both fell into silence. Along the shore, a male peleguin glided in for a landing and began searching for pebbles. The poor creature was a bit late at his nest building.

"I still think she's changed."

I told you—Crowned Ones don't change. But the rest of us, well, we've all changed since we met you humans. Kahali raised his stump and waved it. *Not always in ways we've wanted to.*

"Sorry." Bleu's face clouded with emotions.

Are you the one that did this to me? Kahali's heart launched into a gallop.

Bleu raised his hands in innocence. "No. No, no, no. That's one thing I didn't do."

Kahali believed Bleu. But even so, his body shook inside. The last thing he wanted to do was travel with the humans. Especially Savas and Zach. Had one of them done this to him?

His breath became jagged. A tumult of images from the day he was hunted cascaded through his mind's eye. *Not now. Please, not now.* But it was already too late. He ducked his head, not wanting Bleu to see his weakness.

Somehow over the sounds of the hunting sticks blasting and his own screams as the humans shot him and the cave collapsed, he heard Bleu sliding closer to him on the log. "Kahali? Is it your arm? Are you in pain?"

He managed a small shake of his head, but his mind was a jumble of twisted horrors, and mind talk was beyond him.

"Okay, but what's wrong? Should I get another star being?"

Kahali yearned to be safe in his own hut, away from the human, but even there, he wouldn't escape from the torments of his own mind. Sweat trickled down his spine, and he shook. What if Bleu panicked and shot him?

Over the thumping of his own heart came the rustle of fabric as Bleu flipped up his hood. *One In All, please don't let him attack me.*

A mechanical crackle ripped through the air, making Kahali's whole body jerk.

"Girak? Girak? Tell a Crowned One to get to the lake now. Something's wrong. Kahali is hurt or something."

Kahali wanted to tell him to stop. But his body trembled so hard, he couldn't. It took all his strength to withstand the horrors unfolding in his head. He wrapped his arm around his legs and hid his face in his knees. He must look the fool. These stupid humans had ruined him.

"Kahali? Girak is getting someone. What should I do?"

Unable to form mind talk, Kahali just grunted. His whole body shivered.

"You're freezing." A moment later, Bleu wrapped his strange coat around Kahali's shoulders.

The unexpectedly kind act was both touching and repulsive. Kahali couldn't respond. Even through his clenched eyes, the bright flash warned of an arriving Crowned One.

"Kalakanya." The formal iciness in Bleu's voice fueled Kahali's tremors. The misunderstandings of humans had gotten him hunted in the past, and while part of him knew Bleu couldn't be armed, his body didn't trust that reality.

What happened? Kalakanya asked. The crunching of snow beneath her boots signaled her approach.

Bleu murmured a reply, but Kahali couldn't hear him over the sounds of hunting sticks and crashing ice in his head.

Kalakanya's warm hand touched his back. Warmth and calm flooded him. The images faded, but the terror remained.

"I'm...not...sure." Bleu's voice shook from either cold or anger. "He wanted to know if...if I shot him, and I said no."

But why are you two out here? You could both be hurt.

The heat from her hand seeped through Kahali, replacing his fear with love, cell by cell. The tension that had racked him evaporated from his body and seemed to pool itself between Bleu and Kalakanya.

"You wouldn't answer me. You leave so much out that you might as well lie," Bleu huffed in the cold.

Despite the tension swirling between the human and Crowned One, Kahali's heart slowed and the pressure that had squeezed his lungs released.

Kalakanya's hand still rested on his back, sending calmness. She clearly had no fear of Bleu, but when Kahali raised his face, Kalakanya pierced Bleu with that Crowned One look. Bleu glared back in defiance. As if that would help him.

It was kind of you to lend your coat, Bleu, but it's not coldness that's making him shake. Take it back before you get hypothermia.

Bleu cast a questioning glance to Kahali.

He'd had enough human drama for today. *I'm okay.*

He pushed against the log with his arm to stand up and pulled Bleu's bright coat off his shoulders. As he handed it back to Bleu, the human gave him a concerned glance.

Kahali ignored it. He was done being seen as the sick and weak one. *Thanks. Both of you.*

No problem. Kalakanya flashed him a smile that melted his annoyance. *We should get back.* She grasped Kahali's hand and extended the other toward Bleu.

The human took a step backward. "I'll walk."

Kahali rolled his eyes. *It's not safe. Give her your hand.*

"The Crowned Ones planned out making me commander. So, I'm sure her scans"—Bleu nodded his chin toward Kalakanya—"show I don't die before we leave. Right?" His last words came out a bit sharper than the rising wind.

Kalakanya's lips tightened, and she gave a tight nod. *I look forward to seeing you tomorrow at the launch.*

"Yes, since you've left me no choice in the matter."

Kahali glanced from Bleu's ashen face to Kalakanya's firmly set one. Whatever had happened between these two had left them both a tangled mess of emotions. He wanted to be as far away from both of them as possible. If only his strength had returned to allow him to leave them here to settle it.

Kalakanya stood completely still, a nonresponsive statue. Kahali felt the whirl of conflict within her and also knew the human would remain unaware of it. Bleu'd only see the cold stillness.

"I never thought the star beings would be the issue." Bleu's eyes welled with betrayal. "I thought I could trust you."

Kahali swallowed. He was definitely missing something here. How had the star beings been a problem? Why wasn't Kalakanya telling Bleu he made no sense? He loosened his grip on Kalakanya's hand, but she didn't let him go.

There's a difference between knowing what's going to happen and being able to control it. You don't know the whole story, Bleu.

"Because you won't tell me."

It is my burden to carry. She looked away. *I hope you can forgive me.*

Without warning, she star beamed Kahali back to the village. Her rush left Kahali wondering if she couldn't bear to hear Bleu's response. Because it was pretty clear that he *hadn't* forgiven her. Not yet.

A horrible thought clawed its way up to his awareness and perched in front of him.

Kalakanya saw future outcomes.

She had planned the Calling of the humans.

Had she foreseen that when Kahali Called them, he would end up like *this*? Had she calculated the loss of his arm as an acceptable loss?

Kahali stumbled away from her.

Suddenly, Bleu's anger toward his cousin made a lot more sense.

Chapter 17

Peleguin-Rookery-By-The-Lake: Atsushi Collins

"I'm ready," Atsushi said to Luminary Vadin, grasping his hand. Kahali's father had agreed to star beam him back to Northern Haven's door.

Vadin nodded, and a flash later Atsushi wobbled to stay upright outside the massive door of Northern Haven. He sucked in a deep belly breath as Kahali had taught him, and the ground stopped shifting.

"Thanks." Atsushi reclaimed his hand and straightened up. Since yesterday's meeting had made him a member of the expedition, he had to deal with Northern Haven's requirements: a medical exam, vaccinations, and school assignments. He considered the door. It remained closed, and no elevator shaft noises clanged from the other side. "Should we knock?"

He was joking, of course, but the Crowned One shrugged as if it was a real option.

Commander Savas said they would be waiting for you. I am not familiar with human protocols. Perhaps we should sing?

Atsushi snorted. "No, that would definitely keep the door locked."

Vadin grinned.

"Oh, I see. You were joking." Atsushi blushed. Crowned Ones, with their super serious attitude one minute and then dry jokes the next, kept him on his toes.

Beside them, the door rumbled, creaked, and began to open.

Luminary Vadin clasped Atsushi's shoulder. *Our threat of singing worked. I'll return for you in a few of your hours?*

"Yes, please. Thank you."

The door opened fully, revealing three armed men squinting into the bright daylight. Luminary Vadin's hawk-like gaze narrowed as the men waved their rifles in his general direction.

Vadin turned to him. *You're okay on your own?* Vadin tilted his head. *You don't require an escort inside?*

They had already discussed this. "No, I've lived my whole life here. I'm fine. Magic genes, remember?" He was referring to his unique and valuable genes that always earned him special status. Educator Girak had explained the value of good genes to Northern Haveners at the meeting where they'd discussed Atsushi's safety in returning.

Someday, you will need to display this magic. Luminary Vadin's eyes glinted with mischief. He touched his heart and extended his palms in a bow. *Be safe, Atsushi.*

Atsushi began raising his hands toward his chest to return the star being gesture.

No, son. They're watching you. Luminary Vadin turned to the men. As he also gave them the gesture, Vadin continued mind speaking to him only. *Do not anger them. Don't risk their anger on my behalf.* He gave Atsushi an almost Girak-like paternal smile and disappeared in a flash.

As Atsushi stepped toward the men, he gave them a nervous smile, but at their judgmental scowls, his gaze fell to the ground. Like his father, they also judged him as having chosen the wrong side. All his previous anxieties surged out of the elevator shaft and engulfed him as if they had been lying in wait for him since the night Ayanna, Girak, and he helped Rana escape through this same door.

"Hurry up, kid. We're freezing."

He recognized the voice—his classmate Sera's father. What was a cook doing, holding a gun?

Atsushi stumbled across the threshold and onto the elevator. *Kid?* In silent fury, he took off his goggles and headpiece and sucked in the bitter cold air.

Because after living for two weeks on the Surface, he could breathe unwarmed air. And because he wanted them to know he could do something they couldn't. He didn't even cough.

One of them grumbled something about crazy teens while another radioed for the door to be closed.

It clanged shut, exchanging vibrant sunlight for buzzing sterile bulbs. The elevator lurched down, returning him to his parents. He imagined their usual sugar-sweet smiles and stiff hugs. So different from Luminary Vadin's warm concern after only having spoken with Atsushi twice. Swallowing the lump of sadness in his throat, he realized a warm reaction from his own parents probably wasn't awaiting him below. Did Kahali know how lucky he was to have a dad like that?

Thinking of his mentor made him remember a lesson in managing strong emotions. Atsushi sucked in a few steadying breaths and focused on his ability to control his own breath. Breath he could control, but he had no control over how his parents judged his choice to save Rana. He would never choose to let someone die, and if they couldn't accept that, then so be it.

He could survive a few hours of their anger. A quick medical exam. A few shots to protect him from whatever viruses may lurk in the other Havens. Picking up his schoolwork. All while hopefully avoiding his brother, Liam, and his bullish friends.

His stomach lurched as the elevator continued its rapid descent, but his deep breathing seemed to help the elevator nausea as well. The surrounding men scrutinized his every breath as if his time on the Surface had suddenly transformed him into a feral animal.

A soft clicking noise behind the wall to his left caused him to step closer to it, searching for the source of the sound. As the clicking stopped, a fine spray came from all directions, and he startled.

"It's just to clean you of any wild pathogens you may be carrying," Sera's dad explained. "Otherwise, you might infect us all."

Atsushi considered reminding them that the star beings had accepted all the Sickness patients, but decided it was better to return to his old ways and remain silent. *Only a few hours...*

"Can you feel it when they're reading your mind?"

Atsushi looked up. "What?"

"Do you feel it? When they're prying into your head?" The man shook his head. "Must be terrible. No privacy." The man shuddered in revulsion.

"No, it's not like that at all." Atsushi's blood boiled at the suggestion.

"It's creepy. That's what it is." They all laughed.

The door opened, and Atsushi plunged into the corridor, more than happy for the escape. Rounding the corridor, he ran smack into the always sharply dressed Dr. Medicci.

"Ah! Just the young man I was coming to meet," the doctor said, smiling. "We have a lot to do this afternoon. Follow me." He did an about face and led Atsushi toward the medical corridors.

Atsushi sighed with relief that Dr. Medicci didn't seem angry that he, Girak, and Ayanna had helped Rana escape the doctor's lab. "It's just a couple of shots, right?" He peeled off his parka as he strode after the doctor.

"A couple of shots? You make me sound like a simpleton. My team and I have been working round the clock to recreate all the vaccinations people used to take on the Surface. We have no idea what you may run into."

Atsushi groaned. "So, a ton of shots, then. Sounds like fun."

Dr. Medicci waved him into a suite of medical rooms. "Actually, it's a bit overwhelming for the immune system. We've treated everyone that's going except Bleu and Girak, and everyone has had a mild reaction."

"So maybe we should skip it. I mean, if Bleu and Educator Girak are skipping it..."

"Girak's a Deplorable, not an Educator. Don't let him con your young mind into forgetting he's responsible for the death of two people."

"Not directly responsible. Educator Girak doesn't have a violent bone in his body."

"He had his hearing with the Council." Dr. Medicci pulled the door shut and held up a medical gown.

Atsushi grimaced and stepped backward. "I don't need a gown for a few shots."

"A battery of shots. And it's standard procedure. I don't have time to debate. Change into this." He tossed the gown onto the medical bed. "I'll be back in a minute with the first few." He pulled a few large vials from his pocket. "I'll need you to fill these as well."

"Huh?" Atsushi took them and turned them around in his hand.

"In my opinion, they never should have agreed to let you go on this trip. Too risky for someone with your genes. These are just a precaution. In case...well, you know, if you don't come back."

"You want me to..." Atsushi grimaced. He knew this day would arrive, but he still wasn't prepared.

"Yes, semen collection. I'll be back when you press this buzzer with the shots."

✻ ✻ ✻ ✻ ✻

Atsushi forced his eyelids open. The medical room spun, a swirl of silver equipment and lemon-yellow walls. "What? Did I react to the shots?" He'd been okay with the first four vaccinations but couldn't remember finishing up the last set.

"Oh, sweetie, you're awake." His mother's face hovered over him, more embellished perfection than concern. "You passed out during the final shot."

"Give him some air." His father's voice drifted across the room. "He's fine. Just the predicted reaction."

Atsushi rubbed his face as if waking himself up to hide his fury at his father's lack of concern. The predicted reaction was to pass out? Didn't anyone care?

Footsteps approached. "Well, you look better." Dr. Medicci grinned, while another woman held a device to Atsushi's throat and took his vitals. "Don't worry, Zach and Neviah passed out on the last one as well. You'll be fine."

"I've never passed out from a shot before." He sat up. His body felt like the Surface elevator had landed on him. "How long was I out?"

"You had a nice rest, dear," his mother said, patting him on his back. "Long enough that that nasty star being up there got tired of waiting and started sending his mental control down here asking about you." She shivered. "Simply dreadful."

His father put a comforting arm around her.

"Luminary Vadin? What did you tell him?"

"Nothing." His mother clucked her tongue and shook her shoulders in revulsion. "None of us are going up there with that *thing*."

Dr. Medicci grimaced at the mere mention of Luminary Vadin.

"Mom! He's worried. I told him it'd only be a few hours." He looked about for his clothes, but all he saw was a closed cabinet and a rolling cart with medical supplies.

"Well, we can't help it if you're so sensitive to the vaccinations." His father gave him a disappointed look.

Dr. Medicci cleared his throat. "As I said, both Zach and Neviah had similar reactions. There's nothing wrong with your son."

His father growled in disagreement. "There *is* something wrong with him. His traitorous decision to help that creature escape your lab ruins his chances of ever following in my footsteps as a Councilman, or of gaining any responsible job position." His father glared at him. "You had a brilliant future, and you threw it all away for some irresponsible teenage adventure."

"What? I *was* responsible. I saved Rana's life and helped prevent a war," he shouted. Something inside him cracked, and that anger that Kahali had warned him of bubbled out. "And if given the choice, I'd do it all again." As soon as the words were out, he knew it was a mistake. Dr. Medicci stepped back with a look of horror, and his parents gasped.

His father's nostrils flared. "Atsushi, we have tried to be good parents to you, but at times like this you truly test my patience. Your mother and I have faced a lot of criticism for what you did. I expected you to be apologetic. I hoped we could repair your reputation with you going on this expedition, but if you have no loyalty for your fellow humans and prefer those *things* up there, then perhaps you're not really my son anymore."

"Huh? I..." Atsushi's gaze dropped to the cold floor, and he struggled to breathe. What was he talking about? He'd only wanted to save Rana's life, he'd never deserted Northern Haven. Yes, he'd spoken in anger, but hadn't he had every right to be angry? Couldn't they see he'd helped Northern Haven by helping prevent war?

Perhaps you're not really my son anymore...

"Are—are you saying..." He couldn't form the words. His father had been so quick at the meeting to agree to let him go on the dangerous journey. To not care for his safety. He knew his father had been mad at him, but to be so angry that he didn't want to be his father anymore? Could parents do that?

"Dear, I think he's not quite right. It's the vaccinations..." His mother gave Atsushi a warning side-eye and patted his father's arm.

"Right," his father said, though his disapproving glare at Atsushi showed he didn't actually agree it was the vaccinations. He cleared his throat. "We collected your school stuff and your music while you slept." He dropped a few hand computers on the foot of the bed. "While on the expedition, we expect you to be responsible and do as Commander Savas says, not Bleu. I don't know how those creatures made you and Bleu—two of our brightest kids—so readily betray our interests. I don't want to hear of it happening again." His father shook his head in disgust and gave him a dismissive wave. "Go. Get up there and get *him* to leave with you so he stops invading our minds."

Atsushi turned away in disgust, covering his face. They wanted him prepared and gone as soon as possible. "Feel the love," he mumbled, then snapped his hand over his mouth in panic, hoping he hadn't made things worse.

"What?" His mother asked, wringing her hands together. "Are you going to be ill?"

"Yes, I might. Maybe you should leave." He kept his hands over his face to hide the traitorous tears. Why did it hurt so? Hadn't he always known they didn't really appreciate the way he saw things differently than they did? They had never loved him. He made gagging noises to cover his gasps, and his parents fled as Dr. Medicci handed him a metal bowl.

Chapter 18

Northern Haven: Atsushi Collins

As his parents' footsteps fled down the hallway, Atsushi found his lungs no longer worked properly. His parents were more concerned with how he'd made them look bad than they were with his well-being. They didn't want him and had left him alone here, and his constricting throat couldn't take in enough air.

It's called breathing, Atsushi. He remembered Kahali's laughter this morning when he'd spoken that. Atsushi had been sharing how different and out of control everything seemed since leaving Northern Haven, and Kahali had reassured him with jokes. His new mentor's humor cut through his panic, reminding him that even if his parents never spoke to him again, someone—Kahali—would still guide him. And with his parents not really caring and Girak talking about maybe staying to live at whatever haven they found, Atsushi needed someone to keep his mind from spinning off over all these changes.

His mentor had teased that humans were so frail and off balance that they couldn't breathe properly.

I'll show him he's wrong. I can do this. Atsushi sucked in a tremulous breath. And another. It helped.

Atsushi?

Dr. Medicci froze, and the other doctor gasped and dropped the vitals device.

Is Atsushi returning to the Surface this evening?

"That's Luminary Vadin!"

They both turned on Atsushi, incredulous. "It's a horrible violation of our minds." Dr. Medicci glared at him. "He's been doing this for hours. Are you going to puke or not?"

Atsushi wiped his eyes and shook his head. How ironic that his parents had left him alone to get sick while the Crowned One had been worried for hours.

"Good. You don't have a fever. I think you're fine. Get dressed. Your clothes are in that cabinet." He pointed across the room. "You missed dinner, so I'll have someone bring you a protein drink. You need to leave so the rest of us can think in peace."

"Okay." He'd missed dinner? No wonder Luminary Vadin was worried. Atsushi slid to the edge of the bed and lowered his bare feet onto the cold floor. Its coolness soothed the ache in his feet. Maybe the Surface's cold would soothe the rest of him.

Dr. Medicci finished making a note on his hand computer and turned to leave. But at the door, he paused and turned. "Atsushi, regardless of what your parents feel, we need you down here. You're very unique. Come back in one piece, okay?" The doctor gave him a wolfish smile and left him to get dressed.

They didn't need him. They just wanted his genetic contribution.

Breathe. Get up to Luminary Vadin, before they lose patience with him as well.

Ignoring the sting in his eyes, he focused on standing upright without holding on to the bed. His legs wobbled at first, but he found his clothes and then sat on the firm mattress to dress.

The father of a fellow student entered wearing a nonmedical tunic. With an apologetic grin, the man handed him a green drink. "The dining hall's closed. Algae is the best I could do."

Atsushi grimaced but slugged it down. "Okay, I'm ready."

"Don't forget your schoolwork." The man motioned toward the bed.

"Never," Atsushi quipped with mock seriousness. "I'm sure those lectures will be the only excitement I'll have while exploring the Surface."

The man chuckled at his sarcasm and spoke into his communicator. "He's ready. Meet him at the door." He clicked the communicator off and looked back at Atsushi. "Good luck out there. You're a brave kid to risk getting to know them. Even Commander Savas doesn't like staying overnight at their village."

Atsushi shook his head. "It's not bravery. I just realized they weren't dangerous before the rest of you. I watched Rana, the one we captured, heal Ayanna."

"Yeah. And you taking that risk saved my Luanna. She's up there now, and when Dr. Reinier returned, she reported that Luanna's getting better." He grinned and clasped Atsushi's shoulder. "It's a crazy miracle what you kids discovered. I wish I could meet one."

"Volunteer to be my escort back up to the Surface. I can introduce you."

"No." He shook his head. "They require those volunteers to be willing to shoot them dead if they try anything. I couldn't do that. They're saving my Luanna."

Atsushi's stomach turned. "All three of them agreed to that? Even Sera's dad?"

He rubbed his face. "I'm afraid so." He stared at the door. "Though he probably agreed only because he doesn't believe they'll ever try anything. He was there in the crowd when that female brought Ayanna back all healed."

"I guess that's something, at least." Atsushi wasn't really sure it was at all, but he had to get back up to Luminary Vadin before his mind talk was judged as *trying something*.

"Look, most folks here, we're both good and bad. People are scared, and when they're scared, they believe stupid stuff. But all us parents with kids up there being healed, we're counting on you."

Atsushi nodded, but the responsibility landed heavy on his shoulders. At fifteen, he had his hands full with his new mentor and wondering how to keep his budding relationship with Ayanna over the upcoming expedition. But Luanna's father was waiting, hoping for reassurance. "We learn more every day."

"Yes. I wonder just how much they are like us. Maybe they have good and bad ones, too. I love what they're doing for us—healing our kids and all—but we don't really know them. Not much in life is just black or white. There's a lot of gray."

"They're good. I can tell." Atsushi smiled with confidence and ignored the shiver that passed down his spine. The possibility of an evil star being was a nightmare he wouldn't consider. Couldn't. They would be unstoppable.

"Let's hope so. Maybe aliens lack the human penchant for violence. In any case, you get going. Please. I can't deal with him"—he nodded toward the ceiling to designate Luminary Vadin—"yelling in my head anymore."

"Happily." And Atsushi meant it. He missed the Surface already. "But you heard they're not aliens, right?"

The guy laughed. "They certainly aren't human. Wait, you're serious?"

Atsushi nodded. "No one has told you? I thought Savas must have gotten the message back here."

"Maybe to the Council, but I don't understand. What are they?"

"Our relatives. They evolved from the Undescended."

Luanna's father paled. "But they swore vengeance on us. And if they're related, they must have a dark side."

"Trust me. They're completely kind."

He shook his head. "You don't understand evolution. It's survival of the fittest, and we're no longer the fittest." He wrung his hands. "You better be careful up there. Don't trust them."

Atsushi just smiled and shook his head in disbelief of the man's fear. It wasn't worth arguing about. He had to get back to Luminary Vadin before the guy busted in, looking for him.

❋ ❋ ❋ ❋ ❋ ❋

Half an hour later, when the door shuddered open, Atsushi stepped onto the frozen ground with a light heart. Dusk had settled and the Milky Way stretched overhead. Though his body ached like he had the flu, the expanse of the Surface infected him with the thrill of freedom. Up here, he could become whoever he wanted to be.

Luminary Vadin's face lit up when he saw him. *I thought something bad had happened.* He strode closer and his eyes widened. *Did they hurt you? You look sickly.*

"I had a reaction to the vaccinations. I passed out, but I'll be fine. I'm sorry they didn't respond to your mind talk."

So, they heard? I wasn't sure if I was loud enough.

Atsushi laughed. "Oh, they heard you just fine. But it freaked them out."

The Crowned One's brow furrowed. *Interesting. Quite interesting.* He sighed. *Did you get food, or were you too ill to eat? We could have Bahujnana look you over and then get you some food.*

Atsushi stopped walking away from the door and stared at him in shock. "What?"

Do you want our healer to treat you so you feel up to eating? I've heard you really enjoy our food. Luminary Vadin grinned.

"Huh?" Atsushi's eyes teared. He sniffed and looked away. How was this guy so kind when his father wasn't even sure he wanted him anymore, and his mother hadn't argued on his behalf? His own people had only given him disgusting algae, a warning, and sent him packing.

Luminary Vadin watched him, his face a mask of concern. Atsushi looked away, lost as to what to do with such a response.

I'm so sorry that your visit was not what you hoped.

Atsushi got the distinct sense that Luminary Vadin had heard all of his thoughts. He stared at his boots as Luminary Vadin stepped closer and put a gentle hand on his shoulder.

I believe fear has infected your people, and you experienced the blunt end of it. You deserved a warm welcome, not that.

Didn't he, though? Atsushi sighed. He'd clearly gone against his own people to save Rana and now had no idea who or what his purpose was anymore. Was he a son? Part of the expedition? He felt like a piece of an ancient puzzle shoved into this future where he was adrift with no role. His freezer baby self would never fit anywhere.

Beside him, Luminary Vadin spread his arms. *If you were Kahali I'd hug you, but I'm not sure if you'd like that.*

Atsushi stiffened. What did one do when they were offered a hug? A hug sounded wonderful, but had his parents ever offered him one? His mind strained through memories, seeking a time he had gotten a hug. Only Ayanna's hug during their dangerous escape with Rana came to mind, and that had been surreal...

Shast, the Crowned One was still waiting for a reply. Atsushi shook his head. "I'm fine."

Luminary Vadin furrowed his brow.

"Sorry, I'm not used to anyone asking." He waved his hand toward the star being. "I'll be okay."

I was not suggesting you'd die without one. Vadin grinned. *I was suggesting that a hug might help.*

The guy was trying to make him laugh, and it worked. "If the offer still stands, I'll happily accept that dinner you mentioned."

Okay, that's easy. We can be at the gathering hall in a flash. He winked and held out his hand.

Atsushi took it.

A moment later, they were outside the dining hall. The soft firelight and savory scents drifted out the door like a warm invitation. The power Luminary Vadin had to suddenly star beam them from Northern Haven's door to the dining hall astounded him.

Releasing his tight grip on Vadin's hand, he shivered but resisted the urge to immediately enter the buildings glow. "Can I ask you a question?"

Always.

"How do you all think of us? Are we like Neanderthals, you know, cave people, to you?"

Vadin's lips curled upward in mirth. *You live in tunnels, not caves, correct?*

"Tunnels that were engineered, yeah. But still...we are..." How could he say what he feared? His heart raced.

It really changes nothing. I do not consider you to be less than us if that's your fear. But you do have a different level of awareness.

"And that makes us stupid." A chasm separated humans from star beings. That was clear.

No, not at all. Intelligence and awareness are not the same.

"Can my awareness change?" he asked.

Indeed. And it will likely do so, especially with Kahali teaching you lessons. It will be a pleasure to watch you unfold. Luminary Vadin's eyes sparkled with mischief. *Especially with your magic genes.*

Atsushi barked out a laugh. "Right." A bittersweet warmth filled him. This Crowned One wanted to watch his life develop, while his own parents had deserted him at the first threat of vomit.

Are you sure you're okay? You're still very pale.

"It's just a lot to take in. A lot of vaccinations and a lot to think about." Atsushi's mind whirred in circles. His conversation with Luanna's father about star beings having a dark side replayed in his mind. *Maybe aliens lack the human penchant for violence.*

Perhaps they did. But they weren't dealing with aliens. The star beings were humanity's descendants. Could humanity ever truly outgrow millennia of violence? He shivered in the rising wind and followed Vadin into the dining hall.

Like it or not, he was about to find out. Traveling together for months in helicopters would probably bring out the worst in them all.

Chapter 19

Peleguin-Rookery-By-The-Lake: Rana of Peleguin Rookery

On the morning of departure, Rana took Desna's hand and reassuringly rubbed her pup's chin. *It's just a quick flash, and I'll be with you the whole time,* she explained to Digga, a moment before Desna star beamed them to the helicopters. They reappeared in a breezy ice field with the silent helicopters in front of them. Digga growled in surprise at her first experience with star beaming and bounded away, running in circles and biting the ice.

"This is why I thought we should arrive early," Rana said, laughing. She wanted Digga to get any last-minute friskiness out of her system before take-off. The last thing she needed was to be trapped on the huge human contraption with a hyperactive cave digger pup. She carried only her pack, Digga, and the small package Ayanna had handed her to distribute in secret—surprise pictures she'd drawn for Bleu, Atsushi, and Girak.

As she studied the massive black machines, her heart galloped in her chest. She was actually going on this wild journey, and Eka was joining them! She still hadn't spoken to him since he'd left with his brothers, but she'd finally heard from him yesterday. Not from him directly, but his older brother Asav, who was Crowned, had relayed Eka's message.

Asav hadn't told her much, but instead asked her if she was okay with Eka accompanying her and the others on the journey. Such an odd question. *Of course* she wanted him to come. She had never wanted him to leave in the first place.

Then, to top off the weirdness, Asav had recommended she and Digga not leave the village alone until she talked to Eka. She frowned again, pondering the strangeness of it all.

"Looks like we're the first star beings here," Desna announced.

Rana nodded. "Digga!" Digga cocked her head in Rana's direction. *Stay away from the helicopters and the humans.* Digga grunted and rolled in some melting ice. At least it wasn't mud. Rana turned to her maha. "Can you stay until the others get here?"

"Of course." Desna took a few steps closer to the hulks of black metal. "It's amazing that things this huge can fly. Think of the stories you'll have to share when you return."

"I guess…" Rana said. She was excited to see Eka, and it did sound like a wild adventure, but she didn't want to travel with Savas and Zach. She didn't want to do *anything* with those two.

But she'd promised Girak she'd help him find other humans to live with. And now that Eka and Kahali were going, too many people she cared about would be locked inside these metal cages. She needed to make sure everyone stayed alive. At least she didn't need to worry about Balavati and Daman, who would be safe at home, watching out for Ayanna.

Desna walked up to the nearest helicopter and touched it, then turned and smiled at Rana. "Wow. This is a lot of that metal substance they're so fond of." She stroked the strange surface of the machine.

Rana gave a backward glance at Digga and then walked up to the helicopter and leaned inside. The entrance required a step up into a large enclosed area with a bunch of strange gray identical padded shapes in rows with black straps. To her right, toward the front of the helicopter, was an entrance to another area with two more of the padded shapes and a bunch of symbols and the big curved windows. To her left was another entrance to another large area with more padded shapes. "What do you think those are?" Rana asked, pointing to the shapes.

Savas, wearing his usual goggles and orange parka, ran around the outside of the helicopter, yelling about Rana checking out his precious helicopter. No one translated for him, but it was clear he believed she would damage it.

She only touched it. Desna nodded in approval at Savas. *They are quite miraculous inventions.*

Savas glared at where she had touched the entrance, then looked back to her and said something that sounded like a threat. He looked about, as if he were confused why she and Desna were there. "Zach!"

Rana shivered in recognition of that name.

Zach's head and shoulders popped out of the side of the other helicopter. "Yes, sir?" Thankfully, Zach didn't seem to have the same device that Savas wore, so she could understand his thoughts and grasped what he said. Maybe that would make it easier to avoid angering him?

Savas yelled something and then motioned for Zach to get out and stay with Rana and Desna as if they required supervision. Rana growled softly. They had just arrived, and already, Savas was angry at her. Where were Eka, Kahali, and Kalakanya?

As Zach climbed down from the helicopter, Lion Master Sandor and his now nearly grown cub, Sukti, star beamed in. The two white lions nodded in greeting to them all. Zach furrowed his brow at them but said nothing. Rana hadn't seen Zach and Sukti together since he had hunted the cub. The fury Rana had worked so hard to release flared inside her, and she instinctively took a protective step toward her lioness friend.

Sukti's eyes lit with joy as she spotted Rana and bounded toward her, all traces of her previous wound gone except for some missing fur. She rubbed her muzzle against Rana.

Be safe, friend, she purred.

Rana knelt and gave her a hug. *You, too. I wish you could come.*

Sukti side-eyed the helicopters and gave the lion version of a snort. *No.* With a friendly whack of her tail, Sukti turned and sauntered back toward Zach and sat in front of him.

Zach stepped around the lioness, ignoring her, until Sandor grunted at the human's rudeness. Zach tightened his jaw in fury and then yelled to Sandor, "You said I was *free*."

You are free to go on your trip, Sandor replied so that everyone heard, *but if you were free of your anger, you would know that she only came to wish you a safe trip.*

Zach's face reddened. "Fine." Clearly, Zach still resented his forced stay with the lions. He'd seen it as being kept against his will, just as Savas had despised staying with Ameya's family. With a groan of frustration, Zach faced the young lioness, thrust his hands into his pockets, and grumbled, "You know, I'm fully capable of taking care of myself."

Sukti stared at him in complete stillness except for her tail, which beat a rhythm on the snow. Whatever passed between them shifted something in Zach. His eyes widened, and he became as still as the lioness.

Finally, Sukti turned. With a quick bound to her father, they star beamed away. She hadn't even said goodbye.

Behind her, Rana heard the sounds of the others arriving, but she forced herself to ignore them for a moment. She cautiously approached the guy, eyeing the gun holstered to his thigh and watching for any telltale signs of danger. He had to be mostly safe if the Crowned Ones wanted her and the others to travel with him, right? *You okay?*

Zach blinked and then looked at her. "Yeah." His suspicious gaze narrowed to her eyes, and she felt his fear as he obviously studied their larger size and different pupils. He'd spent his time with the lions, but maybe he hadn't spoken to enough star beings to be used to them yet?

She attempted a reassuring smile. *Did she give you a vision or something? Was their journey in danger?*

He huffed and looked away as waves of annoyance pulsed off him. "It was nothing. Just some warning about a white bear. Everyone knows polar bears are dangerous." Zach scowled at the spot where the two lions had disappeared and then stormed back into the helicopter.

As Zach slammed the helicopter door shut, she found herself agreeing with the human's statement. A warning about a white bear did seem odd.

A gentle hand touched her arm. "Hey, you okay?"

She'd know that voice anywhere. Her whole body warmed as she spun to face Eka's incandescent smile. "Oh, I missed you!" She pounced on him, hugging him fiercely. Over his shoulder, she saw Kahali raise an eyebrow at her exuberant greeting.

"Rana, it's best not to tackle our fellow travelers," Kahali called. "Besides, Eka's good at shielding, and we might need him later."

Eka gave a deep laugh, his chest rumbling against hers. "I feel his love."

Rana chuckled. "Yes, that's Kahali."

She glanced over at Kahali, who raised an eyebrow at her and Eka's continued embrace before turning and discussing something with his fathers. She stepped back and patted Eka's firm chest. Oneness, it was, as Balavati would say, a very nice chest.

"I've been worried about you. When we get a chance," she said, sparing a wary glance at the humans gathering around them, "you need to let me know what happened."

Eka put his gloved hand over hers. "You have no idea how much I have to tell you. I've been wanting to talk to you every day since I left, but things got a bit...chaotic. I'm sorry." His glance dropped to her chest, then the ground at her feet. "Wait. Where's Digga?"

Rana shrugged. "Around here somewhere. I thought it best that she run around and dig a bit before we get inside those things," she said, motioning at the helicopters.

Eka's usually calm face had grown tight with worry, but when she opened her mouth to ask what was wrong, he shook his head and sighed. "Sorry, I'm sure she's fine. There's lots of us around. I'll explain everything as soon as we can talk in private." He nodded in acknowledgment at Desna, who was approaching.

"Rana, dear, I'm not sure how the humans are going to handle this," Desna said. "I'm going to hug you goodbye now, and I'll be over there if you need me." She motioned to where Eka's maha and brothers stood with Kahali's dads and sister.

Desna wrapped her in a warm hug. "Trust your connection to Digga and the animals, okay? And I know you might not be able to Call us over the long distances involved, but I want you to know we are here. I'll be there in a flash if I possibly can, okay?"

Rana nodded against Desna's shoulder, suddenly panicked that she'd be as vulnerable out there as her Uncrowned parents had been. She hadn't even considered that only Kalakanya could locate people who were not actively Calling, and that she, Kahali, and Eka couldn't Call over the vast distances they'd be traveling. Oneness, they really would be on their own with the humans.

"I love you, Maha." She kissed her maha's cheek. Sniffing, she pulled back. "We'll be okay."

"I know." Desna's eyes were damp. "You be careful, too, Eka."

"Thank you." Eka started to bow, but Desna scoffed and pulled him in for a hug.

"I'll be praying for you all." She winked and motioned at something over Rana's shoulder.

Rana turned to see Commander Savas jump down from one of the helicopters and yell for Neviah. The icy commander waited for Neviah to join him and then strode over, gaze narrowed at Eka.

As he got closer, he slowed, staring at Eka's long hair. "I've never before seen hair like yours on a man."

Neviah rolled her eyes in embarrassment as she translated. Eka laughed, but Rana could only sputter.

I've never seen hair as short as yours on anyone but babies, Eka responded with a grin.

Savas' jaw twitched, and Rana almost sparked a shield, but then Savas' upper lip quirked as if he might actually laugh before his usual coldness returned.

"So, you're Eeka?" Savas asked.

Eka laughed. *Close.* "E-ka." *And you're...* "Savas?"

"Commander Savas. Bleu's in charge of this mission, but I'm still Northern Haven's commander." Again, Neviah translated.

Okay. Well, you can just call me Eka. Eka bowed in the traditional greeting.

"Yeah, don't expect me to do that back. I've got work to do." Commander Savas spun and left.

Neviah translated and then added, "Please don't hate me for parroting his words. I'm only saying them, so you know what he's saying. I'm not agreeing with him. I want to make that clear, okay?" She grinned. "Okay, I've got to go get ready to fly."

I vote that we get on hers, not Savas' helicopter, Rana said, and Eka chuckled. He must have had quite the adventure if this was all so funny to him.

Chapter 20

Peleguin-Rookery-By-The-Lake: Bleu Reinier

Bleu was going to be late on his first day as commander. Grabbing his bags, he ducked under the flap of their guest hut and hurried after Girak and Atsushi into the too bright light. Kalakanya stood waiting outside. *Shast.* He'd planned to walk to Kahali's hut and to travel with his reluctant friend and fathers to the helicopter. But *she* was already here, waiting.

He narrowed his gaze at Kalakanya. It pierced him to his core to keep her at arm's length, but her lack of disclosure at the meeting had betrayed their previous open communication. He wanted to believe her. Trust her.

But he couldn't. Not yet. The problem was that today, he wasn't just Bleu. He was Commander Reinier, and commanders needed to maintain team cohesion. If he couldn't get along with all the star beings, how could he expect Savas and Zach to? He gave her his best smile, a forced mutation of one that Stamf would have laughed out loud at.

Are you ready, Commander Reinier? She beamed at him. *I can transport you all there now.*

Damn, she was hard to be angry at. Everyone needed him to make this work. Ayanna needed him to make this work. He shoved away his hurt and considered her offer to transport all three men.

"You sure about this? All three of us at once?" They were running late. Girak, Atsushi, and he all needed to star beam to the launch site in the Valley of Ice.

Yes. Kalakanya smiled with amusement. *It's only the mind that makes star beaming three humans seem more difficult than one. As long as we have physical contact.* She extended her arms, as Bleu and the others exchanged nervous glances.

"So," Girak said with confusion, "we take your hands? All three of us?"

Yes. Her eyebrows made a delicate arch. *You had no concern when Bahujnana or Luminary Vadin transported a group of you. Is this your false belief that women are less capable?*

"No," they protested in unison.

She laughed. *So?*

"It just seems...ah, disrespectful for three men to grab hold of you," Bleu tried.

Well, unless you want to walk and be late—she laughed—*get over it.* She again extended her arms.

Bleu exchanged glances with the others, and they all stepped forward. Girak took one hand and Atsushi clasped her other one. Bleu froze in confusion until he caught her barely restraining her smirk. He stepped up nose to nose with her and rested his hand on her shoulder. She was short for a star being, only a centimeter or two taller than him. Almost a perfect match.

The corners of her lips twitched upward. "And we're off."

Bleu raised an eyebrow in amazement.

She laughed as they dissolved into nothingness and reappeared in the frigid Valley of Ice.

"You spoke just now." Bleu shivered in the blustery wind that raced the length of the valley, making the Valley of Ice much colder than anywhere else he had visited on the Surface.

Kalakanya grinned as he yanked his hand from her shoulder. "I am learning," she said as if learning another language without lessons was a piece of cake.

"Nice of you to show up," Savas shouted over to them. He was doing final checks on his helicopter while Neviah paced around the second one, doing the same thing.

"Sorry to disappoint you." Probably not the best way to get started, but Savas just laughed and continued checking his copter.

Shast. This trip to the other havens that he and Stamf had dreamed about was happening with him ridiculously in charge. As Bleu foundered for what to do to look commander-like, Neviah stopped her work to approach.

"Remember saying you'd never get into my helicopter?" she teased. "Does that mean you'd rather fly with Savas?" Laughing, she returned to her checklist.

Stamf was supposed to be the second pilot. His absence smacked Bleu in the chest for the thousandth time, and his chest tightened. They were supposed to do this together, to explore the world together. Stamf was supposed to pilot, not Neviah. Beneath his goggles, Bleu's eyes smarted.

"Bleu." Savas strode toward him.

The incoming psychopath kicked Bleu's brain back into gear. He blinked away the memories and straightened up. "Yes?"

"We're all loaded with everything divided evenly between both. The anti-freezing equipment was tested multiple times. You got that report, I presume?"

Bleu nodded.

"Good. Zach is checking that everything's secure inside the helicopters right now. I was thinking you and I should split up, just in case." Savas' eye twitched.

Bleu wondered if that signaled Savas plotting his demise. He had to wrench back control before Savas completely took over this mission. *Make a decision. Quickly.*

He glanced back at Kalakanya and the humans. Four star beings were going on the mission. "Yes. And we'll split up the star beings, because their skills and knowledge may come in handy if we have any equipment issues."

"Our equipment will be fine, Bleu," Savas chided, avoiding using his title. "But if you think splitting them will help, go for it. Just keep that Kalakanya with you. She's a bit too creepy if you ask me."

Bleu stiffened. "I didn't." Here they were, not even on the copters, and the jerk was already insulting them. "We're a team. If you have such thoughts, keep them to yourself."

Savas' eyes narrowed, and he glared back. Tension crackled between them. Then Savas cracked a half grin. "Sure. After all, I'm the only one here who *can* keep my thoughts to myself, right? Might as well enjoy that right."

Bleu bit his cheek in frustration, but it wasn't a battle worth fighting. "How long until we lift off?"

"I'm ready." Savas turned to Neviah. "How long?" he yelled over the sound of the engines.

"Ready as I'll ever be." Neviah grinned and gave a thumb's up. Unlike Savas, she had gadgets stuffed in every one of her orange parka pockets.

"Good." Bleu approached the star beings who huddled off to the side and grimaced with alarm at the rapidly spinning helicopter blades. "Are you ready? It's time."

Rana looked around the ground as if searching for something that had fallen. Eka shrugged at her behavior and smiled apologetically to Bleu.

Rana was still examining the ground and walking about.

Bleu gave her a questioning look. "Rana, what's wrong?"

Digga was just here.

Bleu's heart thumped. "Digga's coming? What if she tears a hole through the copter?"

Rana raised her eyebrows and snorted with amusement. *She goes wherever I go. And she'd never do that.*

Rana seriously expected them to transport a cave digger in their brand-new helicopters? Was she mad? Bleu looked back up at Eka for help.

Digga goes everywhere with her. She has to. Eka gave him a playful shrug and began walking around calling out to Digga.

"What in the world are you doing? We're on a schedule," Savas yelled over at them.

This was exactly the kind of craziness Bleu had feared. "Look, Rana, we can't wait. She can stay here at the village with your maha."

Desna shot him a nasty look. *Oh no. She goes with Rana.*

Neviah screamed from where she stood on the far side of her helicopter. Savas had his rifle on his shoulder in an instant, and a second later, Kalakanya threw a shield around him. They all ran toward Neviah as Savas yelled every curse word in existence at Kalakanya.

The snow near Neviah's feet shifted as if there was a small earthquake. It tugged at Bleu's memory. Savas continued to curse, and Zach appeared, gun out but not yet raised.

Don't hunt! It's Digga! Rana threw herself in front of Zach as a snout popped out of the snow. Growling and huffing snow from her nostrils, the pup emerged.

Kalakanya turned to Savas and released the shield. *I apologize for that, Savas. We can't have any more hunting. That was agreed at the meeting.*

"You stupid wench," Savas growled. "There's a difference between defending my team and hunting!"

I will not let predators harm you. You must trust us. There will be no killing. Simple.

"Get that stupid animal out of here." Savas snapped his mouth shut and narrowed his eyes at Kalakanya. "Did you just understand what I said without someone translating?"

Everyone turned to Kalakanya except Neviah. She continued to back away from Digga and toward the other helicopter door. Kalakanya turned to Neviah, who usually translated for Savas. Neviah looked up at the silence, having missed the whole question.

"Could you understand Commander Savas?" Zach translated for Kalakanya.

Not specifically. But he was clearly furious about me shielding us from his long stick.

Zach coughed at the last two words and struggled to keep a straight face. "It's called a rifle." He turned to Savas and smirked.

"Ah, guys." Neviah waved to get their attention. Digga licked at her insulated pants, rubbing her snow-covered snout against her knee.

Sorry. Rana rushed over to where Neviah had flattened herself against the helicopter. *Digga, stop.* Digga grunted and began eating snow near Rana's feet.

"She's trained. Right, Rana?" Bleu asked. *She had better answer yes.*

All the star beings chuckled.

Shast. They had heard him. Or was she that obviously untrained? He willed his face to stop blushing. "Well, is she?"

Yes. Rana smiled. *Though she's also only a few moons old, she's started to hunt for her own food and will do whatever it takes to protect us.*

"I bet Ms. Peace doesn't put a shield around *her*," Savas muttered.

Bleu glared at Savas. "Good, Rana. She travels in the same helicopter with you, and you keep her far away from the pilot and supplies. That work?"

Rana nodded and scratched the cave digger's brown-and-white-striped head.

"Okay, I don't care how you split up, but we need two star beings to help on each helicopter. Get on." He waved his arm toward the helicopters in a manner he hoped looked worthy of a commander.

Neviah and Savas went to their helicopters, and everyone else followed Neviah. Awareness seemed to dawn on them that half of them needed to follow Savas, and they floundered. Bleu, watching them from behind, grimaced and waited to give them a chance to choose. Zach shook his head at the others' indecision and hurried after Savas.

The four star beings and four other humans darted glances at each other. He could command them, but he waited, sensing this moment might provide valuable information on the group's interactions.

They stood rooted as if a deep chasm existed between where they stood in safety and Savas' helicopter. No one wanted to cross it. Was he wrong? Should he jump in?

Rana's head swiveled between the door to Savas' helicopter and where Digga had terrified Neviah. Bleu could imagine how unappealing either option was, but she'd be safer with Neviah, who wasn't itching to hunt. Unable to take the tension anymore, he strode over to Rana.

But as he reached her, she tugged on Digga's ruff and they stepped toward Savas' helicopter. What was she doing?

"Digga might be better off with Neviah," he whispered.

Rana spun, her eyes wide. *Yes, she would be. But if she scared Neviah, we would all crash. Savas isn't scared of her.* She gave a strange snort. *And this time he hasn't drugged me, so I can shield.*

"Right." He exhaled a breath he hadn't realized he was holding. "That's very logical."

And brave. Thank you. He hoped they all heard this time.

While they talked, Kahali and Eka stepped behind Rana and Digga to follow.

Kahali, I need you in the helicopter with Bleu and me, Kalakanya mind spoke. More of a command, actually.

Kahali spun, eyes flashing. *I'm not leaving Rana with him.*

She has Digga. And Eka.

This resulted in a stare-off between Kahali and Kalakanya. Clearly, a private debate was underway, and by his darkening expression, Kahali was losing. He glanced in Bleu's direction, and Bleu remembered Kahali telling him how one should never argue with a Crowned One. So, what was he doing?

As the two of them stood there in a completely silent battle of the wills, on their left Atsushi and Girak argued about the safety of an educator turned Deplorable around Savas. Atsushi, not waiting to be declared winner, rushed to Savas' helicopter. Girak grumbled and then slogged his stuff to Neviah's copter and boarded.

As Kahali trembled with emotion, Bleu feared he was about to go into another of his episodes.

Zach stuck his head out the door. "They're still at it?" He shook his head in disgust and gave Bleu a dramatic wave. He slammed their door shut, and Kahali startled.

"Come on, Kahali." Bleu risked touching his shoulder. "Please. I'm sure if Rana was in danger, Kalakanya would have stopped her."

Kahali stiffened and gave Kalakanya a snarling glare. *Yes, just like she stopped me from Calling so I wouldn't get shot and lose my arm.*

Kalakanya's face drained of color. *I...Kahali, I didn't know. There were so many threads, many of which were deadly. I chose the safest. I swear.*

Kahali, tears welling in his eyes, just grunted and carried his pack to Neviah's helicopter. Bleu felt gutted. His concerns with Kalakanya paled in comparison to Kahali's issues. And he had never fully considered the responsibility burden of Kalakanya's gift. He turned to her, but she avoided meeting his eyes, and with shoulders slumped, she climbed in after Kahali.

"And we're off to a great start," Bleu muttered.

He retrieved his pack from where he had dropped it when Neviah had screamed. He needed to board, and inside sat his team members, ready to tear each other to shreds. The open door waited for him.

When he had stared at the door to the Surface a few months ago, just getting out under the sky was all he dreamed off. Now, by going through this door, he would not be under the sky, but soaring through it. His heart thumped with excitement, and he ran the last few steps and climbed aboard. Grinning at the others, who were all still in their funk, he poked his head into the pilot compartment.

"Ready?"

Neviah turned, communication headset on her head—meaning Savas could now hear everything she said—and she gave a thumb's up. "Savas says you're slow." She rolled her eyes.

"Of course, he does." Bleu grinned. "So, why don't you take off first? After all, you're transporting the commander, right?"

"Sounds like a plan. As soon as you are seated, Commander Reinier." Smirking, she jabbed her thumb over her shoulder.

Bleu grabbed the extra headphones—the set that didn't require the implant at the back of the wearer's head. "I'll listen in periodically, just in case he gets, uh, crafty."

Neviah nodded, and her lips moved in a silent *thank you.*

Bleu sat near the others, and as soon as his seatbelt clicked, they lifted off. First.

Chapter 21

In Flight: Commander Kern Savas

"Neviah," Savas bellowed as her helicopter soared into the air. "Safety protocol!" *Stupid, stupid kids.* "Straighten out and check your list. This isn't a holo-game."

He scanned down his checklist. Someone had to be the responsible adult on this mission. "Preparing for liftoff." He clicked off his radio and yelled over his shoulder, "Rana, now's a good time to keep your monster under control." He clicked his radio back on. "Neviah, stay parallel to the surface. Lifting off."

For luck, he touched his chest where his mother's antique compass hung beneath his parka. He grabbed the lever, pulled, and the helicopter soared upward.

His stomach sank as the ground blurred into a smear of bluish-white grays—the beautiful drabness of the Surface. Up here, everything was clear and real with none of the fake brightness of those dreadfully idealistic murals covering the walls of Northern Haven. Up here, nature's brutality ruled as crisp as the line between life and death. He loved it.

One wrong move, and they'd die. Push the wrong button, and they would crash. His blood roared with the fierceness of it. He was flying. In control. And he had a mission. He caught up to Neviah's helicopter and flew alongside, waiting.

He'd make her say it.

They flew side by side in the old magnetic northwestward direction. As the icy mountains loomed in the distance, Neviah maintained radio silence. He waited, careful to stay a safe distance but not to lead. He had a point to prove.

The radio crackled. This would be it. A smile played about his lips.

"Savas, you're the only one who knows the coordinates. You need to take the lead," Neviah said.

He nodded, though of course she wouldn't see him. "Of course. I just wanted to make sure you had stabilized after your rapid takeoff."

"Right." Neviah's voice was clipped over the radio.

Good, she had learned her lesson. As the pilot, she held three human lives in her hands. This mission was about finding humans, not losing more of them.

He pulled ahead and settled in for the first leg of their journey. The trickiest part would be not messing up his directions. He'd spent his whole life studying maps, and the old cardinal directions were burned into his mind. In case the navigational computer failed him, he'd stuck a card to the dash, reminding how to adjust for the new polar magnetic changes. Even with the reminder, he suspected he'd always think the old way.

As he turned north—the old north—to avoid the mountain range, the others oohed and aahed at their new expansive aerial view. He found his glance straying from the flight controls to the craggy mountains, the dazzling shimmer of ice, and the movements of animals far below. Animals...

"Zach, is Rana's pet behaving?" he yelled back.

"Ahh, *now* she is..." Zach's reply was barely audible over the flight sounds. The helicopters had been built with more soundproofing inside than old military helicopters, but it wasn't perfect.

Now *she is?* What the hell did that mean? Instant fury coursed through his veins as he pictured his beautiful helicopter shredded. "Get it under control, or we're landing and leaving it," he growled.

"No need to stop. She panicked when we first took off, but now she's lying down," Zach shouted.

"She better stay lying down!" he threatened, but he wasn't sure what to do if it didn't. The ridiculous star beings would probably all desert them if he kicked the animal off, and he sensed that Kalakanya had told the truth about his team needing their help to be successful.

Ugh, what a mess. He sucked in a deep breath and forced his fingers to unclench their grip on the controls. He'd have to wait five hours until he landed for their lunch break to assess any damage that little monster may have caused. Northern Haven's experts—as if anyone underground could call themselves an expert regarding air flight—insisted they could travel for five hours before they risked pilot error.

After rechecking the settings, he grinned wolfishly at the endless expanse below. *All the resources we need, just waiting to be claimed.*

"Commander Savas?" Zach leaned into the cockpit, his face lit with excitement.

"Hmm?"

"Can you tell me where we are? I've seen old maps, but I can't translate all this." Zach motioned at the vast emptiness below.

"Sure, but you should buckle in." He nodded to the empty chair beside him. "Right now, we're travelling north, toward the Black Sea. If you remember, Northern Haven lies hidden within what used to be the eastern half of Turkey." Not exactly the far north compared to humanity's old range, but it was the farthest north of the four havens SHAST had built with the world's pooled resources.

"Right," Zach said, belting himself in. "It feels weird discussing that out loud up here. You know, all those stories about the Undescended trying to find us."

"Yeah," Savas nodded. "And here we are, giving *them* a ride." He grunted in disgust and jabbed his thumb over his shoulder back toward where Rana and Eka, descendants of the Undescended, sat.

The land they now soared above once teemed with humanity. Now it held salt deer, birds, arctic rabbits, wolves. Star beings. No humans. His fingers tightened their grip on the controls. No humans. None.

"I hope these pretentious star beings aren't all that remain up here." he grumbled. If Northern Haven was the only haven to survive, was humanity doomed?

Zach scoffed. "I mean, we're up here now, so as long as you don't crash us, they'll no longer be the only ones up here, right?" Zach said, chuckling.

Despite his seatbelt, Zach sat on the edge of his chair and ogled the scenery below.

"I didn't spend my whole life trying to get these expeditions going only to crash the first day. It's safe to sit back and relax."

Zach nodded and leaned back. "Wait." He leaned forward in excitement and got jerked back by his seatbelt. "*You* got the Council to start the expeditions to the Surface?"

Savas grinned. "You think they were going to risk it without a shove?"

"But the Sickness made it necessary, right?" Zach cocked an eyebrow. "Find a cure, expand the gene pool..."

Savas smirked as Zach recited what he had learned in his expedition training. "Exactly. But they were shaking in their boots at the idea of coming up here. It still took a shove." Savas snorted. "Years of shoving, to be exact." He shook his head at the memory. "Look, I appreciate this conversation, but I need you to return to your seat in the back and keep an eye on Rana and Eka. Let me concentrate on flying."

"Yes, sir." Zach returned to his regular seat, gushing to the others about the view from the front cabin.

He wasn't the official commander of the mission, but he appreciated how well Zach listened to him. He'd always prided himself on his ability to remain in control of situations and in control of his own emotions. It had saved his life as a child. And with Bleu smitten with the star beings, someone on this mission needed to stay in control and focus on protecting human interests.

He clenched his jaw and glanced back through the open door to the main compartment where Rana and Eka sat, and then glanced back at his watch. As long as the green dot on its display glowed, no one knew his thoughts or could control his mind. Not even the mind-reading star beings. Everything was under control. He was safe.

He inhaled deeply, savoring the scent of manmade materials, heated air and technology that had been lacking in that forsaken ice hut he'd been forced to live in. Looking over the controls, he blew out his breath. If only this watch technology had existed when he was a boy, it might have saved him years of...

He shuddered, unable to go back there. No. Not even in his mind. It had taken years to learn how to fully hide his memories. To convince the doctors they had *saved* him. To act like everything was fine. His eye twitched, and he blinked rapidly as if that could wash away the images. No kid should have to live through that.

He shuddered with a sudden chill. No. No one would ever mess with his mind again. And certainly not these damn star beings.

Unzipping his jacket with his free hand, he pulled out the compass that had hung from his mother's bedside lamp that day. It was a miracle she hadn't put it around her neck as usual. If she had, he would have lost it, too.

The familiar, cold metal soothed the old emotions that roiled beneath his silent exterior. He held the heirloom to his lips and then slipped it back into his parka.

No. No one would mess with him. Or humanity. The star beings with their pompous evolution be damned. Real humans survive without superpowers. He'd find Western Haven and return humanity to its rightful place on the Surface.

When he was well out over what he assumed was the frozen Black Sea, he banked left and headed due west. Neviah followed, maintaining a safe distance. "Below us," he yelled to his passengers, "is the Black Sea. Not much to see, is it?"

"It's certainly not living up to its name," Atsushi shouted back in jest.

The Black Sea lay mostly hidden, having become gray-white like everything else. A center of dark choppy water still remained, surrounded by thinner, darker ice before merging with the endless gray-white. But even so, nothing below him even remotely resembled the ancient aerial views of Turkey's coast or the Black Sea.

Useless. The old maps he had spent hours downloading into his communicator were useless. He grunted in disgust. Why was everything always up to him?

No landmarks. No global satellite positioning. No air control.

He'd held out hope that something of the old coastlines would remain. But there was...nothing. Just a useless black splotch of water. A mere puddle compared to the once vibrant Black Sea. His hope of following naturally occurring landmarks had been *naïve,* and a Council's strategist should never be a naïve fool. He pressed his fisted hand into his seat in frustration.

"Nature hates us," he growled under his breath.

Now the navigation was solely in the computer's control. All he had left to find Western Haven were its old longitude and latitude coordinates, and the Flight Management Computer, dubbed Magellan by Neviah. By comparing coordinates, flight speed, direction, and time in the air, Magellan calculated their current position and route.

Everything now rode on the engineers of Magellan. Despite his respect for scientists, he was not the trusting type. He had no choice, though. He had to trust Magellan, tolerate the damned star beings, and let Bleu play commander. At least he still had a few secrets up his sleeve, including the all-important location of Western Haven and the horrific remote to the nanotech in the vaccines.

He grimaced at the section of the helicopter's dash panel that hid the compartment with the remote. That tech scared him. It was way too much like mind control, and he hated that Dr. Medicci and his team had created it. The only way he'd touch that damn thing was if the star beings turned their mind control on his team and he needed to temporarily knock out his human teammates to save lives. Hopefully, by the time he returned, they would have protective watches for all the humans interacting with star beings, and he would see to the remote's destruction.

Only he and the Prime Minister knew all four haven locations, and they now permanently wore the watches that blocked the star beings from reading their minds. At the time of the havens' foundation, SHAST had killed to maintain the secret. Northern Haven wasn't about to risk the star beings plucking the coordinates from their minds. Or Bleu telling his new best friends.

But Savas knew that their destination, the United People's Western Haven, lay buried in the desert of the western United States, near the old Four Corners. On the other side of the world.

"Magellan, you better get us there. And back." He sighed in frustration. He hated depending on anything other than himself. He had depended on Stamf, and the star beings killed him. *Don't worry Stamf, I'll make sure they never get a chance to betray us again.*

Chapter 22

In Flight: Rana of Peleguin Rookery

R
ana had thought the weird contraptions called chairs would be the strangest thing about the flight. But no, that wasn't it at all. She was actually flying through the air, and what shocked her the most was Eka's awkward nervousness now that they sat alone. He had only been away at his village a few days, but since he'd returned this morning, he carried an almost haunted look in his dark eyes. She'd caught him watching her from his seat bedside hers, but when she smiled, he looked away again.

Bored, she shoved the stuffing back into the hole that Digga's claws had sliced into her seat and wished she could reseal it the way Crowned Ones could mend open wounds. Savas would be angry when he saw it, and all she would be able to do was apologize. She sighed, and Digga whimpered up at her. The pup was listening and staying off the chair, but she wasn't happy that Rana wasn't sitting on the ground with her as usual.

Rana removed the belt tying her to the chair so she could lean toward the floor and scratch Digga's head before the pup panicked and slashed something else in the helicopter. She looked back over her shoulder to see Eka watching the two of them. He was taking too long to be ready to talk, and the noxious smells and vibrations of this helicopter were making her grumpy.

Are you going to tell me what's going on or just keep giving me those eerie looks the whole flight?

Eka's lips curled up into a half-smile, a far cry from his usual dashing grin. He looked about the compartment as if checking on their privacy, and Rana followed his gaze. Atsushi was curled into the last row of chairs with some sort of electronics attached to his ears. They looked like what Kahali had said the humans use to somehow hear music.

Across the aisle, Zach stared out the window, lost in his thoughts. In the cockpit, Savas had remained quiet ever since he had yelled back about the sea below and Atsushi had translated it.

Eka turned back to her, his smile now even tighter. *Okay, now seems like a good time.*

He studied his hands and chewed his lip. The only time Rana had seen him nervous like this was after he'd pulled her out of the collapsed ice cave. He'd explained that he followed her because of his cousin's unexplained death. Her stomach tightened as she considered what he was about to say. He had wanted to come on this trip with her, so his worry couldn't be something bad about her, could it?

She sat up in her seat and wanted to touch him, reassure him, but what if he didn't want that? "Eka, just tell me. Did I do something that upset you?" She had to speak louder than normal to be heard over the noise of the helicopter.

He turned abruptly, his eyes wide. "What? No, of course not." His breath feathered her face. "No, I just don't know where to start. I don't want to scare you."

"You think sharing something with me would make me scared of you?"

His eyebrows rose in surprise, and he grinned. Oneness, she'd missed that grin. "Not of me," he said, laughing. "When I got recalled to my village to figure out why I had spontaneously tried to star beam to you when the humans captured you, I learned a lot. I didn't solve my star beaming problem, though I had lots of practice at not doing it. Maybe I'll be able to resist star beaming if you're in danger again."

She furrowed her brow. "They still didn't figure out how to stop you from doing that? It could kill you. Isn't that the whole reason they called you home?"

"I never had time to think when I star beamed before. It just happened. But now I've learned to recognize the feel and to resist it."

"Am I doing something to cause it?" she said, grimacing.

"No, it's all me. But that's not what I wanted to say." He pressed his lips together and looked from Digga to her. "I think I discovered a new predator out there. Something that hunts cave diggers. Something more dangerous than a lion or a sea bear."

She protectively reached for Digga and buried her fingers in her thick fur. "Discovered it? How?"

He told her everything that had happened at the suns he'd spent training at his own village, Conifers-Greet-Mountain's-Shadows. Her heart raced at how close he had come to death. How close she had come to losing him.

She studied him with disbelief. "So, your Crowned Ones basically gave you therapeutic nightmares of me dying over and over, and then you nearly killed yourself by trying to star beam to rescue me?"

"They stopped me from actually star beaming and dying, but yeah, there were a few...close calls." He swallowed and looked away.

She reached out and rested her hand on his forearm. "I wish I could have been there for you, but I guess that would have made it more difficult for them to train you."

He gave a soft laugh. "Yeah, it would've been a bit hard to convince me you were in danger if you were sitting there with me."

She frowned. "And that experience of seeing me endangered triggered the memories of the night your cousin Gian was killed by the strange predator?"

"Essentially. And I got more information in a conversation with Gian's spirit as well."

She shook her head at the horror of his last few days. No wonder he looked haunted. "I'm glad you came back safe. But I don't understand. You think Digga's in danger from this unknown predator and that it could easily kill an adult cave digger?" She shivered. What sort of creature could easily kill an adult cave digger?

"Yes, but I think it's even worse. Digga is in danger, as well as anyone near her." He glanced at the floor, where Digga had finally fallen asleep wrapped around Rana's feet. He smiled at the pup's snores, then his dark eyes met Rana's. "Rana, you're always near her."

Rana stiffened and then looked out the window, unsure what to say. He was right. She and Digga were usually inseparable. Below them waved the dark-green crowns of a dense evergreen forest. Anything could be in there, hidden under the thick cover, even Eka's terrifying predator that could kill a star being.

No, she couldn't think like that. She never had this kind of fear until the humans emerged, and if she let it overtake her life, she'd never Crown. She had to develop behaviors that helped with Crowning, and fearing the unknown was not on that list.

She sucked in a deep breath. "Well, if this strange predator specifically preys on cave diggers, there are a lot bigger ones to go after with more meat on them. Hopefully Digga won't get noticed. And if she does, we'll simply have to protect her."

"Of course." Eka stared out the window at the wilderness below. "I'm not sure where the humans are taking us, though. I haven't seen any star being villages below us for a while. A predator that has avoided detection for this long probably lives away from everyone...like out here."

Again, he made sense. But fear was not on her mental list of capabilities needed for Crowning, so she would not nurture it, or allow it to take root in her. She would nurture other things, like friendship.

She took his hand. "I'm glad you came along. I missed you."

He nodded, and suddenly he seemed much closer. His skin still smelled of evergreen resin from his forest village, making her feel heady. "It's good to be back," he said, his blazing grin bursting forth like a sunrise.

Oneness, that grin got her every time. She bit her lip and hoped her thoughts were fully blocked. *Friendship only*, she reminded herself. Distracting herself with guys was not on her list to Crown, either. "Between the three of us, Digga will be fine."

Eka side-eyed the snoring pup and raised an eyebrow. "I'm not sure she'd fend off much of anything."

Rana laughed. "I was counting Kahali as the third."

His eyes widened ever so slightly. "Ah, yes, Kahali is much fiercer." He laughed and sat back in his seat, still holding her hand. "Just promise me you'll consider what I said."

"Of course, I promise," she said, squeezing his hand and biting back a laugh. "I'll keep in mind how fierce Kahali can be."

He groaned. "I'm serious, Rana. It's more dangerous than an enraged sea bear. I've never seen any furred one move like that. It was unnatural." After a moment, he turned to her, his expression earnest. "You do believe me, right? What I'm telling you, that it's real?"

Oneness, he was really upset. "Yes, I believe you," she said. "But I don't want to live in fear."

"I'm not asking you to live in fear. I simply want you to *live*."

Chapter 23

In Flight: Bleu Reinier

Given the frigid tension in their passenger compartment between Kalakanya and Kahali, Bleu wondered if it would have been better to fly in Savas' helicopter. He gave a soft snort at the ridiculous thought, and Kalakanya side-eyed him before turning to stare out the window again.

Well, this is going well. He rearranged the small bag and bulky parka in the chair beside him for the thousandth time, sighed, and leaned back against his seat. At least the seat was comfortable.

They all sat in the first passenger compartment nearest to the cockpit. It had an aisle down the middle with two seats on each side. The two chairs converted to a bed in case someone became injured or the weather required them to sleep inside. The cold blasting between his team members was enough for Bleu to consider sleeping outside tonight, regardless of the weather.

He shifted in his seat in the rear right corner, but Kalakanya, siting across the aisle in the other back row, seemed determined to stare out the window and ignore him. Kahali, mad at Kalakanya, had staked out the first row for himself and positioned his pack so that no one could join him. Girak had positioned himself across the aisle from Kahali and sat sideways, probably to appear friendly. But when Girak had noted the tension between the two star beings, he'd given Bleu a concerned smile and put on his headphones. Even Bleu's ambassador had deserted him.

There must be something I can do to help patch this up before we land for lunch. He perched on the edge of his seat, formulating a plan. Could he help them when he still prickled with her betrayal?

Kalakanya cleared her throat. She was watching him. How had he forgotten they heard thoughts? As she raised an eyebrow in concern, he blushed. She patted the seat next to her.

He checked the others. Girak was typing something on his comm, and Kahali sat with his eyes closed but still managed to look annoyed. Not wanting to be like that himself, Bleu scooted over beside Kalakanya.

Were you hoping for privacy? Kalakanya mind spoke.

Bleu nodded, cursing the blush creeping across his face.

She smiled. *We should start some classes in controlling the privacy of one's thoughts. But not just for you. For all of you. Otherwise, this will be a very noisy and embarrassing journey.*

"I totally agree."

Good. In the meantime, if you want privacy, I could construct a small shield around the two of us. Would that be okay with you?

Bleu glanced at Kahali and narrowed his gaze. Would that be rude to Kahali?

At that precise moment, Kahali spun and glared over the seat at him. Bleu covered his head with his hands. Ugh. He couldn't even think.

Kalakanya spoke to Kahali in their native tongue. After she finished, Kahali looked slightly mollified, but now Girak had abandoned his comm to turn around toward them.

"Did I miss something?" Girak asked.

"I just need a moment of mental privacy," Bleu said.

Girak cocked an eyebrow, looked at Kahali, shrugged, and returned to his reading.

Kalakanya tossed up a small shield. Instantly, the two of them were encased in a yellow eggshell of light.

"Guys," Neviah shouted. "Something's happening to the equipment."

"What? What's wrong?" Bleu sprang through the shield toward Neviah.

"Everything just started spinning!" Neviah frantically tapped the gauges, but everything looked normal to Bleu.

"It looks fine."

"Yeah, now it does." Her voice was shrill with panic. "But a moment ago, everything began spinning."

Bleu looked at Kalakanya, who grimaced with guilt. *Is it back to normal now?*

"Yes, but what the hell happened? Did one of you do something?"

I'm sorry. I believe the shield I made may have affected your equipment.

Neviah spun wide-eyed. "Why would you do that?"

"She didn't know it would do that. None of us did," Bleu retorted, surprised at his own knee-jerk instinct to defend the star beings.

Neviah seethed. "You could have killed us! If it had been dark, and I couldn't see the horizon—"

Sorry. I had no idea a small shield would affect your technology. I would never put us in danger.

From behind them, Kahali snorted.

Kalakanya spun toward him. *You're not being fair. I never wanted any of you to get hurt. What will it take for you to believe me?*

Kahali bristled from his seat, static energy seeming to emanate off him.

"Both of you! No energy stuff or we'll crash." Bleu turned to Neviah. "Radio Savas that Rana and Eka can't use energy. I'll handle this."

Neviah raised an eyebrow. "Good luck with that." She clicked on her radio.

Bleu turned back to the others.

Kahali and Kalakanya were engaged in a stare-off. Both their faces quickly changed through a kaleidoscope of emotions. So, not a stare-off. A silent disagreement.

Bleu looked over his shoulder at Girak, who shrugged and turned his palms upward.

Bleu stepped forward. "Look, both of you. Stop it. No one is perfect, and everyone here has done things they regret."

Kahali and Kalakanya both regarded him with annoyance.

The only thing I did wrong was to try to save you ruinous humans, Kahali said.

Stay out of this, Bleu, Kalakanya added.

Shocked by their mental blast, Bleu stumbled backward into the pilot compartment.

Over the radio, Commander Savas was swearing at the star beings. Savas seemed the simpler of the two situations to address. "Neviah, tell him I said to cut that out."

Then he spun back toward the feuding star beings. They were now seated in their original spots, ignoring each other. Bleu looked from one to the other, waiting for something dramatic to occur.

When nothing happened, he turned to Girak, who shrugged and whispered, "We really know very little about their way of handling disagreements."

Bleu nodded, exhausted from the emotional explosion. He flopped into his original seat at the back. Hopefully Kalakanya wouldn't mind, but he avoided looking in her direction just to be safe. Closing his eyes, he rested his head against the back of the seat.

I meant no offense, Kalakanya said.

He opened his eyes. Kalakanya faced him.

I had the situation under control.

"Didn't exactly appear that way." He sighed, wondering how many were listening in this time. "I had to keep us safe."

I know. I'm sorry that happened. Everything I do lately seems off.

"Can they hear you?" He nodded toward Kahali and then toward Savas' helicopter, which flew beside them.

Only you can hear me. Though they can still hear your thoughts.

"Hmm." He took a deep breath. "At the risk of offending you, have you ever considered that Kahali has a point? I mean, how *do* you calculate what risks are worth it?"

She bit her lip and looked out the window. Bleu sensed no anger, but would he?

Everything used to be clear. The right choice was obvious.

"What changed?"

You. She gave him a sad smile.

He sighed. "So, Kahali's right. We humans have destroyed your lives."

I meant you, Bleu Reinier.

He stiffened. "Wh—what have I done to you?"

Are you still wearing it? The necklace that saved your life?

Bleu's hand went to his chest, where the necklace Ayanna had gifted him hung. It was made of lapis lazuli and silver from the ancient Surface, passed down for generations.

Bleu shuddered as his finger ran over the jagged crack in the stone where it had partly deflected Savas' bullet and saved his life. Without this necklace, he'd be dead. Was he supposed to have died that day? A deep chill overtook him, and he shivered.

He'd forgotten that when Kalakanya discovered the necklace, she had looked scared. He held up the pendant. "What does this have to do with anything?"

Kalakanya gazed at it, lost in thought. Her hand reached out, trembling, and touched it with one finger. Instantly, her eyes dilated, and icy prickles tingled along the back of his neck. Was this another transtemporal scan? But the prickles spread as if pointy icicles were stabbing him from every direction.

"Kalakanya?" His head pounded and sweat trickled down his back as panic gripped him. He glanced up toward the pilot compartment, but Neviah seemed oblivious. The equipment must be fine.

He returned his gaze to Kalakanya. Her pupils were normal-sized, but tears welled in them. The icicles that had pierced him evaporated. "What's happening?"

That. She pointed accusingly at his pendant. *That is why choices are no longer obvious. Why nothing I do seems right. But it is not my place to stir the past.* She wiped her eyes. *Put it away. Please.* She turned away. *I'm going to rest for a while.*

Bleu waited, but she remained facing the window, eyes closed. He looked down at his fingers clasped around the necklace, wondering why it bothered her so. And just for a second, his hands strangely shifted their appearance from his own familiar brown hands to older, large-knuckled, worn ones.

Chapter 24

First Landing Site: Rana of Peleguin Rookery

When the horribly noisy and jarring helicopter finally landed and Zach unlocked the door, Rana sucked in a deep lungful of the crisp, fresh air. She and Digga burst past Zach and through the door. As her boots touched the solid ground, relief swelled within her.

Before meeting humans, she had never even thought it possible to *not* have her feet on solid ground unless she had climbed a tree. Her insides still quivered with the mechanical vibrations of the helicopter, and her legs wobbled, but she was free and in her own world again.

Behind her, Eka chuckled from the doorway. "You walk like a newly hatched peleguin."

"Really?" She bit back a grin and waited with quiet glee for him to disembark.

He confidently hopped down and toppled over.

She laughed. "He's quite the peleguin chick himself, isn't he, Digga?"

Digga purred and sniffed at Eka, who lay in a heap on the ground, laughing.

Eka stood and wiped the snow off his pants and gloves. "We better warn Kahali before he gets out."

Above them, Neviah's helicopter continued circling as if she enjoyed flying too much to become grounded again. Poor Kahali must be dying to get out. The sun shone overhead onto the incredibly flat horizon, making the ground appear blindingly bright. Despite the afternoon's brightness, something felt off. Rana scanned the snow field, remembering Eka's warning of a new predator, but only an empty horizon greeted her.

Thrump. Rana spun at the sound. A package of gear had hit the ground behind her.

"Sorry, Rana. Didn't mean to scare you." Atsushi waved from his perch in the open door. Zach tossed another package of gear. Digga huffed in annoyance at the disturbance.

"Aww, Digga! I wasn't aiming for you." Zach smiled down at the pup, who gave him an annoyed grunt that trailed off into a long series of murmuring grunts. Rana cocked her head.

You're speaking to her? Rana waved toward her furry friend.

Zach blushed. "Yeah. I shouldn't?"

It's just...ah...a big change?

Zach shrugged. "I'd never really met animals before I shot your lion friend."

Rana grimaced at his casual reference to nearly killing Sukti.

"Zach," Savas shouted from the front of the ship, interrupting them. "Let Atsushi unload the food. You check out the area. And take your gun." Atsushi translated for them.

I can go with him, so he won't need a gun, Eka offered.

"If you want. But if he needs it, he'll use it. Right, Zach?" Savas hopped out and slammed the pilot door shut. Atsushi translated again, giving them an apologetic smile as he did so.

"Yeah. Of course. I wouldn't want to feed the local wildlife." Zach snorted with laughter at his joke and climbed down to the ground without any difficulty. He strolled past Eka. "Coming?"

Yes. Eka leaned near Rana's ear and spoke in their native tongue. "Maybe hang out with Atsushi until Neviah lands?" He nodded in Savas' direction to insinuate his concern.

"Already my plan," Rana whispered back and squeezed his hand. "Be careful out there. Something feels weird here to me."

Eka cocked his head, sensing the energy. "I don't feel it. Do you think it's all my talk of the new predator?"

"Maybe, but I wasn't thinking about that until after I sensed something."

"Okay, I'll stay on guard. Keep Digga close."

She nodded. Eka walked off with Zach, something that would have been unimaginable weeks ago. She knew Eka could handle himself, but seeing them together only added to her sense of unease. A few weeks ago, she would have never imagined she'd be traveling with humans. Savas, Zach, and Bleu had all hunted and killed her people.

She took a deep breath to calm herself and turned back to Atsushi. *Tents first?*

"Sure." Atsushi stared at the icy landscape beyond the door. "Should we worry about falling into a crevasse? How can Zach and Eka just take off like that?"

Rana followed his gaze. *Eka would sense one. As for Zach...* She held up her palms in the human I-don't-know gesture and grinned when Atsushi understood. She was learning their spoken and body language, and she never wanted to be stuck unable to communicate with them again. *Don't worry, I'd let you know if we were near one.*

"Thanks."

She could do this. "You're melcome."

Atsushi snorted in laughter. "Well, that's better than I could do in your language, but it's a *w*, not an *m*. Welcome."

She nodded. "You're welcome."

"Perfect."

They walked around with Rana sensing the ground. They located a flat spot on the wind-sheltered side of the helicopters for their tents, while Digga snorted up snow and ran circles around the ship, growling and digging tunnels in the ice.

The entire time, the hairs on the back of Rana's neck prickled as if she were being watched, but the ice field and the sky remained clear. Almost too clear.

Eka sensed nothing, so it's probably just my fear. At least Savas busied himself with the equipment and left them alone.

As Rana and Atsushi dragged the tent bags to the sheltered area near the helicopter, Neviah landed. The others tumbled out. Girak's sleep-laden eyes brightened in the fresh air. Despite his exhaustion, he had no wobble. Somehow, the humans seemed immune to the side effects of their helicopter's vibrations.

Kalakanya exited next, looking oddly weary herself. Stepping down, she stood very still, adjusting with grace. She frowned at the ground with concern. Then Bleu and Kahali appeared in the hatch, both looking...ill.

Careful, Kahali. Eka and I both fell, Rana warned from where she stood with Atsushi.

Kahali gave her a strange look and then climbed out, maintaining his hold on the helicopter. He swayed but remained upright.

"What the hell are you doing?" Savas yelled.

They all spun toward him.

"This is our lunch break. You were only supposed to take out the food. We're not camping here." He gave an exasperated groan and returned to checking his helicopter.

Rana couldn't make it all out, but when Atsushi explained, she frowned. *Okay, I'll help you put everything back inside in a moment.*

Over Atsushi's shoulder, Kahali still held on to Neviah's helicopter.

She hurried over to Kahali. *You okay?*

That was not fun. Remind me to never argue with a Crowned One again.

Rana gasped and glanced at Kalakanya. *You didn't?*

I did. And I don't want to talk about it. Not now...with her around. Kahali's eyes narrowed as Savas came around the side of the ship, checking to make sure they had stopped their unloading. *Was he his usual horrid self?*

Rana snickered. *You know, you almost sound like one of them.*

Their hatred is contagious. I've been warning the Crowned Ones of that since the humans attacked me. He meant it.

No. She shook her head. *It doesn't work that way.*

I've lost more than my arm, Rana. We need to be careful.

I agree with being careful. But... Even though the energy of one's surroundings affected them, she refused to believe they were doomed to become fearful and violent. But was that what she was sensing as being off here? Was she simply picking up their fear of the natural world beyond their tunnels?

Look, we'll make sure we do sunrise sit every morning and meditate on the ship during flights. That way, we'll affect them instead of the other way around.

Kahali wrinkled his nose in doubt. *We can't do anything energetic on the helicopters.*

As Rana considered something to say to reassure him, her gaze wandered past him to Kalakanya's odd movements. She tapped Kahali's side and motioned with her chin, and he turned, too. The Crowned One touched her foot to the ground, lifted it with intense thought, and returned it to the frozen ground.

What's she doing? Rana asked.

Kahali chuckled. *A new dance?*

Suddenly, Kalakanya's head jerked up, and she strode to them. *Do you feel it? I don't think this is solid ground. It's very thick, so it's safe, but...* She began her strange foot maneuvers again.

Rana stared at the ice beneath their feet with growing horror.

"What is it?" Bleu strode over. "What's wrong?"

I believe we are standing on a thick ice shelf, not land. Kalakanya glanced at the helicopters, their engines now quiet but still giving off heat.

Bleu's eyes widened. "It's going to crack? Neviah! Savas! We're on an ice shelf!"

The two pilots began running toward them with shouts of, "What?"

I don't think it'll crack. But there's...movement, Kalakanya said.

"An earthquake?" Atsushi yelped and stood on his tiptoes.

Rana stifled her laughter. Then she remembered Eka and Zach were off on their own. "Eka! Eka!"

She turned to Atsushi. *Get Zach on the radio. He and Eka are out there.* She waved toward the distant figures, small on the horizon.

Kalakanya took a few steps toward the distant men, Calling them. She spun back toward Rana and the others. *We need to leave. Start your helicopter. Something's not right.*

Without any warning, Savas raised his rifle and shot at Kalakanya. Rana froze in terror. The gunfire exploded through the air as she and Kahali threw up shields. Kalakanya had erected a shield in front of Savas, knocking him backward onto his butt.

Savas sputtered as he hit the ice, then sprang up and shouted in fury as he pointed beyond Kalakanya. Neviah backed toward the helicopter, wide-eyed and pointing in the same direction. "He wasn't aiming for you. He was aiming at them," she shouted, motioning frantically at something behind Kalakanya and Rana.

❋ ❋ ❋ ❋ ❋ ❋

Heart racing, Rana spun to follow their wild gestures of warning.

The ice had come alive. White *chunks* sprang up into the air and whizzed toward them. As they rose into the air, gray legs became visible beneath the ice clumps.

They weren't chunks of ice. They were oval-shaped, flat insects as large as Rana's hand with a terrifying sharp-pointed mouth part. They sprang into the air between each jump so high that they might as well have had wings.

Digga sprang into action, slicing every insect that hopped toward them. The other humans drew their guns. Rapid explosions erupted around her, filling the air with burning smoke and making it hard to think.

Bleu, did you reach Zach? They're in the middle of that field. Adrenaline ripped through Rana's limbs like flames. She remembered Desna's warning—Eka would die if he tried to star beam to her. She sucked in a deep breath, and holding her shield firm, she began running into the giant insects. Within two steps, Digga joined her inside her shield, loping beside her. Behind her came shouts to stop, screams, and bursts of gunfire, but she continued to race toward the two figures in the distance. She could barely make them out through the air thick with bugs.

Eka, I'm coming for you. I'm okay. Stay put.

As she ran, bugs thumped against her shield, then slid along the curve of it to the ground. She extended the shield below her, wincing as she slipped on the hard outer shell of one and squished its leg. Horror shot like lightning through her body.

Sorry. Oneness, I'm so sorry.

She stumbled, bending to see the poor, mangled creature. It crawled away on its other legs. Nauseated, she pressed the back of her hand to her

170

mouth. Maybe it would live, but her haste to reach Eka had been the cause of its injury.

Desna's other warning about attachment washed over her, leaving her throat thick with guilt. Being too attached to another star being could prevent Crowning. Was this the sort of problem her parents had faced? Being so concerned with each other's safety that in their rush they crushed unfortunate beings along their path?

No, she would not make that mistake. But the closer she got to Eka and Zach, she realized there was only one of them still standing.

"Eka!" She sped up.

He stood, encased in a wobbly shield, with Zach lying at his feet. He was trying to pull Zach up. No. He was pulling something off Zach. A giant bug.

Eka hurled the bug through his own shield as Rana slid to a stop beside him.

"Nice of you to drop by," he said with a hoarse laugh.

Sweat ran down his flushed face as he bent to grab another bug that had burrowed beneath Zach's orange coat. Zach lay on the ice, trembling and pale. Barely conscious and groaning, he kicked and batted ineffectively at the multiple creatures latching on to him. Digga grabbed one with her mouth, and with a sickening snap crushed it in her jaws.

"Falling stars!" Rana's shield merged with Eka's, strengthening it. "You okay?" She eyed him as he yanked another bug off. Digga growled at the swarm just beyond their shielded sphere.

"I'm fine. Can you shield while I—" He twisted another bug, yanking it free as Zach screeched in agony. He placed it into the pile beyond his shield. *Sorry, Zach.*

Rana took over the shielding as the air around them filled with a cloud of hungry insects clicking their mandibles.

"I'm not sure we should be staying here. Can we take these off him inside the helicopter?"

Eka hurled another bug and paused, panting. "That's what I thought, too. But I don't think he'll survive the walk. They're quick, draining him of blood. Look how swollen this last one is." Eka wrapped his blood-covered fingers around the insect's hard shell. "We have to get them off as soon as possible. Where's Kalakanya? I was hoping for a star beam back."

"Probably getting the others safely inside."

Rana focused and Called the Crowned One. *Kalakanya....Kalakanya ...Zach is hurt. Can you beam us back?*

The Crowned One sent a wave of relief. *You shouldn't have run off like that. As soon as Kahali and I get the others inside, I'll come. Try talking to the insects, like Desna taught you. Call them off.*

Okay, but hurry. Zach doesn't look good.

The final, oval-shaped insect had grown even larger and crimson, swollen from ingesting Zach's blood. Eka pulled with all his strength, but the creature's legs had wrapped themselves deep into Zach's thigh.

Zach had passed out, his face damp and pasty. She had to do something. Her hands throbbed with healing power, but to tune into him and heal, she'd lose focus on the shield. She'd run into the same problem if she mind talked to the bug.

"This one won't budge. I can't believe how strong it is!" Dark fear clouded Eka's expression. "Rana, I can't get it off."

"Can you hold the shield?"

He nodded and stood. For a moment, their energy sizzled together around them in unison. The resulting thrill energized her.

She bent and placed her palm on the bug. *Release...*

It ignored her, focused only on sating its hunger. She unfurled the boundaries of her awareness, reaching for the insect's vibration. It was low. A steady thrum, simple and strong. She joined it as if joining in a drumbeat, matching it. Then, still holding that rhythm, she opened her mind.

You've had enough. Release. Release...

Nothing happened. Zach grew even paler, and Kalakanya was nowhere in sight. Eka had grabbed Digga's scruff to keep her safely within the shield as the pup lunged and snapped at the bugs beyond the protection. Amazingly, Digga hadn't eaten his hand.

Digga, stop. Rana tried her best to maintain a calm presence, but the cave digger spun and snarled at Eka.

Wisely, Eka released the half-grown pup, holding his hand out in an I-meant-no-harm gesture. How could she parent a cave digger and deal with these bugs at the same time?

Digga! Come here now. Rana used all the authority she could muster and pointed to the spot beside her well within the shield.

Digga whimpered and rushed over to Rana.

Stay inside the light. She sent Digga a mental picture showing the four of them safe inside the shield, and Digga plopped down beside her, brown eyes wide. *Thank you, Digga.*

Eka, still holding the shield, stepped backward as a bug hit the protective light near his face. *Oneness, there's so many of them.*

Rana only nodded, too distracted by the ginormous bug under her palm. She had never talked to an insect. How large would this creature grow? No one could survive losing this much blood. *Release...release...*

Her bug-free hand rested on her thigh near her dagger. She had never used it to hurt anything. Could she now, to save Zach? Would such an action work, or in the long run only serve to separate her from the One In All? As her gaze darted between the engorged bug to Zach's pale, sweaty face, her vision blurred with tears.

If she didn't try something, Zach would die. Her free hand closed around the grip of her dagger.

Release or you might be injured when I have to cut you out. I don't want to hurt you. Release...

The massive bug, now nearly twice its original size, shifted beneath her palm. Above her, Eka hissed a warning. The insect wriggled. With painstaking slowness, it released its grip on Zach. Relieved, she grabbed the bloated thing and slid it through the shield. Her threat had worked, but the weight of threatening violence made her tremble with shame.

"Impressive," Eka said. "Anything in your pack to help Zach?"

She looked at him blankly. Pack? Then she noticed the weight at her back. She hadn't taken her pack off when they exited the helicopter. She took it off and tugged out a blanket. She spread it over Zach and rested her shaking hands on the worst bloody and swollen bite. As the healing surged through her hands and into his body, she leaned in to see if he was still breathing. *Zach? Can you hear me? Hold on. You're going to be okay.*

He was past the point of responding, but Desna had once said that sound was the last sense to go. But did mind talk count as sound? *Zach, hang on.*

She removed her glove and held her fingers to his nostril, then sagged in relief at the moist warmth on her fingertips. He was still alive.

The bright yellow flash of a Crowned One star beaming cut through the gray bug-filled air, and then Kalakanya appeared beside them. She merged her shield with Eka's. "Let's go." She knelt to touch Zach and Digga, while Eka and Rana grasped her shoulder.

They dissolved into nothingness and then reappeared next to the helicopter. Neither had been started for takeoff. Kahali paced outside the closest helicopter. His shield extended around the door, so that people could enter and exit without letting in bugs. His worry transformed to a relieved grin at their appearance. Until he saw Zach slumped in Eka's arms.

Rana checked the integrity of the shield around them as bugs thumped against it in a desperation and then gave Kahali a shaky smile. She stepped toward him and tripped over a bug body. Dismembered insects were scattered on the ground where the humans had been gathered. They had, as usual, left slain wreckage in their wake. Her stomach roiled at the needless loss of life.

Kalakanya turned and looked over the unconscious human. "You got them all off him?"

Rana nodded.

"Good work." Kalakanya nodded toward the open door. "Climb in with Zach. You, too, Kahali."

Beyond Kalakanya's domed shield, the ferocious bugs whirred in agitation, trying to get at the group. Clumps of them covered the helicopters. The solar panels on the top were collecting energy, but they were also generating heat and attracting bugs. That couldn't be good.

Kalakanya turned to Savas, who stood in the doorway, rifle raised and ready. *Savas. Get ready to close the door as soon as I'm in. Yes?*

Savas, his jaw set in grim determination, nodded in agreement.

Rana shied away from him, waiting for his usual assertion of control. But as she climbed up, Savas slung his rifle over his shoulder to grasp the door handle. With a grim nod to Zach he said, "Thank you," followed by more she couldn't grasp.

His exact words were lost to her, but his appreciation for saving Zach was clear, and she inwardly reeled from this unexpected change. Savas expressing gratitude? And in addition to that he'd disarmed himself and trusted Kalakanya's shield. Savas' newfound cooperation was mind-bogglingly wonderful. Did that make her horrible for not trusting this sudden change?

She managed a shocked nod of acknowledgement to him as she turned in the entrance to help get Zach into the helicopter. Eka strained to lift Zach's limp body up to herself and Bleu.

She and Bleu carried Zach over to a row of seats that had been converted to a bed as Digga scrambled behind Rana.

"I have blankets," Neviah shouted, running out of the storage unit with a medical bag and blankets. As Bleu and she settled Zach onto the bed, Kalakanya jumped inside and Savas slammed the door shut. Bugs thumped against the outside of the helicopter, their legs and mandibles clicking against the metal in their desperation to reach them.

Rana shivered as she looked at Zach's motionless body that had been so full of life when they landed. The bugs had done this to him in moments, and his weapon had been useless. They all stood, crammed into the entrance area of one ship, and the hungry bugs showed no sign of moving on. *What now?* she asked. *Can we fly away from here?*

"No," Blue said. "Not with such large insects covering the helicopter."

Chapter 25

Unknown Ice Shelf: Rana of Peleguin Rookery

Rana eyed the helicopter walls, alarmed by the screeching and scratching coming from all sides. How long would the metal hold against such an onslaught? Kalakanya's shield extended through the exit wall and presumably around the outside of the door. For some reason, the Crowned One wanted to maintain a bug-free zone just outside the door. Was she expecting their mandibles to pry open the door?

Focus, she chided herself. Zach lay before her, dying, and she was worried about the bugs getting in. She closed her eyes, centered herself, and called up healing energy.

She laid her hands on Zach's wound, but at the sudden metallic grind of Savas locking the door, her eyes flew open. He pushed his way between Eka and Kalakanya to reach her and Zach.

"Is he going to make it?" Savas asked Eka as he grimaced with disapproval at Rana. "Kalakanya, shouldn't you do this?"

Rana gasped in disbelief. The human was rude beyond belief.

Eka, too, seemed thrown by Savas' question. Eka turned toward Kalakanya and something was exchanged between them, fast as lightning. Then he responded so that everyone would perceive it, *I'm going to switch with Kalakanya. She can heal Zach the fastest, but then we need to go back out there.*

What? Rana asked, flinching as insects thwacked into the windows. She exchanged a look of horror with Kahali. They should just leave this place.

The bugs could jump to safety as they lifted off. Besides, she didn't trust herself out there. She had nearly killed one in her fear. She'd chosen to threaten another with her dagger to save Zach. Violence was definitely on her "Reasons Why I'll Never Crown" list.

Why go back out there? she asked. Could she do any better communicating with the bugs now than earlier?

"Three reasons," Savas replied. His explanation was too much said too quickly, so Neviah translated. "One, our supplies are still out there. Two, the helicopters won't fly safely with those monstrosities attached to them. We need to clean them off. And three, I'm not abandoning the other ship. I need to get back to it."

Rana's heart sank. No one knew she had probably killed one, but if she went back out there, it might happen again. She glanced at Kalakanya, praying the Crowned One would refute him. Surely, she had a better idea than risking their lives. It had been hard enough to communicate with one bug. There were hundreds of them out there now.

Kalakanya let out a long sigh and gave a side-long glance at Bleu. *I agree with Savas. Commander Reinier, your thoughts?*

Bleu glanced at Zach, wincing as another big bug slammed into the nearest window. "I agree. But first we need to stabilize Zach and make a plan."

"Just remember," Savas said, "the longer we plan, the fewer hours of daylight we have left to solve this. I don't particularly want to engage those things in the dark. And we can't let them mess with the ship's hull overnight."

Why? Rana asked.

"Because we need the solar chargers to work."

But you can fly without them, right?

"Of course. But it will get cold and dark in here."

Rana frowned and again looked at the helicopter walls, so different than the thick, insulated, cozy walls of their ice huts. She didn't mind darkness, but without their heaters, this metal thing would soon be the same temperature as outside.

She would have to go back out there and avoid being reactive like the humans. Normally, that would seem trivial, but her earlier violence weighed heavily on her shoulders. She closed her eyes and sighed.

"You okay?" Neviah asked.

Rana opened her eyes.

Neviah stood before her, holding a container of water. "I got this to clean Zach, but..." She put the bowl down and turned back to Rana. "Did you get bit? Are you okay?"

Rana managed a smile. *I'm not bit. I just don't want to go back out there.*

"Only a fool would." Neviah gave a light laugh and patted her on the arm. "Let me know if you need anything specific for Zach. Or yourself. We have all kinds of things back there in the storage room."

Rana nodded. She assisted while Kalakanya stabilized Zach. Neviah brought them healing supplies as needed, and Atsushi and Kahali scrounged up drinks and snacks for everyone. Eka held the shield around the door while tossing food to Digga. He grinned and flashed Rana a smile every time Digga whined for more. Their half of the room cooperated seamlessly.

On the other half of the room, up by the cockpit, the three human men argued nonstop. The energy of their anger bounced off the walls and prickled her skin like needles.

"We should team up, star being and human. They shield while we blow those bastards off the ship," Savas commanded.

"And damage the hull?" Bleu asked. "No, that won't work. Our guns are useless."

Savas scoffed. "Maybe it's your aim that's the problem. I didn't mean shooting directly at the hull." He shook his head in disbelief. "Shoot parallel—the bug dies and falls off, and the hull is undamaged."

"That's a lot of ammunition. I'm surprised you'd want to use it up on our first stop." Girak gave Savas a look that Rana couldn't quite translate. "Unless you brought along extra without Bleu's permission."

"You are not part of this team, Girak, so shut up. We packed exactly what we need to survive."

"Everyone is part of this team." Bleu glared at Savas.

Rana turned away. She'd had enough human anger for a lifetime. They were wasting time while outside the insects swarmed thicker.

Rana, can you please take over? Kalakanya asked. *I'm going to check the time threads.*

Rana nodded and took her place as the Crowned One walked to the back of the room and sat cross-legged and instantly went into deep meditation. Rana bit her lip as she assessed Zach. His breathing was stronger, but she'd never worked on anyone this seriously injured before and didn't know how fragile humans were.

She glanced over to where Kahali and Atsushi sat munching snacks and grimacing at the men arguing up front. "Kahali, can you help me?"

His face brightened into a beautiful smile. "Of course." With a concerned glance at the planning men, he positioned himself opposite Zach's body to her, his back to the humans. He took a deep breath, calming himself.

"Eka's between them and us. We'll be fine."

"Right." But his smile was laced with anxiety.

Rana called up the healing energy of the One In All and with closed eyes focused on Zach's bone marrow, encouraging the rapid rebuilding of his blood. She sensed Kahali's energy bloom as he focused on the largest wound.

She didn't need to see his energy; she knew it intimately from years of training together. She even sensed the energy of his missing arm, now filled in by the stiff, wooden prosthetic Atsushi, Girak, and Bahujnana had rigged up for him. She gave her head a slight shake and refocused on Zach.

Atsushi sidled up to her. "Is she going to have a seizure?"

What? Rana's eyes flew open and glanced around for Neviah, worried that she'd missed Neviah having an injury. But Neviah sat perched on the edge of a chair, grimacing at the men's endless, unproductive bluster.

Rana tilted her head at Atsushi. *She looks okay to me.*

He pointed toward Kalakanya.

Kalakanya, still in deep meditation, sat with her eyes open but focused elsewhere. They rapidly moved side to side as if dreaming. *She's fine*, Rana told him. *She's reading the time threads to see what our safest option is.*

But Rana had never actually observed Kalakanya use this gift. Usually, the Crowned One disappeared to do this and then returned to announce her findings. Was it good that it was taking her so long? Did it mean they had many options? Or did it mean they all died in every option she had checked so far?

Rana refocused on Zach while the argument spun on and on around her. Bone. Marrow. Flowing health.

Zach muttered something in his torpor, but his mind was too messy to read. His starting to regain consciousness was a good sign. She sagged with relief until another insect body hit against the hull near where she stood.

"…Kalakanya eating?" Savas asked.

Rana looked up. She had nearly understood him again. Savas had stopped arguing long enough to eat some of the snacks.

"She's doing her thing with studying the future," Bleu answered. "And she told us she hardly ever eats much."

Savas grumbled something that sounded suspicious. Rana could only imagine how weird the Crowned Ones' lack of eating must appear to the humans.

Rana had done about all she could for Zach. Some things just take time. Yawning, she sent to Kahali, *I need a break.*

Same. He withdrew his hand from Zach's abdomen and gave her an intense look. *You okay?* He shifted sideways to eyeball the angry humans as Savas again yelled at Girak. Fear flashed in Kahali's eyes as if he were cornered prey before her normal, concerned friend reappeared. *What happened to you out there?*

She tensed, shame keeping her lips pressed together. A glance at Eka told her he was watching her and Kahali, though he wouldn't hear their mind talk. She gave Kahali a strained smile and looked away.

You can tell me anything. Kahali, sensing her need for privacy, shifted to stand somewhat between her and the others. Real privacy didn't exist when crowded on a helicopter and surrounded by hungry insects.

I…I think I killed a bug. She couldn't meet his gaze. *And then, when I thought Zach was dying, I threatened to cut another one out with my dagger if it didn't detach. I don't know what's wrong with me.* She wiped a tear from her cheek.

Kahali had become very still. Too still. *Did you...?*

No, it detached. She sucked in a shaky breath. *And if I had trusted the One In All to keep them safe, I wouldn't have tripped on the other one and hurt it.*

She risked a glance. His face radiated concern, not judgement. Not anger. *What if I become like...them?* She nodded her chin toward the humans.

That will never happen. He stepped around Zach's bed until he was close enough that his warmth reached her. *I'd stop you. Just like you would stop me.*

She swallowed, unsure how a friend could stop such a horrid transformation.

Kahali tapped her arm playfully with his wooden prosthetic. *If I got up and asked Savas for a gun, you'd stop me, right?* His question rang with humor.

She laughed. *Of course.*

Then we have an agreement. Look, I told you I think they're affecting us. And you said we need to switch it around—so that we're affecting them instead. Mischief sparkled in his dark eyes. *Think we could get Savas to do sunrise sit tomorrow?*

She snorted in laughter. Everyone except Kalakanya turned to her. At Savas' pompous glare, she giggled. Him meditating at sunrise sit? "Sorry."

This whole situation is so bad it's funny, she sent to them all.

Bleu sighed in exasperation, clearly not getting the funny. By the time the humans agreed to a plan, she'd be too exhausted to be of any use.

With an exasperated sigh, she stepped around Kahali and approached Savas and the others. *Since Zach is now stabilized, may I offer a suggestion?*

Girak gave her a pleading nod, as if any intervention to stop their endless arguing was appreciated.

"Of course," Bleu said. "We want your feedback."

But behind him, Savas snorted in annoyance.

If we clear one helicopter at a time, the first can fly above the swarm while we clean the second. We'd need a star being on each helicopter, enlarging the shield around it as the bugs are removed. They'll probably need to be outside to see what's happening and protect the bug remover until the whole thing is clear. The other two can shield while you pick up the supplies. Then we can take off. That work? She rubbed the back of her neck, which suddenly tickled.

Savas shook his head. "There are only four of you. That would take six."

No. Eka still held the shield around the door with no sign of exhaustion. *Two can focus on getting the supplies in while two clear the first helicopter. Then two of us take off with half of you in the debugged helicopter while the remaining two of us help clear the second helicopter.*

Bleu pushed his fingers through his cropped hair. "That'd be great. But getting the bugs off is the sticking point. How would we do it without damaging our helicopters?"

Rana shrugged and looked back where Kalakanya still meditated. The Crowned One's gaze was locked on to Rana, her eyes still distant. Rana shivered at the ongoing prickle on the back of her neck. No wonder the Crowned Ones scared the suspicious humans. The need for a transtemporal scan couldn't be good. Was Rana's life in danger if they chose this plan? "Kalakanya?"

The Crowned One's eyes cleared, and she blinked, taking a moment to re-orientate herself. *Getting the bugs off? Leave that to Rana and me.*

Rana's stomach clenched. No. Not only would she have to face the blood-thirsty swarm, but she'd have to avoid the dangerous mistakes she had made earlier. Mistakes that would not only keep her from Crowning but would lead her down a path entirely different than where she wanted to go. She'd be...violent...reactive. Human-like.

What about us? Kahali asked, stepping up behind Rana. *Eka and I can help.*

"Me, too," Atsushi added. "I can stand inside your shield and push them off the helicopter with a stick or something."

Kalakanya shook her head. *I appreciate your offer, Atsushi, but we want to avoid any more violence, and shoving them might injure them.*

"Worried about the damn bugs..." Savas scoffed.

You two, she said to Kahali and Eka, *need to protect the others while they load the supplies, and while Savas gets to his helicopter. Rana's the best with animals. She and I will handle it.*

"Now wait just a minute," Savas growled. "This is a Northern Haven mission and—"

"They're right, and you know it," Girak interrupted. "We knew we'd need their help up here."

"Don't you—" Savas began.

"Enough!" Bleu held up his palm to Savas.

Savas was so startled that he actually stopped arguing.

"It's settled," Bleu snapped. "If Kalakanya says they can do it, we let them try." He divided them up into two teams to collect the supplies.

"Wait." Savas spun around, searching the room and narrowed his eyes at Rana. "Where's Zach's gun?"

The force of his aggression stunned her. It took both Neviah's translation and a full moment to realize what he was talking about.

Where he dropped it.

"Why didn't you bring it back? He needs it. We don't have your flashy powers, you know. We need our guns." With an apologetic frown, Neviah translated.

Zach's gun didn't do him much good, Kahali noted.

"Everyone stop." Bleu walked between them. "Are we sure no one brought it back?" He raised his eyebrows hopefully at Eka, Rana, and Kalakanya.

They all shook their heads.

Savas walked over to Kalakanya. "If Zach survives, he'll need his gun."

We can keep you safe, Kalakanya responded. *Violence is not necessary.*

The muscle twitched in his jaw, and he checked his wrist. "How did you understand me? Neviah didn't translate yet."

I'm learning your language.

Savas' bristling energy surged through Rana, but his face remained impassive. "I don't want any of us to be dependent on you. Get the gun."

He glanced over at Zach. When he looked back at Kalakanya, his face had shifted. Softened, almost. "Please?" As the word passed through his lips, he twitched as if it pained him.

He and Kalakanya stared at each other in silence. If Rana didn't know better, she would think they were two star beings in a silent argument. She exchanged nervous glances with Eka, who stepped closer as if expecting trouble.

Finally, Kalakanya gave a curt nod. *I will star beam you there, and you can retrieve it. I will not touch a weapon of death.*

"Thank you." His crisp, official tone belied the shift in his stark-blue eyes. Asking Kalakanya for help had taken its toll on him.

*But if you insist on wearing your device—*Kalakanya nodded toward his wrist—*I feel I must advise you that I'm not sure how the energy of star beaming will affect it.*

Savas' nostrils flared as he regarded her. Would he lay aside his distrust to retrieve the gun he believed Zach needed? Rana said a silent prayer that he'd finally choose to not see the star beings as a threat.

Savas narrowed his eyes. "Then take Girak."

Kalakanya's smile faltered. *At some point, I hope you will learn to trust me.*

Savas smirked. "Like you trusted me earlier when I shot the bug leaping at your back? As I recall, you sent me flying backward to protect yourself from my supposed assassination attempt."

Kalakanya blushed. *I believe I previously apologized for that reaction. Girak, are you willing to go get the gun?*

Girak grimaced as he glanced from the gray insectoid legs pressed against the window to Zach's still form on the makeshift bed. "Yeah, I'll go."

Commander Reinier, is it okay if Girak and I leave?

Bleu jumped at her question, clearly not expecting it. "Uh, yes. Be safe."

Come on, Girak. Kalakanya held out her hand, and they were gone.

Rana sagged with relief. Exhausted, she plopped down onto a chair.

Eka claimed the chair beside her, still holding the shield. "Would you like some real food?" He offered her an open sack of dried cinnaberries and pine nuts. Chuckling, he shook his head. "Are humans always like this?"

"Yes." Her voice rang bitter as she popped some of the dried mix into her mouth.

His laugh cut off, and he gave her a concerned look. "You can tell Kalakanya you're too tired. She can probably do it herself."

"Really? You believe that?" As she spoke, another bug thumped against the outer hull.

"She might be able to."

"Not even she's that good, and you know it." Rana marveled at his reclining ease while still holding the shield. "You're going to Crown soon."

"No. Shields are just my thing, like animals are your thing. Remember when you sensed something was wrong out there, and I sensed nothing? Animals are definitely your thing."

"My thing is still in hiding," Kahali joked, joining them.

As the three of them laughed, the humans cast them suspicious looks.

I'm making fun of myself, not you, Kahali reassured Savas.

The humans returned to their small discussions, though Savas continued to scrutinize the star beings' every move. Rana turned away from him and faced the guys.

"Wow. They really are touchy," Eka observed.

Rana gave him an I-told-you-so smirk.

Kahali jumped as another bug smacked the hull beside them. "Rana, do you really think you can get all those bugs to listen to you?"

She turned to stare out the small bug-free section of the nearest window. Not facing her fears and not helping the rest of the team stay safe would both contribute to her "Reasons Why I'll Never Crown" list. It was doubtful she could get all the bugs to listen, but anything she tried would be safer for the bugs than Savas shooting them. Sighing, she gave Kahali and Eka a shrug. "Do I have a choice?"

Chapter 26

Unknown Ice Shelf: Rana of Peleguin Rookery

A few moments later, Girak and Kalakanya star beamed back inside the helicopter with Zach's gun, and everyone else breathed a sigh of relief. Rana only heaved a sigh of exhaustion. She hadn't doubted Kalakanya's abilities.

She questioned her own feeble abilities, though. Well, that and her recent destructive impulses.

Kalakanya rechecked Zach's condition and turned to face them, chipper and full of energy. *Everyone ready?*

Rana shrugged.

Bleu, Savas, and Girak readied their guns. Atsushi eyed the handgun Savas offered him, glanced out the window, now covered with dark insect bodies, and then extended his trembling hand.

"He's too young for a gun," Girak said. "He doesn't even know how to use it."

That got Kahali's attention. His full attention jerked to Atsushi, and he leapt to his feet.

Careful, Rana sent Kahali as he strode toward his human charge.

Kahali stopped just short of pushing between Savas and Atsushi. That would have involved touching the gun. *Hey. I kept you safe earlier without that, right?*

Atsushi nodded.

You don't need that. Remember the chant I taught you?

Atsushi nodded.

"Chant?" Savas snickered. "You've *got* to be kidding."

Somehow, Kahali stood his ground. *Good. Stay near me and practice that chant. It builds your energy so you'll have more strength and intuition.*

Savas scoffed. "Don't be fooled by his silly song. You're not a star being; you're a young man." He waggled the gun in front of Atsushi. "Take it."

Atsushi's glance bounced between the gun and Kahali's face. Then, with a final, dubious look at Kahali, he cracked a crooked smile. "Don't let me down."

I won't.

Rana's heart soared. Atsushi might be different from Savas, but without shielding, those insects had to be terrifying. Maybe there was hope for humans learning to be nonviolent after all.

Atsushi turned back to Savas. "I can't use that, but thanks for thinking I'm old enough to handle it,"—Atsushi raised an eyebrow in jest at Girak—"unlike some people ."

Savas sighed and tucked the extra gun into one of the many pockets in his coat.

Eka readied himself for this expedition by positioning himself by the door.

Kalakanya gave Rana a reassuring smile, the type of smile Crowned Ones gave when they were about to teach you something new.

Rana was not reassured. This would be more than difficult. It would be a dangerous, on-the-spot teaching.

I think it'll be easier to get them off the ship than off Zach. They're not getting any food from the ship.

Yes, Rana said, *but that also means they're starving. We've never dealt with them. We have nothing to offer them for cooperating.*

"We offer their lives," Savas interrupted. "If they don't cooperate, we shoot them to high heaven. Seems plain enough to me."

Guilt rushed through Rana. Her earlier threat to the bug on Zach had been horribly similar to Savas' violent suggestion.

Kalakanya's face tightened. *Leave the bugs to us, or you'll put everyone in danger out there.* She turned back to Rana. *If they won't leave, we'll have to remove them manually.*

Bleu strode to the door lock. "All right, here we go. Watch each other's backs." He unclicked the lock mechanism and shoved the door open.

The full clicking and scraping of the swarm, no longer blocked by the closed door, hit Rana. She stepped backward onto Eka's boot, nearly tripping. Off to an excellent start.

Checking that Kalakanya was ready, she climbed down onto the snow and into the extension of Eka's shield. A scrape of claws on the snow behind her told her that Digga had followed. She closed her eyes to Call the insects, trusting Kalakanya to have her back. But the noise of the insects was so random that she couldn't connect with them. It was like trying to find a pattern in the particles of campfire smoke on a blustery day. Impossible.

She walked farther, nearing the edge of Eka's transparent gold shield. The closer she got to the swarm, the more tangled her awareness became as she searched for a pattern in the flurry of vibrations.

The clicking of their legs and mouth parts against the helicopter's metal skin carried no decipherable communication. She stretched her awareness further, seeking understanding. Desperation and hunger flooded her. Oneness! The poor creatures had been in a near hibernation state until they sensed the presence of blood-warmed bodies and mechanically warmed helicopters. No wonder they were so determined to feed.

Connecting with the low thrum of their minds, she sent calming.

Nothing happened. Nevertheless, she continued. The overall noise quieted a bit. Behind her, boots crunched on ice as the team exited the helicopter. Muffled whispers murmured as Bleu gave orders that the supplies be checked for bugs and then loaded.

Refocusing on the insectile thrum, she asked the bugs to leave. The most distant ones responded by hopping away. But the hundred or so that clung on to the two ships and enjoyed the heat radiating from them remained.

It's not working with these. She motioned to the nearest ones.

Kalakanya looked at the nearest ones thoughtfully. *Try giving each one a nudge.*

Rana did. The bug she focused on would grow still but wouldn't leave. She sighed. This was way beyond her. She gave Kalakanya an apologetic shake of her head.

An idea forming, she approached the nearest bug on the helicopter, just beyond Eka's shimmering shield. *I want to try something. Eka, can you extend the shield in an odd shape in one direction?*

Whatever you need, he responded from behind her.

Good. Expand your shield in this direction as I clear the copter's surface. She wriggled her fingers in the proper direction for him, concerned that a larger gesture would startle the closest bug.

Got it.

Targeting the nearest bug with calmness, she took another step closer. The massive gray-white head swiveled, its mouthparts trembling in anticipation as it clung to the warm ship.

To grasp the huge tick-like creature, she'd need to risk leaving the shield's safety. *One In All, please let this work for both of us.* She took a deep breath and stepped beyond the shield.

She got within an arm's length. When the bug's head swiveled toward her, its legs shifted as if preparing to jump. Her body heat must have become more alluring than the copter's warmth. Or maybe it smelled her blood?

Careful. I'm trying to help you get off safely. If you stay attached, you will die. She left out that if it stayed put it would also trap the ship, eventually making the humans and star beings available for dinner.

Thankfully, the bug didn't jump on her, lulled by the ship's warmth and her communication. With a grimace, she stepped closer and wrapped her fingers around the hard shell, holding tight so that it couldn't turn and latch on to her with its mouth. Still sending calmness, she walked about ten strides from the helicopter and placed it on the ground just outside of the shield.

Rana, watch out! Eka warned.

She looked over her shoulder. All the bugs turned and sprang toward her. She rushed back inside the shield as they smacked into it behind her.

"Great work," Savas exclaimed. "Seriously, it's impressive. But if that's your technique, we'll be stuck here for days."

Normally, his comment would have angered her, but looking at the hundreds of bugs still in need of safe removal, she could only sigh. He was right.

She turned to Kalakanya, hoping for some support...some congratulations...anything. But the Crowned One only looked at them all with amusement. *You're right, Savas. Rana, how many can you hold in your focus at once?*

Not only did she consider the answer to the question, but she also sensed that she was teetering on the edge of whatever lesson Kalakanya had planned to teach her. She wasn't in the mood for a lesson. *Maybe three of four if they're close together. Why?*

Because what we need is more hands, not more star beings gifted in interspecies communication. She turned to grin a bit mischievously at the others. *We can all carry calmed bugs to the perimeter. We'd make short work of it.*

The humans collectively gasped, but Rana chuckled with relief. The anticipated lesson had not been for her. Kalakanya was stretching the humans' minds, not hers. They had to trust the star beings and learn that they could effectively remove the bugs without violence.

Bleu recovered from the shock of Kalakanya's suggestion first. "Okay, everyone, you heard her. This way we don't risk damaging the hull with our guns. Rana, how should we start?"

Rana explained how to approach the bloodsuckers without anger and to each gather their bug near each other so that Eka only had to extend one part of the shield at a time. Kahali, who couldn't properly restrain the large bugs with his wooden hand, kept a close eye on Atsushi while assisting Eka with the shielding. Even Kalakanya carried the bloodsuckers.

Rana discovered she could lull five at a time, and if they quickly deposited the bugs at different edges of the shield, they could safely return to the shield before ones outside noticed their body heat and attacked. Soon, Neviah's ship was cleared and loaded with half the strewn supplies. Kahali and Atsushi were reluctant to leave the others behind to clear Savas' helicopter, but Bleu convinced them to ride in Neviah's helicopter with Zach.

"But what about the shielding?" Neviah asked. "Last time we were flying and Kalakanya made a shield, its energy threw off my equipment readings. I don't see how I can fly with Kahali holding a shield around the helicopter, but if he removes it, we'll be covered with bugs again before takeoff."

Everyone turned to Savas, but he looked stumped.

"Wait. Did it mess with all your equipment?" Bleu asked. "If I remember correctly, when Kalakanya shielded, you said you would have crashed if you hadn't been able to see the horizon. Am I remembering that correctly?"

She nodded. "The dials and needles spun like crazy, but the engine was okay."

"Good memory." Savas had actually complimented her and not winced in pain at the effort. "If the engine could run, you're going to have to take off using only your sight. Kahali can drop the shield as soon as you're above the height the insects can jump."

"O-kay," Kahali said, grinning at his grasp of the human word.

The humans did a double take.

Bleu shot him an appreciative grin. "That was cool, man."

"You all sure do learn language quickly." Neviah translated Savas' words, but Rana had grasped the gist of it on her own. Savas seemed more concerned than impressed by their learning.

Could she allay his fear? *It helps that we get a running translation every time you all speak. Spending time with everyone is a constant language lesson.*

"Of course." His smile quirked, mimicking his inner conflict. "You're studying us."

We're learning so we can communicate better, Rana tried, hoping the small correction would keep his paranoia from building to a dangerous level.

Neviah looked unsure. "Savas, we never practiced with the holographic helicopters taking off without all our equipment. I'm not sure I can do that."

"You can do it, Neviah." Savas gave her an encouraging nod. "You did a great job staying aloft before, and you weren't expecting to have that problem. Plus, it's still daylight, so you can see your position relative to the ground."

Neviah furrowed her brow. "All right."

As Neviah approached the cockpit, Rana studied Savas. Was it possible that Savas might be learning a stitch of kindness?

Savas, seeming to notice her watching him, turned to give her an icy glare. No, forget that. Savas needed Neviah to succeed, and he knew she'd react best to kindness. He manipulated them too easily.

Chapter 27

Unknown Ice Shelf: Rana of Peleguin Rookery

Rana grinned with pride as Kahali held a shield around the bug-free helicopter and, with only one jerky movement, her new friend, Neviah, managed to lift off. Digga pressed against her leg as the noisy thing rose straight up and circled above them in the bug-free sky. Kahali, Atsushi, Zach, and Neviah were now safe, and Rana hadn't injured a single bug.

One more helicopter to go. Using the same technique, they began to clear and load Savas' helicopter. But when Rana led the others to the ship's far side, she gasped. Two bugs had somehow climbed the convex-sloping metal surface to the top of his ship. No one could simply reach up and remove them.

"They're not near the engine," Girak observed. "Maybe we could take off with them still attached?"

"No." Savas pulled out binoculars and studied the two bugs. "They might be able to chew their way into the engine section. It's one of the warmest areas." After seeing Rana's confusion, Girak translated. She had grasped most of the words, except the engine part.

Nodding at the translation, she approached the ship and rubbed its surface. *I might be able to climb up there.*

Too slippery, Eka countered.

No, I can do it.

"But, Rana, you need to focus on calming them, not climbing." Bleu screened his eyes from the sun with his hand and studied the surface. "I think I could do it."

"But if you slid," Savas said, still eyeing the bugs through his binoculars, "not only would you fall and break your neck, you also might hit something crucial on the way down and damage the ship."

I'm not sure there's a better option, Kalakanya sent. *I could buffer a fall. I'd probably have to lower whoever climbed up there anyway, because you wouldn't be able to climb down holding the bug. And there's two of them, so we need two climbers.*

Savas gave Kalakanya a disgusted look. Was he that upset that Neviah no longer had to translate for him? You would expect him to be grateful.

"Or you could just do it all yourself." Savas added. His face had become a mask of fury.

Concerned, Rana took a step backward away from Savas. What had she missed?

Kalakanya tilted her head as if confused as well. *No. I'm better at catching others than catching myself.*

Savas' face turned nearly purple. "Stamf would beg to differ, seeing as you dropped him to his death."

At his accusation, everyone froze. Rana and Eka exchanged a confused look.

You dropped a human? It was out before Rana could stop herself.

Bleu's shoulders hunched, and Girak had gone even paler than normal. Savas' finger twitched on his gun. And Kalakanya had tears in her eyes.

It was a horrible accident. I had caught his fall and was lowering him when someone shot at me. Kalakanya's glance flickered to Savas. *I lost control of his descent.*

"Lost control of his descent?" Savas mocked. He turned to Rana. "She let him fall. My son plummeted two hundred meters to his death."

Your son? Rana asked, unsure she had understood properly.

For the first time, Eka lost focus, and the shield flickered. The bugs increased their clicking as they flew toward the warmth. Eka gathered himself and steadied the shield.

"My eighteen-year-old son. Only a year older than Kahali, whom you seem so fond of protecting. So, yes, I doubt your capability or willingness to protect Bleu or whoever else climbs up there."

Bleu turned to gape at him.

Kalakanya looked ready to cry. *I am so sorry. It was an accident. I would never allow another to come to harm.*

"You already did. Stamf's dead. There's no way in hell I'm climbing up there. I'll take my chances with my aim and use the rifle first." Savas raised it to his shoulder and began walking around, trying to get the correct angle to not damage the hull.

"Stop it, Savas. I said I'd go." Bleu's quiet tone could barely be heard in the surrounding insect din. He sounded desperate, like it was hard for him to form words at all. Since the mention of Stamf, his whole demeanor had changed.

He turned toward Kalakanya. Something unsaid passed between them. Something powerful that left both of them distraught. "I can trust you to catch me?"

Rana scowled. What kind of question was that? Rana gave Eka a questioning look, but he only shook his head and shrugged.

Of course. Kalakanya's mind speak carried a shaken tone, as if whatever Bleu had just apparently mind spoken to her about had completely undone her. *Just because I can't share everything doesn't mean I'd ever allow you to come to harm if I could do anything to stop it.*

"And to be clear, as long as no one shoots at you, if I fall, you can catch me?" With tears in his eyes, Bleu bit his lip and glared at Savas, then turned back to Kalakanya.

Yes. I had hoped to still save your friend but had to shield myself first so I'd be alive to catch him. Kalakanya looked from Bleu to Savas.

Bleu narrowed his gaze at her for a moment and then without a comment paced around the helicopter, trying to find a good angle to hunt the tick. Savas' shoulders were hunched, his mouth pressed into a straight line. Rana wasn't sure if he was about to kill or about to cry. Maybe both?

"Okay, I trust you. I'm going up," Bleu said, shooting a tight smile toward Kalakanya. Then he turned to Savas. "I know you want me out of your way, but if you shoot toward Kalakanya now, it's obviously murder."

Savas spun around and strode back toward them. "You think I would just randomly cause your death, for no reason, when humans are nearly extinct?" he bellowed.

Bleu blinked and swallowed slowly. "Maybe…"

He and Savas glared at each other. They were both so twisted up over Stamf's death that Rana had no idea whether Savas would ever hurt Bleu or not.

Finally, Savas grunted and shook his head. "Bleu, you don't have to do this. We can't afford to lose any more healthy teens. I can shoot the damn thing."

"If you damage the helicopters, we risk losing more than just me. I can do this, I trust Kalakanya, and it's my decision." Bleu narrowed his gaze at the helicopter. "Anything specific that I should avoid grabbing?"

Savas grimaced. "It's not a climbing wall, but it's made to withstand a lot. I'll give you a lift." Savas interlocked his gloved hands together and lifted Bleu up high enough to grasp a ridge of the door and pull himself higher. He began climbing.

Hmm. So Savas could help the others and be kind if it suited his purposes. Good to know, but she still wasn't about to trust him. Rana approached the helicopter to climb up as well. This was a two-person job, and she wanted to be as close to the bugs she was calming as possible.

She looked down at Digga. *Stay with Eka so you're safe.* Digga grunted and waddled over to Eka.

"Do you want a leg up as well, or can you float or something?" Savas asked her. It felt like a test of her capabilities disguised in an offer to assist.

She didn't want him to touch her, but since Eka was holding the shield and Kalakanya was watching Bleu, she relented. *If you don't mind, I could use an assist.*

Savas tightened his jaw. "So, you can't float?"

He *was* gathering information on their capabilities, probably to use against them. Or, maybe her fears were getting the best of her. She shook her head. *No floating.* What strange thoughts he had about them. Grinning, she added, *And before today, none of us have flown.*

He grunted, gave a soft chuckle, and boosted her up.

Kalakanya sent up to them, *Don't climb too close to each other. I can only catch one at a time.*

"Great time to mention that," Savas said.

Rana ignored him and kept climbing. Her boots, slick with ice, slid on the sheer metal. This would never work. She perched on top of the door and pulled off her boots and socks, tossing them below. She returned to climbing and easily caught up with Bleu.

Throw your boots and socks down, she suggested as she passed him.

Nearing the bugs and panting from exertion, she stopped to center herself. Despite the metal's warmth, the cold breeze made her bare feet stiff with cold. While she calmed the insects, Bleu climbed up beside her, also barefoot.

"Are they good? Should I go up?"

Should be good. But be careful.

Bleu climbed slower now until he reached the almost flat top. He pulled himself over. Rana did her best to ignore him. The bugs needed to be her focus. Currently, they rested sleepily from the heated hull and warm sunlight, but that could change in an instant.

Bleu crept close and grasped the closest one. Holding it tightly, he crouch-stepped over to the edge of the top where the descent became sharp. He took a deep breath and nodded to Kalakanya. "Ready? Can I come down now?"

Bleu's face twitched, and his smile for Kalakanya turned to a grimace. "Shast. Not now," he mumbled.

What? Rana asked.

Despite his legs being firmly planted, he wobbled as if dizzy.

Bleu, what's wrong? The other bug lay still behind him. What had happened?

His eyes widened, and he moaned as if in pain.

Hold on. Rana climbed upward, quickly closing the gap between them. Bleu threw his arm out as if avoiding a blow from an invisible attacker. The bug twisted in his grasp and latched onto his arm. The other one jumped at him from behind.

In her panic, she had forgotten the other bug!

Bleu fell toward her, all kicking boots and flailing arms. Shouts from below soared up to them. But he was moving too quickly. If she tried to stop his fall, they'd both go down. Kalakanya couldn't catch them both simultaneously.

He slid past her, bug still attached, eyes wide. As Bleu flailed, he knocked the second bug off the back of his parka. The bug skittered down toward Eka and the others.

Light enveloped Bleu as Kalakanya caught him. Rana watched through teary eyes as he was lowered to the ground while shaking and pulling at the first bug. The other insect soared through the air, outside the shield.

Guilt washed through her as the soaring bug, that had been hers to hold, bounced on the lower section of the helicopter and sprang at Girak and Savas. But they couldn't shoot without directly hitting the ship. Savas fell to the ground, firing his gun to get it from below.

Girak whipped the bug away with his gun, and Rana winced at the horrid crunch.

Savas fired again. The second insect, hers to safely remove, was blown to bits before it ever landed.

Rana trembled against the warm ship. She had messed up again, and this time her inattention had killed the insect. If only she had kept her calming energy focused on the bugs and let Kalakanya keep Bleu safe. Why couldn't she ever concentrate properly? Pressing her shaking hands against each other to stop their shaking, she let out a sob of regret. She'd killed it, and now she'd never Crown.

"Rana, you okay?" Eka yelled.

She crouched and through the blur of her tears examined the ground below with revulsion. The snow around the helicopter was littered with dead bugs. She could no longer say it was all the humans.

Rana. Eka's mind talk somehow reverberated through her entire body. *Rana, breathe. It wasn't your fault.*

She sucked in a shaky breath. And another. *I'll be okay*, she sent, immediately struck by how unconvincing it sounded even in her own head.

And Bleu is going to be okay, too. We'll get you down in a minute. Hold on.

Falling stars. Bleu had been fine one moment and then lost it. What had happened to him?

Rana. Stay put. Give me a minute and I'll get you down, Kalakanya sent.

Rana was so exhausted and ashamed that staying put sounded just fine. She curled her feet under her legs, protecting them from the rising wind. Below, Savas, Girak, and Kalakanya removed the bug from Bleu and tried to help him stand. Eka still shielded them all and the ship. Digga paced back and forth, her sharp, black eyes watching Rana as she rested on the smooth metal.

Rana?

She looked around, confused.

Up here. You okay? She glanced up at the flying helicopter and made out a star being in the window—Kahali.

She waved, too tired to communicate.

Is Bleu okay?

Rana watched as Bleu stood with Girak's support. *I think so.*

Neviah won't land. Can I do anything?

Distract me. Tell me a joke.

A joke? Okay. Once there were some best friends. And they believed they could help some humans...

She laughed a bit maniacally until it was her turn to slide down.

Chapter 28

Midflight: Commander Kern Savas

For the first time, Savas wished someone else would pilot the helicopter. His helicopter. He needed to know what was happening in the main cabin right now. Behind him, out of sight, Bleu was recovering from whatever had happened to him. Savas needed to question Bleu while he was still shaken. Once he recovered, he'd be able to lie and cover the truth more effectively—like he had after flailing about in the star being dining hall.

It had to be the Sickness. What else would make someone freak out like that? And how could he keep the mission going if Bleu was losing it? Sure, he could take over command, but the star beings had been clear they wouldn't allow that.

And after that display of power with the bugs...

He couldn't rid himself of the image of the four star beings saving their asses. Kahali and Rana had at least had the grace to break a sweat. But Eka and Kalakanya barely seemed put out by using their supernatural abilities.

The whole experience was terrifying. Awe-inspiring. Their raw power...

We need them. He glanced at his wristband, making sure Dr. Medicci's device still worked. It was hard enough to admit that to himself. He certainly didn't want the star beings knowing it.

He needed them more than ever. Bleu was getting ill. Zach would recover but was currently too weak to walk steadily. And Neviah, Girak, and Atsushi were totally inexperienced with weaponry. That idiotic

Girak had actually used his gun as a bat to whack away the giant tick. Atsushi wouldn't even hold a gun. Neviah had real potential, but lacked confidence...

He blew out a long breath. First things first—find a safe place to camp for the night.

Who was he kidding? He had no idea how to prevent landing in another bug-infested spot. He needed those uppity, *more-evolved* humans. Again.

He needed their help again. *Shast.* How had it come to this?

He ran his fingers through his hair, pulling it to stay alert. The day was never-ending, but he'd never admit exhaustion when Kalakanya was just fine.

He could do this. They would probably see his asking for help as a sign that he was becoming more like them. He snorted at that unlikely scenario.

"Kalakanya?" he called. "Can you come up here?"

Would she come or choose to stay with Bleu? Something was going on between those two. Whether it was sexual attraction, mind control, curiosity, or friendship, he hadn't decided. But he was damn sure she'd rather stay back there with Bleu than come up and help him.

Yes?

He jumped at her sudden presence beside him. "*Shast!* Don't startle me, or we'll crash. Make a little noise or something." She was like those creepy white lions, totally silent when she walked.

She raised an amused eyebrow.

"Can you tell if we've gone far enough to be away from those monstrous insects?"

We've been flying for...what do you call your time units?

"Hours. Yes, since I've been doing the flying, I'm aware of that fact." He shook his head in annoyance. "Can you tell from up here if it's safe? Is it solid land down there? No bugs?"

She walked to the side window and placed one palm on the glass. Below, the shadows of trees and hills bloomed like bruises across the snow. The sun would set soon, and he had no intentions of landing in the dark.

She remained quiet. For too long.

"Don't do something to mess with my equipment."

She turned, an unreadable look on her face. *I have no intention to cause a safety issue by messing with your equipment.* The side of her mouth quirked upward.

She wasn't messing with the equipment; she was messing with him. He wasn't about to play her games. "Can you tell or not? You're distracting me from piloting, so if you're not going to be of assistance, get out of here!"

Her face fell. *I believe it will be fine to land. However, I should exit alone and check the area while you go back up into the air to remain safe. Just in case. Is that agreeable?*

"Fine."

She removed her hand from the glass and wiped it on her long, leather vest as if his helicopter were filthy. Nothing manmade was ever as damn perfect and pristine as their ice fields and evergreens, clear sky and mountains.

He ignored her insult. "Is Bleu okay back there?"

He's recovering. He'll be fine.

He scoffed. "I wish it were that simple. Go buckle in, and I'll land this bird."

❄ ❄ ❄ ❄ ❄ ❄

In the absence of the giant ticks, his team set up camp in the Kalakanya-approved site in no time. Even with two men down. By the time Savas had checked everything on the helicopter and shut it down for the night, Bleu was up and engrossed in the activities.

Still, Savas couldn't leave Bleu's strange episode alone. Individuals with early cases of the Sickness often felt fine after an episode. That's how the Reiniers had hidden Ayanna's condition. He wasn't sure how he knew, but he had concluded Ayanna had caused the commotion near the Surface door weeks ago. This time, the Reinier kid involved didn't have the buffer of a medical-specialist mom to cover for him.

The kid kept avoiding him whenever he got near. Savas finally cornered Bleu inside Neviah's helicopter as he grabbed the sleeping bags. "We need to talk."

"I just have a sec. Rana's teaching fire-making skills." He grinned, but not quite with his usual care-free attitude. "Don't want to miss it."

Yeah, that's what he should be worrying about. Making a fire when his own brain is slowly being fried inside his own head.

"Sounds useful." Savas smirked. "For when all our lighters somehow malfunction."

Bleu laughed, but there was no mirth in it. "It's good to learn as much as we can from each other."

"What have they asked for you to teach them?"

Bleu's face went blank.

"Yup. That's what I thought." He sighed. "We have nothing of value to them."

Their unearned helpfulness never ceased to irk him. Even Zach's ability to sit in a chair and stay conscious this soon seemed unnatural. Another thing owed to them.

Savas gazed out the window. Girak was walking their way. He didn't have long. "Look, what happened up there on top of my helicopter?"

Bleu's eyes widened ever so slightly. "I lost my balance."

Savas narrowed his eyes and just stared. Maybe he could make him squirm enough to tell the truth?

Bleu met his gaze. "It was windy. And I couldn't let go of that stupid bug."

"I was there. Are you aware of that?"

"What?" Bleu's anger flashed. "Of course, I know that."

"So, what really happened? If something is wrong, I need to know." He paused, his next words burning like acid in his throat. The insult to his pride was too much, especially speaking to a damn eighteen-year-old who was clearly losing his mind. "I'm your second in command. How can I support you if you don't let me know what's going on?"

Bleu's gaze had become downright steel-like. "There's nothing to know except what I already—"

"Bleu? Need help with those?" Girak climbed in, clearly checking on his ex-student.

Savas ignored the intruder, keeping his focus on the kid. "You need to be honest with yourself. If you're compromised, we need to deal with it."

"I'm fine." Bleu tossed a sleeping bag toward Girak. "Thanks, Girak. I got the rest."

The two of them left, joining the others at the spot where Rana had set up a fire pit. The window framed the whole scene. On each side of it stood two large gray tents, one for the humans and one for the star beings.

The star beings had yet to enter theirs. Of course. Built by humans, so therefore useless.

As he watched Rana coax embers, blow on them, and create orange flames, he felt only the dropping temperature within the cooling helicopter. It settled in his bones while outside the team cheered her on. He was on his own. The others trusted these creatures completely.

Hopping out of Neviah's helicopter, he closed the main door with reverence. These machines were works of art, and regardless of the sudden leisure of the others, his exhausted bones still had work to do.

Secret work that a sudden door slam might draw attention to.

He strode over to his own helicopter, entered his cockpit, checked again for observers, and then removed a panel. He pulled out the metal box and opened it. Quickly, he typed his message to the Prime Minister. *They have learned human speech. Test one commencing tonight.* He hit send and replaced the device.

For test one, he withdrew a piece of paper and pen from the same recess, and wrote, *I know how to kill Kahali. He is the least useful and should be the first to go.*

He stared at the words for exactly two minutes according to the experiment design and then put the note with the communication device and resealed it behind the panel.

If only his words were true. Actually, the part about the one-armed one being the least useful was true. But he had no idea how to kill any of them unless he and his gun miraculously caught them all in a deep sleep.

The truthfulness didn't matter. Northern Haven needed to test their abilities. Would Kalakanya know he'd written that? Could she see what he saw when he stared at what he'd written? Or could she see the thread of time where he contemplated killing Kahali?

Rap. Rap. Rap.

His heart skipped a beat. *Shast. That was fast.* He drew his small gun and looked about for Kalakanya. Only to see Atsushi standing at the door to the cockpit, looking sheepish.

"Atsushi." He waved the boy in, blowing out a sigh of relief at the humanness of his visitor.

"Am I interrupting you, sir?" Atsushi's eyes widened at his drawn gun.

"Not at all." He holstered it. "I was just finishing up and getting ready to join you. How's Rana's fire?"

"Great." Atsushi shifted foot to foot, then looked over his shoulder, checking something.

"What's wrong?"

"Well, uhm…" He looked over his shoulder toward the fire. "Those bugs were pretty dangerous, and it's only our first day." His words came faster, as if afraid he would be interrupted by someone walking up behind him. "Would you still be willing to teach me how to use a gun? Just in case, you know…"

Savas grinned. "Of course. Offer still stands. You interested?"

"Yes." He leaned closer. "But I don't want to upset Kahali. Do you think we could do it…uhm…on the sly?"

Savas' grin grew. Not only was the kid going to learn to handle a gun, but he was willing to keep information from the star beings. What potential. "We could probably figure that out. Though you shouldn't worry so much about what that guy thinks. He's not always going to be around. You need to protect yourself."

"Yeah. I mean, I trust him, but a gun seems safer than a chant, you know?" He shot Savas a shy grin.

"I'm glad you're using your brain. I can start teaching you now. They seem pretty distracted by the fire." Strange sounds drifted across the ice field. "Is that singing?"

Atsushi laughed. "Yeah. They all have great voices."

"Of course, they do." He pulled out his gun. "This is—"

"Sir? There's one other thing. Before someone comes over…" His faced pinked. Even his ears.

"Okay." Savas checked the safety and rested the gun on his lap. "What?" The boy was super talkative tonight.

"Do you have a way to get messages back home?"

Savas' smile froze. "Why would you think that?" No one else on the expedition had clearance to know of his experiments.

Atsushi shrugged. "Just wondering…"

Did this mean the star beings knew what he did when out of sight but not what he thought? Were they planning right now to harm him to keep Kahali safe? He slipped off the safety on his gun while checking over Atsushi's shoulder. Seven standing silhouettes and the hump of Zach's occupied chair. No one was sneaking up on him yet. "Who sent you to ask that?"

"What? No one!" His blush deepened.

Savas watched him, saying nothing. Waiting for him to break.

"I just had a wild idea." He shook his head. "I'm sorry. Forget it." He turned, in a hurry to leave.

"What wild idea?"

Atsushi turned, his expression tight with anticipated rejection. "I wanted to know if I could get a message to Ayanna. She left me a picture in my sleeping bag, and I didn't leave her anything. But it's silly." He brushed at the air as if ridding the idea from their presence. "I'm sorry to bother you. It's stupid."

Savas chuckled. "Sounds like you found a girlfriend."

"No, well…maybe." The kid grinned. "I think the picture was a good sign."

The boy was clueless. "Depends on the picture. What's she doing in it?"

"What?" He looked horrified. "No, she just drew me a picture of her face."

"Oh. Well, still, I bet no one else got pictures." An idea hit him. "I might have a way to get something to her."

"Really?" His face lit up like the headlights on the copter. "That would be so great."

"It'd be tricky, though. Maybe you could help me with a project in the meantime?"

"Sure."

"Great. I can't seem to get a straight answer out of the star beings about what the Crowned Ones eat. Think you could keep an eye on Kalakanya for me? Maybe ask Kahali about Crowning?"

His lit face dulled. "Like, spy?"

Savas shrugged and held up his palms. "Think of it as research. They're a new species. You're doing field observation."

"I don't think she eats at all. None of the Crowned Ones seem to. They go to the gathering hall to socialize."

"You do realize that's impossible, right? They're alive. They need an energy source."

"Kalakanya said she eats air or something."

Savas snorted. "Well, be curious. Ask Kahali when you're alone. Later, ask the others. We'll compare answers."

Atsushi grimaced. "They'll know what I'm thinking. I don't want to upset them."

"No, you don't." If he had another Medicci device, he'd offer it to him. There must be something the boy could do to stay safe. A tiny, guilty voice rose within him at exposing the boy to the dangers of mind-control. His fingers drifted inside his parka and found his mother's compass. No kid should go through that. He had to give Atsushi options.

There had to be a way to create some background noise in his head that wouldn't cause suspicion. "The chant!"

"Huh?"

"What if you keep that chant Kahali taught you running in your head? Maybe then they won't catch on?"

"Maybe." Atsushi was silent. "I'm supposed to be chanting that all the time, but I'm horrid at remembering."

"You work on that and get me a short message for your girlfriend. I'll see if I can figure out how to get it to her without having the whole Council see it first."

Atsushi nodded with excitement. "Thank you, sir." He glanced toward the fire, where the star beings suddenly sang more loudly. "You still don't trust them, do you?"

"No, I don't."

"But why? They're so nice."

"There used to be a fish that lived in the depths of the ocean. It evolved a beautiful light that shone magnificently in the darkness. Other fish would swim close, mesmerized by the beauty, feeling completely safe. And then the light-bearing fish would tear them to pieces."

Chapter 29

Unknown Surface Campsite: Bleu Reinier

Bleu and Girak tossed the sleeping bags onto the floor of the tent for humans, but as Bleu turned to leave, Girak clasped his shoulder.

"What?" Bleu asked, turning around.

"Savas is doing something over by the helicopters." Girak had kept his voice soft, barely a whisper. Out by the fire, someone began making repetitive thumps, like a drum.

"Yeah?" He assumed Girak was warning him of an impending Savas scheme, but as he recognized the concern in Girak's eyes, he realized this had nothing to do with Savas. Girak was eyeing *him* with concern, assessing his every move and expression. This was about how he'd freaked out earlier. *Shast.* He didn't have time for this. Kalakanya had insisted on an explanation for his fall and was already waiting to meet him. "I'm fine."

But Girak still held his arm. "Look, I've known you all your life. You are not the overly dramatic type. Or clumsy. What happened to you back there?"

Bleu sighed. How had his mother dealt with this all her life? Lying to friends was not his thing. But he also couldn't tell the truth. He didn't even know the truth. But Girak deserved some sort of explanation.

"I..." He shook his head. "I don't know how to explain it. Maybe it's like you seeing Josefina, but different."

"You saw someone? Josefina?" Girak's eyes had regained a bit of their old spark at the mention of her. "Or Stamf? Abdul?"

"No." He gripped his temples in frustration. "Look, I'm going to go talk to Kalakanya about it now. I'm hoping she can help me figure it out. I'm sorry."

Girak's eyes narrowed. "Fine. But I think you should let one of us mere mortals know as well. It's going to be hard to keep Savas off your back about it if I don't understand it myself."

He gave him an apologetic look.

Girak put his hands up, as if fending off more excuses. "When you're ready, when you're ready."

"Thanks." As he watched Girak lift the tent flap to exit, inspiration hit him. "Girak?"

The older man turned.

Bleu grinned. "When Savas gets back, if my ambassador can get him to leave Kalakanya and me alone, I'd appreciate it."

Girak smirked. "Make sure you address the actual issue, Commander." He good-naturedly dropped the tent flap in Bleu's face, and as his footsteps receded, he called out, "Zach, you need anything before I grab a seat?"

Bleu lifted the flap and peered out. Kalakanya sat on the opposite side of the flames, her white hair luminescent in the fire's glow. *Shast*, she was beautiful. He closed his eyes, wishing for mental privacy and his heartbeat to stop galloping off like a salt deer every time he looked at her. He was being absurd. And he was about to make a total fool of himself.

As he ducked under the tent flap, Ayanna's reminder to act like a commander came back to him. But how did he do that when he seriously liked the mind-reading woman he was about to confess his crazy visions to?

"Not by hiding in the tent," he mumbled. Throwing back his shoulders and plastering what he hoped looked like confidence on his face, he strode out into the sensuous wafts of wood smoke. Glowing orange sparks flitted up from the crackling logs to warm the cold stars twinkling above. Was there no end to the wonders of life on the Surface?

"Bleu!" Rana called in greeting. *Come on. Kahali's just getting warmed up.* She grinned and motioned for him to join them.

Bleu waved back and gasped as Kahali's drumming took flight. Gripping the tall drum between his knees, Kahali struck his single hand like lightning against the drumhead and sides. He created not just an infectious rhythmic complexity seemingly impossible for a single hand, but also tonal differences. Everyone tapped their feet or danced, caught up in the spell of Kahali's music. Even Zach, still too weak to stand, bobbed his head from his makeshift chair.

Bleu's earlier exhaustion evaporated. He half-walked, half-danced his way around the circle toward Kalakanya while Eka began strumming a small string instrument. Rana taught the lyrics to Neviah and Girak as they laughed. Kalakanya began a complicated chant-like tune that coordinated with Kahali's beat. Her ethereal voice reverberated through the smoky air, enchanting him.

He tried not to stare, but his gaze kept returning to her. He yearned to be close to her, to sleep spooning her and have her be the first thing he saw when he woke up. But given that she wasn't even human, he probably looked like a cave man to her, and most women wanted someone who was sexual, the odds were against him.

He was being a fool already.

Stopping his magnetic drift toward Kalakanya, he turned back to Kahali. "Where'd the instruments come from?" he shouted over the performance.

Kahali snorted in laughter. *Someone never checked what we brought, did they?*

Bleu blushed. That had been his job. He scanned the fireside gathering. Noting Savas' absence, he relaxed. "Busted. Anything else you brought that I should know about?"

You mean the lions? Kahali couldn't keep a straight face.

Bleu rolled his eyes. The guy was really fun when he wasn't ready to damn his whole species.

"Is there another drum? Can you teach me?" Atsushi called out.

Kahali arced one eyebrow playfully toward Atsushi. Laughing, Kahali handed Rana the drum and danced past him to grab Atsushi's hand. Bleu stepped back, curious to see if he could pick up any pointers in star being dance techniques.

First, you need to learn to move to it. Feel it move you. Kahali began dancing, his feet barely touching the ground while Atsushi floundered around, trying to keep up. It wasn't fair, this music was nothing like what they usually danced to in Northern Haven.

"Wow! You can really dance," Atsushi shouted over the noise.

Wow, you are really trying. Kahali doubled over, laughing at Atsushi's attempts to mimic his latest movement. *Stop thinking about it. Just let the music move you.*

Girak cheered them on while Zach laughed so hard that he nearly toppled out of his chair.

As amusing as his team was, he had promised to tell Kalakanya what had happened today as soon as they set up camp. He dreaded telling her of his out-of-control visions that made no sense. Maybe she'd forgotten? She seemed quite happy for the moment, weaving her voice among the instruments. Was there anything she couldn't do? Listening to her, his heart pounded as fast as Kahali's drumming had. She wanted to talk to him privately, and he'd be a fool to pass up that opportunity.

Sucking in a deep breath of the cool air, he maneuvered around the dancing duo until he reached her. She smiled and stood, took one look at him, and then teased, *I don't bite.*

He chuckled but couldn't think of a witty comeback. Standing so close to her in the darkness and suddenly unsure of star being social norms for flirting, he turned to watch the dancing. It seemed safer. His brain raced through all the things to say or do, but they all seemed trite for a conversation with a Crowned One.

A moment later, Atsushi tripped and fell, pulling Kahali down as well. The music paused to check for injuries, but the only tears were from laughter.

The chaos resumed.

Bleu leaned in close so she could hear him over the noise. "Do you want to talk here?"

She raised her eyebrows in amusement and then seemed to think better of it. *This*—she motioned to the dancers—*is going to get wild. Are you up for a walk?*

He nodded, though being wild with the others seemed the safer bet.

Walking under the starlight with her would only make his interest crystal clear. She'd read his mind and probably politely excuse herself. The last thing he wanted was to mess their connection up the first day of their mission.

Kalakanya scanned the dark ice field around the fire and tents. *Let's try this way.*

She led him in the direction opposite the helicopters. She probably didn't want to deal with Savas either.

He began following her when someone grabbed his arm.

"Bleu?"

He turned to look into Neviah's sparkling eyes, her face flushed from the merriment. "Huh?"

Neviah looked from Bleu to where Kalakanya had stopped and turned around, waiting for him. "You're leaving? *Now?*"

"Yeah, we need to discuss something."

"But..." Neviah motioned back to the music and dancing. "We're just getting started, and you're commander." She raised an eyebrow. "*You* should be leading the dancing."

By the fire, Kahali was doing a way better job than he could have. Bleu chuckled. "Ah, no. Sorry. This is important. I have to go."

Neviah pressed her lips together, grunted in frustration at the two of them, and spun away.

Bleu shrugged and hurried to catch up with Kalakanya. They strolled, side by side, away from the firelight and into the sea of blackness and stars.

It was so dark he could barely see his own hands. "You're sure there's no bugs here?"

They will not surprise me again. She turned to him, her hand brushing against his.

His breath froze at her touch. "Good. I'd rather focus on...just being out here."

Even in the near blackness, he felt her gaze searching for his. *If I were Neviah, would you be so nervous talking to me?*

"Neviah doesn't read my mind."

She laughed. *Thoughts are funny. Stop thinking I'm holding you responsible for each one. We have strange thoughts, too, you know.*

"That's not really helping."

She shrugged. *Okay, if you prefer to be self-conscious...* Her voice tailed off as a star shot across the sky.

"Whoa!" In his amazement, his hand reached toward her. But as his hand brushed the edge of her cloak near her hand, he came to his senses and yanked it back. "Sorry," he mumbled, but she hadn't seemed to notice.

So beautiful. In the near complete darkness, a soft glow emanated from her, reminding him of when she first appeared to him and his mother in a vision. This inner light was nothing like the slight pink glimmer she got when she did her calming energy thing. Tonight's glow seemed like pure joy.

"It's almost like something from a dream." He was torn between watching her and the sky above. The sky was safer to focus on. "What was that?"

A meteor. In myths, people used to make a wish when they saw one. She turned to him. *I wish you would just be yourself and not worry what I think. I like when you're yourself.*

Did that mean she liked it when he had almost touched her just now? He needed to make a wish. A safe wish that wouldn't mess anything up. "I wish I knew how to lead this team safely. Today was a bit more than I expected."

She nodded. *Today was a big test for all of us. Everyone was a bit stretched beyond their comfort. Which reminds me, I really appreciate your trust this afternoon. I was not entirely sure if you truly trusted me when you climbed up on the helicopter or if you were trying to keep the team functional, but I appreciate it either way.*

He nodded. Her gratitude somehow became energetic, radiating toward him like a warm, comforting hug. It flooded him to his core, making him a bit tipsy. "You saved my life. Though I never planned on falling for you like that."

He flushed with embarrassment. That hadn't been what he meant to say. Must've been the energy. He'd known he would probably make a fool of himself tonight, but this was worse than he'd imagined. Chuckling softly at himself in the darkness, he wondered if she got the pun. He couldn't make out her face. She was a warm, black silhouette beside him.

I got it—just so you know. Her smile was tangible, even in the dark.

He gave a nervous laugh. "It's rather…embarrassing when you do that."

She laughed. *As I said, I like your thoughts.*

Now he really wished he could clearly see her. Was she joking? She *liked* him falling for her? Did she really get what he was saying? *Shast.* Was she listening to this, right now? He wanted to run but knew distance made no difference. Maybe Savas had the right idea with a wrist device.

You just need to learn to shield your thoughts. You don't need a machine. She grew very still. *I probably shouldn't say this, but I've seen that you have the ability. So, I'm not accepting any excuses.*

"Seen it? Like, in the future?"

Yes, if you choose that path.

"So, why do I need to talk to you about what happened on Savas' helicopter? You must already know."

I do not. And since you have not wanted to share, it would be rather rude of me to research it against your will.

"I appreciate that, but now I'm confused. How do you make your decisions? You decided it was okay to research whether or not I have the ability to shield my thoughts, but not to research what happened today?"

I wanted to know how best to have us all get along. It's noisy with five humans transmitting thoughts nonstop. And it clearly terrifies Savas, which makes him more reactive, and therefore dangerous. I wanted to see how much could be taught and how much was evolution.

"It'd be *great* if we could talk now without the others all knowing what I say. Should I be able to shield now?"

Kalakanya smiled and shook her head. *You'll all require lessons and practice to shield your thoughts.* She looked back at the shapes dancing around the fire's glow. *Theoretically, they could hear you. But they appear rather distracted.*

He had been hoping for privacy. Just for once.

I can shield us, so we have privacy. Is that okay?

"That's fine. You don't need to keep asking."

It's only polite to ask before I enfold you in my energy field. Some might view it as an intimate act. She gave a soft laugh.

Was that star being humor, or was she flirting with him?

She laughed again.

"Stop it." He groaned.

She stifled her laughter. *Okay,* she said, giving a small sigh of disappointment. *If you prefer, we can just talk about what we need to.*

A golden orb of light sprang around them, and her earlier mischievous attitude evaporated. She waited, watching him closely. He preferred the earlier her. The teasing Kalakanya in the dark, not the now serious Crowned One who surrounded them both with a shimmering yellow shield.

She raised an eyebrow and tilted her head. *You asked me to stop joking around, and I did. So, tell me what happened on the helicopter.*

But with her beautiful light suddenly surrounding him, his thoughts seemed darker by contrast. How could he confess the strange things that were haunting him? He looked beyond her shield into the darkness to avoid her question, but the heat of her gaze still fell on him, making his heart beat erratically. He stared at the toes of his boots, letting his parka hood partially shield him.

Hey. She touched his arm.

The electricity of her touch scattered the pathetic explanation he'd been piecing together in his mind. The surge of energy from her hand raced through his thick coat and into his body, making him light-headed.

She stepped back. *Sorry. What just happened?*

As if he knew. He wanted to crawl into a hole. Now he couldn't explain *this* or the helicopter. Maybe the intensity was because she was a star being and it was some strange energy thing. But maybe it was because, despite the ludicrousness of it, he had never felt this way before. It wasn't sexual, it was as if he'd been transported somewhere else. Which, of course, made no sense since she hadn't star beamed him anywhere. He blinked at the familiar icy field and the stars. No, he hadn't actually seen something else, had he? It had simply been that he'd *been* someone else. Which made even less sense.

Did I offend you?

He met her worried gaze. "Nothing I think is private, right?"

Whatever just happened, it was like you disappeared. Like you were here physically, but your thoughts were elsewhere. Beyond reach. I meant no offense. I thought humans touched.

"It was fine. I'm not offended. Humans touch, but...it didn't feel like regular touch. Or, it had a different effect?" He shook his head, trying to fathom what he'd just felt.

She gave him a quizzical look. *How so?*

Why hadn't he just shut up when he was ahead?

Did my touch make whatever happened to you those two times start up again?

"I've been having visions." He snapped his teeth together, having not planned to just blurt it out like that. And now that she was gaping at him with alarm, he couldn't take it back.

Chapter 30

Unknown Surface Campsite: Bleu Reinier

Bleu winced at his own sudden reveal of having had visions.

A series of emotions flashed across Kalakanya's face like clouds on a windy day. Only none of her clouds were bright, fluffy, happy clouds. *Visions of...?*

He shrugged. "They make no sense. Like, they're dreams. Or maybe symbolic."

Could you share one?

"Today, on the helicopter...it started when I asked you if I could come down. And then this wave of...no, not a wave...a tsunami of emotional devastation hit me. I was somewhere else. Someone else. And what had just happened, the people I had lost, it was so overwhelming, and I was being dragged away. I could barely breathe. I wanted to die. And then...I was back here. But I can still see it. Still feel it." He shivered, and then it turned into a tremble. He shoved his hands into his pockets to hide it.

Are you seeing it now?

"No, just the feelings. I'm fine."

To his chagrin, she didn't agree. She remained silent, watching him.

From her concerned look, she clearly thought he'd lost it. "See? This is why I didn't want to tell you." He spun and took a step back toward the fire.

Wait. She grabbed at his coat sleeve.

He jerked as if shocked, but he felt nothing. He was kneeling on the ground, blood dripping from his face, numb with grief as soldiers yanked him up and dragged him away from his shouting wife and children. He blinked in horror as reality flickered and his screaming blond wife's face merged with Kalakanya's face. Another blink and he was back in this reality with Kalakanya.

She let go. *Oh, my Oneness! I'm so sorry. Just stay. We need to talk.*

He glared at her. "Why?" It was bad enough to experience these horrific images over and over, but he couldn't deal with her thinking he was crazy in addition to it all. He had to get back to the others.

He took a step toward the distant fire, but the devastation of his vision hit him again, and he could barely breathe. Gasping, he bent over, willing the tears pricking his eyes to evaporate. The woman he loved and their four children were being forcibly torn from his him. He roared and struggled against the soldiers. But there were too many of them, beating him. They were being parted, and his soul split in two...

Still gasping, he forced himself to open his eyes and see his real surroundings. This, with Kalakanya, was real. He sucked in breaths and waited for it to pass. Her concern surrounded him, but she didn't offer any comfort. She was probably afraid of setting his visions off again if she touched him. Finally, it passed.

He stood and crossed his arms to hide his trembling. "What's wrong with me?"

She shook her head. *This shouldn't happen.*

He began stumbling in circles, too hyped up to stand still but too exhausted to argue. Because whatever "this" was, it had definitely happened. And it seemed to be getting more frequent.

At least she hadn't said he'd lost his mind. She seemed to take the whole thing seriously, as if he really was seeing something important.

I think I understand what's happening. But I don't know if you will understand because I'm not supposed to tell other star beings this stuff.

He stopped pacing and furrowed his brow.

Or humans. I don't talk about what I see.

"I'm seeing stuff because I'm around you?"

No. It's not the same way I see stuff.

"My mom sees visions. I've inherited it, haven't I?"

She plopped down onto the ground and shook her head at the heavens. *Falling Stars. This complicates everything...*

"What?" He stopped pacing and sat beside her, somehow closer than he had planned. They were both cross-legged, but their knees touched.

She looked up at him. At their touching knees. *That doesn't set off the images?*

"Oddly, no." Her closeness was the one thing holding him together right now. The emotions from that other man's life ripped and pulled at him with gale-force winds, pulling the breath from his lungs and threatening to shred him until nothing remained. Her proximity calmed the winds. Her presence somehow returned to him what the other man in his vision had lost.

He caught her gaze. "Other than making me miserable, how do my visions complicate things?"

You're seeing another time. Can you tell if it's past or future?

Another time? *Shast.* His mom saw the future. She had seen Stamf and himself standing on the Surface together. But she'd missed the key piece that Stamf died hours later. If she'd seen that, they could have done something differently. Stamf would still be alive.

But no, visions were useless nightmares...curses...

Bleu?

He blinked and shoved his grief aside. "I think from the past. The clothing looks old...maybe twenty-first century, as the Ice Age hit?"

Alarm flitted across her face. She gave a slow nod, but the same dread showed in her eyes as when she'd first seen the pendant from his mom.

"What?"

Nothing. She rubbed her face. *It's just, that was a tragic time. I've seen it myself.*

"Wait. How old are you?"

She laughed. *Not that old. I was only five when I first came upon your pregnant mother during one of my dreams. I didn't have any control of my capabilities and didn't even know what I was doing when we started talking.*

His mother had always told him her visions started when she was pregnant with him. "So, you're only five years older than me? I thought all the Crowned Ones were ancient." She was twenty-three? That wasn't so different than eighteen.

Some of us are a few hundred years old. But we evolved, so no star beings were alive at the time of the Ice Age's start. I've just seen it in the time threads. Is there anything that might be a clue as to why this is happening to you now?

"It happens only when you're around. When Ayanna got sick and you were with Mom, when we were together at the gathering hall, and then again twice today. Why is that? It's like it's all connected."

She grew very quiet and stared at the miniscule space between their knees as if an answer big enough to explain all this was somehow crammed into that small space. He waited, consoled by their quiet closeness.

As much as he enjoyed being with the other star beings, he had something different with her. A connection that went beyond simple romantic attraction. It wasn't sexual, either. Their connection felt almost sacred and timeless, though that sounded ridiculous. He had no words for it.

He just needed her to validate it. Because he was pretty sure she felt it, too. He could wait for an answer. Especially if waiting meant sitting here with her under the star-strewn canopy.

At the risk of angering you, I think it's best I don't answer how it's all connected. Please trust me that it's for your own good.

"It's something about the two of us, isn't it? We have a connection? Because of something that happened way back in time?"

We should probably get back to the fire. The others might start to worry.

"I'm going to take that as a yes unless you tell me I'm wrong right now."

She raised a brow, stood, and waited for him.

She hadn't said he was wrong about them having a special connection.

"So, yes, it is." He grinned and jumped up.

Her stern expression made it clear that she didn't find it amusing. His grin evaporated. Her openness had frosted to stiffness.

"Look, you're the one that wanted to talk about what happened to me on the helicopter."

She remained silent.

He threw his hands upward in a gesture of surrender. "Why do you do that? You just cut yourself off from me like you did at the meeting with Savas. I hate that."

She winced at the word *hate* and shook her head. *I don't know what to do with you, Bleu.*

"Be open. Isn't that your thing? Tell me what's going on"—he gestured with his hand between the two of them—"here. Between us."

If only that would make it easier. A flicker of sadness escaped from a slight crack in her Crowned One exterior. For the first time ever, she seemed unsure of herself.

What had Kahali said? That she sees things about others and has to carry that massive burden alone. Bleu couldn't imagine how hard that must be. How lonely.

"Let me help." He wanted to touch her, to offer some small crumb of comfort, but he was unsure how it'd be received.

A sad, wistful smile formed. *You've got your hands full with this team, Bleu. I'm not sure that you're ready for the full truth.*

"What?" Frustration and disappointment surged through him, but as he tried to form a cogent response, she held her hand up in a motion to stop.

Before you take that as an insult to yourself, let me add that I'm not sure I'm ready to deal with it, either. The crack in her Crowned One façade sealed up completely. She gave him a tremulous smile. *We really should get back. Savas already suspects you are developing the Sickness or being mind-controlled by me.*

"He said that? To you?"

I don't have to read his mind to know his fears.

"But that should make him happy. I wouldn't be able to lead in either of those situations. He'd have an excuse to do away with me."

She grimaced. *Yes. That's my concern.*

Chapter 31

Unknown Surface Campsite: Bleu Reinier

Movement startled Bleu awake. In the disorienting blackness, it took him a moment to remember he was in a tent with his team.

Beside him, Atsushi sat up and groaned.

"What's wrong?" he whispered.

"My personal Kahali Alarm for sunrise sit." Atsushi yawned.

What had Kahali done to awaken poor Atsushi? Tell a joke? Mess with his dreams? Just say his name over and over? He watched as the kid stumbled upright, nearly stepping on Savas as he pulled on his parka.

"We have to cross the whole Atlantic today," Savas groused. "If I hear a peep from any of you, you can all walk home."

Atsushi actually laughed. "I'll make sure we're not too close." He unzipped the tent.

As Atsushi stepped out and began to close it, Bleu sat up. "Leave it open. I'm coming."

Savas groaned. "Bleu, you're a commander, not a schoolboy. Get some shut-eye."

But Bleu rose, grabbed his parka, and followed Atsushi outside. That might be a horrid idea, but Kalakanya had said he could learn some mind stuff. And that might give him a better chance of...of what?

He'd never Crown. He was being a fool.

But if he went back inside and woke Savas again, it wouldn't bode well for their trans-Atlantic journey. Savas and Neviah needed their sleep. So, he stumbled after Atsushi, having no idea what he'd just volunteered for.

The scant moonlight cast the ground in blue shadows, but it provided enough light to follow Atsushi. "How do you know where to go?" Bleu whispered.

Atsushi murmured something as if he were talking to himself and then chuckled. "It's a game. I can hear Kahali giving me directions in my head, so I have to listen to him. And I'm supposed to try to respond in mind talk, but I have no idea what I'm doing." He yawned. "Basically, he makes jokes in my head until I stumble."

Bleu groaned. "That's a lot of mental work before you've had even one cup of tea."

Atsushi laughed. "Stop distracting me, or we'll end up in a crevasse."

He was kidding, because this time they had been careful to land on an icy field, not an ice shelf or glacier. Moments later, they found the others gathered in a semi-circle, sitting on their furs.

Bleu frowned, noting Atsushi held a rolled fur that Kahali must have given him the night before. "Was I supposed to bring something to sit on?"

Atsushi yawned and nodded at the same time. "We can share."

He managed a thumbs up and then turned to the star beings. "Good morning," he said, careful to keep his voice low. They were a way off from the tents, but there was no reason to risk annoying Savas.

The others nodded, and something dark shifted on Rana's mat. Digga.

Sit, Kalakanya said, motioning to the ground. Atsushi flopped down the fur pelt he'd brought between Kalakanya and Kahali and shifted to one side of it, making room for Bleu.

Before Bleu was fully seated, Kahali began beating a drum. *Savas is going to love that.* Unlike the night before, this rhythm was a steady beat, constant and hypnotic. Kalakanya began chanting, and the other star beings all joined in.

Bleu side-eyed Atsushi, who had closed his eyes and moved his head slightly to the rhythm but was not chanting.

Kahali leaned forward to peer around Atsushi and grinned at him. *You don't know our language, so just listen for now. Notice how the sounds affect you, how it affects your body and mind.*

Bleu nodded. That's it? How was this going to do anything? He'd assumed they *did* something at sunrise sit, not just...sit? He tried to focus on the words, but his attention kept drifting to Kalakanya, whose silhouette beside him began to glow. Her beauty made it hard to care about the words of a language he didn't know. He squeezed his eyes tight as if that would keep a mind reader from hearing his thoughts and inwardly groaned. He should have stayed in bed.

The chanting went on and on. His legs cramped, and he tried to shift without kicking the others. It must have been an hour already.

He stifled yawn after yawn and then leaned over toward Atsushi's ear and whispered, "How long does this go on?"

"Forever," Atsushi said through his yawn.

From across the semicircle, Eka gave a soft chuckle. Digga shifted to put her head on Rana's thigh.

Until the sunrise, Kahali answered without opening his eyes.

Bleu stifled a groan. What had he been thinking, volunteering for this?

Finally, the torture ended and the sun peeked over the pink horizon. Bleu sagged with relief as the others all stopped chanting. If this was what powered the star beings, it wasn't worth it. He was happy to be a mere mortal. He'd do anything for a warm sleeping bag and a mug of tea.

Kalakanya rose and chuckled. *You survived, Commander Reinier.*

Bleu laughed as he shook out his legs that had fallen asleep. "I'm sorry. I didn't mean to be disrespectful, joining without asking. Was that bad?"

She shook her head. *Quite the contrary. Will you be joining us every morning?*

He tried to hide the horror from his face. Doing this every morning? "As commander, I need my sleep."

"Hmm." *Is more sleep what you really want?* She stood in front of him, crossed her arms, and gave him a mischievous smile. *Or would you prefer to learn the benefits of mental privacy?*

All he really wanted was sleep, but she was challenging him, and her attention pleased him more than he'd care to admit. "Is this what you meant last night when you said that, if I got training, I could learn to block my thoughts?"

She tilted her head. *It would be a good start.*

Please, start, Kahali begged with fake desperation as he passed them.

Bleu chuckled. He really didn't want to do this ever again, and certainly not every damn day. But some mental privacy would be incredibly useful, and he didn't want to remain a cave man in Kalakanya's eyes. "I like my rest, but I'm willing to learn more."

That earned him a smile.

Atsushi came up behind him and threw his arm around Bleu's shoulders. "Good, then maybe the Kahali Alarm can wake *you* up tomorrow morning."

❋ ❋ ❋ ❋ ❋ ❋

The star beings built a fire and prepared breakfast while Bleu and the others packed up and prepared the helicopters. The team was really coming together. The only issue he noticed was his own exhaustion, and Neviah seemed a bit off, almost like she was annoyed with everyone. When she climbed aboard her helicopter to begin her pre-flight checks, he followed her.

He entered the doorway to the cockpit and waited for her to turn around, but she completely ignored him. "You okay?"

She used her stylus to push her hair behind her ear, tapped a button several times as if it weren't working, and acted as if he wasn't there.

"Neviah?"

She spun in her seat. "Oh, you're talking to me now? I thought maybe you'd become a star being and lost your language skills."

He scoffed. "What are you talking about?"

"Let's see. You sit with Kalakanya on the helicopter. You desert us at the fire to hang out with her last night. You leave in the middle of the night for sunrise sit." She glared at him. "I lost Stamf, too, you know. It's not all just you. You can't avoid all us humans and pretend it never happened."

His jaw dropped. What did Stamf's death have to do with any of that?

"Yeah, he was *your* best friend. But we went to classes together. I know I wasn't as cool as you two, but you've totally left me back here with Savas."

"Oh, *shast*. Did he do something?" Guilt rushed through him.

"He's a jerk, Bleu. You know that. He gave me chocolate to help keep me awake on the flight, supposedly." She shuddered and pointed to a golden bag filled with individually wrapped chocos tossed in the co-pilot seat. "Ew."

He frowned. "But you *love* choco. Everyone knows you love it. You fix electronics for choco."

She rolled her eyes. "Bleu. Why would Savas give any woman choco?"

Oh. He grimaced. "He's hitting on you?"

"Thanks. Like that's so unbelievable," she said, glaring.

"What? I didn't mean that. You're...pretty." He shouldn't have paused. She *was* pretty, but it was weird telling her.

Oh, crap. The look she gave him bordered on lethal.

"He's not hitting on me. Not really, though I suppose I *am* the only human woman in his vicinity. That's not the point."

"Then, what is?" He glanced out the window. Rana was putting out the fire. The others would be boarding soon.

Neviah stared at her computer board and stylus, checking something off. "I thought we were at least friends."

"We *are* friends. I don't understand. I'll try to make sure Savas stays away from you. I'm sorry I didn't think of that before."

"I said that's not the point." She stared at him as if he were daft. "Bleu, you nearly died back there when you fell from the helicopter. I can't lose you like Stamf." Her dark eyes shimmered with tears. "Why don't you get that I care about you?"

Oh, *that. Shast*. He sucked at this relationship stuff. And he and Neviah would never work. He'd noticed her checking him out, and she definitely seemed physically attracted to him. He had no interest in sex. "Look, you're not going to lose me. I'm in your helicopter, so unless you get annoyed and throw me overboard, you're stuck with me." He grinned.

"Don't tempt me." She gave him a suggestive look and twirled her hair around her index finger slowly as if contemplating tossing him. "Are you really okay?"

"Yes." But the word tasted bitter, untrue. He owed her honesty. Girak, too.

He couldn't forever push them away and expect to not lose them.

Outside, the wind blew sparkles of snow across the desolate ice fields. Without his small team, he was just another helpless speck of life struggling to survive on the Surface. And despite the hordes of bugs they'd seen at their last stop, nothing else alive stirred on these fields. He needed her. Maybe not the way she wanted, but still...he valued her friendship.

He didn't want to push away his friends by not telling them anything. But everyone from Northern Haven focused on science, and his visions would be seen as a mental liability. The best he could do was share the minimum. "Can you keep a secret?"

Tapping the stylus on her computer board, she raised an eyebrow. "I believe I've already proven that."

"Of course, sorry." He took a deep breath. Now or never. "I'm not getting the Sickness, but I can't tell Savas the details. I'm trying to avoid the discussion for now."

"He won't let you avoid it. He senses a weakness. Like a wolf sensing an injury in its prey."

"It's not necessarily a weakness." Again, the bitterness of the untruth stung him. But everyone said he had to be a leader. And maybe the visions wouldn't turn out to be a weakness, so it wouldn't be a lie? "I don't understand it. It's something...new. Like a latent ability awakened by being around them." He thumbed out the window toward the gathering star beings.

She furrowed her brow at him. "*Latent ability*? Could you possibly be a bit more terminally vague?"

He shrugged, a smile tugging at his lips. "Seeing stuff. Not hallucinations...just stuff. Visions." *Shast*. Had he said too much? He had to get her attention off of him. "Girak has had some strange stuff happen as well. You're not?"

"No." She tucked the rebel strand of hair behind her ear. "I *might* be looking at things differently. Like, seeing a bigger picture, maybe? But you—you were scared when you were up there, Bleu. I could see it from the cockpit."

"It's because I'm *literally* seeing things differently. And it's disorientating." It was the closest he'd let himself get to the truth. "But it's not the Sickness. That's why I talked to Kalakanya last night—to make sure I'm okay. I wasn't avoiding all of you. If I was getting ill, I swear I'd tell you. And then we'd get them to heal it, right?"

She nodded. "I guess. But don't leave me in the dark. Savas and Zach are constantly pressuring Girak, Atsushi, and me. Looking for ways to undermine you. I can't help you if I don't know what's happening."

He had expected Savas and Zach to question the others about him, but hearing about it made his stomach roil. "I give you my word. And I appreciate you having my back."

She nodded. "Of course." Her gaze narrowed. "You do know you're doing a good job, right?"

He snorted. "So far, we've managed not to kill each other."

"Considering Savas tried to nuke them a few weeks ago, that's a huge accomplishment."

He laughed, but she was right. It *was* amazing they hadn't yet attacked each other. "Okay, let's hope we can all continue to stay alive." He turned to leave, then spun back. "Listen, if the choco doesn't work to keep you awake, call back to me, and I'll come entertain you. All right?"

Her smile was radiant. "Entertain me? Hmm. That sounds good. A whole lot better than stressing about flying across an ocean that hasn't been crossed in centuries. Perhaps I should just give the choco back to Savas now?"

"Noooo. Choco is too amazing to lose."

"Oh, so now we're sharing it, eh?" She poked him with her stylus. "You want some of my choco?"

"Only a fool would say no to that."

"Hmm. To the choco or to sharing it with me?" She lifted an eyebrow expectantly.

He shrugged and looked away, too riffled by her mood to answer properly. Her persistent flirting embarrassed him, and she always interpreted that to mean he liked her back. "I need to help pack up." He left before she saw him blushing. *Shast.*

✳ ✳ ✳ ✳ ✳ ✳

As they boarded for the long stretch across the North Atlantic, Bleu stood in the main cabin of Neviah's helicopter, making sure that each person properly secured their gear.

"Hold on. Don't close the door yet," Zach called, huffing as he hurried toward them. Still a bit weak, he struggled to pull himself up onto Neviah's helicopter.

Eka, the closest, hurried to assist him. *Take my hand.* The guy effortlessly pulled Zach up through the door.

Bleu frowned past Zach toward the spinning rotors of Savas' helicopter. His gaze snapped back to Zach. "You're coming with us this time?" It sounded suspicious, which he was but hadn't wanted to show.

Peaked and sweating from the exertion, Zach collapsed into a chair and gave him a questioning look. "That a problem?"

"No," he said a bit too fast. Managing a smile, he added, "Not a problem at all. Welcome aboard."

Was he now supposed to send someone over to Savas' helicopter to keep the numbers even? He looked over his travel mates, unwilling to force any of them to leave. He made an executive decision to ignore the uneven status. Still, curiosity played at him. "Did Savas send you over?"

"Yeah, he thought just in case I had any, you know *issues*—" he waved at his injuries, "—I should be on the same helicopter as Kalakanya."

Are you in pain? Kalakanya asked from her seat.

"Nope." Zach gave a tired grin. "I'm fine. Just pretend I'm not here."

Guilt pressed Bleu into the seat next to Zach. "Nonsense. Let's go, Neviah."

They soared into the air, carefully following Savas, who still hadn't even hinted at where they were ultimately heading. Just that they were going over the Atlantic.

Bleu sighed in exasperation and sat back into his seat. Neviah had given him credit for the team not yet killing each other, but it was getting harder and harder to lead when he didn't even know where they were going. And now he had Savas' minion, Zach, on his helicopter, watching his every move.

Chapter 32

Midflight Near the Old Atlantic Coast of Europe: Bleu Reinier

The rhythmic quivering of the helicopter lulled Bleu into wanting a nap, but the excitement of crossing the Atlantic Ocean negated the vibrations' effect. The team, no, *his* team was crossing an actual ocean. He wasn't sure how much credit he personally deserved, but maybe some? Assuming they survived, it would be a huge accomplishment, way bigger than winning gaming tournaments or getting the agriculturist position.

Remembering back to their first time flying as a team, when no one but Zach had wanted to get on Savas' helicopter, he snorted. *At least we've gotten past that.* Neviah had credited him with the team not yet killing each other, but they needed to go beyond that, to function as a true team. Was there a way he could assess how well they were all really getting along?

He sat forward and twisted in his seat to assess this morning's seating arrangement. Unlike yesterday, when everyone was annoyed and sitting apart, today everyone clustered together. Even Kahali perched only two seats from Girak, on the far side from Zach. But that positioning made sense as all the Northern Haveners except Atsushi were armed. And Girak, unlike Bleu and Zach, had never attacked star beings.

Kahali fiddled with headphones and a comm. Since when did any of the star beings touch technology?

"What's up? Can I help?" Bleu asked.

Kahali grimaced. *Atsushi told me, if I was going to teach him to dance, he should teach me about human music. But I still don't understand these.* He held up the headphones and comm.

"He didn't show you how to use them?"

Kahali grinned. *Only about ten times. Could you show me again?*

"Sure." Bleu took the comm and started flipping through the music Atsushi had downloaded from the stored internet. Old music from before the ice age. There were all kinds of playlists including one called "Ayanna." *Ugh.*

Bleu shook his head and asked, "What did he want you to listen to?"

Kahali studied the comm with suspicion. *How much can fit in there?*

"A lot." Bleu grinned at Kahali, then back down at the playlist. "I'll set it up to play a bunch of dance music. If it's not your style, let me know." Bleu turned it on and handed it back.

As Kahali slid the headphones over his ears, his eyes grew wide, his face a mixture of horror and fascination. "Wow."

Bleu laughed. How strange the electronic music must sound to Kahali's ears.

"Hey, everyone," Neviah shouted from the cockpit. "Welcome to the Atlantic Ocean!"

Bleu stood, his hands on the back of a chair as he leaned toward the closest window. Everything remained white below. "How can you tell?"

"Magellan, the navigational computer, says we're now over it," Neviah shouted, her voice breathy with excitement. "We should see open water soon…" Below them, the ice began to be broken into chunks in some areas, bobbing and swirling in dark-gray water.

"Josefina would have loved this," Girak said.

Flying like this is almost like being a feathered one, Kalakanya said, her face pressed to the window as they flew above the dark gray endless waves.

Even Kahali, still wearing the headphones, stared at the water with rapt attention.

"Congrats, Neviah. You're making the history books." Bleu moved back into the aisle. Hoping to build on the new camaraderie, he removed his gun and left it on a recessed shelf in the front. Then he slid into the seat between Girak and Kahali, earning himself a half-smile from the star being.

Girak, his faithful ambassador, looked up from his small computer with an unreadable expression and rose.

Puzzled by Girak's closed-off expression, Bleu glanced at the computer screen left open on his seat. At the top of the page was, *Dearest Josefina.* Below, in letter format to his dead wife, he had written and sketched scientific observations on yesterday's insects.

Bleu straightened and checked that Girak hadn't seen his nosiness. But the older man stood at the front of the cabin with his back to Bleu, checking his safety and placing his gun on the shelf. Bleu risked another glance at the letter to Josefina. Had Girak been writing to her every day since her death?

As Girak returned to his seat, his eyes lit with curiosity. Thankfully, his inquisitiveness was directed toward the star beings, not at what Bleu had read.

Girak turned to Kahali and Kalakanya. "If you don't mind, I have a question for you about yesterday."

Kahali pulled off the headphones and massaged his arm stump, clearly listening but not eager to engage. His usual wooden prosthetic was nowhere in sight.

"Does it hurt? Want me to do something?" Bleu whispered.

Kahali shook his head but looked pained. *I got it.*

Taking the cue to leave Kahali alone, Girak turned around in his seat toward Kalakanya. "What you all did yesterday was amazing. Are there limits? Like how far can you shield? Does it make you tired? Could you use your powers to move things? Do these powers increase in scope your whole lives?" He paused to catch his breath and picked up his computer to take notes.

Kalakanya's face remained expressionless.

Girak flushed. "Okay, I guess I have a lot of questions. Is that bad?"

Kahali sneered. *Those sound like things Savas wants to know so he can use them against us.*

"No." Girak paled. "No, I am just...so impressed. It seems you are almost god-like." He shook his head. "Forget those other questions if they threaten you. Please don't answer anything if it doesn't feel safe." He looked from Kalakanya to Kahali.

Neither said a word. The tension in the helicopter crackled like a looming storm.

Girak shot Bleu an apologetic glance. "Am I the only one that wants to know more?"

Bleu gave an imperceptible shake of his head, watching the two star beings. He wasn't surprised at Kahali's reaction, but Kalakanya's silence unnerved him. Was the team's newfound rapport that fragile?

Kalakanya stood and moved closer to Kahali in front of their row so they could all see each other. Kahali's foot tapped a rapid beat on the floor, and he looked ready to burst.

She glanced at Kahali with concern, then turned toward Girak. *Try asking your question differently, Girak. Our capabilities come from years of practice. We cannot possibly explain decades of training in a few words.*

Girak nodded, then furrowed his freckled brow. "I appreciate all you have done for us. And I instinctively trust you. It's why I risked everything to bring Rana back when you asked." He glanced at Kalakanya. "But I feel like we are only liabilities to you. You can do what our technology can't. So, I guess my real question is, how do we...?" He groaned in frustration. "I don't want to ask your weaknesses, because that is something that some humans, not me, but perhaps others"—his gaze flickered to Zach, acknowledging that he may well be spying for Savas—"might use against you. But it seems like you don't need us at all."

We don't. Kahali's foot stopped tapping. *We were just fine before you crawled out of the dirt.*

Kahali, stop.

Girak held up a hand to tell her it was fine and gave a dry, sardonic laugh. "I'm okay if you're mad, Kahali. I get we messed up everything. You have every reason to hate us and question my motives." He sighed and tossed his hands up in surrender. "Is there any way we can support you? Like, if we run into trouble again, I get you hate our guns. But I don't see any way to help in a dangerous situation. We're not going to just stand around while you endanger yourselves."

Guns never help. Kalakanya turned and smiled approvingly at the discarded guns. She ignored the one still worn by Zach.

"In general, I agree. But sometimes, they save lives. The fake ones from the gaming room helped us get Rana out of Northern Haven. And I would be dead beside Stamf if we didn't have guns to keep those cave diggers away."

Our ancestors developed these capabilities because they work better than guns. They made life better for our ancestors and all life on the planet. It is as the One In All wished—for all to live in peace.

"But we haven't developed the same skills. So, if there's trouble when we land, how can we help?"

You always expect trouble? Kalakanya asked, a challenge in her mental tone.

Given Kahali's previous warning, Bleu wanted to spare Girak a possible argument with a Crowned One. "We are seeking humans that may never have seen star beings. They may be frightened. Or they may think we are Undescended and have come to attack them."

Puzzlement covered Kalakanya's face.

"We don't know where they are, so we have no way of contacting them," Bleu explained. "We might initially scare them until we explain where we're from."

Kahali groaned in disgust and buried his face in his palm. *What have you dragged me into?* He rubbed his face with trembling fingers and then glared at Kalakanya with a mix of fury and terror. *All they know is war. They will battle those they claim to seek, and we'll all die in the crossfire!*

Bleu's jaw dropped.

"Stop thinking of us as such idiots just because we do things differently," Zach interjected. "SHAST made protocols for the Havens contacting each other. I'm sure Commander Savas knows all about those things. He just doesn't share the details with us because we don't have clearance."

Everyone turned to Bleu, probably assuming as their Commander, he had clearance. Of course, Northern Haven and Savas had neglected to tell him any of this. He hated this game. He couldn't pull off any cool, leader-like response, so he just shrugged. "It wouldn't surprise me."

Beside him, Kahali had begun shivering like he had that day at the lake when he'd experienced the flashback. Kahali sat hunched, his hand balled against his thigh, his breathing ragged.

"Kahali, we aren't going to have a battle with this Haven. They'll probably throw us a welcome party."

But Kahali didn't seem to hear him. He leaned forward, nose to his knees as he gasped.

Bleu gave Kalakanya a startled look. She met his gaze and then glanced out the window. They were well out over the Atlantic Ocean. There would be no landing the helicopter, and no soothing energy.

She stood and reached over the chair back between them, touching his back. *Kahali, you're safe...*

He didn't respond.

Something crashed behind Bleu, and he spun. The cupboards holding supplies had burst open. A giant container of water smashed to the floor, bursting and spraying them. *What the hell?* Bleu twisted toward the windows, assuming they must be spinning downward, but the horizon was stable.

"Hey!" Neviah shouted. "What's going on back there?"

"I don't know!" Bleu shouted back.

Dry food packs, canteens, and gear flew across the room. Everyone ducked the sudden swirling storm. Hands protecting his head, he raced toward the cockpit, terrified something would knock Neviah unconscious and they'd all crash into the sea.

But as he burst through the doorway to the cockpit, he found everything calm inside. "You okay?"

"What's happening?" Neviah shouted, eyes frozen on the instrument panel.

"I don't know. Keep us in the air. I'll deal with it."

He raced back into the storm of supplies, slamming the cockpit door shut, hoping to protect her from the flying debris. Crouching closer to the ground to avoid the swirling tornado, Bleu hurried toward the center of the storm, where Kahali lay curled in his seat, shaking as if having a seizure.

"Is he doing that?" Bleu yelled.

Kalakanya paled and gave him a slight nod. "Kahali!" She continued to rapidly speak in their native tongue.

Items continued flying off the shelves, whacking them in the head. "Stop this now, or I'll shoot," Zach threatened as he attempted to stand.

Girak pulled Zach back down, blocking something large from hitting the injured guy.

The helicopter lurched to the side, knocking Bleu on top of Kahali, who somehow curled up even tighter under him.

"I'm so sorry." Bleu scrambled back onto his own chair, getting smacked in the mouth by something in the process. Metallic-tasting blood dripped into his mouth as the helicopter swung back the other way.

"Hello?" Neviah shouted back at them. Despite his having latched it, the door had swung open. "What's happening?" Then she said, "Shut up, Savas, I'm doing my best."

Bleu, heart pounding, nodded to Girak. "Go help her."

As Girak sidled out the aisle, Bleu wiped his bloody mouth on his sleeve.

"He's going to kill us all," Zach yelled, drawing his gun.

"Zach, cut it out," Bleu shouted.

Girak had stumbled to the front of the cabin, but as he passed the shelf with the guns to reach Neviah, both guns floated into the air.

"Shast." Girak froze, palms forward in surrender.

"Kahali, you're going to kill us." Bleu struggled to sound calm. "You need to stop."

But Kahali was still curled in a ball, unseeing of Girak's surrender, unhearing of Bleu's words.

Kalakanya spun toward the floating guns. *Neviah, hold on.*

She flicked her hands, and a shield formed around the weapons.

The helicopter swerved and dove toward the icy waters, slamming Bleu into the seat in front of him. Someone screamed.

"Kalakanya, we're going to crash," Bleu yelled. But she ignored him and instead exchanged a long, panicked look with Girak. Probably more than a look, as then Girak narrowed his eyes and then nodded. Whatever they were doing, they needed to hurry. Each chopping of the helicopter blades brought them closer to hitting the waves below.

The helicopter jerked again. "What the shast are you doing? I'm losing control!" Neviah shouted.

Bleu gripped the seat to keep upright. He braced for the worst, watching Girak step behind the still-floating guns. Careful to only put his hands inside the small shield, Girak grabbed both weapons. Bleu heaved a sigh of relief as Girak removed the magazines and then enclosed the guns in a storage unit.

Kalakanya dropped the shield. Neviah struggled to right the copter, still cursing at all of them.

As the enclosed guns thrashed against the locked door, Zach let out a string of swear words at Kahali, raising his own gun at him. Bleu and Kalakanya exchanged horrified glances. Her powers were useless—another flick of Kahali's energy would send them into the icy waters with no rescue team.

Bleu stepped between Zach and Kahali. "Zach, put it down. You're making things worse."

"Worse than us all dying?" he shouted. "He's going to kill us all." He leaned to the side, aiming around Bleu.

Bleu stepped forward. Something heavy smacked his back, nearly knocking him over. "Give me the gun." He struggled to remain upright as he held out his hand. "That's an order, Zach."

Zach glared at him. "You're not my commander."

Bleu met his gaze. "Didn't you learn anything from shooting Sukti?"

Zach winced at the reminder of his incident with the white lion but steadied his aim at Kahali.

Bleu swayed to block him. "If you shoot, you will be responsible for all our deaths. Kalakanya will need to shield, and we will fall into the freezing ocean." He had no idea if Kalakanya would make that decision, but Zach would believe that he knew. "And if we crash, Northern Haven—"

A swirling tent bag slammed into the open cockpit door. The helicopter jerked to the left, knocking Bleu and Zach to the side. Bleu hit the seats, but Zach, standing in the open, stumbled and fell. Bleu dove for the gun.

Bleu closed his sweaty hands around it, attempting to lock the safety as Zach's fist smashed his jaw, smacking his head against the chair. Stunned, he couldn't resist as the gun was pried from his fingers.

The cabin spun. His eyes couldn't focus, but Girak yelled.

Everything stopped flying through the air.

Bleu? You okay? Kalakanya asked from somewhere above where he lay crumpled on the ground.

He nodded instinctively but remained on the floor, legs splayed before him, wondering who had the gun. If he moved too much, he feared the dizziness would cause him to fall over. Closing his eyes, he sucked in a breath. And another. The ship hadn't crashed. The gun hadn't fired.

From behind him, Zach let out a string of curse words at Girak. Which meant Girak held the gun.

"Gir-ak?" Bleu croaked.

"Yeah?"

"You...have the gun, right?" His words were slurred. Must have really hit his head.

"Yes." He knelt next to Bleu. "Can you get up?"

"Eventually." He laughed, but that made the pain in his head worse. "But it's not bad here on the floor. Kahali?"

Girak grunted. "We've all been better. But he stopped whatever he was doing, and Neviah kept us flying."

"Only until the freak loses it again," Zach sniped.

"Zach." Bleu forced himself to sit up against a chair leg, even if he couldn't stand and the room still spun like crazy. "If I ever hear you say anything like that again, I will personally throw your gun overboard."

Zach muttered something under his breath.

"I meant that, Zach." *Shast*, it hurt like hell to speak.

Zach quieted, though the star beings probably still heard the injured man's furious thoughts. Bleu couldn't do anything about that. And he was sure Savas had hidden extra weapons on the helicopters, so his threat held no real teeth.

But for the moment, they were all still alive and flying toward Western Haven. And Girak had the guns. Bleu remained on the floor, waiting for the cabin to stop spinning. He hoped that, if it didn't, Kalakanya could fix whatever had happened to his head.

Chapter 33

Midflight over the Atlantic Ocean: Kahali of Peleguin Rookery

The violent images had slowed as soon as Rana Called to him, checking on why their helicopter was flying out of control. Her familiar mind burst into his like a ray of warm sunlight. It burned away the fear and left him able to breathe. To reason. And with that clarity came the knowledge that his emotions had somehow recreated the chaos in his mind outside him.

He had become a living tornado—out of control and dangerous. Lost in the chaos. What had he done? Sweat trickled down his spine, and his breath came in ragged pants. Everything had toppled to the ground in a horrible discord of clanks and thumps.

Kahali tried to uncurl his body, but his muscles remained tightly spasmed. He couldn't open his eyes. He couldn't raise his nose from his knees even a finger's width. He couldn't move under the weight of what he had done. No matter what he tried, he remained locked in a panicked balled up mess on the helicopter chair.

Rana still Called, asking if he was all right.

If everyone else was all right.

His eyelids remained clenched, but from the shouts and groans around him, the others weren't okay. He'd hurt them. Scared them. Nearly killed them all.

Rana's mind's voice drowned in the waters of his sorrow, distant and distorted. He should respond. Reassure her. But nothing in him worked properly. A chaotic force had exploded from him and shattered him. He seemed nonexistent, lost in the ruins of himself.

Individual voices filtered through. Something about guns and crashing the helicopter. Kalakanya sat close, waiting with the infuriating patience of a Crowned One. But darkness had clutched him, and he lacked the strength to struggle free of it. She waited in vain.

The sweet release of exhaustion offered escape. He slipped into the deeper darkness and left them.

✳ ✳ ✳ ✳ ✳ ✳

The endless drone of the engine pulled Kahali back to the horrible destruction his actions had wrought. The swirling energy of his teammates' fear and pain filled the compartment. His muscles cramped and burned, and his head throbbed. He wished for death. But the horrible human machine thrummed on, relentless in its vibration. It buzzed a reminder that he still lived. That despite the violence he had inflicted on his fellow travelers, the One In All had somehow helped the others keep him safe from Zach's gun.

Sucking in a deep breath, he turned his head. Not toward them, because he couldn't bear to see their hatred. Instead, he turned toward the wall. That little movement would alert them to the danger he presented as an awake being.

Kalakanya, no longer beside him, murmured something about healing Bleu. Falling stars, he'd hurt Bleu badly enough to need healing. Kahali somehow tensed even more, wanting to race away, but he was too exhausted to support the effort. Besides, there was nowhere to go.

He waited, but no one said anything. No one accused him, not even the humans. Perhaps he was too horrible for even them to bother with?

With terrible effort, he turned his head toward them. Bleu, Girak, and Zach no longer sat beside him. Scattered supplies lay strewn and smashed across the seats and floors. His explosion had been real.

How had he become a tornado? How had he sent his inner chaos out to them? He would never do something like that. Never.

Except he had. Somehow, the helicopter hadn't crashed. Its droning continued, a rhythmic echo of his thoughts.

You lost control. You hurt them.

You lost control. You hurt them.

Each swirl of the helicopter blades proclaimed his guilt.

Tears streaming onto his lap, he addressed them all. *Sorry. I'm so sorry.*

Anger from Zach's mind instantly slapped him.

I'm so glad you're back. Kalakanya's relief was like a balm to Zach's slap.

"You okay?" Girak asked with sadness.

"I never meant to scare you. I'm sorry," Bleu said with a wave of regret.

"You think an apology makes this okay?" Zach said, his words rippling with fury and fear.

And from Neviah, he got nothing but a sigh and exhaustion.

Kahali was too hollowed out to respond but lifted his head enough to fold his arm under it. He understood Zach's fear.

"Would you like some water?" Girak appeared at the end of the aisle. Apparently, he had taken shelter on the floor.

It was too hard to be seen in this loathsome state, so Kahali shut his eyes again and managed a nod. The urge to disappear overcame him again.

"Here." Girak shook the canteen.

At the sloshing sound, he opened his eyes to risk a glance at Girak. The human's face was surprisingly filled with warmth, not hatred.

"I made up a bed in the row behind you if you want it." Girak unscrewed the water canteen's top and held it near him patiently.

Kahali unfolded his stiff arm and accepted it. His hand was so unsteady that he nearly spilled the water all over himself as he took a long drink.

"I used the furs, not blankets. I figured after expending that much energy, you probably could use some sleep." Girak still stood next to him. "If you need help getting back there, I can do that. Kalakanya's busy with Bleu."

What did I do to Bleu?

"He got injured. He'll be fine. Right, Bleu?"

Bleu grunted his assent.

He didn't sound good. If only Kahali could manage to sit up and see him. To see what abominable injuries he had caused.

Sorry. Tears of shame rolled down his cheeks and soaked into his lap.

"Hey." Girak's tone was gentle, as if he were talking to a child. "Your swirling storm of supplies did clunk us all a bit, but Bleu's real injury is courtesy of Zach, not you. Give yourself a break on that one."

Zach?

"Yeah, me." Zach said. "Bleu nearly took a bullet for your out of control—"

"Neviah?" Bleu shouted. "Which one of these trap doors open in flight?"

"Hey. I cut myself off." Zach yelled. "He should know how close to dying we all came when he lost it."

"Girak," Bleu ordered, "go get Zach's gun."

Why? Kahali shouted, sitting up with a painful jerk.

Bleu stood, pale and blinking at the end of the aisle, holding on to a chair back for balance with one hand and grasping a bruise on the side of his head with his other hand. "No worries. I just told Zach that if he wasn't going to be nice about what happened, I'd throw his gun overboard. I don't find his current wording to be *kind*."

Kahali looked from Zach's wild eyes and turbulent energy to Bleu's pale, pained face. Despite what Kahali had just done to them by letting loose his energy, Bleu still sought to protect him from Zach's wrath.

But Zach had a point—he had been more out of control than the humans. The others would be better off without him further endangering them. He yearned to fold into himself, becoming smaller and smaller, less dangerous, until he ceased to exist.

Girak studied the three guns at the front of the cabin and then held up one. "This one's his."

"Bleu, please." Zach swallowed. "I mean, Commander Reinier. Please don't throw that away. We don't know what's going to be there when we land. I won't be disrespectful to you or Kahali. You have my word."

Bleu narrowed his eyes. "What do you think, Kahali?"

Me?

"Yes." Bleu said. "It's your life he threatened and you he's now being rude to, even though I warned him. It should be your decision."

Kahali glanced from Bleu to Zach and then to Kalakanya. But she had on her unreadable mask face. He wanted the gun gone. Wanted it more than anything he could dream of, other than never having found the humans in the first place.

But he had also promised Atsushi that he'd keep him safe. And now, he only endangered everyone. He might have killed Rana if she had been on this helicopter. He was a danger to them all. His mind needed a safety lock like their guns.

If I say you keep it, will you make me a promise, Zach?

From Zach's wide eyes, this was not something the human had expected. He shrugged. "Depends."

If you get your gun back, will you promise to stop me if I ever get out of control and hurt anyone?

What? Kalakanya's thought blasted at him.

"No, I don't like that." Bleu said, holding up his hands. "That's not okay, Kahali."

Kahali turned to Bleu. *I can't live with violence. I will not allow myself to become an abomination.*

"But you just lost control!" Bleu shouted. "I've never seen any of you move things with your minds. Is that even something star beings normally do?"

No. You're not an abomination, Kahali. Kalakanya's face pinched with concern. *You experienced some sort of new ability, perhaps brought on by your trauma. Certainly nothing you'd be expected to control without training.*

She turned toward the humans. *We can't usually pick up objects and move them with our minds, but Crowned Ones can use our shields to help buffer a fall, like I did with Bleu the other day when he fell with the bugs. The only time I've seen us move objects with our minds is when we coordinate as a group. Crowned Ones can coordinate to move ice blocks to build ice huts. But that's a capability based on a ball game we play as kids, which usually takes at least eight players, all coordinating, to lift and move the ball. I've never seen someone do what Kahali just did.*

She sighed. *Kahali, you could never have been expected to control a new capability emerging with such force. Especially under these*—she waved her hands up at the helicopter—*conditions. It took me years to learn to control my skills.*

"Years?" Zach's face hardened. "I promise, Kahali."

Kahali gave him a small nod of gratitude as the others looked horrified.

"We don't have years," Zach defended himself. "Next time, he could kill us all."

Thank you. Remember, only if I'm going to hurt someone.

Kahali ignored the protestations erupting around him and stumbled back toward the bed. The arguments twisted his stomach. Even Kalakanya was emotional. He couldn't get away from them, and he couldn't tolerate the agitation. He fumbled into the bed, blessing Girak's thoughtfulness, and pulled the furs over him.

As he drifted in the grayness between wakefulness and sleep, it occurred to him how odd his traveling companions were. They were angrier about him putting *himself* in danger than they were that he had already put *all of them* in immediate danger. Even Kalakanya, the other star being, was no longer fathomable to him.

The Crowned Ones had told him to come on this trip to learn to forgive the humans and to gain compassion for their bumbling ways. Instead, every day he spent with them, he became more like them. More angry. More reactive. And now, he'd been violent.

He was losing himself, transforming into a monster. Rana would be horrified when she learned of his actions. His dads would be disappointed. Ashamed, even.

Curled and trembling beneath the furs, he drifted into sleep, wondering if they wouldn't all be better off if Zach simply put him out of his misery. A quick death seemed preferable to facing another den of reactive humans. Because, in this state, who knew what he might do?

Chapter 34

Midflight Over the Atlantic Ocean: Commander Kern Savas

"Neviah! What the hell is going on over there?" Savas shouted over the radio. At the first sign of trouble, he'd dropped back to fly alongside, though at a safe distance.

Now, as suddenly as the whole fiasco had started, Neviah's distant helicopter had straightened out. Its flight pattern steadied, and it turned to shorten the distance between them. Savas blew out a long breath.

The comm device crackled. "Savas? Everything here appears under control, thanks to Rana."

"Rana? What the hell happened?" Had the helicopter malfunctioned, or was this some sort of star being attack?

"Still trying to clear that up. Bleu and Kahali are injured."

Bleu and Kahali? Savas turned to Eka, who had run up to offer his assistance when Neviah had lost control. "Can you close the door on your way out?"

Eka furrowed his brow. *You don't need anything?*

Savas flicked his hand for him to leave. As Eka closed the door, he addressed Neviah. "Am I on speaker?"

"No, sir. Just took you off. And sorry about the language earlier."

Savas gave a humorous snort. "Least of our problems. Is Bleu okay? Kahali attacked him?"

"Girak says Bleu will be okay. His head got knocked against something pretty hard. But Kahali...I don't know..."

He hadn't asked about the damn freak. "Kahali attacked Bleu?"

"No, sir. We had an...accident. If you don't mind, I need a few minutes to just gather myself. Thought we were goners for sure, there. How much longer is this flight?"

"Rana said she had to stop Kahali. Our mission has been compromised. What the *shast* happened?"

"I don't know, Savas. Asking me over and over isn't going to get you a new answer. I just almost died, and we have injured. I need to focus on piloting. We can sort it all out when we land."

"Hmm." He considered the ramifications. "Is Bleu conscious? Is he still capable of leading?"

"Uhhh..." she became silent.

"Neviah?"

"Hold on, sir. I'm working on that..."

Her flight was fine, so either she was gathering info or protecting Bleu. Could taking control of the mission really be this easy? He chuckled, shaking his head in wonder at his good luck. The kid was compromised on only the second day out, leaving Savas in charge? Or had Bleu been the one to attack Kahali? Those with the Sickness often attacked others. Either way, this simplified everything...

In celebration of his unexpected success, he kindly bestowed on Neviah the time she needed. He would become official mission commander as was only his just due. He had planned every bit of this search for years. Bleu and the star beings were the recent, unwanted additions.

Though if they ran into trouble, Bleu had been quite handy with the gun. The kid had killed the Crowned Ones that first day on the Surface faster than they could materialize on the battlefield. A strange sensation, almost regret, formed in his stomach. The kid had really shown potential. Such a waste for him to end up crazy from the Sickness or brain-injured from an "accident" before he helped them find Western Haven.

The next few hours passed uneventfully. As his earlier adrenalin rush waned, he found his eyelids getting heavy. "Atsushi!"

The cockpit door clicked open and Atsushi's head popped inside, his short, high pony tail now much longer than Northern Haven's regulations allowed. "Yeah?" Atsushi said. "Everything still okay since...whatever happened to them?" The kid motioned out the window toward the other helicopter.

He nodded. "Seems so. Can you get me one of those high caffeine teas we brought?"

"Sure. Did Neviah tell you what happened?"

Savas grunted. "No. Bleu and Kahali are injured, but I don't know how it happened or how bad off they are. Have the two lovebirds back there said anything?" He thumbed back toward where Rana and Eka sat together.

"No. Rana's been trying to reach Kahali but can't. I hope he's okay." A look of panic crossed Atsushi's face. "I mean, I hope they're *both* okay, but Bleu usually is, you know?"

"Hmm." Savas took his gaze off the controls to watch the kid's reaction to his next words. "I told you to stop liking that Kahali so much. We don't know enough about their intentions to completely trust them."

Atsushi's eyes narrowed with anger, but he didn't talk back. "I'll go get the tea," he mumbled and left.

❋ ❋ ❋ ❋ ❋

It had been two hours since the tea, and Savas really wanted to land and stretch his legs. They had known this cross-Atlantic flight would be the longest, most exhausting part for the pilots, but now he was more antsy to know what had happened than he was tired. The longer Neviah remained silent, the more confident in his success he became. Bleu was injured, and he'd have to take over.

He always led the flights, so there really wasn't a need to rush this. Still, he wanted to know the details so he could plan appropriately. The blue-gray, ever-shifting waters below him took on golden edges toward the horizon. The sun was descending, and soon they would step onto the North American continent.

He checked the navigation equipment. They should be landing somewhere near the border of the old United States and Canada. Western

Haven would still be almost two days' flight away, but the enormity of his accomplishment swelled his chest.

In the distance, a smudge of blackness formed on the horizon. They must have flown faster than he thought. *North America, here we come.*

"Neviah, I believe I see land. You see it?" The water had become sluggish, slushy. Soon it would be frozen solid, extending the coastline out to meet them.

"Maybe?"

His excitement grew at what *must* be land, but he was flying ahead of her. His heart beat nearly as fast as the rotor blades whirled above. *Come on, Neviah...*

"Yes! Savas, we made it."

He laughed at her enthusiasm. "Yes, we did it. Just a bit more, and we'll have successfully crossed the ocean." He was grinning so wildly that his cheeks hurt. If only his mother had been allowed to live to see the coastline now surging below them, rising into a stout row of mountainous sentinels guarding North America.

"You can't stop us," Savas teased as his helicopter effortlessly rose before them.

"Sir?"

Damn. He'd forgotten to turn off his microphone. "Nothing, Neviah."

"Okay. By the way, Bleu is doing better. Kalakanya thinks he'll be fine."

"What?" No, that couldn't be. His stomach churned. Bleu was seriously injured and would need to yield command.

"He's doing much better now," she said brightly, as if it were great news.

He cleared his throat, giving himself a moment. "That was a quick recovery. Let's see how he's doing when we land and—"

A blinking green light on his pilot console turned on and off in tandem with sudden, screeching beeps. He stared, gaping at the flashing light.

When he had asked the engineers to install the alarm, he'd never dreamed he'd be lucky enough to witness its activation. It measured a special proportion of carbon dioxide, oxides of nitrogen, and volatile organic compounds. It could detect the burning of a wood fire miles from the source. And, barring a recent lightning strike, wood burning meant humans.

His fingers found the compass hanging around his neck. This might be it. Maybe the Western Haveners had resurfaced ages ago and reclaimed the continent?

"Neviah?" He dared to hope that the sensor was correct. "Are you detecting the wood smoke?"

"Yes. It just started. Woohoo!"

"Hold on. Remember protocol. Spread out a bit, and let's try to find its source. Just stay in view. And if Bleu's up and about, get him up there with you."

"Yes, sir!" He could picture her doing one of her strange dances in her seat, and he chuckled at the image.

"Neviah, ask Kalakanya to see if she picks up anything as well. We can't assume they're friendly. If they survived, they may not want visitors overhead."

He kept his eye on the circular red light of the electromagnetic field detector. It remained an inactivated, deadened crimson. If only the EMF detector would light up, they could expect human activity nearby. Not just any humans, but humans with technology. Possibly Western Haveners that had resurfaced. Or Undescended that had managed to eke out a living this far north and not evolve, which was probably a near impossibility.

Last night's campfire had been lit by the star beings. Not humans. Groaning, he rubbed his temples. *If* any humans survived on the Surface, they probably had evolved into star beings.

Still, as he and Neviah spread out, his gaze kept darting to the EMF detector. It remained dead.

"Come on..." His index finger tapped the crimson circle whose lighting would change everything. "Show me some technology."

He stared at the complex console before him with its computer screens, gauges, and buttons, giving him the godlike ability to soar over the Surface. But below him lay only a desolate wasteland of windswept trees and ice fields, fenced in by jagged rocky peaks.

As always, it appeared they were alone.

Chapter 35

Over the Eastern Coast of North America:
Commander Kern Savas

As Savas circled his helicopter above the proposed landing site, he continued tapping his EMF detector as if that could awaken any hidden technologies below.

SHAST survivors who had resurfaced would never attack visitors from the other Havens. They had special protocols—a code on a specific frequency broadcasted when entering each other's airspace and before landing—to identify each other. They were probably still too far from Western Haven to be considered in its airspace, but he broadcasted the identifying code now as Neviah landed, just in case.

Neviah touched down on an ice field on the inland side of the mountain range—the nearest suitable landing site near the smoke source. Evergreen forests framed the field on all sides and continued their green lushness up to the jagged, white mountaintops. Their camp would be boxed in and hopefully sheltered from the worst of the icy winds.

"Come on," he coaxed the EMF detector. "Show me something signifying technology."

The last thing he wanted to tell Prime Minister Pridbor was that they'd only found more star beings. Could the wood smoke have been blown great distances and then collected in the flat field, trapped by the forest?

Maybe the smoke he'd detected came from a fire set by lightning. Keeping an eye on Neviah's landed helicopter, he scanned the evergreen giants for a victim of lightning. Nothing caught his eye. Then again, he'd never seen a lightning-struck tree. Would it be burnt and shriveled? Eka or Rana would know, but his stomach roiled at the idea of depending on their knowledge.

He continued flying, his helicopter's lone mounted gun guarding the grounded chopper in case whatever caused the smoke wasn't only lightning. As agreed, Kalakanya exited Neviah's helicopter first and scanned the field. She paced around the frozen ground, testing it with her walking stick and looking off for long periods in all directions.

He despised that her skills were necessary. Without her and the other three, they might have all perished in that first tick-infested stop. And with both Zach and Bleu now injured, and him and Neviah piloting, the only humans left to scope out the dangers were Atsushi and Girak, one a fifteen-year-old kid and the other a fool. He had no choice but to trust the pompous Kalakanya, whose motives for helping still mystified him.

Ms. Perfect circled the icy field near Neviah's helicopter. She appeared intent on assessing safety, but would he know if she was mind speaking to the local star beings? Was she ensuring their safety for now, only to pull off a bigger betrayal after she learned the location of Western Haven?

His helicopter hovered above, facing her head on. One squeeze of the mounted gun's trigger, and he'd be free of her higher-than-thou attitude and highly evolved DNA bull. She wouldn't even know it was coming. He stared down at her, his skin crawling at his mixed revulsion and awe of her power.

Why couldn't he figure her out? From this height, she passed for a tall human dressed in pale leather pants, boots, a matching tunic vest, and a long fur cape. Her white spiraled braids were uncovered, the hood of her cape thrown back, probably to improve her peripheral vision.

At moments like this, he understood Bleu's interest. She strode about with the grace of a salt deer and the confidence of a lioness. Too bad she wasn't human and had such an impossible attitude. *Damn, I wish we didn't need them.*

She stopped and turned to look up at him. *Right* at him. He glanced down at his wrist. Medicci's device still worked. Just a coincidence. Her arm waved at him in a beckoning manner.

All clear. Nothing dangerous in the immediate vicinity.

He snorted. *You're forgetting me.*

Removing his hand from the big gun's controls, he sighed in frustration. He needed her. In truth, she'd always been nothing but damned pleasant to him. Could evolution have actually changed humans that much?

What did she feel, standing down there, exposed in the open, looking up at him hovering above? He had the tech to blow her skyward. She had shown herself to be too smart to trust him, so what was going on underneath her damn braids?

She knows as well as you do how much you need her, he told himself. *And, when the insects attacked and we needed to retrieve Zach's dropped gun, she warned me that if she star beamed me, the energy might ruin my Medicci device. So maybe she really does want to help?*

He groaned. Either he'd lost his touch at analyzing others, or he needed to consider that selflessly helping others might be an actual motivation for star beings.

Savas, did you hear me? Kalakanya stared up toward him. *The area appears safe.*

It's the appearance of things that has me concerned, he thought to himself.

He flashed a thumbs up to her and then called over his shoulder, "Okay, we're landing. Get belted in."

In the mirror, Atsushi raced from the large window to the closest seat, while Rana and Eka just grinned at each other. Those two lovebirds sat so close together they probably shared a single seatbelt.

Savas landed a fair distance from Neviah's helicopter but facing it. That way, if his EMF detector had missed the presence of technology, their mounted guns could defend both directions. Though only bears or wolves would likely stroll out of the tree line.

Part of him didn't care if that was the only life they found at this site. They had almost made it to Western Haven. He would save humanity. Hope and exhilaration surged through him until he was nearly giddy.

Wait. What the hell was wrong with him? Just because he'd successfully crossed the Atlantic, he couldn't afford the luxury of hope—he'd seen how that ended for his mother.

"Being hopelessly hopeful doesn't work." He touched his mother's compass in apology. *All your lessons about hope, and you ended up murdered by the very people you were protecting.*

"Savas, Digga needs to get out and do her business," Atsushi said from the doorway.

Savas blinked. How long had he been just sitting here holding her compass? Behind him, the lovebirds chittered with excitement while Atsushi shouldered his bag impatiently at the door.

"Give me a moment."

With another glance at the tree line, Savas began shutting things down. He turned off the mounted gun last, just to be safe. He gave the wilderness a final examination, scowled at the EMF detector, and sighed.

"All I need is some regular humans," he whispered to the detector, as if he could will it to find them.

Stubbornly, his gaze again sought the sky for a telltale column of smoke. It seemed only reasonable that, if Western Haven had never developed the Sickness, then maybe they had already begun exploring and repopulating the Surface. Or maybe some of the Undescended had avoided evolution and had built campfires out in the woods? "We're probably too far from Western Haven for humans, anyways," he grumbled to the empty cockpit.

He zipped up his parka and slipped on his outdoor gloves. He still had to deal with Kahali and Bleu. If he wasn't going to get the thrill of the EMF detector going off, maybe he could at least take the command from Bleu.

"Can I help in any way?" Atsushi leaned into the cockpit. "I can watch the sensors while you check your shutdown list."

The kid stared wide-eyed at the still lit green light. The two detectors had their own batteries and would work even if the helicopter was turned off. "That's it, right?"

"Yeah." He grinned. "You interested in learning to fly?"

"Maybe." Atsushi shrugged noncommittally, then his eyes lit. "Hey, could this bird fly to Japan?"

Savas laughed out loud. "I like how you think. But there's no more Japan. No countries survived."

"I prefer to keep an open mind. It makes life more fun."

"Perhaps. But it also leads to disappointment." Savas looked around. All that existed here was an endless wasteland. Across the field, the evergreens' tops bowed low under the bitter wind as if acknowledging the truth of his words.

"I'll take the risk," Atsushi said, his gaze never leaving the green light.

"We have enough risk as it is." Savas waved Atsushi closer and whispered, "Have either Rana or Eka said what really happened on the other helicopter?"

Atsushi stepped back and glared at him. "No."

"Well, we need to find out. I know you think Kahali is your friend, but he nearly killed everyone on that helicopter. He's dangerous."

Atsushi's eyes narrowed, and he shook his head. "You don't know him."

The kid was pissed. "Atsushi, I just want you to be safe."

"I can take care of myself."

"I'm not doubting your abilities. My concern is we have no way to rein in *their* abilities."

Chapter 36

Eastern Coast of North America: Rana of Peleguin Rookery

As Savas had touched down the helicopter, Rana sat on the edge of her seat, cape tied, pack slung over her shoulder. Digga sat alert by her knee. She hadn't heard a peep from Kahali. She'd only gotten a brief message from Kalakanya that he was stable. What did that even mean?

Atsushi had slid into the cockpit, probably to see how angry Savas was. Her human friend was fearless.

"Maybe I should stay here with Savas?" Eka nodded toward the cockpit. "Maybe I can help him out here and calm him down before he gets to Kahali."

Rana raised an eyebrow. "You realize who you're talking about, right?"

Digga, as if agreeing with her, grunted and leaned against Rana, raising her muzzle to be scratched.

"Everyone has the potential to change. Even him." The hopeful smile Eka gave her was radiant, but if Savas were to see it, he'd probably only notice Eka's teeth and think he was a threat.

She inwardly cringed at her own negativity. Was she being influenced by the humans, as Kahali had feared they might be? Before, she would have wholeheartedly agreed that everyone had the potential to change. But now?

"Everyone has the potential to change if they *want* to change, but I think Savas is happy with the way he is." She sighed. "Look, I knew him before he wore his gadget that blocks his thoughts. I know how he thinks, and it's worse than you imagine."

"Fair, but don't you think staying with Ameya's family and talking with the Crowned Ones might have changed his thinking?"

Remembering how walled off Savas had been when she could read his thoughts, she grimaced. "Maybe. Stay if you want. I need to make sure Kahali is okay."

Alarm rippled across his face. "I thought Kalakanya sent that he's okay? Don't you think she'd keep him safe?"

"Hey." Atsushi exited the cockpit and approached as Savas turned off the engine. He leaned over and whispered, "I'll stay with Savas and unload. You both go check on Kahali. That work?"

Rana furrowed her brow. Had he understood their discussion?

But before she could ask, Savas strode into the main cabin. "The equipment suggests humans or star beings are nearby, so be on guard out there. Atsushi, this might be a good time for me to show you what you asked about."

Atsushi's eyes widened as if he had been caught doing something wrong. He glanced from her and Eka to Savas. "Right, of course."

Thanks, she sent to Atsushi.

She sprang out the door after Digga. Eka followed. As she paused to adjust her pack, she glanced at the helicopter. In the still open door, Savas pulled his gun from his thigh holster. Her heart leapt into her throat, and she froze. But he wasn't looking in their direction. He talked to Atsushi while pointing his gun.

You okay? she sent to Atsushi.

Atsushi startled at her question, then nodded, blushing as if guilty. Why would he feel bad at stalling Savas for them?

"I'm fine," he said, waving for them to go on without him. Humans were still sometimes undecipherable, but this odd behavior in her new friend seemed off.

Everyone was off today, but she was most concerned about Kahali. His refusal to respond to her mind talking meant something huge had happened to him. Her heart thudded more from that unknown than from her jogging across the barren, frozen stretch of field.

"Hey," Savas yelled after them. "Where are you going? Help secure the area and unload our stuff."

Unloading... Without turning, Rana held up her own pack that she had unloaded and hurried on. Kahali needed her. She could feel it. Beside her, Digga loped and rolled with the joy of being on solid ground again.

But Eka, always the dutiful one, stopped and answered Savas. *As soon as we check on Kahali, we'll help.*

Savas snorted in disgust. "He was the problem, not the victim. He better have a great explanation for nearly killing them."

He'd never hurt anyone. I will let you know what we learn, okay? Eka didn't wait for his reply, but instead hurried up to Rana. *Any trust we'd gained with him has evaporated.*

She harrumphed. *We never had a drop of his trust. His heart hides behind a wall of ice, unaffected by anything we do.*

Eka raised an eyebrow at her judgmental pronouncement.

A few more suns with Savas would teach Eka how right she was. *Wait,* she thought to herself as her steps slowed and she fell behind. *Now I'm justifying my judgments? Another behavior for my Reasons Why I'll Never Crown List...*

Eka paused to turn back to her. "You alright?"

She sped up until she jogged side-by-side with him again. "Yeah, just letting my past stuff with Savas get to me."

He watched her as she ran for a moment. "I suspect you're being too harsh on yourself. He stole you, kept you prisoner, and threatened your life. You can't just *get over* something like that."

She gave a strangled laugh. "I guess," she mumbled, making a mental note to add "not yet forgiving Savas" to her ever-growing list.

Neviah's helicopter sat at the edge of a huge ice field near a cluster of larch trees. Beyond them mixed evergreens spanned upward to the mountains beyond. If anyone lived near here, they had plenty of cover.

Rana skidded to a stop in front of the helicopter's steps.

Kalakanya sat in the open door at the top of the steps, barring it, with a finger to her lips for quiet. *Let him sleep. I'll keep Zach away while you help Bleu. His concussion is worse than he's letting on.*

Kahali's sleeping? Now? It was late afternoon, and he had regained most of his strength before they started this trip.

Kalakanya nodded. *He had a rough time.*

But he's okay? Rana peered around Kalakanya but couldn't see Kahali sleeping on any of the seats. She should be allowed in to see him. This was ridiculous.

Let him rest, Rana. Trust me, he needs it.

Why must Zach stay away? He had nearly killed her lion friend Sukti. She glanced down at her feet as Digga rolled over them. *Should we all be careful?*

I think...always. Kalakanya responded, her usually bright eyes dulled with exhaustion. *I don't want to scare them further by mind speaking and appearing to exclude them. Their fear of us has reignited as it is. I can update you while you help unload. Everything needs to go over there.*

Kalakanya pointed where Neviah, Girak, and Bleu were setting up the two tents. Really, Neviah and Girak were doing everything, while Bleu pointed and managed to look busy. But with every step, his arms moved slightly outward as if he expected to fall over. If Bleu looked like this, was Kahali really just sleeping?

Annoyance flared at the Crowned One's presumption that she had the right to control Rana's access to Kahali, but she took the bags and turned away. Kahali was her friend. She was the one who should be sitting with him, not Kalakanya.

Eka gave her a gentle bump with his shoulder, his arms as full as hers. *I'm sure he'd appreciate your anger on his behalf, but even he'd tell you to not argue with a Crowned One, right?*

Rana sighed and nodded. As they unloaded the humans' ridiculous amount of supplies, Kalakanya used mind speak to update them. With each new piece of information about Kahali's trauma reaction and dangerous new ability, Rana grew more and more tense until she began tripping and dropping things.

She had never seen any sign that Kahali could move things. Had he been keeping secrets? And how could he have asked Zach to kill him? What was he thinking? She needed to see him and talk to him. To get answers and end this madness between him and Zach *now*. Yet Kalakanya continued to insist Rana stay outside and let him sleep.

Falling stars, Crowned Ones could be annoying! Didn't she understand the danger and Rana's need to be with Kahali? She was growling under her breath so much that Digga stopped eating ice to give her a look.

I'll be okay, she reassured her furry friend. Yet every time she returned to the helicopter for more stuff, it was all she could do not to call Kahali's name and awaken him.

To make matters worse, Zach and Savas were nowhere in sight. Were they plotting against Kahali right now? She began scanning the open field and tree line for the two of them.

She handed a crate to Girak.

"Zach's pretty worked up over there with Savas." Girak pointed behind her toward Savas' helicopter. "I can't believe Kahali gave him back his gun."

"Why is it so hard for them to try to understand he didn't mean to hurt anyone?" Atsushi griped. "I tried talking to Savas, but he's convinced Kahali's a danger. Told me I'm *too naïve* to recognize the threat. I swear, if Zach hurts Kahali…" Atsushi's fists balled at his sides.

We won't let him. Rana put her hand on Atsushi's shoulder in reassurance and then glanced back at Neviah's helicopter, where Kalakanya still sat in the door, legs swinging.

Neviah finished setting up the tent and joined them. "No, we won't let them hurt him. We're all going to protect him, right?"

"Of course." Girak shook his head. "Zach used to be a good kid. I don't understand why he's so eager to impress Savas."

Eka sighed in frustration. *How can we be a team when they're still acting like we're the enemy?*

Enemy? Rana raised her eyebrows at him, surprised. *So, you see it now?* she asked.

"They can walk their anger off." Bleu tapped his communicator. "Savas? I need you and Zach to check the perimeter. See if you see any signs of humans. Or star beings."

He paused, closed his eyes, and swayed slightly. "Let me know if you find anything. Either way, check in every fifteen." He grew silent as Savas must have responded. "Right. And keep your locators on. That way, in case you run into trouble, we'll be able to get there quick."

He gave a soft, mirthless laugh at whatever Savas said. He tapped his communicator off and wilted onto a nearby crate.

Rana put her hand against his shoulder to steady him.

"Bleu, you look like hell," Girak observed. "Stay put there and just answer his check-ins. We'll do the rest."

"Yeah." Bleu gave a weak smile. "But don't go far, 'cause if I have to go anywhere quickly to save them, they're goners."

"Bleu."

Rana spun at Kalakanya's voice from right behind her. The entrance to the helicopter was open and unprotected. Rana stiffened.

Come back to the helicopter. Kalakanya offered her hand to Bleu. *I can work on you until Kahali wakes up.*

Rana narrowed her eyes at the open helicopter. Did Kahali know he'd just been deserted to help Bleu? *She* would never have left Kahali alone. Never.

Kalakanya followed her gaze. *He's sleeping, and they're both over there.*

She motioned with her hand across the field, where Savas and Zach stomped off into the trees with footsteps heavy enough to scare off all intelligent life. Rifles slung over their shoulders, they turned to glare at Neviah's helicopter.

Where Kahali was.

Rana's anxiety curdled. Girak was right about how worked up Zach and Savas were. It showed in their stride and emphatic hand movements. Waiting for the trouble that brewed on the far end of the field twisted her stomach into knots.

In desperation, she turned to the others. *We need to do something to stop this from escalating.*

They nodded, but the ensuing silence showed they were at as much of a loss for solutions as she was.

She snorted in exasperation. *That's it. I'm waking up Kahali now, and he's going to learn to control his new ability before they come back.* She tossed the gear bag in front of the nearest tent and stomped off toward Neviah's helicopter.

Rana! Kalakanya ran up behind her. *Don't startle him. Slow down.*

Kahali would never hurt me.

Not on purpose, no. He loves you.

Rana grimaced. *I know. We've been friends since forever, and he'd never hurt me. But I'll risk it if that's what it takes to help him learn to control it.*

Eka stepped up beside her. *Me, too.*

"Me three," Atsushi said, raising his hand. "Let me help Girak and Neviah finish with the other tent, and I'll catch up with you."

Rana grinned at them in appreciation and strode with Eka to the helicopter.

Kahali must have heard them, because his slouched, blank-eyed figure appeared in the door. Rana froze. With a fur wrapped around his shoulders, his black eyes met hers only for an instant, as if the very sight of her pained him. His normally burnished skin shone pale in the late afternoon light, and his gaze remained averted.

This was worse than she had feared. As he sank into the chair nearest the open door and hung his head, her heart likewise sank. His morbid silence cast an impenetrable wall around him.

"Kahali?" Her voice scratched at the distance between them.

His head remained bowed in listless silence. The only response to her call was his eyes closing.

"Kahali..." She climbed up past Kalakanya and sat beside him. *Falling stars, what happened?*

All traces of mischief, humor, and playfulness—the Kahali she had known all her life—had evaporated, leaving only this shell of her friend. Only he wasn't a shell, because the waves of guilt and sadness that wafted off him nearly knocked her out of her chair.

Her heart broke seeing him like this. She remembered the first time she had seen him after he had been hunted. This was worse. He blamed himself for whatever had just happened. More than blamed. Despised himself.

Slowly, she leaned her head against his good shoulder, pouring all she loved about him into the gesture. Tears ran down her face. She sniffled.

His hand rose and brushed the tears from her cheek. Somehow, this made her cry more.

How can you not hate me? His mind talk was tremulous, as if his mind loathed this small mental connection.

She burrowed her face in his shoulder. *Nothing you do could make me hate you.* She clasped his hand, still on her cheek. *Remember my fiasco with the bugs?* She choked out a sardonic laugh. *I messed that all up on my own.*

She switched to her voice for emphasis. "But you. You were having a flashback. And your special talent showed itself while you were trapped in a metal bird flying over the ocean." She laughed for real this time. "You should cut yourself some slack."

"You didn't see it. I was horrid. I made the guns point at Girak."

She stiffened. Kalakanya hadn't given her that detail. But did it change anything? Kahali was terrified of guns. He'd never do that, normally, which was her whole point. "Have some compassion for yourself."

"I gave Zach his gun back."

She sat upright. *"That* part I'm mad about."

His quick, sideways glance was full of remorse. "I couldn't live with myself if I got out of control and killed someone. What if next time you were next to me instead of Bleu?"

She put her arm around him and leaned into him. "I'm not afraid of you. If I needed to, I'd shield myself and talk you down."

He gave a dry laugh. "Of course, you would. Do you know how unbelievably amazing you are?"

She blushed, suddenly aware of Eka watching them. Her head still rested on Kahali's shoulder, and their fingers were interlaced.

"Speaking of how amazing you are, it's the second sun of our journey, isn't it?" Kahali asked, giving her an exhausted grin.

She had forgotten the day's significance to her. How had he not, given everything that had happened?

He attempted to bend over and grab his pack, but Rana had to grab his shoulder so he didn't fall. "Help me?" he asked, nodding to his pack. "There's something in the side pocket wrapped in red cloth."

"Kahali, you didn't have to..." She pulled out a long package.

"Best friends don't forget. Go on."

"It's your birthday?" Eka asked, looking a bit flustered.

Rana nodded and unwrapped the cloth. "Seventeenth," she whispered.

Inside was a long leather case that hung on a cord meant to be worn around the neck. She undid the tie and gasped at the small wooden flute, perfectly carved.

"Kahali, its gorgeous." She turned it over, feeling the smooth, polished wood and fingerholes just her size. She looked at him, full of wonder. "How did you make this?"

He laughed. "I started moons ago, when I still had two hands. Vadin had to help me with the last few steps, but I did most of it. I thought we could...make music together."

She nodded, her heart too full to speak. She leaned over and gave him a hug. "Thank you, I love it." She slipped the cord over her neck. "Come on. You can't hide in here forever." She pulled him toward the door. "No one's mad at you except Savas and Zach, and..." She shrugged. "That's not really new for any of us, is it?"

With only a glance at their still-clasped hands, Eka gave Kahali a huge grin. "Glad to see you up. Kalakanya and I have an idea."

"That's alarming," Kahali quipped, giving Eka a hesitant smile.

Eka chuckled. "You need to practice this new capability of moving things with your mind. That was Rana's idea. But we should go into the woods now, away from the humans, so you can learn to control the movement. Maybe try with sticks, like the ones you and Atsushi use."

Kahali's smile evaporated. "No. I've done enough damage for one sun."

Kalakanya leaned in from outside. "We can all shield. You need to practice away from the humans for everyone's safety. We may not get another chance like this."

"But—"

"Kahali, you know you need to do this. I don't want to explain to your fathers that someone got hurt because I let you shun training. How would they feel about you avoiding your gift?"

Whoa. Rana's eyes widened. Kalakanya was going to bring his fathers into this?

"It's violent," Kahali argued, apparently forgetting his own rule to never argue with a Crowned One.

"It's a gift from the One In All," Kalakanya persisted.

"Try telling that to Neviah," he mumbled, looking away.

Rana put her arm around him. "Neviah's not mad at you. You're the one who's mad at you."

Kalakanya nodded in agreement with her. "Crowned Ones do something similar to your new gift to build ice huts, but it takes cooperation. Imagine what you could build!" She gave a mischievous grin. "I bet the kids would love some big ice creation to crawl around on. Once you're trained, you could probably shift an entire avalanche."

His gaze met Rana's.

She winced but held his gaze. Her parents had needed that gift. Such an ability should never be squandered. She gave him an encouraging nod.

"Fine..." He studied the three of them for what seemed an eternity. "As long as you all promise to use shields."

Atsushi slid to a stop at the door, his face lit with excitement. "Hey! Savas and Zach just radioed Bleu. They're in the woods, and they found boot prints!"

Chapter 37

Eastern Coast of North America: Bleu Reinier

Back in Northern Haven, Bleu had been mocked for studying how animal tracks used to look on the Surface. Today's discovery justified his obsession. As soon as Savas had radioed him of the tracks, his exhaustion faded in a deluge of adrenaline. But Kalakanya proved more difficult than his exhaustion.

You have a serious concussion. You can't go traipsing around the woods.

"If you beam me there, I won't have to traipse." He gave her his most winning grin. Stamf could convince anyone with one of his grins.

But she simply laughed. *You're showing so many teeth you look dangerous.*

"I see." He grew serious. "Then how's this? You Crowned Ones wanted me in charge. As commander, I order you to star beam me there so I can properly investigate."

She frowned.

Had he gone too far? He knew she was right. He should rest. But as commander, how could he *not* be involved in the greatest discovery of the mission? He had to see them for himself.

Fine. Just remember, if you make your injury worse, I'm the one that has to put you back together.

For a second, guilt made him reconsider his order. They all depended on her too much. But then he remembered—possible human tracks. Nothing would keep him away. "Thank you. I'll just take a quick look. Promise."

She raised an eyebrow in skepticism, then turned to the other star beings. *You three okay here if I go?* Her gaze lingered on Kahali.

Kahali shrugged, looking like he'd never again be okay.

Rana nodded and grabbed his hand. *We can start to practice, right? Maybe you could practice throwing snowballs and sticks for Digga, and Eka can shield in case anything goes...wrong.*

Kalakanya narrowed her gaze at them. *Call me before that happens. And, Rana, keep Digga in sight. This is a new continent, and we don't know what kind of predators might be around. Hopefully, they aren't the ones Eka may have discovered.*

"What? What new predator?" Bleu asked. "I thought you knew everything about life on the Surface?"

Kalakanya chuckled. *It's a vast planet. Anyone who tells you they know everything thinks too much of themselves.*

That wasn't reassuring, but he had boot prints waiting in the snow. Slowly, to avoid making himself dizzy again, Bleu turned and strode back to his fellow humans. "Girak, I'll be back soon. Can you and Atsushi get a fire and dinner going?"

"Probably." Girak laughed. "No promises on the taste, though. Take pictures of the tracks. This should be documented."

Bleu nodded. "You have your gun, just in case?"

"Yes. If dinner gets out of control, we'll be ready," Girak said, laughing and patting his holster.

"Neviah, can you come with us and operate the camera?"

"Is it too high tech for you?" she teased.

"No, but"—he looked guiltily at Kalakanya—"my vision is still a bit off."

Kalakanya huffed at his confession but said nothing. Atsushi ran back to get the camera for Neviah, and then they star beamed away.

As soon as they reappeared, Bleu slipped on the crusty ice under the massive trees, landing on his butt. The heady scent of some unknown evergreen flooded his nostrils. As he tried to stand, he slipped again. From under the trees, Zach and Savas whispered conspiratorial comments to each other.

Your grace is alarming.

Bleu looked up, surprised. Was that star being sarcasm?

Her face threatened to smile as Kalakanya offered her hand to pull him up. *You could hit your head again.*

He chuckled and brushed himself off. "What I lack in grace I make up with charisma, right?"

Neviah snorted and checked the camera. "It's interesting that your energy messed up the helicopter but, after star beaming, the camera seems fine.

Kalakanya shrugged.

"Hey, Savas. Zach." Bleu nodded in greeting and slipped again on the few steps to reach them. Smashing his head had turned him into a hopeless klutz. But he *had* to see the prints.

"Damn, Bleu, you're a mess," Savas said, looking him over. "What did Kahali do to you?"

"This"—Bleu motioned to his face—"was all Zach. Where are the tracks?" Who cared what he looked like with such a momentous discovery?

Savas looked doubtfully at Zach, who shrugged. "I was trying to stop Kahali from killing us."

Bleu groaned. "Where are the tracks?"

Savas smirked at his impatience. "If our *esteemed commander* can stay upright long enough to not smash all the evidence, he'll notice them here and there." Savas pointed to a spot behind himself and another spot further up the slope.

Bleu's eyes widened in awe at the boot-shaped indentations. Others actually existed. He had hoped, but...

"Can you document it?" he asked Neviah.

She clicked her tongue in annoyance. "That's why I'm here, right?"

"No, I could have asked Zach. I thought you'd want to see this. You've been searching for ways to contact the other havens for years, right?"

She slowly lowered the camera from her face and nodded, a grin bursting forth. "Yeah, I have."

"See? I actually pay attention..." He grinned but slipped again and Kalakanya grabbed his elbow to steady him.

"...to the women," Savas grumbled under his breath.

Bleu ignored him, too excited about the tracks. "Let's see if we can tell how many people were here…" He studied the prints, trying to differentiate them with his still messed up vision.

Despite Savas' and Zach's tramplings, they soon identified three sets of boot prints. As Neviah took pictures and video, Bleu squinted down at the clearest print, about the same size he or Kalakanya would make.

"Can you tell if it's human or star being?" he asked Kalakanya.

Kalakanya knelt and studied it. *They were running and have soft-soled boots like ours, not yours.*

He already knew that. But humans living on the Surface wouldn't probably have the same materials for boot soles like they possessed in Northern Haven. "Yeah. But given our species' different heights and builds, can you tell from *how* they ran?"

She grinned without looking at him. *They run well on slippery surfaces.*

He chuckled. It had to be a good sign that she teased him, right?

"So, star beings?" Zach asked.

She stood, narrowed her eyes, and scanned the area. *Did you two touch those bushes?* She pointed at a briary patch that no one in their right mind would mess with.

"No." Savas grimaced suspiciously at the patch. "There's no footprints there, so how could we have?" He pointed to the crusty snow that covered the ground near the bushes. Every step left a crunchy crater.

Bleu strained to see what had caught her attention, but he came up empty as well. "Why? What are we missing?"

She picked up a stick and walked over to the twisted, leafless briar. Touching it to the ground, she wriggled it and then pulled up a loose, thorny stem.

No, a leather snare. *A trap. Star beings do not hunt.* She tossed the stick and snare away with a grimace. *Humans were here.*

Bleu, Neviah, Zach, and Savas exchanged celebratory grins and bumped fists. Their previous entanglements melted away. They had done it. They'd found humans.

Zach let out a loud whooping noise that bounced off the nearby hills.

And now, if they happened to miss your helicopters, they know exactly where we are. Kalakanya shot Zach a stern look.

Zach scoffed at her. "Don't you guys ever loosen up?"

"She's right, Zach," Bleu said, glancing around them. "What if they're hostile?"

"If they're Undescended, then we wow them with our technology. We'll be like gods." Savas seemed unfazed. "If they're from Western Haven and they got the message I sent out, they'll be sworn to assist us."

"What? What message?" Bleu swallowed his fury at Savas' comment and struggled to stay calm. Savas had endless advantages granted to him by Northern Haven up his sleeve, while it was all Bleu could manage to stay upright. But he had to. If Savas took over, Girak and the star beings would never follow him.

He cleared his throat. "You should have spoken to me before sending any message. When did you send it?"

"It's the old SHAST protocol." Savas gave a smug shrug as if it was common knowledge that Bleu lacked. "I sent it out before Neviah landed to let them know we're friendly."

Bleu glared, but he didn't have any fight left. The adrenaline was wearing off.

We should get back to the others. It is best that we stick together until we know these new humans' intentions.

She was right, of course. But he also had to know what Savas had learned. "Did you hear anything back?" Bleu asked.

"No. And as you know, the EMF detectors found nothing." Savas shrugged. "They could be Undescended." From his tone, Savas didn't believe that for a second. Savas probably believed the Undescended were dead or evolved into Star Beings.

But in the previous already-past ice age, humans *had* survived. Anything was possible. Also, the snare was all leather and twine. No metal. Surely, if the people of Western Haven had resettled the Surface, they would have a more efficient way of getting food than snares?

Bleu narrowed his gaze back at the way they had come. Long, blue-gray tree shadows reached like fingers across the field toward their camp. "It's getting dark. We need to get back. From now on, we stay together. Kalakanya, would you beam us all back at the same time?"

Yes, we are safer together. She extended her arms to them.

"No." Savas shook his head. "You said before that it might mess with my tech," he said, raising his wrist bearing the device to block mind reading. "I can see the helicopters from the edge of the woods. I'll be fine." Without waiting for an argument, he strode off. Zach drew his gun and scrambled to follow him.

Bleu opened his mouth to shout something, but it was too much effort. His head still pounded, and Savas wouldn't listen to him anyway. "They'll be safe, right?" he asked Kalakanya.

She dropped her hands to her side and frowned. *We need to be careful, but it is true that I'm unclear on the effect of star beaming on his device.*

"So?" Bleu pressed.

I will not force my will on them. She turned and scanned the woods in all directions. *Let's hope they're safe. Shall we go?* She again extended her arms toward them.

Neviah took Kalakanya's hand, but he waited, biting his lip as he watched Savas and Zach trek across the huge field. Out in the open, they'd make an easy target, but he was more concerned that he had no way to get those two to listen.

"Bleu?" Neviah tapped his arm with the camera. "Let's go."

He cleared his throat. "Right. Of course." Reaching for Kalakanya's hand, Bleu raised his gaze to meet her sparkling jade eyes, and the Savas problem evaporated from his mind. When his gloved hand took hers, the air seemed to spark between them. Why did she always have this effect on him? As his fingers tightened around hers, he could only grin stupidly and mumble, "Uh, ready."

Kalakanya raised a playful eyebrow and asked, "You sure? It would be a pity for you to be distracted and fall on your butt in front of the others again."

"I'm not distracted." *Liar*, he thought, then blushed, realizing she probably heard that. Bleu forgot about finding humans. The electric thrum between their gloved hands was too intense. Star beings used energy to connect a lot. What it would be like to stand closer to her, to allow their energies to merge and become one with her? Breathe her in. Just be one with her.

As they faded to nothing, he could have sworn the corner of her lips curled up.

❈ ❈ ❈ ❈ ❈ ❈

The discovery of human activity had sucked the anger from Savas and Zach. The escalation Bleu had feared now seemed a distant rumble of a storm that had passed them by. Instead of the previous anger and tension, the camp buzzed with the thrill of other humans. At least, for the Northern Haveners.

Kahali had been on edge since Kalakanya had reported finding the snare. He threw up his shield at every unexpected clang of metal cookery or pop of wood sap from the campfire. To make it worse, he tried to protect those around him. They'd find themselves suddenly startled by the flash of light blazing around them. His panic made everyone jumpy.

Neviah made him a cup of tea from the Northern Haven supplies, but Kahali only held it suspiciously while it grew cold. The next time the fire popped, he startled so badly that he spilled the brew on Digga.

His panic killed the celebratory mood and made Bleu's heart ache. "Kahali, I don't see any reason why we'd be attacked. We're safe. You're safe."

In my experience, humans don't need a reason to attack.

Bleu frowned. The guy had a point and a missing arm to prove it. But still, Bleu couldn't feel anything but the anticipatory thrill of meeting new human faces. For his entire life, everyone had been familiar. A known commodity. The idea of newness seemed almost unfathomable.

To Kahali, new humans meant new threats. He needed a distraction before he set off Zach.

Bleu caught up to him near the campfire. "How did your practicing go?" Bleu asked. "Can you move stuff at will?"

Kahali shrugged. *A little.* His glare never left Savas' rifle, laid across the older man's lap as he cleaned it. *It's not something I really want to develop.*

Savas narrowed his eyes in keen interest but kept his gaze on his work. He was up to something.

"Why?" Bleu asked. "It seems like a pretty cool thing, once you learn how to control it."

Seems like a weapon. Something like that—Kahali pointed at the rifle—*has only one purpose. To shoot a bullet at something. It only kills. What I do is similar. It's offensive.*

Atsushi added some wood to the fire. "If you're starving and shoot a salt deer to feed your community, that rifle is life-saving. One life to save a community. Isn't it all perspective?"

Tell that to the deer and its fawns.

Atsushi frowned down at the dried meat he was tossing into the stew.

"Okay, maybe it's just my weird human brain," Bleu said, "but can't anything be used to give or take life? You could save lives with this new ability. What if you couldn't reach Atsushi to shield him, but you could displace the bullets zipping toward him? Isn't it then like an extended shielding?"

Savas abandoned all pretense of not listening. He watched Kahali with an intensity that gave Bleu chills.

Kahali just stared at the flames.

"Maybe think of it like, your mind now moves what your arm can't?" Atsushi suggested as he stirred the stew.

Kahali's face tightened as he watched the flames. *I could learn to control it, probably. But what about my panic and flashbacks? What if we get attacked by these new humans and I lose it?*

"That's not who you are, Kahali." Bleu would bet his life on it. He had, when Kahali had made everything fly around and he turned his back to him to ward off Zach's aim.

"He does raise an interesting question, though." Savas clicked his gun back together.

Kahali sparked his shield, then dropped it just as quickly.

Bleu shot Savas a warning look, but he ignored it.

"Kahali," Savas continued, "any of the powers of the Crowned Ones could kill us off if they chose. So, can you understand why we'd be threatened by your new skill?"

We are not violent.

"But you just said you feared losing control. What guarantees do we have that we are safe around any of you?"

We are not violent. Kahali trembled with emotion.

"Savasss," Bleu hissed in warning.

Savas tossed up his hands in surrender. "It's a fair question. I want to hear it from him myself. I know he doesn't approve of me. So, Kahali, am I safe around you? Are there guarantees you can give me?"

"That's not fair." Atsushi stood and glared at him. "He just discovered this ability today. How can he guarantee anything?"

We are not violent. I will never purposely hurt someone. You have my word. He turned from the fire toward Savas. *Can you promise the same?*

Savas grinned. "Ah. But I never claimed to be against violence. I believe it has its place in life. I will, however, hold you to your word. Thank you. Northern Haven needs powerful allies, and I believe you are just such a man." He laughed. "Sorry. Such a star being."

Kahali shook his head as if Savas was incomprehensible. Bleu, too, wondered what was up. Why would Savas take the word of a star being now?

Savas stood and slung his rifle over his shoulder a bit too casually. "Perhaps you should go practice some more so that you can keep your word?"

Kahali gave Savas a puzzled look, then turned to Atsushi. *How long until it's ready?*

Atsushi looked into the pot and grimaced. "I have no idea." He waved him off. "Go. We can call you."

As Kahali left to practice more, Savas grinned triumphantly behind his back.

Bleu gaped, amazed at Savas' manipulation of Kahali. "You did that on purpose, didn't you?"

Savas smirked. "We can't risk crashing. And it would be a shame to leave such a powerful ally behind."

"We're not leaving anyone behind."

"No? Well, neither Neviah nor I are willing to fly him across the ocean again unless he's mastered that. And he has a long way to go."

Chapter 38

Campsite, Eastern Coast of North America: Bleu Reinier

As the sun descended behind the mountain and darkness crept across the frozen field, a strange dread seeped into Bleu's bones. Would his concussion cause symptoms like that? His vision had returned to normal and he could walk slowly, but he still felt weird. That was all physical. The strange dread felt like a warning, an alarm that danger lurked nearby.

He had known safety in Rana's village, and he'd lost the spatial anxiety caused by the wide-open spaces of the Surface that differed so much from the cozy walls and tunnels of home. No, this unease wasn't spatial anxiety to the openness of the sky and horizon.

This was different, and perhaps a bit similar to what Kahali feared. Bleu had never faced the possibility of other humans with guns. His team sat out in the open, exposed. The meager light from the cooking fire did nothing against the shroud of blackness surrounding them. No safe walls protected them from physical attacks or bullets. And then, there were the unknown predators of the region.

His earlier excitement of finding the footprints evaporated, leaving behind a gnawing awareness of their vulnerability. The darkness beyond the campfire could be punctured any moment by monstrous claws or gunfire. Childhood tales of the evil Undescended crowded his mind with images so ludicrously terrible that he wanted to laugh at himself.

Instead, he checked that they were all armed and sent Savas and Neviah to make sure the helicopters were locked. Then, he divided them up into shifts. After dinner, half would sleep while the other half guarded, and then they'd switch. Animal calls and crunching footsteps drifted down the mountains as if something were encircling them. Even the confident star beings kept glancing out into the night. They should be comfortable in such wilderness, right?

He watched as Kalakanya kept gazing out at the mountainside with the faraway look he now recognized. She was scanning for danger, and since she hadn't said anything, they must be safe. Even so, his intuition kept whispering that something was very wrong.

"Okay, I think the stew's as good as it'll get," Girak said, laughing.

They gathered around the fire's light while Girak and Atsushi handed out steaming bowls. No one broke out the drums or sang. No one even talked.

The fear was tangible. He had to do something, or his team would never get any rest tonight. "Is everyone tired, or are we all listening to the same noises and wondering what's out there?" Bleu asked.

Zach's nervous laugh and the scrape of spoons in the bowls answered him.

When Atsushi approached Savas with his food, Savas waved the proffered bowl off. "I'll sit up here and keep watch while you eat. Just save me some." He climbed up onto a boulder beyond the fire's light and tugged on infrared goggles. His rifle lay across his lap.

"Kalakanya, you haven't sensed anything, right?" Bleu asked. She sat right next to him, but he spoke loudly enough that they'd all hear. They all needed some reassurance.

There are small animals nearby. I do not sense humans. And yet...

The humans all leaned closer even though her mind talk was heard inwardly.

Something is watching us.

Not exactly the hoped-for reassurance. He cleared his throat, hoping to make his voice sound less shaken than he felt by her comment. "Watching us? Like a predator?"

She tilted her head and made a strange face. *As soon as I catch its mental vibration, it's gone. And yet, it's still there.* She shook her head in frustration. *It's as if someone screamed at a mountain and mid-scream someone covered their mouth, cutting off the scream. The scream is gone, but its echo lingers.*

"It's screaming?" Neviah's eyes had grown large.

She laughed. *No, sorry. Bad analogy. It's like it's there, but as soon as I find it, it's gone. But not really, because there's still an echo of its vibration.*

Wait. You're Calling it? Rana asked, wide-eyed.

No. I have no reason to request its presence. But they keep attracting my attention.

"They?" Bleu asked. He shivered, not from the cold.

Well, it was initially high up the mountain. She pointed to the mountain beyond Savas' helicopter. *Then it was over there.* She pointed in the opposite direction. *So, unless it flies or is much faster than any animal we've ever encountered, I'd guess it's more than one.*

"That's it." Atsushi crossed his arms. "I'm not getting any sleep tonight."

Eka threw up a shield around all of them, including Savas. It was an impressive size. When everyone looked at him, he shrugged. *Can't hurt, right?*

"No complaints from me." Bleu flashed him an appreciative grin.

You can't maintain that all night, Kalakanya sent.

There's four of us. I only need to do a quarter of the night.

"Appreciate the thought, Eka, but you're messing with my night vision goggles. Maybe leave me outside?" Now surrounded by the golden shield, Savas no longer blended into the darkness.

Rana looked at her feet and then sprang up. "Digga! Where's Digga?"

"She was right beside you, sleeping." Eka, still holding the shield, stood and looked about, his face clouded with worry.

"She was." Rana spun in circles and then gave Eka a panicked look that gave Bleu the sense that the two of them shared a specific concern about Digga. "Digga!" she shouted. As she hurried off, she sparked her own shield.

Bleu and Kalakanya joined the search, and they checked the tents and under the closest helicopter.

"Here's some prints," he shouted across camp to Rana.

Rana hurried over and squinted at them. *Those might be from earlier. She raced into the woods when we landed.* She turned back to the helicopter she and Digga had been on and seemed to analyze the path. *Eka? Is this the way she ran when we got off?*

Loud, crashing noises thundered from the woods beyond Savas' helicopter. Then the snapping of wood and growling came from the mountainside.

Rana ran toward the terrifying cacophony. "Digga? Digga!"

Kalakanya, take over the shield! Eka took off after Rana. *Rana, be careful! It might be that weird predator I discovered in my training.*

Kahali looked torn between the safety of the group and following.

Bleu shuffled past him, annoyed at his own inability to run, and then turned. "Come on. I've got a gun."

Kahali grimaced, but when Rana yelled in the distance, he took off after her. Bleu followed as best as he could, still a bit light-headed but gun drawn. What if that growling wasn't Digga?

Rana stood at the edge of the woods under the purplish moon shadows of the larches. She paced the edge of the tree line. "Digga!"

The crashing noises grew closer, as if a growling boulder rolled straight at them.

Bleu's heart thumped harder in his chest. The darkness under the trees hid anything that could be charging them. Unless she was sensing the energy, Rana wouldn't know until it was too late. All his earlier fears flashed through his mind.

As if hearing his fears, Rana enlarged her shield. A moment later, Digga raced out of the shadows, nearly falling over herself on the steep decline to escape whatever pursued her.

But as Digga neared Rana, she slammed into the shield's side and roared in anguish as she fell backward.

"Digga," Rana screamed, and then took a step backward, horror on her face.

Another cave digger smashed down the slope, tearing up the undergrowth, and staggered out from under the trees. It limped on its hind leg but otherwise looked identical to Digga, with an identical fur pattern and size.

Hadn't Rana said they all had different markings? The injured one charged the other one, snarling and swiping its muzzle. Blood sprayed the moonlit snow, and the first one shrieked with such force that the hairs stood up on Bleu's neck. As it twisted to retaliate, the limping one dashed inside Rana's shield.

"Digga?"

Eka threw up a shield around the rest of them, making Savas curse. Bleu turned. Savas had his rifle raised and had been about to shoot the unknown cave digger. Now, contained inside the shield, he couldn't fire.

The strange cave digger charged Rana's shield and bounced off backward. It really wanted Digga. Or Rana. Digga stood beside Rana, transformed into a hair-bristling, snarling monster that looked nothing like the murmuring furball that slept at Rana's feet. The first one snarled in fury and then, with a glance at Savas' raised rifle, raced back up the hill under the cover of the trees. It released a blood-curdling deep growl as it raced into the underbrush, but as soon as it was out of sight, silence returned. Was it waiting, watching them behind the curtain of darkness?

Ah, where did it go? Kahali asked with the same unease Bleu felt.

Digga growled threateningly in the direction the cave digger had run, ignoring Rana's attempts to calm her down.

"Rana, can you get her back to the fire?" Bleu didn't want that other vicious thing circling around them in the dark. And since it was small like Digga, that might mean its mother was nearby. A cold chill raced up his spine. Stamf had died trying to escape one. Would their campfire even faze it?

"Rana, can she walk back?"

I think so. Digga, let me see your leg. She squatted and hovered her hand near the nasty gash, then bit her lip. *Ew, that's deep.* She frowned from Digga to the others. *Was it me, or did that cave digger look just like her?*

I couldn't tell them apart. Eka gave Rana a sidelong glance, as chagrined as a dad who couldn't tell his kids apart.

Me, either. She patted the pup's head. *Sorry, Digga. Come on, let's get you back and take care of that.*

"You sure that's the right one?" Savas asked. Frustration painted his face as he lowered his rifle.

Yes. Rana chuckled. *The other one would have killed me by now.*

"How come the other one couldn't get through your shield, but she could?" Bleu asked.

Shields keep out anything that would enter with ill will. I knew if whatever was running down the hill was dangerous, it wouldn't get through. But Digga would have no problem.

Digga was still puffed out in fury, her short tail raised straight in the air. She aimed a low, continuous growl at the dark woods.

"You might have mentioned that before," Savas criticized. "I mean, if we were attacked, I would never have thought that I could have ducked inside one of your shields for safety."

Rana scowled, clearly not thrilled with the idea of Savas hiding inside her shield.

Bleu bit back his mirth, grateful for the darkness.

"What?" Savas laughed. "It's tactical knowledge. We should know how to stay safe together."

Oh, the irony... Kahali groused.

All of you, get back to the fire as soon as possible. Kalakanya's mind talk carried a fearful tone. Bleu shivered at what might make a Crowned One afraid.

"Rana, can you carry Digga if she won't follow you?" Bleu asked.

I'm not sure that's a good idea with an injury. If she squirms in pain, her claws could be dangerous. Rana knelt and took a moment to get Digga to follow.

When the pup finally obeyed, she did so walking backward, growling at the woods. Bleu kept looking over his shoulder, waiting for the wild cave digger to charge them.

When they got back to the fire, Kalakanya was pacing. She stopped and looked them over. *That sounded like a cave digger. What was it?*

A cave digger, Rana answered, shaking her head in dismay. *But it looked just like Digga.*

We need to stay close together and use shields. She nodded to Eka, and his golden shield encased them in in its protective light. Kalakanya bit her lip. *It sounded like a cave digger, so I checked. However, other than Digga, there is no cave digger within scanning distance of us.*

Her gaze checked the darkness around them. *Whatever that was, it was not a cave digger.*

Chapter 39

Campsite, Eastern Coast of North America: Rana of Peleguin Rookery

Rana, standing amidst the others in the flickering light of the campfire, stiffened at Kalakanya's statement. *But it was a cave digger!* She turned to the others for validation. *We all saw it, right?* She found her waterskin and began cleansing the deep cave digger claw wound in Digga's leg. Her pup was lucky to still have a leg.

Definitely, Eka confirmed. *But it was odd that it had the same markings. Exactly the same.* He shook his head at the improbability.

Kalakanya sighed. *It was not a cave digger. After I heard the growls, I scanned. There was only Digga. Check for yourselves. Rana, you can scan for them, right? I would be thrilled to be proven wrong.*

Rana removed her gloves and dug through her pack for the healing salve. She knew cave diggers were nearly indestructible, but she wasn't taking any chances with Digga's wound. Her heart hadn't yet slowed to normal, and she still flushed with guilt over misidentifying the other cave digger. What kind of a Digga-Maha was she?

She squatted and gave the trembling Digga a long stare, wondering what she had missed that must have looked different with the other cave digger. The pup whined and rubbed her nose and muzzle across Rana's cheek. Digga didn't hold grudges.

Rana? Kalakanya pressed.

Oh! She had fallen back into her old pattern of spacing out. *Yes, Desna showed me.*

Try scanning for cave diggers. Now.

Rana nodded and felt everyone fix their gaze on her. Except Digga, who kept looking back towards the forest, her ears pricked. Rana massaged her fingers into Digga's ruff to make sure she wasn't tempted to investigate whatever she sensed, but instead, Digga whined and pressed closer to Rana for protection.

She took a few calming breaths and expanded her awareness. The fear-filled humans surrounded her like a sludgy fog, but once she got beyond that, she unfurled her mind with ease. Her awareness went in all directions at once, like ripples extending from a rock tossed into a summer lake. The trees and rocks felt denser here than at home, their energy thick with a heaviness similar to the humans' fear. She pushed aside that sensation, seeking any trace of a cave digger vibration.

She found nothing.

She sucked in a breath and tried again. She started back at their campfire and rippled outward.

Her mind's awareness hit a flash of danger. Human danger. But then, like a live, wet fish clasped in her hands, as soon as she sensed it, it had squirmed away and was gone. "Oh."

How weird. She cast about searching, but no echo of the human remained. Had she misread the energy?

She screwed up her face in concentration, now seeking any sign of the cave digger or the human, but again, she came up empty. She blew out a long breath and opened her eyes.

Everyone was still watching her.

No cave digger. But there was something human for a moment.

"Human?" Savas stepped closer to her, his blue eyes ablaze with excitement.

I sensed that as well. Kalakanya met her gaze. *Did you feel it...disappear?*

A chill ran up Rana's back. She nodded. *I thought I was imagining it. But when I checked again, it was gone.*

That's the sort of thing I kept sensing before. But until now, it hadn't been a human vibe that I sensed. Kalakanya turned to Bleu, her face tight with concern. *This is unlike anything I've encountered before. We should take precautions.*

"Okay. But what are we expecting?" Bleu asked. "Humans with a trained cave digger? Humans with some sort of jamming like Savas has?"

Rana shook her head. *No, there are no cave diggers in our vicinity other than Digga.* She puzzled over the possibility of a jamming device. But Savas with his wrist contraption felt like a blind spot. If he were on the mountain side, she would sense him as a human, but nothing else about him. And he wouldn't just fade away. Unless maybe the contraption worked differently?

Kalakanya furrowed her brow. *I can't explain it, but it doesn't feel like technology.*

Are they spirits? She strained to remember how Josefina had felt at the Lion Circle.

"Ghosts are real?" Atsushi's eyes grew wide as saucers, and he stepped closer to Girak.

Zach turned in a circle, watching the shadows beyond the firelight, and Bleu shifted from foot to foot, watching Kalakanya.

Kalakanya furrowed her brow. *I am unclear on what we are dealing with. But from what you all experienced with the thing that appeared to be a cave digger, our shields provide protection. Everyone should stay inside the shields until we gain clarity. Eka, is this anything like the strange predator you saw in your training?*

"What predator?" Zach asked, drawing his gun and resting it on his lap.

Eka exchanged a nervous look with Rana. *I only got a glimpse of it, and it was in a dream. It didn't look like a cave digger. It wanted to kill the cave digger.*

Savas snorted. "Tell me you're not going to start recommending strategies based on dream analysis."

It was not a regular dream, Savas, Kalakanya said. *Eka, do you think it could be the same predator?*

Eka stared at Digga's injured leg and grimaced. *Maybe?* He stood so close to Rana that his shudder bumped her. *Nothing about what I saw in the dream and what they found at the site where my cousin was killed made any sense, kind of like what's happened tonight. But the Crowned Ones from my village did find a dead cave digger, which is an odd coincidence with Digga's attack. I mean, why would a young cave digger attack another young one? They're too young to mate or be defending their territory. Something's not right.* Eka hadn't left Rana's side since the second cave digger sighting and protectively interlaced his fingers with hers.

As the others around her continued to toss out their opinions of what had just happened, the warmth of Eka's strong hand re-centered her. She hadn't realized how much the second cave digger, charging her shield over and over, had jangled her nerves. Oneness, his hand felt unbelievably good. Good enough to want to never let go, except then how would she practice her capabilities for Crowning?

Someone coughed, and she became aware of the conversation whizzing around her still. From across the fire, Kahali scowled at her and Eka's intertwined hands.

He's right. What am I doing? she thought. She released Eka's hand, feigning a sudden need to recheck Digga's injury. But when she glanced up, Kalakanya was frowning at her. No one seemed happy with her tonight.

Neviah cleared her throat. "Don't take this the wrong way, but if your shielding energy can mess up the helicopter's controls, perhaps the helicopters can mess up you? Maybe our helicopters shook you all up, and now you're not scanning properly. Would that explain these disappearing humans? I mean, maybe the humans are watching us and startled a young cave digger down the mountain."

Rana shook her head. *Cave diggers don't fear humans. And as uncomfortable as the helicopters were to ride in, I don't think they affected me that much.*

Savas grimaced. "We can't just follow you around and stay inside your shields forever. If they're humans, we need to meet them. That *is* why we travelled all this way."

Rana gave a silent snort at Savas' reminder. As if any of them would forget why they had come. Why had she thought joining this hopeless team of distrustful humans would help Girak? She wasn't even getting better at her capabilities. Instead, she'd trampled a bug and was always annoyed at Savas.

"Think it'll be safer to explore in the daylight?" Bleu cocked his head at the Crowned One and then glanced at Rana. "Maybe we could send a few people out tomorrow looking for them, and the rest of us could keep an eye on the helicopters."

As long as we take precautions. Kalakanya answered. *But for now, should we sleep in the helicopters?*

"That divides us up, doesn't it?" Atsushi's gaze kept twitching around the border of the ice field. "Shouldn't we stay together?"

Rana glanced at Eka. He could hold a shield for hours with hardly any effort. But she and Kahali couldn't. And Kahali was already drained. *I agree with Atsushi. We will get more sleep if we only need to shield one group at a time. It would be safer to explore this unusual land tomorrow if we're not all so exhausted we can't shield properly.*

"Okay," Bleu said. "Is it easier for you if we stay out by the fire or on a helicopter?"

High on the mountain, something boomed so loudly that the snow vibrated under her feet. Rana jolted and spun around, but the mountain remained dark. Digga let out a low, throaty growl, and Rana followed her gaze. A cracking noise followed, and then a tree crashed to the ground, knocking over several others on its way down. Kahali sparked his own shield inside Eka's, then dropped it. The humans all drew their weapons. But there was nothing to see but darkness. And Rana sensed nothing but a rumble of anger, cascading down the mountain toward them.

"What the *shast* was that?" Neviah whispered.

The welcome committee, Kahali quipped. *Don't you feel right at home with the friendly humans you so wanted to find?*

Rana bristled at his angry words.

"What?" Neviah looked terrified. "I've never been rude to you."

Kahali shrugged but looked contrite.

"The helicopter has walls." Atsushi looked at Rana, a pleading in his eyes. "What about we stay in there?"

I prefer Nature. And that way, I don't have to worry about damaging your ship's equipment, Eka said.

Kahali nodded.

"Eka, what if we sleep inside and you stay outdoors and shield the helicopter?" Bleu asked. "Because if this is humans, they might mess with the ships in the dark. Would that be too hard? I don't want to ask the impossible, but if something happens to the helicopters, we have no escape."

"Good thinking." Savas gave Bleu an approving nod.

Rana stiffened. Did they think she, Kahali, and Eka could all make huge shields and endlessly protect them without exhaustion?

Eka cast her a concerned look.

That was no problem for him and Kalakanya, but she and Kahali had never even tried to extend their shields that much. She sent him a *No, don't agree to that. Kahali and I can't help.*

Eka and Kalakanya exchanged something silently.

Kahali sent Rana a panicked, *Are they kidding?*

Kalakanya cleared her throat. *Eka and I can shield like that tonight, but he will need to sleep tomorrow and won't be able to help you explore. Rana could go on the exploration group tomorrow.*

What about me? Kahali fumed.

You are in training. You need sleep tonight. Tomorrow we'll reassess. Fair?

Kahali glared at Kalakanya. *You can't send Rana off alone.*

Yeah, Rana thought but kept it to herself. She couldn't encourage Kahali in his rebellion, because he didn't stand a chance. But her heart warmed that he argued on her behalf.

She's capable, Kalakanya said with a "don't-question-me" edge to her mind talk. *And if you are up to it, Kahali, so are you. But I will need to still shield the helicopters and those that stay behind.*

Bleu looked troubled. "But when will you sleep?"

Like food, I don't need much sleep. She grinned. *I'm pretty easy.*

Savas grumbled something and shot a suspicious look at Atsushi, but Rana missed the rest.

They decided to protect both helicopters. Eka took the one closest to the fire with all those sleeping. They agreed that Kalakanya would shield the second one at the edge of the woods. She could take care of herself, but Bleu seemed uncomfortable with the decision. It took Kalakanya reassuring him multiple times that she would be all right on her own all night before he approved the plan.

As the others clambered aboard the helicopter, Rana watched Kalakanya turn toward the gloom. She didn't even hesitate at the danger. Oh, to be Crowned.

Suddenly, as if thinking better of her stroll into the darkness, Kalakanya turned back to them. *Rana, come with me. I'd like a word with you.*

Chapter 40

Campsite, Eastern Coast of North America: Rana of Peleguin Rookery

Rana stiffened at Kalakanya's request to speak with her. First, Rana had no interest in following Kalakanya into the darkness after all the weirdness they'd experienced tonight.

Secondly, Rana had a feeling she was somehow in trouble, though she had no idea what she'd done wrong. Kalakanya had shot her a look when Eka had held her hand, but why would the Crowned One care?

She turned and gave Eka an only half-joking *save me* look before following in the Crowned One's wake.

Don't argue with her, Eka teased.

She gave a quiet snort and hurried after Kalakanya. Digga limped beside her, hanging close as if terrified to not be brushing constantly against her leg. As far as Rana knew, cave diggers had no known predators except the one Eka may have discovered, and Digga's fear unnerved her. Eka's predator had killed an adult star being, meaning his cousin's shielding hadn't worked. Such a situation had never occurred before, that she knew of. She shivered at what that might mean.

Kalakanya leading them both into the darkness didn't exactly improve her mood. "What's wrong?" Rana asked.

Kalakanya chuckled. "You sound like Bleu. I want to share an observation with you. You may do with it what you wish."

Rana frowned. "About the impossible cave digger?"

Kalakanya laughed again. "No, the disappearing cave digger *is* a problem, but this is about you."

"O-kay." So, she was in trouble.

They had reached the helicopter, and Kalakanya extended her shield to surround not only them but also the enormous machine. As if in annoyance, whatever stalked them from the mountainside let loose a deep, throaty growl. Rana shivered as a chill ran up her spine.

Kalakanya gave a hard look in the direction of the threatening sound, then let out a huff and turned back to her. "I know I'm not that much older than you, so forgive me if this seems more something Desna would usually talk to you about."

Oneness, what was this about? Rana's heart thumped against her chest. "Okay…"

"It's normal to wonder when one will Crown. If one will Crown. How one will Crown."

Rana's heart sank. Of course, this wasn't just about holding hands—this was about her parents.

"I imagine, since your parents didn't Crown, that these concerns might loom larger for you. Am I correct?" Kalakanya leaned against the helicopter and looked up at the stars.

She had to be asking out of politeness. Clearly, she already knew. Everyone in their village probably knew.

Rana sighed. "Everyone knows that."

"Hmm. Maybe." Kalakanya looked back over toward the fire, where Eka remained invisible in the darkness. "You and I have similar problems. I avoid love because of what I know. You avoid love because of what you fear you don't know." She turned back to Rana. "Do you agree?"

Rana's head was spinning. "I…I don't know anything about you and who you've dated."

Kalakanya smiled. "I thought everyone has noticed that I haven't dated. Not really."

"What exactly are you saying?" She winced at the defensiveness in her voice. "Sorry, that came out wrong."

Kalakanya gave a soft laugh. "I think those helicopters have made all our nerves raw, though I agree with what you said earlier that their energy didn't impact our abilities in sensing those humans." She pushed a stray white lock that had escaped her braids behind her ear. "I'm saying that your beliefs about Crowning may be inaccurate. Crowning isn't a goal that you can achieve by completing a long list of activities. Or by avoiding certain things." Kalakanya gave her a pointed stare.

"Oh." Her face grew hot. She must know about her list and how hard she struggled to not date. "You know about Kahali and Eka."

"Yes, the tension between you three is enough to distract the deepest meditator." She grinned. "I understand, mind you. I'm just saying that it's probably more of a distraction to pretend you're only friends than dating one of them would be."

For a moment, she stared at Kalakanya, too shocked to respond. "You...you're telling me to date them?"

"I'm saying that to reach enlightenment, you can't pick which feelings you want to experience. The One In All has given you love. You must experience it"—Kalakanya grew silent as if she had to drag the words up from her depths—"whether or not it seems convenient." She put her head in her hands and groaned in frustration.

Oneness! She'd never seen Kalakanya so distraught. "I'm sorry I'm so frustrating. Are you hearing all three of our thoughts? I talked to them and said we should only be friends so I can focus on Crowning. I didn't mean to be such an obvious failure."

Kalakanya, her face still in her palms, shook her head. "No, *you're* fine, Rana." She looked up, and appeared...embarrassed? "That groan was my frustration at my own relationship conundrum."

"Oh." Kalakanya had never really dated anyone so what was her conundrum? "Do you want to talk about it?"

Kalakanya gave a sad laugh. "No, I can't reveal what I know. You know me—my name should really be the Bearer of Secrets, not the Daughter of Time." She sighed, and Oneness, she had tears in her eyes. "The One In All will help me figure it out." She made an audible swallow.

Kalakanya's glance strayed to where Eka's shield glowed softly against the looming darkness. "I just don't want you to think that tormenting yourself is going to help you Crown. You need to be honest with yourself. If you're in love, you're in love. The issue with dating happens when your mental attachment to the other person becomes so great that it entrenches your identity in that relationship. Attachments make it very difficult to Crown. But avoiding your feelings won't work either. Denying love doesn't make it go away. It may, however, push them away."

Rana inhaled sharply. "Did I cause Kahali's problem on the helicopter?"

Kalakanya shook her head. "No, that was his trauma and the emergence of a sudden, unusual capability. From what I understand, your connection to him calmed him and saved us all."

"So, you're saying I should pick one of them and be with them?" Her mind reeled at the idea. Had she been doing this all wrong, needlessly tormenting herself, Eka, and Kahali? Could she actually enjoy dating and still Crown?

"It's not my place to tell you what to do. But Crowning isn't something you can control. It happens when it happens. All you can do is always be as aware as possible, improve your capabilities, and live with love in your heart."

Rana let out a huge sigh. "That sounds too simple."

From the mountainside opposite the one that the growl had come from, came a sharp crackling of trampled undergrowth. It carried across the still night air, a warning that they were surrounded. Both of them turned toward the noise, but nothing showed itself in the blackness. Part of her wanted to energetically scan the area, but this conversation was too important. Besides, they had shields. "If Crowning is that simple, how did my parents mess it up?"

"Maybe you shouldn't assume they did. Maybe they did exactly what was right for them."

Exasperation filled her. Why were Crowned Ones so cryptic? "But they never Crowned."

"No, they didn't."

"You're saying I should just live my life because I'm like them and will never Crown either?" *Please, don't say yes...*

"I have never done, nor do I intend to do, a transtemporal scan on when or if you Crown, Rana. I'm simply sharing what I know about the path to Crowning."

"You were the youngest to Crown, ever. You also just said you never really dated. You don't think *not* dating and becoming attached helped you?"

Kalakanya blew out a deep breath, creating a steamy plume in the cold air. "I don't recommend you strive to be like me. I don't recommend that at all." She cleared her throat. "You should probably create a shield and walk back over there. It's late and you need to rest."

That was a sudden end to the conversation. Rana turned to examine the Crowned One in the pale moonlight. "Are you okay?"

"Yes, I'll be fine." Kalakanya ran a hand back over her usually perfect braids, tucking in the loose strand. "I have a lot to think about, too."

"The cave digger?"

"That's one of the things. Try to get some sleep. Good night."

She was clearly being dismissed, but she still had so many questions. "Okay, thanks. May the One In All keep you safe tonight." Creating her own shield, she turned back toward where Eka shielded the other helicopter and Kahali recovered from his new capability. She loved them both, but in very different ways. Her steps quickened. The possibility of being able to date without messing up her chance to Crown changed *everything*.

Chapter 41

Campsite, Eastern Coast of North America: Rana of Peleguin Rookery

Using the light of her shield, Rana stumbled back through the blackness toward the other helicopter. Kalakanya's talk had left her a jumble of emotions. Digga stayed so close that Rana nearly tripped on the anxious pup. Eka's shield was stretched so large to surround the helicopter that its light was barely noticeable as a murky dome.

As she walked toward the firelight at its center, her heart sped at the thought of Eka waiting there for her. But with her emotions running amok like this, she needed a moment alone to think. But she also wanted to see him. Ugh. She shook her head in frustration. Kalakanya's suggestion that she could date and it wouldn't interfere with her Crowning had sent her mind into a tither.

"Is Kalakanya *really* okay over there?" Bleu's voice startled Rana. She had assumed everyone but Eka had already gotten onto the helicopter and gone to bed. "I know she's Crowned," Bleu continued, "but she's not invincible."

"She is safe," Rana said, pleased that she knew the words.

She sent to Eka, *Has he just been standing out here, worrying the whole time?*

Eka gave a slight grin and nodded.

"But..." Bleu paled. "I...killed a bunch of the Crowned Ones with my gun. And she's all alone, and there are unknown humans around."

Rana's stomach grew queasy. How had she so quickly forgotten his murderous past? She found it easier and easier to forget their past violence, lulled by the sharing of space and food, but Bleu had hunted her people.

He's a killer, she reminded herself. *Only Atsushi and Girak aren't.* Bleu stood right in front of her, armed. She took a deep breath. *He's not like Savas and Zach,* she reminded herself.

He stared at the darkness in Kalakanya's direction, apparently worried that Kalakanya might face violence, yet his solution was to keep his hand near his gun? Clearly, his instincts to solve things with a gun hadn't changed as much as Rana had hoped. But he *was* attending sunrise sits and trying to change. And he was worried about one of them.

From what I've heard, you killed them as they star beamed into the area. Before they could put up their shield.

Bleu winced. She watched as, in response to her words, his energy curdled in horror.

Despite his past, she liked Bleu, and part of her wanted to say something to make him feel better. But she had lived her whole life with those hunted Crowned Ones. And nothing she could say would take away what he had done to them or his guilt.

She remained silent. It wasn't the kindest thing to do, but she was sick of dealing with human chaos. Maybe she was more like Kahali in her anger than she cared to admit.

But still, Bleu wore his worry like a smothering cape, so she relented a bit. *Unlike the ones you hunted, Kalakanya is already shielding and has no need to star beam.*

"Right." He nodded but remained planted outside, gaze fixed on where Kalakanya had last stepped through the veil of darkness to disappear. A long howl echoed down the mountainside. They all glanced in its direction, and Eka looked around at his shield as if checking it.

Bleu, get some sleep, Eka said. *She wouldn't want you staying up, worrying about her. She's been worried all day about your concussion.*

"Really?" Bleu looked strangely happy about that.

Rana looked at him anew. His energy was excited in a hopeful way. The guy had lost his mind if he was falling for a Crowned One. Especially Kalakanya. She'd just said she'd never really dated. *Bleu, give it up. Crowned Ones are in a different league than us*—she pointed to herself and Eka—*and you're not even a star being.*

"What?" He blushed. "Oh, of course." His shoulders hunched. "I'm just concerned. We humans care about others, too, you know."

He hurried on board, not meeting her glower as he did so. A screech followed by terrifying deep grunts rolled down the other mountain. What furred one was that?

Eka raised his eyebrows at the scary noises, then blew out a long, dramatic breath. *That wasn't very kind.*

She wilted at his scowl of disappointment. She had shown how far she was from Crowning. How petty she was. How unlike him.

"Yes, it was mean." She looked away. How had she messed this up? She finally had a moment alone with Eka. And even if he had to hold a shield, no one else was around. And instead of...whatever she had hoped for, she had chosen to be rude to Bleu and disappoint Eka with her lack of civility. No, not a lack of civility—pure fury suddenly pumped through her veins when she thought of Bleu and the other humans.

"Why are you so angry?"

"Because we are out here risking our lives for them, and they're so ridiculously obsessed with violence that they're going to get us all killed." She motioned toward the hill. "And now there's that. I never wanted to deal with all this. It's only been a few suns, and I'm *so* sick of their ways." She kicked the snow, and it spurted up onto Digga's muzzle. The pup sneezed and grunted at Rana.

Falling stars, what was wrong with her? She had been excited to spend time alone with Eka, and now she was nearly in a rage. *Sorry.* Rana squatted and rubbed the pup's ears, avoiding Eka's gaze. This anger made no sense. What was happening to her?

A cold wind blew down from the mountain and swirled around them. She shivered under her cape.

"I don't think your anger is about any of that," he said with the annoying confidence of a Crowned One.

She glared up at him. "Reeeally? Then what's it about?"

He sighed. "Look, I'm trying to help. I think something else is going on, because this isn't like you."

Falling stars. Her fists clenched Digga's thick fur in tight fists. She shook them out.

"Sorry, I can't seem to lose this anger." She froze. "Hold on…" Something wasn't right. She scanned her body and then scanned the mountainside. Whatever watched from the mountain was furious, and she somehow had empathically connected with it, picked up its anger, and taken it on as her own. She shrank in horror of what she'd done to Bleu. How she'd snapped at Eka. She buried her face in her palms. "I owe Bleu an apology. And you. I'm sorry. That wasn't even my anger."

Eka's brow furrowed. "Why would you be picking up another's anger?" he asked, tucking his wind-wild locks back inside his hood to see her better.

Another wave of anger hit her and she snorted, her body stiffening at the surge of fury. She glanced at Eka, who seemed completely unaware of the wave that had nearly knocked her over. She looked up at the mountains and sensed a questioning. Almost a *why?*

"I…I think it's trying to communicate." She managed a stiff wave toward the mountain.

"It?" Eka's gaze followed her gesture, and then he looked about with unease. "You don't think it's humans?"

She shook her head, then reconsidered how unpredictable her human team members were and shrugged. "I don't know. I think it tried to mind speak. Humans don't do that." She shook off the dregs of its anger, freeing herself and blocking it. Her whole body relaxed. Much better.

"You'd normally never pick up another's anger, right?"

"No, but all rules of normalcy seem off since we landed."

Eka gave a tense nod and scanned their surroundings again. "If there's any chance it may understand mind speaking, I'm not sure we should discuss it in detail with Kalakanya via mind speak, in case it overhears. But maybe you should let her know?"

Rana nodded. "Good thinking." *Kalakanya?*

Yes? the Crowned One answered immediately. *Is everything okay over there?*

Yes, but I think whatever is making those noises just tried to communicate with me. I received waves of anger and then maybe a "why." Just wanted to let you know.

For a moment there was no response. Rana wished she could see Kalakanya, get a sense of her reaction to the news.

Then, Kalakanya sent, *I wonder why it's only trying to communicate with you?*

Assuming this is the same type of predator that killed my cousin, Eka responded, *maybe it's because she's the one who's always with Digga? Based on what my cousin's spirit told me during my training back at my village, I think there's a link between this predator attacking and cave diggers.*

I don't like this, Kalakanya responded. *Rana, you and Digga stay inside the shield. Hopefully we can get some answers tomorrow when we better explore the area.*

Rana got the sense that was all their Crowned One would say tonight.

Eka again looked his shield over and then gave her a worried smile. "Since you're our expert in animal communication, you might want to look around tomorrow and see if whatever they are tries communicating again."

"Only if they come up with a better method of getting through to me." She shivered at the memory of their rage. "I'm not getting ill on their anger for no reason." She sighed and glanced upward at the overhead dome of his shield. "Of the three of us, you seemed to get the best special capability."

"Huh?" Eka tilted his head in question.

"Your large shielding is quite the special capability. Kahali's ability to move things with his mind seems a bit of a nightmare right now, and I certainly don't want to be the one responsible for communicating with these...creatures."

"Of course not. They're not exactly...friendly." He turned back to her. "Were you okay earlier when Kalakanya mentioned that Kahali's capability would be useful in an avalanche? It seemed a bit..." He shrugged and gave her a concerned look. "Balavati told me how your parents died."

Avalanche. And leave it to her talkative friend to have told Eka everything about her parents' death. She'd completely pushed that avalanche reference aside in her concern for Kahali. "Why did she choose that example for him?"

Eka cleared his throat. "Because it worked, I suspect. Kahali agreed to try because he thought of *you*." With a little huff, he shook his head. "He'd do anything for you."

"We've always looked out for each other." It was true, but only half the truth. In the last year, their emotions had ventured beyond what they had always been. And from the concerned frown on Eka's mouth, he was thinking the same thing. Kalakanya's advice drifted through her mind.

Her gaze lingered on his lips. What would they feel like on hers? "Kahali and I will always be close. I can't imagine not being so."

Eka's face softened. "I'd never come between your friendship with him, no matter what might happen between us. You know that, right?" He tilted his head, awaiting her response.

Oh, she knew that. His kindness and maturity had been duly noted by both Balavati and herself ages ago. Despite the howling creatures on the mountain and the armed, volatile humans just inside the helicopter, she nodded and stepped into his warmth.

Somehow, their adventure of rescuing Digga and all their deep conversations on the helicopter coalesced into a knowing. She'd always love Kahali, but she wanted Eka to hold her, to share secret moments with her, to kiss her.

She yearned to wrap her arms around him, but he was shielding the whole team. She was afraid to even brush against him because everything whirled like a chaotic lightning storm within her, and they needed his shield. Could he hold a shield and kiss? No, first kisses shouldn't be distracted kisses.

"I wish you weren't holding a shield right now." She bit her lip and then grinned.

His eyes widened in recognition of what she was hinting at, and his whole face lit up. "That makes two of us. But it's not really negotiable, you know?"

A curdling screech rolled down the mountain and echoed around them.

"Right." She resisted pouting and settled for standing so close together that their body warmth mingled.

"So, to be clear, you've changed your mind? If I wasn't holding a shield, would you be interested in...getting even closer?" Oneness, that grin. It somehow exuded joy, mischief, wanting, and innocence all at the same time.

"Yes." She looked into his eyes, their warm brown reflecting sparks from the firelight. She drew closer, then put a hand on his chest to stop herself. She cleared her throat. "But not now. Now I need you to shield so we all survive until...later."

He gave a throaty laugh. "You just made this the longest night of my life."

She frowned, then laughed. "I'm sorry."

"No, you're not." He didn't touch her. But his steady breath warmed her face. He gave a sad chuckle. "I'd hug you, but..." He nodded toward the shield enclosing them and the helicopter.

She smiled. "Yeah, we don't need everyone else in on it."

"Exactly. So, later?" He cocked an eyebrow in question, his expression flickering between hope and playfulness.

"I'll hold you to that," she teased.

"Good. Since we're left with talking...may I ask you a question?"

She nodded, curious what he suddenly wanted to know about her.

"You were afraid dating would ruin your chances at Crowning. What changed your mind?"

Oh, *that*. How could she explain it? "I realized that..." She stopped, definitely *not* wanting to tell him about her list. "Not dating gives me more time to focus on developing my capabilities toward Crowning, but it also means I'm avoiding my feelings for you. And that's not helpful either, so I may as well do what I want, right?" She grinned, hoping her thought process didn't sound too strange.

"You don't expect me to talk you out of that, right?" he asked, his eyes twinkling.

"No," she said, laughing. Another set of gurgling screams rained down from the mountain, and she trembled. "Are you okay out here shielding alone? I mean, she's a Crowned One. You're—"

"I'm good at shields. I'll keep you safe."

"I wasn't worried about myself. Aren't you scared to be out here alone?"

He scanned the impenetrable black wilderness beyond the fire. The humans or whatever she had sensed on the mountain could be anywhere. Behind wind-flapped tents. High in the trees. Or creeping closer in the shadows, furious and watching.

And then there was the cave digger that wasn't a cave digger. Animals didn't misrepresent themselves. That was just so *wrong*. Eka shouldn't be out here with that...thing.

"Fear will keep me alert," Eka said.

"Want me to stay?"

"Want?" He laughed. "Of course, I do. But no. You'll be out searching for humans tomorrow. You need sleep."

"I could get a fur and sleep out here."

He grinned. "Because *that* wouldn't distract me at all."

She smiled, but inside, her frustration at their need for the shield strangled her. "Okay. Well, I'm grabbing a chair as close to the door as I can. If you have any problems, call me."

"Thank you." With his hands to his heart, he bowed in the traditional farewell. "Sleep well."

But the slow, smoldering smile he gave guaranteed it would be quite a while before she'd sleep.

Chapter 42

Campsite, Eastern Coast of North America: Kahali of Peleguin Rookery

Out of guilt, Kahali had insisted Neviah take his bed. After all, he'd not only nearly caused her to crash, but while he lay in the bed recovering, he'd realized that the converted chair-beds were sized for the shorter humans, not star beings. So, she got the bed, and he shifted his furs to a chair nearest the helicopter door. Rana and Eka were still out there, and his body refused to relax with them in danger.

Finally, Rana stumbled in, looking a bit dreamy, as if she'd already fallen half-asleep. A moment later, Digga jumped up after her, grunting in pain at her injury. As another lion-like roar filled the air around them, Digga darted under Rana, who tripped and grabbed a chairback to keep from falling.

Nice moves. He grinned and patted the empty chairs near his own. *I got your furs so your searching for them won't wake everyone up. Everything okay out there?*

She nodded, her earlier humor gone. She slipped into the chair beside him. He passed over her stuff and waited. She had a strange look on her face that he couldn't read, like she was fighting with herself about something. The turmoil coming off her competed with what wafted off Bleu two rows away as he worried about Kalakanya. *What happened?*

She bit her lip. *Eka's going to Crown soon. Nobody can hold a shield that large and carry on an intense conversation without being close to Crowning.*

Intense?

She waved away his question as if it were unimportant.

Crowning isn't a bad thing. It's our goal—he playfully poked her with his elbow— *right?*

She gave him a withering look.

Oh, it's no longer our goal? We've decided to go the other way? Lower our vibration by learning to kill?

She covered her mouth to stifle her laugh. *That's definitely not the promise I remember making.*

So, then the problem with him Crowning is...?

She pressed her lips together in a flat line and looked away.

Oh, no. She'd picked Eka.

He couldn't breathe. Nothing around them had changed, but his world imploded. *No. No no, no,* his heart stammered in his chest. Her expression as she checked out the window on Eka's safety screamed *yes.*

His insides spun and twisted, contorting as his dreams collapsed. He pulled further inside himself, unwilling to show his devastation. She was his best friend, and he loved her more than he'd ever believed was possible. He would not ruin her happiness.

He stared at his clenched hand in his lap. Eka was amazing, and she had every reason to choose him. Eka had it all together, unlike him. He'd been a fool to think he had a chance with her given his anger at humans, refusing to see her after he'd been shot and lost his arm, and now this out-of-control tornado thing. But ever since that magical night last year when they'd watched the meteor shower together on their favorite boulder...

He forced himself to breathe, blinking as she gazed out the window to check on Eka. Kahali took another slow breath and touched her arm. *Hey. If it's meant to be, it'll work out. Even if he Crowns now.*

He avoided what they both knew—romantic relationships didn't survive the transition of one partner Crowning before the other. It was just too life-altering and created too large a chasm between the partners.

Maybe that could work to his advantage, but he didn't want to be chosen as a leftover. No, if she had chosen Eka, he'd lost his chance.

She turned back to him, her eyes damp. Maybe he hadn't hidden his devastation, or maybe she simply knew him too well. Knew what her decision meant to him.

He attempted a smile. *Just because I hoped for something different doesn't mean I don't want you to be happy.*

You're the best...

He waited, knowing the word *friend* was coming. Except it didn't.

Instead, she laid her head on his shoulder and nestled deeper into her chair. *Eka said he'd call if anything happens...* She drifted off to sleep.

He watched her breathe, each breath fluttering the loose, amber wisps of hair around her face. Could he ever not ache when he looked at her? Was there anyone, anywhere, that he'd ever love as much as his best friend?

❋ ❋ ❋ ❋ ❋ ❋

Somehow, Kahali awoke early for sunrise sit, which was good because Rana never would have. She was adorably hopeless in the mornings. Once, he had hoped to experience clumsy mornings with her for the rest of his life. But Eka would get those mornings he had dreamed of.

He woke Rana and Atsushi with mind talk so the others could sleep in. As they quietly exited, Bleu followed them out the door.

Don't you need to rest for your concussion? Kahali asked.

Bleu gave him a smile that turned into a yawn. With his mouth still covered, he mumbled, "Can't sleep with this headache."

The sudden, bizarre turmoil over Kalakanya that had clouded Bleu's energy last night still lingered, but now it carried a hint of resolve.

Kahali wished for resolve of his own as he forced himself to turn and greet Eka.

Mr. Perfect leaned against the helicopter, holding the massive shield faithfully. *Of course.*

Eka greeted them with a sleepy smile. Sure, he had missed a night's rest, but whatever *intense* conversation he had shared with Rana last night made them both blush when they saw each other.

Kahali wanted to vomit, but that wouldn't do. Instead, he led Bleu and Atsushi to a flat area, where they could meditate within Eka's shield. Rana joined them after a private moment with Eka.

Suffice it to say it was one of the worst sunrise sits of Kahali's life.

By the time they were done, Savas had taken it upon himself to divide the team into two groups.

"Hold on," Bleu said, a bit annoyed as he joined the others at the campfire for breakfast. "It's not your decision, Savas."

Kahali sat off a bit from the rest of them, waiting for the sure-to-follow power struggle.

Neviah joined him on his fallen tree, far from the others. "I was spoiled with your cot." She smiled and handed him a small golden bag. "Thanks again."

He accepted the small bag and shook it. *What is it?*

"Choco, the best treat there is. It's pretty rare, and I thought it might cheer you up." She gave him another smile. "Try it."

He wasn't in the mood for sweets. He had no appetite. *Thanks, I'll try it later.*

Disappointment radiated from her, but he was much more concerned with Rana and Eka and the fight about to break out in front of them between Savas and Bleu. Both had puffed out like angry peleguins fighting over a nest.

Neviah followed his gaze. "Yeah, this should be fun."

It took Kahali a moment to realize she was being sarcastic. Despite his foul mood, his lips curled into a smile at her statement. Human sarcasm charmed him. Probably another sign that he was damaged beyond hope of Crowning.

Savas took a gulp of his tea as he studied Bleu with a smirk. "Bleu, you can barely stand, and you vomited this morning. You're in no shape to be leading a search."

Bleu stiffened. "I'm commander, and I already planned everything while you were still asleep."

"Now what's that supposed to—"

"Stop." Bleu held up his hand. "I'm not in the mood for this game. I meant nothing except that I've already decided how we're doing this."

"I see." Savas' face twisted into a deadly smile. "And what are *we* going to do today, Commander?"

"You, Savas, are going to take a small team up the mountain and see if you find humans. A short trip so you can be back before dark. Rana can shield, and if Kahali is up to it, he can join as well.

"Neviah, you need to stay behind so we have a pilot, just in case something horrible happens to them." He nodded toward Savas, meaning the search team. "With Eka sleeping, we'll need Neviah and Zach to guard the far helicopter. So, Savas, you'll have yourself, Atsushi, Girak, Rana, and possibly Kahali."

"That's a pretty small team," Savas said. "If we run into trouble—"

"Then you have Rana to shield, and you get back here as soon as possible. Just don't go so far that you can't be back before nightfall. I don't want anyone out there in the dark."

Savas narrowed his eyes at Bleu, opened his mouth, and then seemed to reconsider. He watched Bleu and took another swig as if he needed time to think.

Everyone waited to see if Savas was going to argue. Everyone except Rana. She hadn't looked up from where Digga rolled at her feet.

"It's not a bad plan." Savas put his empty cup on the ground. "We'll need guns and the portable sensors so we're not wandering around uselessly. Okay."

Savas stood as if ready to head out, leaving his empty cup behind as if the local wildlife would clean up after him. "And while we're gone?"

He smiled at Bleu as if it were a simple question, but the insinuation that he would do nothing while Savas did everything rang in the air between them.

Bleu clenched his jaw. "We need to check out the tree that fell. There should be either humanoid or animal prints around it. We'll wait until Eka wakes up, and then if I'm still feeling like this, Zach and he will go. It's not that far."

Kahali watched for Rana's reaction. On the surface, she appeared fine with the plan. But the way she sat perfectly still and kept her gaze locked on Digga... She hadn't even glanced at himself or Eka. No mind talk to him. Just silence.

Whenever Rana acted like that, she was far from okay. There was no way she thought this was a good idea, and he agreed. How could traipsing off to meet humans that had already threatened them be considered wise?

Kahali?

He looked up, surprised that Eka was singling him out. *Yes?*

You okay today? Can you go with Rana? I don't think any of us should ever be alone with them.

He should have been relieved that he wasn't the only one looking out for her, but after last night, it ached like salt rubbed on his torn heart. *Even if I were half-dead, I'd never leave her alone with them.*

On the other side of the fire, he could just make out Eka near the helicopter. He had turned at Kahali's message and was assessing him with concern. *You know I'd go with you both if I could, right?*

Of course, you would. Perfect Eka would always do the right thing.

Are you mad at me?

Kahali closed his eyes. The anger was taking over. If only they hadn't met Eka at the Spiral Ceremony and he had remained a stranger to Rana.

Kahali, what did I do?

Nothing.

What was he going to say? "She loves you, not me, even though I've loved her before you even knew she existed?" He had to breathe. Stay calm. He had a big day, and this was no way to start it.

Is this about Rana?

Annoyance surged through Kahali. Rana was right—Eka was about to Crown. Kahali's own sister, Sohana, had gotten annoying with her intrusive questions in the moon before she Crowned. Sohana had been testing, but this was...

I'll take your silence as a yes?

Yes.

Kahali tried to still his racing heart. He opened his eyes. Atsushi was collecting dishes. Neviah had locked the guys out of the helicopter to change her clothes. Bleu was picking at his food.

And Rana was watching him.

Numb to the core, he returned her gaze. She quirked her mouth slightly in a failed smile, stood, and left.

Kahali sighed and then shoveled in the rest of his food. Its bland taste and congealed texture gagged him, but he'd need his strength out there.

"Hey."

Kahali nearly jumped out of his skin. Eka stood beside him, his face unreadable.

He grunted in acknowledgement and forced down the last horrid swallow of breakfast.

"Can I sit here while I eat?" Eka sat before he could protest.

Emotions swirled inside him. Eka was a good guy. He knew that. He just didn't want to be anywhere near him right now.

"Look, I'm not really in a social mood, so I'm going to go get ready." He began to stand.

Eka went to grab his arm, but he was on Kahali's armless side. He had already grasped his empty sleeve before he realized.

"Oh, sorry." He released it. "Please. Just hear me out."

"You weren't saying anything." Kahali looked over his shoulder. "I have things to do."

"I know. Bear with me. I'm kinda slow. I'm exhausted, but this is too important to wait, so hopefully I won't mess it up." He turned to look right at Kahali. "You are her best friend. I know that. And I know how you feel, so I'm sorry. Is there a way we can..." He waved his hand about aimlessly. "I don't know...not be awkward? Not argue? I like you. I think we've become friends, right?"

Kahali grimaced. They *had* been friends, but he wanted this conversation over with.

"Okay, maybe we weren't friends? Maybe I was wrong?" Eka had the nerve to look sad. He never got mad. No wonder Rana picked him. "If things were reversed, I'd probably be looking at you the way you're looking at me."

Kahali grunted.

Eka gave him a half-smile. "Just think about it, okay? There's only four of us out here. I think it'd be best if we stuck together."

Kahali let out an exasperated sigh. "You're right. And we are friends." He let out a laugh that sounded like a sob. "I just don't want to be around you right now, okay?"

"Okay, that's fair. But I still have your back. You're not alone out here."

"I know." Did he know that? He had said that a bit too quickly. He did feel alone. He turned to leave.

"Kahali, we were being watched all night by whatever is out there. I think it's…" He tapped his head as if trying to remember something. "What was the word you used to describe the humans when they attacked you? Rabid? This felt dangerous like that. But calculating. I'm telling you this because I think Kalakanya is minimizing the danger to keep down the humans' reactivity."

Rabid but calculating? Kahali laughed, this time in the human sarcastic way. "Sounds like a joy."

Eka didn't share his humor. "Just stay safe. Rana told you about the new predator I had a dream about, right?"

"Rana tells me everything." His tone betrayed his anger. Oneness, he was an emotional wreck.

Eka nodded. "I know. Look, whatever is watching us from the mountains feels like that same predator. I know this sounds impossible, but I think it preys on cave diggers. We both know Rana won't leave Digga behind. I wish there were some way I could go with you."

"I'll keep Rana safe. You keep yourself from panicking. If there's danger, you need to trust us to take care of it. Don't attempt to star beam and kill yourself, okay?" Kahali frowned. Maybe he still had a heart, somewhere, even if it was shredded to ribbons.

Eka attempted a smile about as effective as the one Rana had tried earlier. "I'll do my best not to die."

"You're not going to die, because as much as I love Rana, I don't want her to be with me only because you foolishly got yourself killed."

He turned, eager to put as much space between himself and Rana's choice as possible.

Chapter 43

Campsite, Eastern Coast of North America: Kahali of Peleguin Rookery

Nothing Kalakanya said would keep him from helping Rana explore the mountain today, and the last thing he wanted was an argument with a Crowned One. So, he bypassed her requested check-in and climbed aboard the helicopter to load his pack with food and water. He tossed in his knife and stared at his fake clunker of an arm. It was usually just an annoyance, but Bahujnana had advised him to wear it daily to maintain his shoulder strength. Would it be too heavy for a full-day hike?

His entire body still ached from his freak-out yesterday, but the possibility of the unknown humans shooting at them made him pause. The wooden arm would protect his side. Sad, how he now expected violence as a daily part of his life.

"I choose the One In All, not fear," he mumbled. But that was easier said than put into practice. He glared at the wooden arm and then the mountain beyond the helicopter window that possibly contained humans.

He opted to follow Bahujnana's advice. He'd wear it to strengthen his shoulder but throw in some rope to tie it to his pack if necessary. Focusing on his health meant choosing love, not fear.

As he struggled to attach the arm's leather straps, Atsushi climbed aboard. "Let me help."

Rana and Atsushi were the only ones Kahali would let touch his fake arm straps.

With a grateful nod, Kahali held out the wooden arm. Atsushi did the straps in a quarter of the time it would have taken him.

Atsushi stood back, brow furrowed. "Is that right?"

Yeah. Thanks.

"You know, Eka could probably carve you a hand that might work better than it just ending like that."

I'm sure he could. Kahali took deep breaths to dissipate his rising anger.

Of course, perfect Eka could carve him a fake hand because he had two hands to carve and two arms to hug Rana. He swallowed the growing lump of fury at Rana's choice. Eka had never done anything to him. The humans had been the ones to take his arm and steal Rana. Eka had been the hero to save her for both of them because he himself had been still too weak to go. *Eka has always been a friend.*

He shook his head, hoping to escape the anger, but it was useless. He forced a crooked smile. *I don't think we'll have time for our lessons today. Sorry.* He caught Atsushi's narrowed gaze. *What?*

"Something happen I should know about?" Atsushi continued to study him.

No.

Atsushi winced as if slapped. Then, heaving his shoulders in a big sigh, he turned to leave. "It's okay if you don't want to tell me. But you can't teach me to read energy and then deny what I'm picking up." He whipped his pack over his shoulder and hopped out before Kahali could respond.

What kind of mentor was he being? He hurried down the aisle, trying to catch Atsushi, when Kalakanya's head and shoulders popped through the doorway. Kahali froze.

She raised an eyebrow and grinned. "Hiding from me?"

"Just getting ready." That was true, but his flush of guilt confirmed the truth for both of them.

She nodded. "How's your arm today?"

"Still missing." He grinned the first real grin all day.

"Aha. Back to normal, I see." She nodded and grew serious. "You going to be okay out there?"

He shrugged. "Only one way to know. But either way, I'm not letting Rana go alone with them. Regardless of what you say."

Ignoring his challenge, she tilted her head. "Did the practice help yesterday? Can you control it?"

He shrugged noncommittedly. "At least now I know there's something to control." He shifted to his other leg, impatient to get outside as Savas called his team together. "Savas' love for me won't increase if I'm late."

"Of course." Still blocking the open door, she handed him a small leather pouch.

"What's this?"

"Dried Eldinberries. If the pain in your arm gets bad, chew one at a time. It'll help." She tilted her head, assessing him in that penetrating Crowned One way.

Outside the window, everyone had gathered around Savas.

"Thanks. I have to get going."

She nodded. "I know something happened between you three last night. Don't let your emotions scatter your focus. If you want, we can talk when you get back."

"I'm fine."

She gave him a sad smile. "No, you're not. And if we hadn't been hanging out with humans so much lately, you would never have tried using such denial with me. Be careful out there, Kahali. Don't forget who you are."

He blinked at her, surprised by her bluntness. Was it that obvious that he'd lost himself to the anger and hurt? "I'm not sure I know anymore," he mumbled, and hurried past her.

✳ ✳ ✳ ✳ ✳

Kahali and the rest of the team started toward the horrible trap they'd found yesterday, hoping to pick up the trail in the morning light. The slight breeze ruffled the trees' boughs overhead, filling the air with pungent scents of damp tree bark and evergreen sap. Kahali stuck close to Rana, their bootsteps nearly synchronized on the crunchy snow. Digga raced in circles around them, batting with her long claws at the miniscule seed cones scattered across the snow-covered ground.

"Here they are," Savas said, his voice tense with excitement as he pointed down at the boot prints. "Looks like they go straight up the mountain."

I never thought I'd be seeking out humans again, Kahali joked to Rana.

Her immediate smile almost made this whole nightmare worth it. *You and I seemed destined to be with them.*

Kahali made gagging noises until Atsushi shot him a concerned look. He laughed and waved off the human's concern. He'd been afraid he would have lost something in his friendship with Rana, but it seemed intact. Despite his shredded heart, he breathed a bit more freely in this weird, new world where she hadn't chosen him. Wincing, he focused instead on the forest floor, which now rose at a steep angle.

The mountain resisted them, its slippery mountainside and thorny undergrowth hindering their progress. The humans' footwear fared poorly, being so bulky and stiff that the incline made each step hard work. Girak huffed and unsnagged his puffy parka from the strange thorny undergrowth.

Their progress was painfully slow. This strange forest seemed determined to keep them out. Since when had such thorny bushes grown beneath evergreens? He scowled as the thorns seemed to reach for him until he noticed the small, twittering feathered ones sheltering within the brambles. The feathered ones' colorful plumage and bright calls cheered him.

They hiked the slope at an angle, following Savas as he held his sensor aloft before him. Kahali had no idea how it worked, but Savas was convinced the light on it would flash if anyone was nearby. The sensor's light remained steady, and the human grew grumpier with each step. Kahali and Rana hung back a bit to keep an eye on everyone. If there was a dangerous predator afoot, as Eka believed, it would most likely attack from the rear.

The sun rose higher as they climbed up the side of the mountain. The humans stomped with each step, breaking fallen branches and loosening stones. He still spotted several new furred ones scampering off and pointed them out to Rana and the others. If there were a dangerous predator around, it certainly knew where they were.

As they climbed, Atsushi cast him concerned glances. As much as he regretted his earlier rudeness, Kahali couldn't apologize and tell him about Eka and Rana with her hiking beside him.

At Atsushi's third glance, Kahali couldn't take the guilt anymore. *Sorry I snapped at you. You were right, something happened, and I'll explain later when the others aren't around.*

Atsushi nodded, relief blooming on his face.

Kahali managed a smile. He really did like the kid. *Now, stop worrying about me and stay alert to your surroundings like I taught you.*

Atsushi gave a nod and the biggest grin he'd seen the whole trip. If only Kahali could fix his own troubles that easily. Every time Rana smiled or spoke to him, a new shard of pain stabbed his chest.

Friend. After years of hope, he had his answer. She considered him a friend only. His eyes stung, and he studied the ground, biting his lip to keep from losing it. He had to stay focused. They were in danger out here.

"What should we name this lovely mountain?" Girak said, breaking the tense silence. "I suggest Too Steep. Or Destroyer of Parkas."

Atsushi laughed. "Maybe you should stop trying to be one with the brambles?"

Ahead of them, Savas stopped and cursed under his breath. He had lost the boot prints in the rocks. "Rana, what do you see?"

As Rana moved forward to check, Kahali shifted his pack. His arm ached, and the dried Eldinberries called to him. From past experience, they made him light-headed, a risk he didn't want among humans. He'd had enough of his wooden arm for today, and since they had stopped and everyone was occupied, he quickly removed it and redressed while keeping an eye on their surroundings.

While Rana searched the ground, he extended his awareness, scanning for human energy. The area seemed devoid of life. Even the usual scurrying nut-gatherers were absent.

There should be some sort of furred or feathered ones, unless a predator was nearby. His neck hairs prickled. It was too quiet. Something was off.

Chapter 44

Mountainside, Eastern Coast of North America: Kahali of Peleguin Rookery

Kahali turned in place, scanning the too-quiet mountainside. What did the furred ones sense that he was missing? Heart thumping wildly, he walked over to Rana as she crouched, studying the ground. *You picking up anything odd? I'm not getting anything. Not even furred ones.* While he had addressed Rana, he included everyone in the mind speak, just in case they were being stalked.

Rana glanced up, her eyes wide in alarm. She stood and scanned.

"You're not sensing any animals?" Atsushi stepped away and scrutinized the slope below them.

No. It's odd, Kahali confirmed, scanning again. Only a large eagle soared above, too high to scare away prey.

There's something, Rana said, tilting her head as if hearing a distant sound. She wandered off a bit toward a patch of the thorn bushes and put her palm near one.

Savas swung his rifle to his shoulder, ready to kill as usual. He nodded to Kahali. "What are you picking up?"

There are no feathered or furred ones around. It's unusual. Might be nothing, but it might be... Kahali shrugged, trying not to worry the reactive human with the already-raised gun. *It's just weird.*

Still watching the slope, Atsushi slid his hand into his pocket, and his energy noticeably calmed.

Curious, Kahali tuned into Atsushi's thoughts. In his head, Atsushi chanted one of the mantras Kahali had taught him. Maybe he wasn't such a bad mentor. He smiled in pride.

Suddenly, Rana jerked and fell. She lay crumpled and still, unconscious or...

"No!" Kahali threw up his shield, but before it reached the others, Atsushi spasmed and collapsed to the ground. Kahali spun, trying to locate Girak. He lay unconscious as well, splayed on the cold ground.

"Stay close!" Savas yelled. Only he remained upright and inside Kahali's shield. He had his rifle to his shoulder.

You can't shoot from inside!

Savas nodded. "Can you get them inside your shield? Can you do that?"

Kahali had already stepped toward where Rana and Atsushi lay near the far thorn bushes. Savas hustled alongside. As Kahali took another step, bullets splayed the snow between his shield and the others. Thin, scraggly humans camouflaged in leather and furs rose from the bushes.

How was that possible? He had just scanned. A wave of terror washed over him, and his shield flickered.

"Get it together," Savas hissed. "It's just us. They can't fire through this, right?"

No. Kahali tried to step forward again, and the bullets again sprayed the ground between him and Rana. *I can't get to them. They're alive, but I can't reach them!*

Panic built in his chest. He had to get to Rana. He turned about, seeking Digga, but she'd vanished. Why had she deserted Rana?

A small whimper reached his ears, and a trembling nose shoved out from under Rana's abdomen. Digga had somehow dug a hole under Rana.

Stay hidden, Kahali warned her. She was outside the shield and would get hunted if she emerged.

The strange humans walked closer, their guns pointed at Savas and Kahali. They both stepped backward, but from the crunch of seed cones behind him, they were surrounded.

"Whatever happens, don't drop our shield." Savas stepped in front of Kahali, facing the human male who seemed in charge. "Do you speak Standard?"

Their leader, the only one with a fur cloak, narrowed his calculating gaze at Savas and then motioned to Kahali. The hostile men mumbled to each other. Their minds were strangely silent to Kahali. He couldn't sense their energy, even though they stood right in front of him. The nothingness of their presence unnerved him. Even ghosts gave off a presence. These humans had to possess some sort of tech like Savas', but stronger.

Between their hats, hoods, and wild beards, he couldn't see much of their faces, but fear and rage showed in their eyes as they motioned toward him and Rana. They didn't look surprised to see star beings, but more like they couldn't wait to kill them. *One In All help me understand what they fear so I can save Rana...*

After making sure the others were still breathing, he almost Called Kalakanya. But images from the day they had met the Northern Haveners careened through his mind. Crowned Ones had been shot as they star beamed in, killed before they could shield themselves. He couldn't Call her to her own slaughter. And with the humans this close, he couldn't extend his shield enough for her to star beam inside.

Instead, he focused on holding the shield and observing their attackers. They poked at Atsushi, then Girak. They seemed happy about something. Did they enjoy hurting them?

They ignored Savas' attempts to communicate and picked their way toward Rana, who lay face down with Digga hidden beneath her. Kahali bristled with energy as he mind screamed for her to awaken. All their guns now pointed at her. "Rana!" he shouted, but she was nonresponsive. He couldn't reach her, and they approached as if to kill.

GET AWAY FROM HER!

They cringed at his mind yell and spun toward him, fury on their expressions. Rapid gunfire exploded against his shield, filling the air with a noxious smell. He winced but held his ground. And his shield. His ears rang from the deafening thunder of them trying to kill him. He roared in anger as his shield brightened.

"Kahali, get it together, or we're dead."

He couldn't stop shaking. Images of being shot and losing his arm filled his vision. *Just hold the shield. Just hold the shield.* The gunfire stopped. He still breathed. He opened his eyes and glared at the humans.

Against his will, he glanced at Rana, and their leader grunted something. All their gun shafts shifted to point at her.

NO!

The leader sneered at him and poked Rana's face with the tip of his gun. She didn't grimace or react. Something like tiny arrows poked out of her in several places. Whatever they had done to her was serious. Digga must have dug deeper, because her nose had disappeared.

What do you want? he mind yelled in desperation toward the despicable humans.

"Kahali, I said to let me handle this." To the men, Savas said, "We don't collar our friends."

What? They don't understand you. They're going to kill Rana.

"They do understand me because I can understand them."

Kahali turned toward Savas to make sure he was serious.

Savas' grim expression softened a bit as he nodded. "Let me handle it."

He was serious.

"They're checking for something, but don't ask me what," Savas whispered and then raised his voice. "She's no danger. Doesn't need a collar. Are you from Western Haven?"

At his last two words, they spun as one and gaped at him. The only beardless one, who had been approaching Rana with a strange circular thing, froze mid-stride to study at them.

Savas pointed to himself. "Northern Haven. We're from Northern Haven."

The leader stood straighter and adjusted his cloak. He nodded and said something that sounded vaguely like Western Haven.

Savas smiled.

Kahali couldn't understand most of what their leader had said, but from Savas' pleased reaction and the words "Western Haven," these were the humans they had been searching for. If they were speaking the same language, it was angled differently. Without reading their minds, he was lost.

"If you put that collar on her, I won't cooperate," Savas warned, narrowing his gaze at the man who approached Rana with the strange metal circle. "They're our allies. I vouch for her."

The men began arguing among themselves. The beardless man holding the circular thing that must be the collar stilled but remained squatting beside Rana. Kahali struggled to keep his breath normal. If they were to survive, he had to keep up his shield.

The younger guy squatting beside Rana flipped her over onto her back. Digga released a terrifying growl. The man shouted something and reeled back, gun pointed at the now visible tunnel. The others ran over, pointing at the hole where Digga hid.

No, Kahali shouted. *She's just scared. Don't hurt her.*

Savas grunted. "Now I have to save the damn cave digger?" Louder, he called, "Look, that's just her pet, and it's not completely tamed. I'd back off."

The leader laughed and said something to Savas and his men.

Savas' eyebrows shot up, and he snorted. "It's not a child. It's a cave digger. A mammal. You don't need to shoot it."

Savas rolled his eyes as the leader said something and an older man with long, stringy gray hair approached the hole with a bow. He nocked an arrow, similar to the ones in Rana and the others.

What are they doing? Kahali asked.

Savas groaned. "For some stupid reason, they think Digga is Rana's child. They want to capture a child for testing."

What? No!

By the time Kahali turned back, they had fired several arrows into the hole, pulled out an ax, and begun hacking at the frozen ground until they yanked out Digga, limp and unconscious. They prodded the pup with their guns, confused that she was an animal.

"The family resemblance is remarkable, right?" Savas snarked. "Will you believe me now? It's a damn animal, not a kid. Seriously, are you all on drugs?"

The older guy dropped Digga beside Rana and scanned the area, fear in his eyes. Kahali stared at the pup, relief flooding him when he made out her rising and falling breaths. The other men stopped arguing, and their leader said something to Savas.

Savas looked mildly relieved but not truly at ease. He turned to Kahali. "Think they're telling the truth?"

Was he crazy? *I don't understand a word they're saying, but you can't trust them.*

Savas asked the leader, "How can I know it's safe?"

The man responded, holding up a metallic stick. It looked like another weapon.

Savas seemed deep in thought. "Show me. On one of yours."

The leader made a face and raised an eyebrow at his team. They looked...-uncertain? Fearful? Disbelieving? A few took a step back from their leader.

Kahali shook his head in frustration. Whatever technology these humans had, it blocked even more than Savas' wrist cuff.

The leader pointed at a man with a single black braid and a scar running down the right side of his face. The man grunted and stepped forward with a grimace. The leader raised the stick, and it flared lightning-blue on the end. He touched it to the man's shoulder, and he screamed in agony. His whole body shook as if lightning had struck him. He toppled to the ground, his braid writhing on the snow, but his leader only stepped closer, bending to torture him further.

Stop it. Please, Kahali begged.

The leader looked up, surprised, and stopped. The man continued to spasm on the ground in silence for a moment. When he stopped, their team assisted him to his feet.

The leader narrowed his eyes at Savas and raised an eyebrow in question.

Savas snorted. "Well, that's not fun. How could that possibly serve a purpose?"

The leader grunted something, and all the guns were once again trained on Kahali's shield.

Kahali gasped. *Savas? I can't hold this forever.*

"I know. That's why I'll have to go along with them."

What? You're leaving?

"They need to test me for whatever they're testing for." Savas looked at the other's stick and grimaced. He stepped closer and lowered his voice.

"I'm going to thrust my arm out there. They're going to electrify me, or whatever that thing does. If I fall, you need to make sure I fall inside your shield. Got it? Pull me in if you need to."

What? That's the worst plan I've ever heard.

"Got a better one?"

He didn't. They could slowly walk down the mountain toward their camp while inside Kahali's shield. But that would mean leaving Rana, Atsushi, and Girak behind.

I don't understand. No one should hurt anyone like that. How does letting them hurt you help us?

"They need to test me to prove I'm really human. Just do what I said." Savas thrust his arm out of the shield.

The leader smiled and strode forward. He clicked on his blue lightning stick.

Savas, what if it destroys my shield?

Savas looked over his shoulder at Kahali, eyes wide at that horrid possibility. Before he saw it coming, the blue stick struck his arm.

Savas yelled and jerked, trying to pull his arm back, but it seemed attached to the glowing stick. Kahali's shield flickered, and he jerked as well as a shock passed from the shield to him. He fell to his knees, gritted his teeth, and called out to the One In All. As Savas jerked savagely, his shield held. The leader held it longer on Savas than on his own man, not letting go. He was going to kill him.

Stop it, Kahali screamed. *You're killing him.*

Savas' face grew red, and blood dripped down his chin from where he had bit his tongue. As Savas spasmed beside him, Kahali twisted to avoid Savas' flailing limbs.

The men outside cheered, and the weapon flared even brighter. Savas screamed and crumpled to the ground, struggling to breathe. Kahali had never liked Savas, but he couldn't let him die.

Terror rushed through him, infusing him with strength. Ignoring the pain, he yanked Savas away from the weapon, and the human popped back inside his shield. The sudden release from the weapon knocked Kahali to the frozen ground. Savas flopped over him as if dead.

Savas?

With Savas on top of him, Kahali held the shield. His heart raced as fast as a snow hare. If Savas died, Kahali faced the humans alone. He couldn't understand what they said. And Rana still hadn't moved.

The enraged humans gestured wildly as if confused by his concern for Savas, but Kahali ignored them.

"Savas!" he yelled.

Savas sucked in a deep breath and cursed. His eyes opened, but his pupils were too dilated. He blinked at Kahali in confusion.

You okay?

"You saved me?" Savas sounded absolutely surprised. Shocked.

Of course, I did. He panted as hard as Savas.

Outside the shield, the humans cheered, happy with whatever sick piece of this was joyous to them. His stomach railed against their cruelty.

"You saved me," Savas repeated, his face a confused grimace. His icy blue eyes locked onto Kahali's face and studied him as if seeing him for the first time. "Well done."

Savas spit blood onto the snow, pushed himself off Kahali, and struggled to his feet. "Do you understand them?"

Kahali shook his head.

"They're saying you're next."

Kahali froze.

"Shield!"

He refocused. *Never!*

"Right. You couldn't hold our shield through that."

Tell them never. Pinpricks of rage flickered behind his eyes. *Savas, tell them never. I will not do their test.*

Savas stared at him a moment, gave a small nod, and turned to the humans.

"He is the same as she is." Savas pointed at Rana. "They're star beings. Safe. You don't need to test him. You already tested me. I'm human and I vouch for him. He's safe."

It was Kahali's turn to be shocked. Never had he expected such glowing praise from Savas. Though, as Savas had said, testing Kahali would mean shield failure and total exposure for both of them. Probably death for both of them.

The humans laughed and shook their heads. The leader approached with his stick weapon. If he touched his horrible weapon directly to their shield, Kahali feared it wouldn't hold. He was too weak.

Savas, stop him.

Savas pointed his rifle at the man. "We can do this another way."

The leader said something, and half the guns pointed toward Rana. The other half pointed toward Kahali's shield.

Savas turned to him. "Our options appear to be to fight, to surrender and let them use that stick on you and then collar you, or…" He swallowed. "Or they kill Rana."

The pinpricks of rage nearly blinded him. *What?* He couldn't breathe. He had to save Rana, but he couldn't fight armed men. He'd have to kill. He was a star being. Killing wasn't an option. The very idea sickened him.

He needed Kalakanya, but he couldn't risk her life as well, could he? Wait. She had risked his life. She had decided he should Call the Northern Haveners, regardless of whatever the threads of time showed happening to him. Was it okay to ask her to risk it all?

Wouldn't that make him as cold in his decision as Kalakanya had been to let him Call when she knew the risks?

He had to save Rana. That one truth he knew in every cell of his body. Kalakanya had said to remember who he was.

He was Kahali. A star being. And he loved Rana.

He looked up at the rocks surrounding them, searching farther up the slope. Loose rocks and boulders of various sizes were everywhere. He had no idea if he could do what had just popped into his mind, but they were not going to die without him doing his best.

Savas, get ready.

"For what?"

He Called Kalakanya, warning her that guns were present and they were about to die. Then, he noted the position of Rana, the one he loved. Atsushi, whom he had promised to keep safe. And Girak, who had risked everything to sneak Rana out of Northern Haven. Remembering them and their locations, he called on his rage.

As he did so, he remembered his truth. He was a star being. A star being fueled with rage. And rage was raw power.

Chapter 45

Campsite, Eastern Coast of North America: Bleu Reinier

Bleu rested on a log near Neviah's helicopter and kept Kalakanya company while she protected their escape vehicle. "You've been guarding out here forever. Want me to get you something to eat?" Bleu didn't have high hopes Kalakanya would accept his offer. She'd never eaten in front of him.

Yes, thank you. I could really use some berries.

"Really?" He probably looked silly, grinning this much over getting berries. "Great. From your star being supply?"

You grow berries underground?

He laughed. "Yeah, but they're nothing like yours. You're really going to eat? Too bad Atsushi isn't here. He's been really wanting to see this."

Her face twisted into an amused grimace. *Why?*

Bleu shrugged. "We are talking about Atsushi. You must have noticed he keeps trying to give you food, right?"

Her eyes sparkled with mischief. *Take a picture for him. You humans enjoy documenting everything. Savas can use it for his studies.* She laughed her unusual laugh that he was starting to treasure.

"Okay, if you say so. I'll be right back." Bleu had never found something he could do for her. And he'd made her laugh. Thrilled at his sudden usefulness, he strode off toward Neviah's helicopter. Each steady step was a joy compared to yesterday's dizziness.

A blasting series of booms reverberated through the air around him.

He froze in his tracks and spun back toward Kalakanya. "That's gunfire on the mountain," he shouted, his heart racing. That couldn't be good. Unless maybe they decided to hunt despite the star beings' request? Another volley of answering shots dashed that hope.

Her eyes were wide with concern. "I'll contact them. Go get Eka."

Bleu raced the rest of the way to the helicopter, where Eka was catching up on his sleep. As he climbed aboard, he noticed Eka sitting up. "Hey. Did you hear that?"

Eka gave no response, instead staring into space in an unnatural daze.

"Eka?" Bleu hurried over and shook him. His clothes were soaked with sweat, and he was nearly steaming. "Eka!"

Light sparked around Eka, and he started jerking as if having a seizure.

Bleu jumped back, unsure of what had just happened. He raced to the door. "Kalakanya, something's wrong!"

She was there in a flash. Literally. *What?*

Bleu pointed to Eka.

Oh, no. She hurried to Eka and gripped him as if he were going to fly away. *Eka, you're doing great not star beaming. Stay with us, okay?*

She turned back to Bleu. *I can't reach Rana or Kahali. Try to reach Savas' team on your radio. Make sure they're okay.*

"Okay. have you seen Neviah or Zach?"

She shook her head.

He flipped up his hood and turned on his radio. "Savas?"

The radio crackled, but there was no response.

"Savas? This is Bleu."

Only a brief crackle sounded again.

"Think they're out of range?"

She looked out the window toward the mountain. *No, they're in trouble.* She shook Eka again. *Eka. To help Rana, you need to tell me what's going on.*

Eka blinked, and his eyes slowly focused. "Rana..."

Yes, what about her?

"Rana…" He jumped up and started yelling in their native tongue.

Bleu stepped back, alarmed, and called Zach and Neviah on the radio. "Something's wrong with Eka. He's picking up something about the away team. Did you hear the gunshots? I think…"

If Savas was hunting, it shouldn't make Rana and Kahali unreachable unless he'd attacked them as well. Or had the people whose footprints were found attacked them all?

Kalakanya turned toward him, her one arm around Eka and her other outstretched to him as if about to star beam. Zach was complaining about gunfire being normal. Bleu didn't have time for that. He clicked off the radio.

"We're going, right?" Bleu asked Kalakanya. "Hold on…" He rushed to the wall and grabbed his handgun and rifle.

Kahali just Called. We'll be going into a battle. Grab my hand and stay close so I can shield us all.

Before he could radio back Neviah and Zach, she had star beamed Eka and him to a steeply banked area. As Bleu stumbled on the uneven slope, bullets and rocks zinged the trees around them, showering them with splinters.

Kalakanya shrieked and fell over, sparking a shield as she fell. Bleu grabbed her as Eka tossed up a shield around the three of them.

"Are you hit?" Bleu pulled Kalakanya toward him, horrified at how limp she felt. Blood poured from her shoulder. More from her arm. "Oh, *shast.*"

Her head lolled against his chest.

"Hey. I got you." Yeah, he did. But he lacked a first aid kit and had nothing to use as a bandage. He pressed his gloved hands to her wound. She was the healer, not him. "Eka, what do we do? Can you see past this tornado of rocks?"

It's Kahali. He's trying to keep the humans away without hurting them.

"This is him?" A huge rock flew by and splintered the tree beside them, covering them with wood shards.

I've gotta help him. Can you get Kalakanya behind there? Eka, still pale and trembling from whatever he had experienced in the helicopter, pointed toward a large boulder. His gaze fell on Bleu's rifle. *If she can't shield…* He grimaced and pressed his lips together, unable to speak the only remaining option.

"I got it," Bleu yelled, shielding Kalakanya as another tree split and rained down upon them.

May the One In All keep you safe. Eka wobbled into the worst of the fray, taking his shield with him.

Coughing from the flying dirt, snow, and wood dust, Bleu carried Kalakanya toward the boulder. The crunch of footsteps surrounded him. Either people were running toward the light from their star beaming arrival, or they were escaping the flying rocks. Either way, chances were they weren't friendly.

He spun, searching for cover. A foot tripped him. As he hit the ground, a boot smashed into his chest, knocking the wind out of him and flipping him over. He lost his grip on Kalakanya. She rolled downhill as he twisted to face his attackers.

A bright blue light swept toward him. As it contacted his hip, ribbons of electric pain shot through his entire body. He couldn't think. Couldn't move except to twist and writhe. Screams tore from his throat. Endless pain wracked every fiber of him, threatening to disintegrate him.

"Stop. He's all right. Check her." The footsteps receded.

A second later, the pain evaporated. Gasping, he searched the smoke and crashing branches for her.

Kalakanya? He feared speaking would redraw the men's attention. *Kalakanya!*

A few meters downhill, a cluster of armed humans surrounded someone. The blue light of their horrible weapon glinted.

"Leave her alone!"

But Kalakanya's scream drowned out his shout. He struggled to his feet, but before he could reach them, another scream pierced the air. Rage curdled his blood.

"Good thing she's old and already injured. None of the light crap that other one's doing. Get her good, Jinhai."

Kalakanya's screams turned to weak moans.

Bleu reached toward his hip, but his hand fumbled at his empty holster. His handgun was gone. He spun, searching the ground for where he must have dropped the rifle when they were attacked.

Only rocks and splintered tree bits littered the ground. Both guns were gone. *Please... stop...* she mentally screamed through the pandemonium. They were going to kill her.

Bleu stumbled toward the three men who snickered over her writhing body. He had wanted to meet other humans his whole life, and now he only wanted these new men dead. Fury raged through his veins, and he charged the broad one leaning over and electrocuting her.

Bleu smashed his shoulder into the big guy. The oaf fell onto Kalakanya, dropping the still activated weapon onto the foot of a younger man with long locs. The loc man jerked from the electricity and fell.

The third man turned and pointed his gun at Bleu's head. "You're supposed to be clear, boy. What's your problem?" He was too close to miss. He sniffed and shook back his long, stringy gray hair.

Bleu froze, his gaze locked on Kalakanya's body. She shifted slightly, and he exhaled. She was still alive. Every cell in his body wanted to crawl to her, but the cold gun barrel pressed against his temple kept him frozen in place.

The older man followed his gaze. "Well, lookey here, Jinhai. He *likes* the monster."

The large man Bleu had knocked over—Jinhai—now rose, glared at him, and rummaged through his backpack while the old guy kept his gun pressed to Bleu's skull.

The man with long locs hissed as he shoved the electric blue weapon off himself. He grasped the safe end and turned it off. "I should kill you for that, you damn fool."

"He may be a fool, but he's human fool." Jinhai grinned at Bleu and pulled out an ugly yellow metallic collar from his pack. "Unlike this one..." He gestured toward Kalakanya.

Before Bleu understood, the man snapped the collar around Kalakanya's neck and touched his wrist. The collar glowed, making Kalakanya groan.

Bleu?

"What are you doing to her? Take that off. She's a human being, not a beast!"

"That's where you're wrong, boy," the gray-haired one jeered. "Man, she really got you good, didn't she?"

They jeered at Bleu as he rushed to Kalakanya's side. The necklace was warm and hummed as he ran his fingers around it, seeking the clasp.

"Don't worry." Jinhai chuckled. "I have a daughter that's a real human. She's looking for a man. A real man. A human."

"You're sick." Bleu's chest constricted as he realized he couldn't undo the collar. It was somehow locked, probably by the thing on Jinhai's wrist.

As his fingers continued searching the collar, Kalakanya's eyes fluttered open and met his. Their usual clarity had been replaced with a terrifying dullness. *Bleu, what...? I can't...* Her eyes rolled upward, and she went limp in his arms.

"What is this doing to her?" he shouted.

"Why do you even care? You're free now." The gray-haired man lowered his gun but didn't put it away. "It keeps us safe from their powers. You'll feel better soon." He stepped closer and leaned in a bit. "Odd, though." His lip curled in disgust. "Her face stayed young but her hair's still white."

"She *is* young, you *shast* fool. And she'd going to die young if you don't take this off her. She needs to heal herself." Bleu took off his coat, removed his inner lighter jacket, and pressed it to her wound, ignoring the bitter wind that cut into him.

Eka? Can you hear me? We need you. Eka...

Eka didn't respond.

Bleu begged the men, "Help me. She's bleeding too much."

Jinhai shrugged. "We kill them after the tests anyways."

Bleu's mouth dropped open in shock. "You...what?"

Jinhai gave Bleu another disbelieving look and turned toward the older armed man with gray hair. "Jeb, keep an eye on them. I'm going to go finish off the violent one." He nodded toward where the rocks spun in a constant orbit around Kahali.

Cold sweat dripped down Bleu's back. Where was Eka? And Savas, Atsushi, Girak and Rana? He searched the mountainside and, finding no hidden teammates, reassessed his older guard. He had to do something. And quickly.

Chapter 46

Mountainside, Eastern Coast of North America: Bleu Reinier

Bleu tied his jacket as tightly as he could manage over Kalakanya's shoulder wound to slow her bleeding. It was as useless a bandage as he'd feared. Her pallor terrified him. He stood, careful to make his step toward the older guard, Jeb, appear natural. Close enough to reach him, if it weren't for his gun. He assessed his chances of escaping the guard and stopping the others from killing Kahali.

"I see what you're thinking." Jeb chuckled. "But I got a gun, and you're gonna only get hurt. You're safe now, kid. Relax." Jeb took a step closer to Kalakanya and eyed her suspiciously, as if she might spring up and murder him.

"You don't understand," Bleu said. Could he talk some sense into him? Otherwise, the next time Jeb looked away, he wouldn't know what had hit him. "We're from Northern Haven. We came looking for other humans. We're not the enemy."

"Northern Haven, eh?" Jeb laughed. "In my dreams, maybe. I nearly believed the SHAST radio signal you sent out, but you've lost all credibility by hanging with the likes of her. Her kind has killed nearly everyone I've known—thousands of innocent people. Damned monsters." At that, he turned toward Kalakanya and spit on her.

Enraged, Bleu sprang at him. The guy spun and twisted like a snake, and Bleu overshot and crashed to the ground. The gun went off, exploding snow millimeters from Bleu's boots.

"I don't want to hurt you, so cut it out." He aimed the gun at Bleu's chest.

Angry curses in Standard and shouts in star being tongue came from the direction of the flying rocks. Bleu's gaze darted from the gun's barrel to Kalakanya and then checked over his shoulder. Kahali still managed to protect himself and Savas at the heart of the tornado. Bleu couldn't just stand here. He had to risk that this old man had enough sense not to kill the first human he spoke to from Northern Haven.

"Look." He held up his hands. "I *am* from Northern Haven. We flew here in helicopters, and we put out the correct radio signal of a SHAST haven to let you know we were honoring the SHAST code, even though we're days from Western Haven."

At this, the older man's eyes widened in surprise, but then he glanced down at Kalakanya and his suspicion returned.

"I have no weapons. If you don't want to hurt me, then don't shoot. But if you must watch me, you'll have to follow. I'm not standing here and watching humans attack each other. There's few enough of us as it is."

He made sincere eye contact with the man, willing him to believe him. Then, in the most nonthreatening manner he could muster, he lifted Kalakanya and hurried toward the swirling tornado. He half-expected a bullet between his shoulder blades, but instead Jeb cursed and followed.

Bleu, leave me. His running had pained her awake. Her eyelids opened slowly, as if they weighed too much to lift. *Help the others.*

"I'm not leaving you." His voice broke. "Never."

But she had passed out again.

Behind him, Jeb had growled threateningly at his words to Kalakanya. He turned to face him. The terror in the old man's eyes made him pause.

Jeb stared at the collar on Kalakanya with terror. "She shouldn't be able to telepath with that on. It's impossible."

"She's a living impossibility." Bleu leaned against a tree, panting. He assessed how best to keep her alive while helping Kahali. Poor Kahali wobbled beside Savas and couldn't possibly keep this up much longer. He needed immediate help, but Bleu was loathe to put Kalakanya down to intervene in the madness of his rock tornado. He muttered to Jeb, "And if she dies, I will personally—" What? He'd dishonor everything she had taught him by killing the man? Of course, he'd *want* to, but would he actually do it?

Her face was so pale and slack. The possibility of losing her forever sent spasms through him. Images of the black man—him?—screaming for his family began to tumble, unbidden, into his mind. *Not now.* He needed to act, not have a *shast* vision.

A rock crashed the tree above.

"Move!" Jeb yanked him out of the way.

Bleu fell on his side, trying not to crush Kalakanya.

"Open your damn eyes, son, or that bastard is gonna kill us all."

"No. He's spinning the rocks around him to keep you away. If he wanted to kill you, he would have a long time ago. I told you, they're nonviolent."

Jeb snorted. But he narrowed his gaze at Kahali's storm. "You're right. He's not hitting anyone unless they walk into the storm."

"Told you. Now get this thing off her neck."

"No. This must be some new trickery." Jeb stared at Kalakanya as if she puzzled him. "Why's her hair white? I've never seen one like that."

But before Bleu could answer him, Jeb shouted, "Good luck!"

Confused, Bleu followed Jeb's grin. Two armed men—Jinhai, who had collared Kalakanya, and another—crawled on their bellies beneath the swirling stones toward Kahali and Savas. "They'll stop 'em," Jeb muttered confidently. He acted as if they fought star beings like this every day and it was almost fun.

Bleu winced at his callousness. Kahali and Savas would be killed. Kahali's tornado of rocks protected them, but it wasn't weapon-proof shield. And were the others—Atsushi, Girak, and Rana—already dead?

Keep it with you always....

Confused, he looked at Kalakanya, but she appeared unconscious. Wait. Those were the words she had spoken when she'd given him the bone dagger, now hidden in his parka. He tapped his coat to make sure the men hadn't removed it when they had taken his guns. The familiar lump lit an ember of hope in his chest. Hopeful, he wrapped an arm around Kalakanya and began crawling his way after the two men.

Jeb grabbed his leg. "Hold on, kid. We fight Ruined all the time. I don't want you getting yourself killed."

They called the star beings Ruined? Rocks flew over Bleu's head. He twisted on the ground to face Jeb and snarled through his teeth. "Your teammates aren't thinking. They're going to kill people who are trying to avoid hurting them."

Jeb again glanced at Kahali, then at Kalakanya. "I think she's still controlling you, even with the collar. Come on, kid, back out of that storm," he said, clearly not wanting to follow Bleu into it.

He had to somehow stop the men trying to shoot Kahali. He drew in his leg back and kicked violently at Jeb, freeing himself, and then quickly shimmied forward on the snow, out of the older guy's reach.

Don't hit me, Kahali. Kahali, I'm coming... Bleu had little hope that Kahali would hear him since Eka hadn't, but anything that might increase his chances was worth the try. He slid forward on his belly, pulling Kalakanya behind him.

"He'll kill you," Jeb shouted, then followed.

Shast. The old guy would follow him even if he believed it meant death? Just his luck. He crawled on, wishing a stray rock would knock out their stalker.

As he crept closer, sticking to the cover of bushes as much as possible, he reached a more level section of the mountainside. Most of it was within range of the rock storm whirling overhead, and the evergreen trees lay broken or smashed, their splinters and needles covering the frozen ground. About forty meters in front of him, Kahali and Savas stood at the center of the rock tornado. Off to Bleu's right, across the ice and parallel to where he wiggled on the crusty snow, he spotted his missing teammates. Despite the rocks' velocity, they miraculously swerved around Eka, Rana, and Atsushi.

Eka's shield around Rana and Atsushi provided additional protection from the rocks and kept away the Western Haveners. Rana lay unconscious, a whimpering, drunk-looking Digga standing at her side. Dazed and pale, Atsushi stared at the whirling mayhem around them.

A few meters beyond the shield, three strange men surrounded Girak, staying close to him to avoid being smashed by the flying rocks. Somehow, Kahali's storm was avoiding his friends. Two other men, the two that had passed Bleu and Jeb, were ahead of Bleu and attempting to reach Kahali and Savas. And behind Bleu slid Jeb, refusing to let Bleu and Kalakanya out of his sight.

Additional men could be heard shouting around them in all directions. They were outnumbered and had no guns. Even if Bleu reached the two men, his dagger wouldn't be enough to stop both of them.

The three crouching men near Girak disarmed him. At their prodding, he groggily rolled and awakened. Girak raised his head, and his hood fell back around his shoulders.

"Whoa. Look at that red hair! The stuff of legends, that."

"He's been unconscious, so he's clear." The young guy bent and, pushing his locs out of his face, plucked a small arrow from Girak's shoulder. "Damn, he's a *real human*." The guy grinned a bit maniacally.

"*Finally*, some good luck, eh, Obi?" The gruff man in a cloak chuckled as the younger one continued examining Girak. "Help him up," he commanded the men crouched near Girak. "It's our lucky day. Real humans and captured Ruined."

"Of *course* he's a real human," Bleu shouted. "Stop attacking us. We're not the enemy."

The men who bothered to look in his direction only shook their heads in pity, as if he were the crazy one. What the *shast* had they thought Girak was? These men made no sense. Why would Western Haveners attack his team? He looked back over at Rana and Atsushi, still within Eka's shield. Atsushi struggled to keep his eyes open and had an identical arrow protruding from his thigh. Rana, face first in the snow, had three in her back. Eka gingerly pulled them out while holding the shield.

They must have been ambushed, and only Kahali's hyped-up sense of danger had kept him and Savas, who must have been the closest, safe. Why was that jerk always so lucky?

The young Obi followed the cloaked man's order and pulled Girak up into a sitting position, grinning at him like he was a living miracle.

Apparently, the guy wearing a cloak commanded him and the others. Bleu memorized their leader's brown-bearded face.

As Bleu crawled to a bush closer to the eye of the storm, another group took out electric-blue weapons and approached the far edge of Kahali's tornado, coming at him from behind.

His heart fell. They weren't going to get out of this. His dagger was useless against so many armed men.

And Kahali looked like hell—pale, sweaty, and wobbling in place. Like he had literally poured his life into the storm that railed around him. It was all that stood between the men and him and Savas.

Every time Eka tried to move forward to help Kahali, they fired at him, and he couldn't carry both Rana and Atsushi and shield at the same time. He, too, looked awful. More of his hair was white, and he barely stood upright.

Bleu, even with his concussion, was in the best shape to fight. Except maybe Savas, whose mouth dripped blood. They couldn't win by force, but the Western Haveners didn't seem open to reason. He had to do something, but he counted twelve armed men and heard shouts in the woods around him. What could he do without deserting Kalakanya and with only a dagger as a weapon?

Kahali began to sway and then fell to his knees. The rocks crashed to the ground, throwing up chunks of ice and snow in all directions. Savas held his rifle ready, but they were surrounded.

Now or never. He was going to get them both shot. But sitting here doing nothing would result in all the star beings getting killed.

"One In All," he whispered, "I don't know you, but she does. Now would be a great time to at least keep her safe, okay?"

He ran forward, bush to bush, half-carrying, half-pulling her behind him. Others pointed him out, shouting and raising their guns.

"He's human. She's collared. I got 'em," Jeb yelled back.

Bleu had no plan, but closer to his friends seemed better, so hoping Jeb had meant that he still wouldn't shoot, he continued to hurry towards Kahali and Savas.

"Stop." Jeb had easily overtaken him and this time took aim at Kalakanya. "You're the stubbornest ass I ever met." He smiled, fine wrinkles spreading across his face. "I like that. But if you move a muscle, she loses her head. Understand?"

Bleu froze, Kalakanya limp in his arms. "Yes."

"Good. Glad we have that understanding. I hate to waste another human. But I have no problem killing one of them. She's collared, so drop her." He motioned to the ground, as if she were a backpack Bleu could just drop.

He carefully placed her on the ice but then stubbornly glared at Jeb. "I'm not leaving her." It was useless, but he couldn't just abandon her, injured and collared.

"Come with me, or I'll kill her, and then you'll stop worrying about the damned monster. What the hell did she do to twist you up so much?"

"I lo—" his eyes widened at what he had nearly blurted out. "She's my friend, and she'd never hurt anyone."

The old man shook his head in disbelief. Or maybe pity? "Move." He shoved Bleu toward the others. Bleu stepped away from the bushes and toward the group of armed men surrounding Kahali and Savas.

As the distance between him and Kalakanya stretched wider, his panic grew. "Do you treat all newcomers like this?"

Jeb laughed. "Newcomers? Ha. We never had real newcomers. Ever." He eyed Bleu up and down, evaluating him against some measure Bleu could only imagine. He grinned, clearly pleased with whatever he assessed.

"Let them go," Bleu said as he pointed to Savas and Kahali. The men were closing in on them, guns raised. For some reason, they seemed loathe to approach Kahali. "They're no danger to you."

Savas, overhearing Bleu, turned and grimaced. "Nice rescue."

Bleu managed a sarcastic smirk. "And I see your diplomacy is as effective as ever."

The men watched their exchange with interest, muttering to each other.

"They ambushed us," Savas snarled.

Bleu nodded. Their argument had distracted the other humans from their advance. Could they keep it up?

"So, your scanning equipment worked just like you designed it to, eh?" Bleu cocked an eyebrow, hoping Savas would catch on.

"No, it didn't. But your lovely star being friends were just as useless."

Hey, Kahali managed.

"Enough of this," their leader shouted. "Take that *thing*"—he pointed his rifle at Kahali—"down."

"Dead or hostage, Ferenk?" one of the men asked their leader.

"Whatever works," Ferenk responded, as if Kahali were an insect that had gotten in his way.

"We're out of drug darts, sir. I say we kill him while he's weak. There's no way we should risk collaring a conscious Ruined."

Bleu tried again. "He's not dangerous. They're all nonviolent. Can you stop a moment and hear me out?"

Their leader, Ferenk, ignored him. Instead, he eyed Kahali and then the shield containing Rana and Eka. "Don't know that we can handle three more anyways. The rock thrower isn't in the light thingy, so he's easier to collar and take alive, though he's already been a real pain in the ass." He sighed. "Let's just shoot him."

The advancing men all raised their rifles at Kahali.

Kahali sparked a pale, flickering shield, so small it only surrounded himself.

Ferenk growled in frustration. "What the hell is this new light trick? Men, use the sticks to destroy the shield, then take him down."

Half the men lowered their rifles and pulled out electric stick weapons. They continued their advance. Given Kahali's current state, Bleu didn't think his shield would last long if they fried it with those weapons from multiple points.

"Now, come on," Savas said to the humans closing in on them. "You've already tested me."

"Right. But with his creepy eyes and rock-throwing, we know he's one of *them.* Step away or face the same fate."

To his credit, Savas stayed put.

"Okay, this is stupid. You didn't shock them." Savas pointed to Rana and Atsushi. "How did they pass your test?"

Most of the men glared at him as if they couldn't fathom how he could ask such a thing. From beside him, Jeb sighed. "What the hell did they do to all of you? The ones that passed were unconscious and stayed human. The kid and the redhead passed. The one with the creature under her is clearly Ruined. She didn't even attempt to hide it from you. And the male holding the light shield around her is as well." He paused, then turned to Ferenk. "We have another two collars, right, Ferenk? She's going to wake up soon."

"Yeah," Ferenk, said, nodding.

"So, if they're unconscious, you deem them safe?" Savas turned and gave Kahali an appraising look. "If Kahali is unconscious, you'll let him live?"

"For now," Ferenk said, glaring at the rocks Kahali had just dropped. "But it's not worth the risk long-term with the Ruined."

"Ruined?" Savas smirked. "Missing an arm, yeah. But he certainly gave all of you a run for your money."

Bleu narrowed his eyes at Savas. Something had changed. He was playing them, like the day he had played Kahali, tricking him into practicing his new skill. But why would he defend Kahali from humans he had spent a lifetime looking for?

"Here's the thing," Savas continued. "He's not going to be conscious much longer. No need to waste a bullet. I'll ensure his safety right now." He clicked his safety and spun his rifle so that the butt of it faced Kahali like a club.

"Savas, what are you doing?" Bleu yelled. "Stop it." His muscles tensed with fury, but he was afraid if he moved, Jeb would turn back and kill Kalakanya where they'd left her lying on the snow.

Savas tilted his head at Kahali. "Trust me, kid. This will hurt less."

"You won't get through his shield. He'll kill you," a man warned.

"Savas," Bleu warned. "What are you doing?"

"No, I can get through it. I know the trick. I'm not a danger, because I'm saving his life."

Savas, stop. Kahali wobbled, and the shield grew a bit stronger. *I saved you!*

"I know." Savas said. And then he walked straight through the shield. "Remember when I said sometimes violence is good? Well, now it's going to save your life."

Kahali raised his arm, eyes wide in terror, as Savas raised the rifle over his head.

Please, Kahali begged.

Savas smacked the butt of the rifle into his skull. Kahali hit the ice face first.

"Savas!" Bleu yelled.

"You monster!" Eka roared.

Savas shook his head at them and addressed the human leader. "Come on. Check whatever you check. He's fine, and he's going home with us. Alive."

Savas threw Bleu a smug look.

Savas didn't understand. They wouldn't just check Kahali like they'd checked Girak. They'd collar him like they had Kalakanya. And then kill him.

Chapter 47

Mountainside, Eastern Coast of North America: Bleu Reinier

Bleu tensed to lunge forward to Kahali's defense, but Jeb's grip on his shoulder tightened. This was all going horribly wrong. The Western Haveners surrounded Savas and him, and the other human Northern Haveners were drugged. Kahali lay unconscious as Ferenk limped toward him, electric-blue stick in one hand, a collar in another. The horrible *thunk* of Savas smacking Kahali's skull still echoed in Bleu's head.

Bleu shrugged off Jeb and ran to intercept. "Stop. Don't put that on him. Wait. Just listen to me."

Ferenk ignored him, but Savas finally took notice of the hatred in their leader's expression. As the other men rushed forward and restrained Bleu, Ferenk bent to snap the collar around Kahali's throat.

"Hold up." Savas grabbed Ferenk's arm, stopping him. "We don't collar our allies."

"Well, your *allies* have hunted my people for generations. We don't tolerate them." He opened the collar and glared at Savas. "If you want to argue, I'm sure my men wouldn't mind shooting you. As exciting as new humans are, you're worthless if you come with more Ruined to slaughter us."

"Jeb." Bleu struggled to pull free, but the three men holding him had iron grips. "Tell them what I showed you. You saw it."

Jeb shook his head and remained silent.

Savas was going to get himself killed, but again, to Bleu's amazement, he stood his ground. Eyeing the rifles now aimed at him, Savas said, "I told you, I vouch for him."

"And you think I'll take your word over the experience of watching thousands of my people die? This," Ferenk said as he held up the collar, "is the only way to deal with them."

The men grunted in agreement.

A flash of golden-red wings above the treetops caught Bleu's eye. The eagle dove down in a blur and tore the collar from Ferenk's hand. The talons sliced his fingers, and blood ran down his fingers. The men began yelling and firing, but the massive bird flashed through the sky like lightning and sped out of range as quickly as it appeared.

"It's an attack! Get in formation." Ferenk yelled more orders.

The men panicked, as if the eagle were evil incarnate. What the *shast* were they so scared of?

The men around Girak argued briefly, and then one handed Girak back his gun. "Shoot first. Question what you see later."

"I don't understand..." Girak began.

The men dragged Girak into the tight circle that surrounded Ferenk, Savas, and Kahali as he lay unconscious on the ground.

In their hurry to join their leader, the three men holding Bleu released him, yelling at him to follow them. Taking advantage of the chaos, Bleu instead raced toward Eka's shield. Had Rana summoned the bird? Could she do that?

He slid into Eka's shield and turned to thank Rana. But she still sat dazed from the three darts.

"Eka, did you do that? The bird?" Bleu asked, panting.

Eka, wide-eyed himself, only shook his head.

A shrill and horrible screech rolled down the mountain like an avalanche, pinning them in place with terror. The animalistic shriek rose and fell, turning Bleu's intestines to liquid. It sounded like what had surrounded their camp last night. Everyone inside the shield—Eka, Rana, Atsushi, and himself—turned toward the peak.

"What the *shast*?" Bleu muttered. The woods had grown eerily still except for the clicking sounds of the men readying their guns.

Atsushi stepped backward, tripping over Bleu's boots. "That doesn't sound...normal. Rana?"

I have no idea, she responded.

Not exactly the reassurance Bleu had hoped for. From far off, the eagle screamed.

"Crap," Ferenk said, "we've got at least two."

"If it's a whole clan, we're dead," someone warned.

"Not yet." Ferenk rechecked his gun.

"You guys know what this is all about?" Bleu asked the others inside Eka's shield.

But their baffled faces and fearful glances told him they were all as much in the dark as he was.

Another howl rang through the woods, ending in an impossibly deep, throaty growl. A second later, another scream—almost human-like—came from directly behind them. Bleu spun but again saw nothing. "Ferenk. What is it?"

"Your fucking allies."

Rana and Eka exchanged a silent look.

Bleu recognized the covert mind speaking. "Talk to me, guys," he whispered. "What are you not telling me?"

Rana's eyes were wide. *That is not a star being. I don't know what he thinks we are, but that's not...* She shook her head.

The cacophony came from all sides now, growing closer, and then stopped as quickly as it had begun. The malevolent silence loomed over them like a storm about to break. A twig broke to Bleu's left, and a few men fired at a shadowy shape that dove behind a tree.

"What was that?" Bleu hissed.

Rana closed her eyes and teetered. For a moment, Bleu thought she'd been hit by more darts, but she was trying some sort of mental star being thing. Maybe some communication with whatever creature stalked them? Eka tried to enlarge the shield toward the men, but their gunfire stopped him. Atsushi pulled a gun from his pocket.

"How did you get that? Give that to me!" Bleu demanded.

Atsushi's shaky grip on the gun tightened. He cast Bleu a guilty look and switched off the safety like an expert.

"Nooooo!"

Bleu spun. A massive white blur sprang from behind a wide tree and plucked one of Ferenk's men from the formation. The man yelped as the bearlike blur yanked him away. Gunfire filled the air.

"It's the White Bear!" someone shouted. A ripple of terror spread through the Western Haveners.

"Stay together. Don't break rank," Ferenk yelled.

The white shape, too large to completely hide behind the massive evergreens, dodged bullets as if it were dancing. Bleu's jaw dropped. *No animal moved like that.* It snapped the stolen man's neck like a twig, dropped him to the ground, and roared in fury.

Bleu reeled back, tripping someone—Rana—as she attempted to stand. She trembled, shaking herself as if she were covered with bugs.

Stay inside the shield, Eka warned, sounding shocked. *This is like the weird predator I saw in my dream.*

Bleu, where's Kalakanya?

"Back there." Bleu pointed along the slope, but he couldn't see her lying anywhere. "We need to get her. Now."

Bleu prepared to dash from the shield's safety toward Kalakanya when a gray-and-white leopard-like creature appeared, stopping him in his tracks. It circled them in flying leaps off the trees, bouncing on the ground to rise again with incredible nimbleness. Its slashing daggers clawed down another two men.

Eka glanced between the carnage and where Bleu had left Kalakanya. *We need to help them first.*

"No," Bleu insisted. "She's not conscious. She can't defend herself."

Doubt clouded Eka's face, and then it hardened. *I'm sorry, but they are dying right now.*

Eka took a step toward the besieged men, forcing the others to follow to stay inside the shield.

Ferenk's men struggled to stay back-to-back, but their circle grew smaller with every attack. The man with the long locs dove to the ground, barely escaping as the shadowy, leopard-like creature dove down from the trees. He fell, rolling away from his peers.

The eagle returned, diving for loc man.

"Obi, watch out!" someone shouted to him. Obi stood and raised his arm. The eagle's talons grabbed him, slicing his arm to shreds while the beak tore through his thick fur hat.

Bleu grabbed Atsushi's gun and jumped out of the shield, shooting at the enormous bird. Rana raced forward and pulled the flailing guy into Eka's shield.

Obi fell to the ground at Rana's feet, losing his hat, and stared up at Rana and Eka, frozen with terror.

Stay inside the shield, and you'll be safe, she commanded. She held out her hand to help him stand.

He shrank from her, nearly pushing Bleu outside the luminous shield. Bleu side-stepped and pulled the guy more toward the center of them.

Eka hurried toward the circle of beleaguered men.

Move together, Rana mind yelled.

"No. Kalakanya!" Bleu ran to the backside of the shield, searching for her. She had been just past this point. A small bloody patch marked the snow where she had lain. "Kalakanya's been moved. We have to find her."

She'll be okay, but these humans won't last long. Eka's doubt was gone.

How could he choose these strangers over her? "No, they collared her," Bleu hollered. "She's dying!"

Eka stopped heading toward the humans, a pained expression on his face. *Rana, can you shield?*

She grimaced in exaggerated concentration. A flash of a shield appeared above her head and then flickered out. *Not yet. The dart stuff.* Tears of frustration filled her eyes.

Another scream rented the air, and blood tinged the leopard's hide.

"Please, Eka." Bleu pulled Eka toward where Kalakanya had last been.

Eka shrugged Bleu off. *They don't know she's there. I'm saving these people.*

"They want to kill you!" Bleu yelled. "You can't bring them inside your shield."

Eka growled in frustration and continued toward the besieged men. *Kahali, Girak, and Savas are in the middle of that mess. If the men want to live, they'll join us as well.*

Rana, Atsushi, Bleu, and the rescued man had no choice but to move along with him or be exposed. Each step took Bleu farther from Kalakanya. He considered running back on his own, but Eka was right. He'd only alert the predators that someone else was back there. Even so, each step pained him.

Kalakanya? Can you hear me?

No familiar lilting voice came to him. Only gunfire and screams of death answered.

"No!" Savas shouted.

Bleu snapped back to the battle. The monstrous eagle dove straight for Savas and Kahali. The raptor's size and speed froze Bleu in place.

Eka grabbed his arm and yanked him along. *Bleu, terror solves nothing. Your friends need you. Now.*

The massive eagle screeched and grasped Kahali in its talons as its wings hit Savas and the other men surrounding him.

It was as if Eka had channeled Kalakanya. Bleu's mind cleared, and new strength surged through him. The cold metal of Atsushi's gun pulsed in Bleu's hands.

"Get as close as you can to them," Bleu yelled to Eka as he stepped outside the shield and took aim. He shot a few bullets, but the raptor seemed to anticipate him and launched upward. It struggled to lift the limp Kahali while the men fought it.

Savas, too close to use his rifle, grabbed Kahali's wooden arm from his pack as the eagle lifted Kahali into the air. Savas slammed the wooden arm against the bird's head, and the eagle floundered and dipped. Girak grabbed Kahali's leg and pulled downward with all his might. As Savas again clubbed the bird, it released Kahali with an un-bird-like screech. It soared upward into the sky on unsteady wings. Bleu fired his last bullet. Screaming, it plummeted into the treetops.

At the eagle's scream, the other two creatures evaporated into the trees as if they had become part of the tangled forest themselves. Shivering, Bleu ran back toward where he had last seen Kalakanya.

"Bleu," Atsushi yelled after him, but Bleu couldn't wait. The creatures had retreated, and this might be his only chance. Stumbling over the uneven, steeped ground, he backtracked, resisting calling out to her in case the creatures returned.

Heart pounding, he stumbled up the mountainside. He passed more and more thorny bushes but couldn't find her. The tightness in his chest grew. Had the creatures taken her like they'd tried to take Kahali?

He scanned one more time. Her pale leather boot, nearly matching the snow, protruded from behind a wide trunk. Had he really left her that far from the others, or had she tried to crawl to safety?

"Kalakanya?" With stinging eyes, he raced toward her. She lay crumpled, unnaturally, as if dropped in a hurry. Blood soaked the ground under her shoulder.

Had she been moved? Was this a trap? He scanned the trees, but everything was still and quiet except for the injured men below on the ridge.

He fell to his knees beside her and pulled off his glove. Holding his fingers to her nostrils, he waited. He prayed for breath. Waited. A slight warmth brushed his fingers.

"Oh, thank you!" He scooped her up as carefully as he dared, scanned the surrounding hillside, and stumbled across the rock-strewn slope.

"Can you save her?" a young child's voice called out to him.

Bleu stiffened and turned. A small, brown-haired girl with green eyes stood a few meters from him. She looked up at him with a tremulous smile. Impossible. Where had she come from? No other humans protected her.

"Can you?" Her innocent eyes filled with worry. "She's bleeding a lot."

Was he imagining this girl? "I hope so," he answered.

"But she's not like us." The girl took a step closer. "She's one of them. You should kill her." Her head tilted, awaiting his reply.

But instead of replying, he scanned the trees for the creatures. "You better come with me. Those things might return any minute."

"What things?" Her little lips curled upward in a smile.

The hairs on Bleu's neck rose. If she were with Ferenk, surely she'd fear those creatures. But she didn't. He noticed blood dripping from her hip and took a step backward, wishing he had a free hand to access Atsushi's gun. But he didn't have any more bullets for Atsushi's gun.

Kalakanya murmured something in pain.

"Whatever those things were that just attacked us." He tried to fight the fear building in him. It was just a kid. A lost human child. "Didn't you see them?"

A slow smile spread over her face. Her face morphed to take on feature after feature, melting and swirling.

"What the—"

The thing sprang toward him with outstretched hands that shifted to claws.

He fell backward, and someone stepped up beside him.

Begone!

A golden shield lit between Bleu and the creature, now a huge, snarling black leopard. It fell back, growling. Bleu looked up.

Eka's eyes smoldered with warning. *We mean you no harm. We are not with those others.*

The leopard's eyes held an intelligence and hatred that made Bleu lightheaded. A throaty snarl came from the creature as it changed into the vague height and facial shape of a livid male star being with short, wavy black hair. The unnaturalness of such wrath on the face of a star being scared Bleu more than anything he had seen that day. Only Eka's thin, shimmering shield protected them.

We are not your enemy, Eka continued, the voice of reason in an insane world. *We desire peace. We are not with those other humans.*

No, but you're protecting him. The imposing creature pointed an accusing finger at Bleu and growled. *What's wrong with you?* His lips pulled back in a snarl as he glowered at Eka.

Despite the feral creature's towering height and bulging muscles, Eka stood his ground. After what seemed an inordinate amount of time, the thing walked right up to the shield and flared his nostrils, sniffing them like a wolf. Ignoring Bleu, he gave Eka a death glare and said, *You will submit to your Hakan, or he will slaughter you as a traitor.*

I don't know what you're talking about, Eka said. *I've never heard of Hakan, but I'm certainly not a traitor. I never betray my friends.*

The creature's jaw ticked with fury. Bleu could feel the powerful rage rolling off him. *You betray your people.*

He glared at Bleu again, studied the shield as if he had all the time in the world, and then grunted as if it wasn't worth the effort. Fearless, he turned his back on them, took a few steps, and merged into the trees.

Bleu couldn't stop his trembling. "Eka? Did that thing just mind talk? Like...like a star being?" Was Ferenk right?

"Yes." Eka had spoken. As if he, too, were too horrified to answer Bleu in mind speak.

"Can it be...? You know, a star being?"

Eka narrowed his eyes at the spot where the thing had disappeared. *It's a good thing Kalakanya managed to Call me, or you'd both be dead.*

Chapter 48

Mountainside, Eastern Coast of North America:
Rana of Peleguin Rookery

Exhaustion filled Rana. Only adrenaline maintained her shield around Digga, Atsushi, the terrified human she'd rescued from the giant eagle, and herself. Eka and Bleu still hadn't returned. She hadn't glimpsed Kahali since the eagle had dropped him between Girak and Savas in the midst of the hostile men. But the eagle had seemed bent on killing. She prayed that its attack on Kahali meant he was still alive. That Girak was now watching out for him.

She had to believe that. The alternative was unthinkable. Rana stroked Digga, murmuring that they were now safe as she squinted at the two figures climbing down the hillside toward them. With the sun setting behind them, they were only dark silhouettes, but she'd recognize Eka's tall frame and flowing mantle of black hair in any light. The one beside him had to be Bleu, carrying a limp Kalakanya.

Eka's golden shield surrounded the three of them, and he checked frequently over his shoulder. Her heart skittered as she scanned the hillside behind them and the branches above them for danger. Those strange creatures had been such rapid predators that her body tensed at every waving branch or turn of a leaf.

Kalakanya's crumpled body lolled with Bleu's steps, but he placed his feet carefully to prevent jostling her. She must still live.

If only Rana could reach Kahali and check, but the Western Haveners weren't exactly going to let her cross the clearing and join them. She remained in place, barely managing the shield and hoping those horrid predators stayed away.

No sign of the rabid creatures remained except for the horror of the dead men the creatures had yanked from the armed formation. Perhaps Kahali, having been unconscious through the attack, was the lucky one. No, she couldn't think like that if she wanted to Crown. It was better to know. She had to believe that, despite the horror clawing its way up her throat.

"You're safe, Obi. She's not one of those things, I promise," Atsushi said to the injured stranger, trying to calm him.

Rana resisted turning because every glance she stole sent the guy into a ridiculous puddle of fright. How in the world could these humans confuse those creatures with star beings?

As Eka and Bleu hiked back down to their level, Ferenk fired a warning shot at their feet. "Hold up. We don't know who you are."

"What?" Bleu fumed.

"We need to test you again, or you will be allowed nowhere near my men." Ferenk stepped forward with a strange electric blue stick.

"Oh." Bleu rolled his eyes in disgust. "This has got to stop."

"There were at least three of them. Now you appear, the three of you walking right up to us. How stupid do I look?"

Eka and Bleu looked at each other as if debating this.

I understand now that they can change appearance, so I respect your fear, Eka said. *But I will not allow you to hurt us. How else can we prove our safety?*

"You speak just like them," Ferenk snarled. "Into our minds."

Because if I speak my native tongue, you would not understand a word I said. All animals understand mind talk, so it's not that unusual that they also seek to communicate that way.

Ferenk muttered something over his shoulder, and several men stepped forward, guns raised. "You stole my last collar, so I'm not taking hostages."

Eka just raised an eyebrow.

Yes, the three of them were still inside his shield, but Rana's heart thudded at the threat.

We stole nothing, Eka stated. *How else can we prove our safety?*

"There is no other way, and you know it."

Rana couldn't hold her shield much longer, especially if she tried to mind talk at the same time. She called out to Eka in their native tongue, "Eka, you need to take over here. If you walk through my shield, after they cleared me and I saved this man of theirs,"—she motioned to the injured man beside Atsushi—"wouldn't that prove something?"

At the sound of her language, the strange humans grew extra attentive.

Eka gave her a nod and then spoke to Ferenk. *These creatures can look like anything. Can they also create light shields like we do? Can they heal?*

Ferenk narrowed his gaze. "I have never seen them do such things, but that is not proof enough for us to risk our lives."

Would they help you? Rana—Eka pointed her out—*left the safety of my shield during the attack and saved your friend. He now sits protected within her shield. I will heal him to prove my safety. Then, after I attend to Kalakanya, we will help anyone who's injured.*

The man behind Rana shrank into an even tighter ball, wrapping his good arm around his bent legs. She squinted at his trembling hand. Pink scars covered the dark skin of his hand, and the last two fingers were missing. This was not the first time he'd been violently attacked, and he looked only a few summers older than her. The poor thing quaked like a dried leaf in a windstorm. Rana smiled encouragingly at him.

He only widened his eyes at her teeth.

Seriously? Humans smiled with their mouths open. She pressed her lips together. How was everything she did so terrifying? Didn't he grasp she had saved his life?

"They won't hurt you. I promise," Atsushi reassured him. "See? She's still protecting us with her shield."

The guy looked anything but reassured.

Eka gave her a worried smile as he and Bleu entered her shield.

"Good luck with that one," she whispered as he passed her and knelt beside the injured human to start healing him.

Ferenk grunted, hooked the lightning weapon onto his belt, and aimed his gun as he walked closer. He had a slight limp, but it wasn't clear if he'd just been injured or he had an old injury. Keen interest gleamed in his eyes though his grip on his gun remained tight.

It's okay. I'm just going to touch your arm. With great care, Eka placed his fingers on the injured man's trembling forearm. His jacket was torn and bloodied from where the eagle's talons had sliced him. The injury was hidden below the shredded layers, but as Eka worked, the man stopped hyperventilating. His shoulders began to relax.

The man's eyes widened, and he blinked up at Eka with wonder. "How?"

Eka grinned. *I can't see the injury, but I suspect if you slip your arm out of your jacket, it will be only a slight scratch. Now, on to your shoulder. That okay?*

The man looked at Ferenk for approval.

Ferenk only narrowed his gaze at the wound, his gun still ready, despite Rana's shield.

"Yeah…" the injured man murmured, "go ahead."

Eka put his palm on his shoulder, and a slight pink glow emanated from his hand.

Still wide-eyed, the man kept careful watch of Eka's hands. The guy's hard face softened until Digga stood and ambled over, sniffing to see what Eka was doing. The guy jerked backward. "Get that thing away from me!"

She's a cave digger, and she's only curious to meet you, Rana said.

"She's not natural. I've never seen an animal even remotely like her," he groused.

Digga, come over here with me, Rana said. *Where we come from, they're quite common.* She conveniently left out the part about them being super dangerous.

As Digga waddled over to Rana and lay down, the man relaxed, closed his eyes, and let out a deep sigh. "It's so warm and tingly…like magic." After a few moments, the man slipped his arm out of his coat and studied it, amazed at Eka's work. "You really *can* heal."

"Or," Ferenk said, "there's more than four Ruined present, and you're not really Obi."

The young man looked offended. "Of course, I'm Obi."

"Prove it." Ferenk's eyes narrowed as he pointed his gun at Obi.

"Do you spend every minute torturing each other with that hell stick?" Bleu asked. "Eka couldn't have entered Rana's shield if he meant her harm. Shields keep out anything ill-intentioned against the shield's creator."

Ferenk glanced over his shoulder toward Savas. "That's what he said."

And note all three of us walked into her shield without an issue, Eka added.

"She did get hit with three darts, Ferenk," Obi added. "And she still looked just like this when she was unconscious. She doesn't hide who she is from them. That alone seems odd for a Ruined to do around humans."

Ferenk glared at them, seeking a problem with their logic. "Prove what you say about those shields."

Rana grunted her frustration. "Eka, can you?"

He nodded, and his own stronger golden shield suddenly surrounded them all. She sighed in relief and extinguished hers.

Digga, stay inside the shield.

The pup raised her head from her paws but showed no interest in moving.

Good. Rana took a deep breath and stepped outside the shield. Ferenk backed up and shifted his gun to her.

She looked Ferenk in the eye. *I will trust you, but I would appreciate not being shot. Now, Obi, you walk out. Can you do that?*

The guy nodded, stood, and exited the shield.

See? Rana said. *Now you, Ferenk, try to go in. You still want to take your fury out on them. Try. You won't get in.*

"How stupid do you think I am?"

If I were one of those creatures, I would have killed you ten times over by now. Try to enter...

"Absolutely not."

But Rana was prepared for that response. She'd spent time with prideful human males like him, namely Savas. *You're afraid? It won't hurt you.*

Ferenk glared.

Rana reconsidered her challenge. The guy had a gun. What was she doing?

"If it rejects me, what happens?"

Rana furrowed her brow. Having never experienced it, she wasn't sure how to answer.

She turned toward Savas and mind spoke in a way they could all hear. *Savas? Can you and Girak bring Kahali over? He needs healing, and Ferenk would probably like to see more of that. Right, Ferenk? And on your way, please, share with him how it feels to not be allowed to enter a shield. Being a nonviolent star being*—she paused and made eye contact with Ferenk to highlight her point—*I've never been repulsed by a shield.*

Savas snickered. "It's nothing like your hell stick, Ferenk. It'll just bounce you backward." He and Girak had stepped from the circle of men and began walking toward Rana, carrying Kahali between them.

Rana gasped at Kahali's paleness. But she had to focus; she had to get them all to safety.

She tore her gaze from Kahali and addressed Ferenk. *See? The shield will not harm you, just repel you because you'd like to hurt us. If you wish harm to anyone in the shield, you can't enter. Eka had no trouble entering with your man, Obi, already inside. That shows we mean you and your men no harm. Try it. Try to enter.*

"No." Ferenk stepped closer to Kahali and shook his head. "Even though that one didn't shift into an animal, he's clearly Ruined, regardless of what the rest of you are. He looks like them and moves stones like them." As Savas and Girak carried Kahali past, he spat on him.

Rana's hands fisted at her side, but she couldn't risk escalating the situation. She had to get Kahali safely inside Eka's shield. She just prayed Savas could enter.

Girak glared at Ferenk's spittle. "Someday, when you look back at this, your own ignorance will horrify you."

Ferenk snorted in derision and held up his hand. All the men pointed their rifles at Kahali. "You really think I'd let you revive him? If he's somehow damaged and can't shift, he may prove useful to study. But to let him go free and be at full strength? Never. He attacked us." He turned back to his men and snapped his fingers. "Bind him."

Chapter 49

Mountainside, Eastern Coast of North America:
Rana of Peleguin Rookery

At Ferenk's command to restrain Kahali, fury surged through Rana. Two men came forward with metal gadgets and cautiously approached her unconscious friend. Savas and Girak exchanged a mutinous look, but Rana was done with this insanity. No one would treat Kahali like that.

As she stepped forward, she garnered all her anger and frustration to flare a shield, pushing Ferenk back and surrounding Kahali, Girak, and Savas before anyone could get a shot off. The men fired, but her shield held. They were safe.

"Finally." Girak grinned at her and Savas. "We've become a fully operational team."

Relief flooded her. She nodded, trying to avoid mind talk again. Shielding took priority.

Savas looked grim. "Yeah, but we've alienated the only humans we've found and made enemies of those creatures."

Girak nodded and whispered to Rana, "I hope you meant it when you said I could live at your village, because I don't think Western Haven is going to work out."

Despite the bullets bouncing off her shield, she chuckled.

As Ferenk realized his men were wasting ammunition, he called them off, and everyone glared at each other.

"Well, this is fun." Girak said. "Can we all just agree today has been one massive misunderstanding and go home?"

"My dead men are a misunderstanding?" Ferenk yelled.

Girak walked to the edge of the shield and looked Ferenk in the face. "Of course not. I meant the idea that our star being teammates are killers. *That* is the misunderstanding."

They glowered at each other. Human males did this a lot, and Rana had never quite gotten the point.

She turned back to Kahali. Poor, dear Kahali lay pale and crumpled, bleeding from his temple. He had the most precarious energy she'd ever seen in a star being.

"Kahali?" she whispered. Every part of her being yearned to help him...

"Rana," Savas growled. "The shield is flickering."

She snapped her attention back to protecting them.

"Rana, we need you," Bleu called.

She turned to see him pointing at Kalakanya. He needed to relax. She would be fine. Crowned Ones always were, unless they were killed instantly.

"Time to move again, Girak." Savas had followed her gaze and had again grasped Kahali under his shoulders. "Grab his legs."

They shuffled past a few more trees and glaring men to fuse her shield with Eka's. Digga rushed her, weaving between her legs and making happy grunts.

Eka flashed her a grin. "That was a bit daft going out there. But it worked brilliantly."

"Daft?" she retorted. The others would have no idea what the two of them were joking about.

"Yup. Brilliantly daft. You got them all back." He flashed her one of his gorgeous smiles.

For a moment, she forgot they were surrounded by humans and guns. Would she ever get that kiss he'd promised?

Bleu tugged at her sleeve. "Guys, Kalakanya. Please."

Bleu, she won't die. You know that, right?

But his panicked eyes and desperate motioning toward Kalakanya said he hadn't known.

She's healing herself right now, not really sleeping. It's how Crowned Ones do it.

"No, you're wrong." He bent and shifted her cloak. "They put this collar on her. They said it would limit her from using her powers."

What? Rana paled at sight of the horrid collar. The metal fit tightly against her skin, and a sickly yellow light glowed from it.

I thought you took it off, Eka said, kneeling to investigate the ugly yellow thing. *When I found you, I couldn't see it.* He touched it and yanked back his hands as if on fire.

"No." Bleu's eyes were panicked. "Now that we're all together, can't one of you shield and the other heal her?"

Eka shook out his hands and shot Rana a startled look. *I can't touch her near it without feeling ill.*

I can try. She bent and touched Kalakanya's shoulder. A horrible vibration ran up her fingers and into her arms, paining her. "Ow!" She jerked backward, flapping her hands to relieve the sensation.

"What do we do?" Bleu looked from one to the other.

Girak leaned in to study the collar. "Hmm. Is your healing like electricity?"

Rana and Eka stared at him, unsure how to translate that.

"Like lightning?" Girak asked.

Rana grimaced and shook her head. *No. That would cause pain.*

Girak shook his head. "No. No. No. I mean, can it travel through things? Like, it can travel through clothing, right?"

Yes? She had no idea where he was going with this.

"Let's try this." Girak put his hands on Kalakanya's wound. "Now you put the healing through me."

She furrowed her brow. *Thet collar's energy doesn't hurt you?*

"No." Girak said, looking a bit embarrassed. "We're definitely not as finely tuned to energy as you are."

Eka frowned, but Rana saw where he was going. *Okay. Eka, you keep shielding. We'll figure this out.* She stood behind Girak and put her hands on his shoulders. *Let me know if this is too much.*

"Whoa." Girak's shoulders stiffened.

Rana pulled her hands back. *Sorry.*

"No, I just wasn't expecting that. I'm fine. Go ahead."

With a worried glance in Kahali's direction, Rana began again. As she worked, Bleu hovered nearby, making her nervous. *Bleu, can you check on Kahali? See if you can wake him up, will you? He's been out a long time...*

Bleu nodded and left. Savas and Eka were talking to Ferenk through the shield. At least they weren't yelling, and no more shots had been fired.

Atsushi, always practical, dug through his pack for food. He pulled out something and turned to her. "Want some?"

Think I'll need to wait. But water would be great.

"You need water?" a strange voice asked.

She turned her head. The guy she had saved from the eagle—Obi, was it?—watched her and Atsushi.

"You need water to clean her wound?" Obi asked.

Rana nodded, afraid she'd freak him out if she mind spoke or smiled.

"I'll be right back." He left.

Looking Kalakanya over, Rana let out a long sigh. She was pretty sure she'd stopped the internal bleeding, but she'd never worked through a human before. *You still okay, Girak?*

He nodded but said nothing. She stopped her healing and watched him wobble a bit in place.

He turned to her. "I'm okay." But his words were slurred and his eyes were dazed.

I think you need a break. Go check on Bleu and Kahali, will you? Maybe Bleu would let me work through him since he's so eager to help?

Girak rose slowly and shuffled off toward Bleu and Kahali. His energy drunkenness from taking in more energy than he was used to reminded her of how Eka had described Bleu and Neviah getting sick from entering the activated Lion's Circle their first day at the village. She'd have to be more careful.

A moment later, Bleu crouched by her side, absently stroking Digga's head. The guy wasn't thinking. The humans did not just absently stroke Digga without asking, but thank the One In All, Digga was still drugged and tolerated it.

How's Kahali? she asked Bleu.

"I cleaned his scalp wound with water, and I tried to wake him. He groaned but didn't quite get his eyes open. Anything else I should do?"

No, I need you here. Hold on... She looked over her shoulder, directing her mind talk to Girak. *Girak, can you wrap some ice on a cloth and put it on Kahali's head wound?*

"Okay." He nodded and slowly began chopping some ice off the ground with his knife.

Obi ran up to the outside edge of Eka's shield. He held out a water skin, remarkably like the ones star beings made. These new humans possessed survival skills the Northern Haveners hadn't yet begun to grasp.

"I got you water." Obi remained outside the shield, shifting from foot to foot. The men behind him shouted insults at him. "Uhm. How do I give this to you?" He eyed the shimmering shield between them.

Pass it through.

Eyes wide, he took a step sideways so he was in front of Bleu and thrust the bottle toward him, not her. So, he wanted to help, but she still scared him? At least he no longer shook at the mere sight of her.

Bleu narrowed his gaze at the water bottle and then at the angry men. He handed it back to Obi. "Drink some first."

"Geez, nobody trusts me today." Obi, flushed with anger, pulled out the bone cork and took a swig, swallowing with gusto. "Still alive. So, we good?" He held it toward Bleu again.

"Yeah, thanks." Bleu accepted it and handed it to her. "Sorry about not trusting you."

Obi grinned. "No worries. I'd have done the same."

The guy was honest. That was always a refreshing trait in humans.

While Rana cleaned Kalakanya's wounds as well as she could, the men continued to taunt Obi from their position along the ridge.

"Are you going to be safe with them?" Bleu asked, motioning toward the men.

Obi pointed at the water bottle Rana still held. "I'm going to definitely get the stick for that." He shrugged as if trying to make light of it, but his fear wafted through the shield. "But you two saved me, and that other one fixed my arm. I don't know what you all are, but I can't believe you're working with the Ruined."

"Thanks for the trust."

"Oh, I wouldn't go that far." He laughed. "But despite the way they're acting"—he motioned to the jeering men—"we're all really excited to meet more humans."

Rana glanced from him to the angry armed men. If they deserted these guys out here, would they survive another attack from those predators without the star beings' shields? But for them all to get back to camp together, Rana and the others needed their trust. All her dart-addled brain could come up with to improve relations was learning to pronounce his name.

"Obi?" This time she smiled without teeth. Not that there was anything wrong with her teeth. Just to play it safe.

His eyebrows popped up, and he laughed. "Ah, yeah, you got it." He almost grinned. "So, if you're not Ruined, what are you? 'Cause you certainly look Ruined..."

I'm ruined?

Despite the insult, Rana laughed, and Obi took a step backward. She shut her mouth to keep from scaring him.

"We call them that because they look beautiful outside. They use that to lure you in. But inside, they're evil and ruined."

Beside her, Bleu shivered. "Like the little girl that appeared to Eka and me."

Obi nodded. "They have all sorts of tricks. But their base form is like you." He motioned to her.

"But what are they, really?" Bleu asked.

Obi shrugged. "We've cut a few up after they're dead. Look pretty close to humans on the inside. Taller, with faces like theirs." He motioned toward Rana. "We thought at first it was illusions, like wicked tech or something. But it's not. All we've found to get them back to their true form is electricity or being unconscious. Or dead." He chuckled. "That works best. They really are monsters."

That is...repulsive.

"Obi, shut up. Get back with the others." Ferenk had appeared beside him. "We're going to let these crazy Northern Haveners go back to their camp. And we're going to follow them. Watch them. And not tell them anything they can use against us, got it?"

Obi nodded. Rana and Bleu exchanged a concerned look. What had Savas told him to earn their free pass back to camp?

"And before we follow them, we're checking you." Ferenk's hand rested on the lightning weapon hanging from his belt. "Don't think I forgot how quickly you healed."

Obi nodded again, keeping his eyes on the ground. "Yes, sir."

Rana wanted to shield the guy, but that would only make his fellow humans trust him even less.

"You could come with us," Bleu offered. Was he being so kind because Obi was a fellow human, or had he changed that much since hunting the Crowned Ones?

"You're *not* stealing my men. Obi will stay with us because he's one of us."

Bleu shot Obi a sympathetic look, but he looked away. His fear had increased.

Rana couldn't think of anything that would convince Ferenk to not test Obi. "One In All, protect him," she murmured.

"Give the kid back his water skin." Ferenk glared at her.

Rana thrust the empty bottle through the shield and dropped it. She pulled her arm back inside before Ferenk got too close.

"And drop your damn shield," Ferenk added. "No crazy stuff. Walk in front of us, and no one gets hurt. It's getting dark, and your damn light shields will be visible for kilometers. No use broadcasting our location to the Ruined."

She scoffed. It'd be foolish to travel without shields. *They already know where we are.*

"Not if we get moving," Ferenk grumbled. "Didn't you notice that they left after several of them got injured? We need to leave this area before they return."

Chapter 50

Mountainside, Eastern Coast of North America:
Rana of Peleguin Rookery

Rana stood inside Eka's shield with her friends, while outside it the Western Haveners prepared to move down the mountain side. She gave Bleu an alarmed look, worried that Ferenk and Savas had reached an agreement without including Bleu. And why would they not use their shields? Surely the Ruined knew where they were going, as it certainly seemed like they were the creatures who had threatened them the night before. *You should have been included in that decision*, she sent to Bleu.

Bleu nodded and grimaced at Ferenk's back as the older man walked away. She disliked this Ferenk as much as she distrusted Savas and wasn't about to follow their orders without good reason.

If Savas agreed to it, I'm concerned. Maybe go check on that? she suggested.

Suspicion masked Bleu's face as Savas exited Eka's shield and laughed with the rowdy men. "He probably just sold us as slaves."

Despite Savas' smiles and jokes, his right hand was never far from his holster. Apparently, he didn't feel confident in his plan, either.

Slaves? Rana asked Bleu.

Bleu waved his hand in the air as if erasing her question. "Forget it."

Turning back to Kalakanya, he touched her hand. "She's freezing." He took off his coat and tucked it around her, pausing a moment to touch her cheek. He stiffened, and then looked up at Rana. "Is she...?"

Rana knelt and touched Kalakanya's cheek. Her skin was too cold, even for this weather. Swallowing her rising panic, she strained to remember what Desna had taught her about injured animals. Something about blood loss and shock, but she had no idea what would help. She had never seen a Crowned One die. Not slowly like this. It didn't happen. They self-healed.

Bleu stared at her, wide-eyed. "Will she be okay? This is all *my fault*. I should have protected her better after she star beamed in." He sucked in a shaky breath. "Tell me what to do for her."

Rana wanted to reassure him, but between not being able to work on Kalakanya directly and the fact that they now had to somehow move her back to camp, she wasn't sure how much she *could* reassure him.

I don't know. If we could get this collar off, I'd trust her healing abilities, but with it on... She bit her lower lip. *Perhaps the real question is, are any of us going to make it back to the camp? Why would they decide now to let us walk away?*

"Right. I need to figure that out." He studied Kalakanya as if he wouldn't see her again and then sighed. "Alright, I'll go deal with Savas and Ferenk. Can you keep her alive and figure out a way to carry her? I know you can't touch her directly, but..." He looked around the forest. "Maybe we can make a stretcher from tree boughs?" Bleu scowled and shook his head. "I don't like this. I'm sure the Ruined can follow us even without shields. It's a huge risk to not use them." From where he crouched beside Kalakanya, he again scanned the trees, then turned to Eka and her. "Do your best to keep up the shield. I'm going to talk some sense into them."

Rana gave him a grateful smile. *Thanks. Eka will be on guard, and I'll figure out a way to carry them.* She glanced over at the armed Western Haveners, and noticed that as Bleu did as well, his hand fell to his gun. Anyone's hands on a gun made her nervous, but Bleu would need some sort of protection to be taken seriously by those desperate men.

With both Kahali and Kalakanya unconscious, they needed not only two stretchers but a whole lot of luck. Because if the angry, hating humans didn't shoot them, they still had to avoid those other creatures.

Creatures, not Ruined. Nothing the One In All created was truly ruined, right? Though if they were as disconnected from the web of life as the humans were and had such strength and fighting capacities...that possibility terrified her.

Bleu placed his palm on Kalakanya's chest and whispered into her ear. He stood, and his face had hardened into fierce determination. "Keep her alive. I'll deal with them." He strode out of her shield, calling to Savas.

Ferenk's men watched him approach like hungry lions watching a peleguin. But she had Kalakanya and Kahali to worry about.

Girak. Atsushi. Can you see if there's any extra clothing or blankets in the packs? We need to keep these two warm.

Atsushi nodded and shoved the food wrapper from his snack into his pocket. He sprang to his feet and nearly tripped on Digga, who had raced toward him at the sound of the wrapper. "Hey, should I feed Digga?"

Rana groaned and rubbed her face. She couldn't even remember to feed her charge, and she expected to Crown? Kalakanya's advice echoed in her mind. She didn't need to check off every perfect behavior and capability to Crown. She could do this. *If you could feed her, that would be great. There's dried meat and a water bowl in my pack. Put it down and walk away. Don't go near the food after you put it down. Understand?*

He nodded. "Consider it done. Is Kahali going to be okay?"

She smiled and nodded, because she wouldn't consider the other possibility.

Girak tapped her arm. "I think Kahali is waking up. Maybe it'd be better if he saw you rather than me?"

Rana ran over and knelt beside him. "Kahali? Can you hear me?"

His eyelids fluttered but remained shut.

She leaned over him and whispered, "Hey, I need you to wake up. Kahali, wake up. It's me, Rana."

His eyes strained open, and he stared straight up at the sky and tree limbs.

She removed her glove and put her palm to his cheek, gently moving his face toward hers. "I'm over here."

He blinked a few times, and his entire body went rigid. "Where? Did I hurt anyone?"

She shook her head, smiling. "No, you did really well."

Atsushi knelt beside them with extra clothing. His face lit up to see Kahali awake. "Hey, you okay? I told Savas to go find your arm."

Fear clouded Kahali's eyes and he bolted up, raising his good arm in front of him. At the sight of it, he sighed with relief.

"Sorry." Atsushi clasped his face with his palm. "I shouldn't have said it like that." He held out his collected goods to Rana. "This is all I could find."

He placed a hat and scarf and a strange blanket-like thing that crinkled to the touch on the ground beside him.

What's this? She touched the creepy material. It was the most unnatural concoction she had seen thus far.

"Neviah told me to pack this. It's a heating blanket." He shifted it around until he found a gray portion. "Press this and it will warm the whole thing up. It's supposed to last twelve hours between charging." He grinned, obviously proud of it.

"Kahali, put these on. You need to stay warm." She handed the hat and scarf to him, but he just blinked. "On second thought, just stay put."

She handed the hat and scarf back to Atsushi. "Help him. I need to take this to Kalakanya. She's not looking too good."

From behind them, Ferenk's voice cut across the clearing. "Let's get it over with, Obi. We do this side of the stick to avoid the other."

What? Rana stood to see Ferenk pointing to where the oldest man knelt over the dead men and used the other end of the electric stick to burn their faces black. The smell made Rana want to retch. Why was he burning the faces of the dead? At a gurgle of pain, Rana turned, scanning the circle of men. Obi spasmed on the ground in the middle of the circle while one of Ferenk's men held the horrible blue lightning stick to him. He jerked, his body flopping. As Obi jerked, the men pointed their rifles at him, apparently waiting for him to reveal himself as a creature pretending to be Obi.

"Stop!" Rana yelled, somehow remembering the human word. It tasted strange on her tongue and must have rang just as oddly in the humans' ears. All the men except Obi and his torturer turned to her.

"Well, look who speaks Standard." Ferenk smirked.

How can you do that to your own friend?

"He would never forgive me if I let his fake self in to kill us all." Ferenk waved his hand to the man hurting Obi.

The man turned his stick off and extended his hand to pull Obi to his shaky feet. "Sorry, man."

Obi and his torturer exchanged a look, and with dawning horror Rana realized Ferenk had spoken the truth about Obi agreeing to the necessity of the test.

I could have made a shield. It would have been a painless test.

"Once that method is fully field tested, yes. But it's too risky right now. Besides, we can't make shields, and despite what your commander says, I don't trust you."

Commander? Oh no. He had looked at *Savas*. They thought Savas was in charge.

Chapter 51

*Mountainside, Eastern Coast of North America:
Rana of Peleguin Rookery*

When Ferenk referred to Savas as their commander, Rana filled with horror. Why would he think Savas was in charge? Her gaze darted to Bleu, who now stood with Savas amongst the Western Haveners.

Bleu gave her the tiniest of nods. He wasn't going to correct Ferenk?

"I told you, they don't like violence." Savas, standing among the new humans, grinned and pointed at her. "See? Rana couldn't tolerate you testing Obi. They're different than your Ruined."

Ferenk snorted, clearly unimpressed.

"Remember, she saved Obi from them," Bleu added. "We may as well shield as we travel. With this many people, they'll easily track us, and besides, the Ruined already know where our camp is. They attempted to infiltrate it last night."

The new humans erupted in a clamor of horror.

Ferenk held up his hand for silence. "First of all, if you don't know how to cover your tracks, you won't survive long out here. And how do you know they tried to infiltrate your camp? I find it hard to believe you would have survived such an infiltration, seeing you knew nothing of their true nature until we told you."

"Rana, explain the Digga incident." Savas gave her an intense, purposeful look, but she wasn't clear what he intended by it.

Yes, but first I must put this on Kalakanya. She held up the distasteful, crinkly blanket. *And if we are leaving, someone needs to make stretchers for the injured. How many do you have over there?*

Ferenk opened his mouth to speak and shut it again. Turning to the man beside him, Ferenk exchanged whispers with his man, never taking his eyes off her. What had she done?

Eka stifled his smile. *I think he's speechless. Didn't expect you to care about the wounded.*

Seriously?

On the bright side, they're easy to impress.

She snorted and hurried to Kalakanya. Searching the weird shiny cloth for the gray portion, she pushed the button like Atsushi had shown her. A slight vibration emanated from the crinkly sheet, the sort of vibration so soft that humans wouldn't notice. But between that and the collar, would Kalakanya be able to stand it?

"Kalakanya? Can you hear me?" She gently touched her good shoulder, ignoring the pain that shot up her arm from the collar. "Can you hear me?"

Kalakanya opened her eyes and met her gaze with dilated eyes that stared through her.

Can you hear me? You've been shot.

The Crowned One continued her unfixed gaze.

Rana shivered. This wasn't good. She had no idea if she understood or not. It was always better to assume she'd heard and talk through it with the injured. She clearly remembered that from Desna's lessons.

You lost a lot of blood, and you're too cold. I'm going to use this human thing to warm you up. It sort of vibrates. I'm sorry, but it's the best I can do right now. Hang in there, okay? Bleu's trying to convince them to take that collar off.

Her pupils focused. *Off. Pleeeease.* The desperation was clear.

It's locked. We need the strange humans to take it off. They think you are dangerous. Bleu is talking to them now.

Bleu... Then she lost consciousness again.

Was she delirious? Why was she calling out for Bleu? *I'm wrapping you in this. It'll keep you warm.*

"How is she?" Bleu reappeared by Rana's side. Ferenk and Obi followed him but stopped outside of the shield.

Not great. She asked for the collar to be removed.

"Of course, she did. They all hate it." Ferenk glared down at her coldly.

"You've seen her unconscious. You've tested me. You know Rana saved Obi's life. Take it off her, please?" Bleu begged. "She's not a Ruined. I promise, you'll like her."

From what Rana had seen of the man, she thought that last bit might be going a bit far. He didn't like anyone.

"From what Commander Savas said"—Ferenk chuckled to himself—"this one's a pain in the ass."

Fury coursed through Rana. She forced herself to suck in a deep breath and release it. To calm. She radiated peace toward Ferenk and Obi. Bleu shot her a grateful glance.

"Explain me this," Ferenk said. "What's up with the young face and white hair? Seems a bit trickish. The Ruined specialize in their damn tricks."

Bleu gave his best explanation of Crowning, and Rana did her best to not show her amusement. It wasn't a bad description, given it came from a human, only he made them all sound like perfect celestial beings. Having been raised with them, she knew how far from the truth that was. Sometimes they were downright annoying with all their knowing.

"So, this one's the most powerful of the four, eh?" Ferenk tapped his gun like he wanted to shoot Kalakanya immediately.

"None of them are dangerous. You're killing her. Please. Remove it." Desperation played across Bleu's face. "Look, you could still place guards between her and your men. You don't have to totally trust me. Just don't kill her before she has the chance to show you who she really is."

"You're smitten." Ferenk cast Bleu a look of disgust. "I saw you with her earlier. Commander Savas!" He motioned to Savas, who said something to the guy nearest him and strolled over.

"How is she, Bleu?" Savas gave Bleu an odd look.

Again, Rana had no idea what to think. Whose side was he on?

"She's going to die if they don't take their *shast* collar off."

"Hmm." Savas glanced at his wrist, as if considering his device that blocked the star beings, then looked out at the trees and seemed to think better of it.

Rana sighed. Bleu was letting Savas play commander. What was wrong with him?

Bleu looked pointedly at her. *If I don't play his game, he might kill her just to spite me.*

Bleu had learned to mind speak? Or had she just read his thoughts? *What?*

Bleu gave her a frustrated look, like he had failed at his attempt to covertly communicate. *Play along. Please, hear me...play along.*

Savas was watching them. She wanted to believe he'd protect his own team but didn't trust him. She cleared her throat and busied herself tucking the blanket around Kalakanya.

"Ferenk," Savas said, "we have two helicopters that could take you and your people away from these Ruined. Do you know what helicopters are?"

"Flying machines?" Obi asked, breathless.

"Yes," Savas continued. "But we can't take people who will not cooperate with us."

Obi grinned broadly, obviously thrilled. Ferenk remained stoic.

"This star being"—Savas pointed at Kalakanya—"saved all our lives at our last stop. Actually, they all did. We work as a team. To be our allies and have us take you with us back to Northern Haven, you must accept our star being teammates."

Rana's mouth opened in shock, and she turned her head to hide it. Savas was playing it both ways. Playing commander but helping? Why?

"Miguel! Cheeks!" Ferenk snapped his fingers.

Two of the scariest men rushed over, guns drawn. The younger one—Cheeks—was the only Western Havener Rana had seen that didn't have a beard.

"If she does anything remotely threatening, you kill her. Got it?"

They nodded.

"Hold on." Bleu stood. "No killing. You shoot her again, and you have no chance at being our allies. You'll never get on our helicopters."

Ferenk shook his head. "You agreed to having guards. Is your word no good?" He looked from Bleu to Savas.

Be ready to shield her if necessary. The thought was clear and crisp, and definitely from Savas.

Rana jerked her gaze upward, just catching Savas as he adjusted his sleeve. Bleu glared at Ferenk, clearly not having heard it.

Was that you? She sent to just Savas.

Without looking in her direction, his lips curled briefly upward. Not in a friendly acknowledgement but as if turning his wristband on and off was a noteworthy accomplishment. But she'd take it. She'd accept any help that kept them safe.

Without missing a beat, Savas waved away Ferenk's accusation. "Of course, our word is good. I understand your need to protect your men. But if your men overreact and kill her, you will stay here, hunted by Ruined. You've got nowhere else to run. They've chased you out of Western Haven and all the way across North America. The Atlantic Ocean is over those mountains. You've run out of options."

Ferenk's men had grown quiet and wandered closer to hear.

"If we can learn to get along, we can answer each other's prayers. We came looking for survivors, and you need help."

"You take us all," Ferenk said, "or the collar remains."

Look, Rana interrupted. *If you have a lot more humans in hiding, those waiting for transport while we fly over the first group will need star beings to shield them. And she's the best. You need her.*

"*You* would shield *us*?" Ferenk looked dumbstruck. Eka was right. They were easy to impress.

I already have. Right Obi?

Obi grinned and nodded, but at Ferenk's glare, he sobered up.

"I better not regret this." He turned back to Savas. "I have your word that you will help us all?"

"Just to be clear," Bleu interrupted, "how many are we talking?" His eyes shone with excitement, not worry.

Ferenk's face darkened as he glanced back at the dead men. "After today, thirty-two. Including the kids."

Rana knew that many might fit in one trip, but she prayed Bleu and Savas were smart enough not to let on to that fact. They needed to give good reason to save Kalakanya.

"It's a deal." Bleu said, holding out his hand to shake.

Ferenk looked from Bleu's hand to Savas, clearly confused by the offer coming from Bleu.

"It's his first mission as commander." Savas smirked. "I'm supervising him his first time out."

Bleu bristled, then chuckled. It rang hollow and painful in Rana's ears.

"Deal." Ferenk grasped Bleu's hand. "But if any of you cross me, I'm holding you all accountable. Jinhai, remove her collar."

A broad-shouldered man stepped forward, grimacing, as if he strongly disagreed with Ferenk.

Instead of being angry, Ferenk said, "This means your daughter could live without being hunted. We'll have a chance."

Jinhai muttered what sounded like a curse and then pulled up his sleeve and fiddled with something he wore. It looked a bit like Savas' gadget that blocked his thoughts. Moments later, the collar's lights dimmed and it snapped open. Cautiously, Jinhai approached Kalakanya, removed it, and shoved it into an inner pocket.

Bleu heaved a huge sigh of relief. "Thank you."

Ferenk pointed over to Kahali, whose expression was a shifting, grim mask of disgust and fear. "And keep that one under control, or we'll kill him regardless of your promises of safety."

Chapter 52

Mountainside, Eastern Coast of North America: Bleu Reinier

As they quietly hiked down the mountain toward camp, pride filled Bleu. His team cooperated as one, with even Savas helping out. Eka and Girak carried Kahali's stretcher while Rana and Atsushi carried Kalakanya's. Despite carrying Kahali, Eka managed to form a shield around almost the whole group. Bleu didn't understand all the mechanics of how the star being shields worked, but since Eka had formed the shield *around* the Western Haveners, instead of having them walk *into* it, Bleu feared the star beings still risked attacks from Ferenk's men.

He and Savas took up formation on opposite sides of the stretchers, guns drawn and ready. Ferenk had taught them to walk so that everyone stayed within eyeshot of several peers. This reduced the odds of a slick grab-and-replace by the Ruined, a hellish occurrence Bleu never imagined he'd need to worry about.

With all the chaos of meeting the suspicious Western Haveners and the attack, he'd forgotten to ask the Western Haveners if they ever had dealt with the Sickness. What had once been his most important quest now seemed irrelevant. Survival came first.

He had made sure his position in the formation was as close to Kalakanya as possible. The horrible possibility of losing her festered within him, tugging his focus from watching for Ruined in the trees to worrying about her motionless body.

Since the deadly collar had been removed, some color had crept into her cheeks. But her usual radiance remained a memory. When they got her back to camp, they'd have no medics or healers to help.

Tearing his gaze from Kalakanya, he scrutinized the tree line on the hillside around them for movement. Next to him, Atsushi studied Ferenk's men and frowned.

"What's wrong?" Bleu whispered.

Atsushi pulled his gaze from them and gave Bleu a sad look. "Nothing."

"You don't look like it's nothing. Are you okay?"

Atsushi managed a half smile. "I always had this silly hope that maybe the other Havens had...you know, people like me?"

Bleu drew a mental blank, and then it hit him. "Oh." He wasn't sure what to say. "I think the odds of that would be pretty low, but I can understand the wish. Maybe the Southern Haven is in an area that was originally Asian?"

"More likely the Eastern Haven, but all races were mixed in all the Havens, so location wouldn't make a difference, right?" Atsushi sighed and shifted his grasp on Kalakanya's makeshift stretcher.

Bleu didn't have the heart to tell him the Eastern Haven was destroyed by Undescended invaders. Not today, after everything that had already happened, and definitely not in front of the Western Haveners. He went back to scanning the trees for Ruined.

"*Shast.*" Atsushi stumbled on a root and nearly dropped his end of Kalakanya's stretcher.

Bleu echoed his curse.

At the stretcher jerked, Kalakanya awoke and gasped. A strange spark came from her—an ill-imagined shield perhaps? All of Ferenks' men whipped up their rifles in well-practiced defense.

"Stop," Bleu yelled. "She's just trying to shield her fall."

She had already drifted off again, but the alarmed Cheeks and Miguel aimed at her from inside the shield. If they shot, Bleu couldn't protect her. He didn't think the shield would either, since they were all inside it.

He exchanged quick glances with Eka and Rana. Kahali was too dizzy to sit, let alone help them.

Miguel and Cheeks approached either side of her stretcher, studying Kalakanya with skepticism.

"I told you, she's not dangerous." Bleu hurried to her side. "But if we stay out here exposed in the woods, the Ruined might come back. Worry about the real dangers."

"Fine." Miguel turned to Ferenk and raised a questioning eyebrow.

After a moment, Ferenk nodded. Everyone lowered their guns, and Bleu could breathe again. They continued descending the mountainside.

"Sorry," Atsushi whispered as Bleu passed him to return to his spot on the left side of the formation.

"Wasn't on purpose." Bleu gave him a tight smile, the best he could manage at this point. "That was an impressive catch—quite the change."

It was supposed to be a compliment, but Atsushi's face clouded.

"That came out wrong," Bleu apologized. "I meant you're getting really dexterous since you started training with Kahali."

"Hmm." Atsushi nodded. Mischief blossomed in his gaze. "Think Ayanna will notice?"

Bleu snorted. "Just watch out for those roots."

❋ ❋ ❋ ❋ ❋ ❋

As they finally neared the clearing with the helicopters, the sun's lingering rays glared off their polished surfaces, making pools of light between the trees. Murmurs of excitement arose from Ferenk's men. Bleu grinned. Their helicopters must seem nothing short of a miracle to people who had fled the Ruined on foot across the continent.

Miraculous and valuable.

Had the Western Haveners followed them to get flown to safety or to steal their helicopters? Bleu scrutinized Ferenk's men as they murmured in awe amongst themselves. They were scarred, battered, hungry wolves looking at the shiny new helicopters corralled by the mountains and stuffed with food and supplies they desperately needed. Savas and Girak also watched them with pinched smiles. Had they also realized the risk that this could still go very, very badly?

They couldn't steal them on their own. Stamf had explained the implant he, Savas, and Neviah had gotten to connect with the helicopters' computers. Without Savas' and Neviah's cooperation, the helicopters wouldn't fly. As long as these Western Haveners didn't out-tech them, they'd be okay.

But there still remained that other danger. The more pressing fear about the Ruined having infiltrated their camp while they were gone.

"Savas." Bleu got the older man's attention and waited for him to cross over to him.

He hated asking his opinion because Savas would see it as a weakness. But Bleu had cycled through the upcoming danger too many times in his own mind and still had found no solution. Maybe none existed. But Savas was strategic, and he needed to know if he had missed any angles.

"What's up?" Savas spoke to him but kept his gaze wandering over their new supposed friends.

Keeping his voice as low as possible, Bleu murmured, "Have you talked to Neviah or Zach since all this?"

Savas locked his gaze on Bleu's. "No. Have you?" From his grim expression, he shared Bleu's fear.

Bleu shook his head. "Think we should let them know we're coming? Or not, in case it's not really them?"

He hated even having that thought. If they had been killed and replaced with Ruined, the guilt of taking off without them was all his. Zach and Neviah had no idea what preyed in these woods.

"Not sure it matters. We're about on them. If they're Ruined, they'll know we're coming."

"But they don't know how much we know, right? I got the distinct feeling the one Eka and I saw with Kalakanya was testing us. It seemed confused that I was protecting Kalakanya."

"You actually think," Savas sneered, "that those monsters are good?"

Bleu snorted. "No. I saw what they did."

"You left people down there?" Ferenk joined them and motioned to his men to expect trouble.

"Two." Bleu's heart hammered as he pictured Neviah and Zach with no shields, no help, and no idea what was attacking them.

"Idiot." Ferenk shook his head in disbelief. "It'd be a miracle if they survived."

He turned to his men. "Spread the word. They've probably been replaced," he warned them. "The camp's been infiltrated."

"They're resourceful," Savas countered. "They may have survived."

Ferenk shook his head. "You didn't even know what they were. They could have posed as you, returning from your mission, and walked right in. And they're mind readers. They sometimes keep the victims alive to pick their brains on how to react to others when imitating them. You have no idea how dangerous these things are."

Bile rose in Bleu's throat. If that had happened, they hadn't stood a chance. *They have to be okay.*

He turned to Ferenk. "No making assumptions and shooting first. It was my responsibility to keep them safe. I'll take the risk."

He had wanted to be a different type of leader than Savas. One that valued life and cared for his team members. Instead, he'd been a fool and raced off to help half the team while deserting Neviah and Zach without any explanation.

Heart pounding, he led the way from under the tree boughs into the dusky clearing. "Neviah? Zach?"

"Bleu? Is that you?" The closest helicopter door slid open, and Neviah's head and shoulders popped out.

"Would Ruined know how to unlock the doors?" Savas whispered, having followed closely behind Bleu. "Do they have tech? Maybe it's really our people."

Bleu shrugged. He hadn't seen any tech on them, but that didn't rule it out. He took a few steps closer to the helicopter.

"Yeah, it's me. Stay right there." He turned to find Eka and Rana in the shadowed crowd behind him.

"Why'd you say that?" Ferenk hissed. "Now they know you know."

"If it's them, they shouldn't run unarmed across the clearing, right?" Bleu responded a bit too harshly, but he wasn't about to put them in any more danger. All Ferenk ever did was assume the worst.

"Rana. Eka." Bleu hurried back to them. "Can one of you shield everyone here and the other come with me to the helicopter? We need to test them. Make sure they can enter your shield. That work?"

They put down their stretchers and spoke briefly in their native tongue. While they talked, Bleu knelt beside Kalakanya, pulling the heated blanket higher around her shoulders. She looked so vulnerable, so unlike herself. Kahali had awoken but lay staring in Bleu's direction, his expression bleary-eyed and pained.

"We're almost back," Bleu reassured him, but Kahali only continued to stare eerily.

Rana tapped Bleu on the arm. "It's you and me. Let's do this."

As he and Rana moved toward Neviah and Zach, Eka pulsed out a shield around the rest of them. Ferenk's men balked at being enclosed within the shield, but Girak and Savas quieted them down. Unfortunately, the shield also lit their location.

Neviah's and Zach's eyes widened in glee.

"You found them!" They both jumped down from the helicopter.

"Stop!" Bleu commanded. "I told you to stay there."

They froze, Neviah giving a strange, eerie laugh. Zach looked fit to kill. An icy shiver rolled down Bleu's back. Foolishly, he glanced about for signs of a struggle or dead friends. But Ferenk had said they were smart. They would never be that obvious.

Rana sparked a small shield around Bleu and herself, and together they treaded toward their supposed teammates. Each step brought him closer to his sentence—either he was lucky and they had survived, or it was his fault their bodies now lay in the thickening darkness. Did the questioning faces of his friends in front of him truly want to tear him apart?

"What are you protecting yourself from?" Neviah's face, backlit by the helicopter's internal light, was shadowed, but her mockery was clear.

"Bleu," Zach yelled, "put your gun down. What the *shast* is wrong with you?"

Bleu and Rana stopped five strides from where Neviah and Zach stood, Rana's shield shimmering in the light. "Neviah, can you enter the shield?"

"Like, I think I can manage that." She rolled her eyes. She sauntered toward them.

Please, let her be all right.

A moment later she stood beside him inside the shield, giving him the side-eye. "Are you okay?"

He grinned. "Now I am." He threw his arms around her.

She laughed. "Okay. You should go hiking more often. I like this."

Bleu blushed and stepped back. Beside him Rana chuckled.

"Zach, come inside."

"No way. You're acting psycho."

From behind him came the clicks of multiple guns. Zach squinted out into the darkness behind Bleu.

"That's an order, Zach," Bleu yelled. "Now."

"What did you do with Savas? Savas? You out there?" Zach pulled out his gun and gave Bleu a wary glance. "Where is he? What's going on?"

"You can't fire from inside the shields!" Savas' voice rolled up behind Bleu. He must have been warning Ferenk's men.

Suddenly, a group of men, rifles raised, stood side by side with Bleu.

"*Shast.* I just didn't want a bear hug from Bleu." Zach cursed at the rifles pointing at him. With a nervous look at the new men, he dashed into the shield with Bleu. "Keep your reunion joy to yourself, Bleu. It hasn't been that long."

Bleu laughed in relief. "You have no idea how happy I am that you're both okay."

"You think we can't survive a few hours without you?" Zach groused.

"That method has not been fully field tested." Ferenk stood just outside the shield, a small gun pointed at Zach and Neviah.

"You saw the Ruined couldn't get through their shields," Bleu reminded him. "Did anything weird happen here?"

"You mean other than you calling us on the radio and then disappearing? Do you have any idea how freaky that is?" Neviah hit his arm. "Don't ever do that again. We thought you were all dead."

"So, nothing happened?" Savas looked around the camp.

It was pretty dark, but all appeared normal.

"We heard some strange noises coming from the trees, like the other night. Since we no longer had the star beings' shielding, we locked ourselves inside." Zach glanced at Savas as if expecting to be criticized. "With our radios on, in case you needed help."

"Good thinking. That probably saved your lives." Bleu released a huge sigh. "We need to get everyone inside, treat injuries, and get something to eat."

"I find it very odd that they are circling your camp and not attacking. Perhaps it's because you already have four of them among you?" Ferenk glared at Rana and Eka.

Fury shot through Bleu. "That's ridiculous. I've lived in the star being village. They are nothing like those creatures. Maybe they just shift into that form to confuse humans that know how nonviolent star beings are."

Ferenk snorted. "Yeah, they're all friendly 'til they rip your throats out."

Rana grimaced in disgust. Eka actually laughed. It *was* ludicrous. Bleu had to end this now. None of his team members would be insulted by the new people, even if they were the first humans seen, ever.

"Look, they're our friends and allies. If you're staying here tonight, you will treat all of us with respect. Otherwise, leave now." He pointed out into the darkness.

Ferenk's men looked furious and terrified at the thought.

"I'm responsible for keeping my men safe." Ferenk glared back at Bleu, his hand near his sidearm.

Bleu clenched his jaw and met Ferenk's steely gaze. "And I'm responsible for keeping my entire team safe. I know my team, and they're not a safety risk. None of them."

Ferenk glanced toward Savas. Savas gave him a slight nod, and Ferenk sighed. "Fine. Just keep them away from us."

Bleu didn't let up. "That's impossible in a small camp, and you know it. They've shielded you and saved Obi's life. You'll have to accept my expertise on them. Same as I now ask for your expertise on the Ruined." He had to focus Ferenk on their common enemy and keep their fear from driving apart their shaky alliance. "How do you suggest we check the other helicopter? Would the Ruined have gotten in?"

"Was it locked?" Ferenk's tone probably fit their situation, but Bleu couldn't help wondering if he were asking how easy it would be to steal for his people.

He filed that concern away for later. "Neviah? Did you unlock Savas' helicopter?"

She shook her head.

"It's probably fine, but we should check it anyway," Ferenk said, ignoring Bleu's request for the specifics on how to check it.

Ferenk walked over to the open helicopter that Neviah and Zach had exited. He leaned in and whistled in appreciation. He grinned at Bleu and then addressed his men. "These really are fine machines. We found some good allies, eh?"

His men laughed but stayed alert, nervously watching the darkness beyond the light spilling from the open helicopter.

Hold on, Rana interrupted their jokes and nervous banter. *We only have two of us star beings functioning, and I'm pretty tired. There is no way Eka and I can do healing and shield two helicopters all night. Can we all fit into one?*

I second that. Eka set Kahali's stretcher down.

Atsushi and Obi put down Kalakanya's.

"Might be a bit crowded, but we can cram in for the night," Bleu responded.

Oh, thank you! Rana grinned at Obi.

Confused, Bleu squinted at Rana. *Oh.* Obi had carried Kalakanya from the tree line to the helicopter for her.

But Obi was staring past Rana. "Who's that?" he whispered.

Bleu followed his gaze to where Neviah stood and chuckled. "Neviah, come here a minute."

Neviah's face lit at the sound of his voice. "Do I get another hug?" she teased.

"No, I wanted to introduce you to Obi." He waved his hands between the two of them. Obi looked like he had never seen a woman before. "Obi, this is Neviah."

"Wow," he gushed, holding out his hand. "Nice to meet you."

Neviah raised an eyebrow and shook his hand. Then she shot Bleu an accusatory sidelong glance.

"Obi was the first of them to help us, Neviah. Maybe he could help you distribute the first aid stuff?"

"I'd love to help. Put me to work." Obi's smile couldn't get any bigger.

"O-kay." Neviah gave Bleu a look he couldn't quite read.

Was she mad or startled by the sudden attention from a strange human guy? None of them had ever met other humans that they hadn't seen every day in the halls of Northern Haven. Did she not want to hang out with Obi? He seemed fine to Bleu, but she had already scolded him for leaving her alone with Savas. Bleu wasn't an expert, but Obi seemed nothing like the womanizing Savas.

"I'll be right here if you need me, Neviah?" *Shast*, it had come out a question.

She gave him another raised eyebrow, the other one this time.

"Sorry to stare." Obi looked away. I just never thought I'd see another human I didn't already know. And a new woman…" He laughed. "I'll just shut up now."

"Actually, I'm thinking pretty much the same. Thought I was stuck with Bleu forever…" She stuck her tongue out at him and pulled Obi toward the medical supplies. "Come on, I'll show you where everything is."

Girak approached, his lips twitching upward beneath his red mustache. "So, now you're matchmaking?"

Bleu shrugged. "I think it went reasonably well."

Girak nodded, but his eyes darkened. "That's not going to work with the rest of them. We could use their help, but I fear for our star being friends. And I think Savas is up to something."

Bleu's gaze followed Savas and Ferenk as they strolled around the far edge of the helicopter. Conveniently out of sight but still within Eka's shield. "Agreed. I'm just not sure what he's up to."

Chapter 53

Campsite, Eastern Coast of North America: Bleu Reinier

Ferenk's men functioned like an efficient machine—assessing the surroundings, setting guards, and dressing wounds. Bleu didn't have to lift a finger. The Western Haveners had survived on the Surface and fought for generations, and it showed in every movement.

Bleu caught Savas' gaze from across the camp, and the two exchanged an amazed grin at the flurry of coordinated activity around them. They had a lot to learn from these new allies, but right now, Bleu wanted everyone settled as quickly as possible so that he could be with Kalakanya in case she woke. He considered striding across camp to ask Savas to take charge for the evening, but the guy had already falsely told Ferenk he was in charge. Probably not best to give him more power.

So instead, Bleu insisted the second, separate section of the helicopter with seats they had never utilized be set aside for Kalakanya and Kahali. Bleu and Atsushi had converted the chairs to beds while Obi and Neviah distributed water and medical supplies.

As he'd left Rana alone, guarding Kalakanya and Kahali from Ferenk's men, she had reassured him again that Crowned Ones were self-healing. That Kalakanya would be fine. But it literally pained him to leave her bedside to organize expanding and protecting their camp for the night.

Her injuries were his fault. He was supposed to have protected her until she could shield. Not only had she been shot twice, but he hadn't stopped them from putting the collar on her.

As soon as he had asked Girak and Atsushi to make dinner, he tasked Savas and Ferenk with figuring out how to divide overnight guard duty. Hoping that would keep them too busy to start trouble for a bit, he left the bustle of the helicopter's main compartment.

Finally, he could open the heavy door to the rear compartment and relieve Rana of guard duty. Their exchange was quick. He yearned to check on Kalakanya, and Rana seemed eager to leave and assist Eka with the shielding. With a sigh of relief, he closed the metal door, enclosing himself in with the two injured star beings. Blissful stillness and silence surrounded him. Not truly quiet—strained, suspicious conversations still drifted through—but enough to mute the swirling tension between the two sets of humans and star beings outside.

More importantly, until the door was next opened, Kalakanya was safe. And having her within arm's length, he could relax. Drooping against the cushioned chair back, one hand on Kalakanya's good arm, his eyes drifted shut.

"Bleu."

He startled upward to see who had called him. Kalakanya still lay unconscious. After a moment's confusion, he looked to his other side.

From his cot, Kahali watched him, eyes wide with alarm. His face had turned purplish-yellow from bruising, and his head bandage where Savas had smacked him with the rifle butt was bleeding through. Kahali was not self-healing. Unfortunately, they had no medic, and Rana and Eka had their hands full shielding the camp from the Ruined while also taking care of their own injuries.

"It's okay, you're safe. We're in the back of Neviah's helicopter. You got hit pretty hard on the head. Do you remember anything?"

Kahali nodded, wincing in pain at the small movement. He said something in his native tongue that sounded like a question and motioned with a finger toward the door.

"What?"

Kahali repeated the question, clearly agitated by the painful effort.

"I'm sorry, Kahali. You have to use mind speak. I haven't learned your language yet."

Kahali grimaced in annoyance and pointed to his head. He was struggling to keep his eyes open.

"You can't? Because your head hurts?" How could Kahali understand him? He considered getting Rana, but he couldn't leave them alone to go outside the helicopter with Ferenk's men all over the place. If only he could mind speak like a star being, he could call her from here. But while he had successfully gotten the star beings to hear his thoughts when he already had their attention, he had no idea how to truly mind talk.

"I can't leave the room. I don't trust Fer—" He stopped himself. Probably not a good idea to let Kahali know the humans that had done this to him were right outside the door.

Instead, he stood. "Have some tea. Rana made it earlier in case you woke up." He carried the mug to Kahali and helped him sit up and drink a few sips.

Kahali pointed to the cup of tea Rana had made, the door and, with a grimace of pain, raised a questioning eyebrow.

Bleu took a wild guess. "Rana and Eka are fine."

Kahali's shoulders sagged in relief.

"She just left to help Eka shield. I'm sure she'll come back as soon as she can. Want some more tea?" Bleu held the cup up.

Kahali shook his head ever so slightly and wilted back onto his cot, wincing as his head touched the pillow.

"This might help." Bleu picked up some ice wrapped in a cloth that Rana had prepared. "She didn't want me to put it on until you woke up. I think she expected me to pass out on guard duty and freeze your brains." Bleu grinned and gently placed the ice pack on the swollen bump. Rana had treated it earlier, but it still looked brutal.

Kahali grimaced at the ice's touch, but then closed his eyes. Within moments he was snoring softly.

Bleu walked back toward his seat by Kalakanya, limping slightly at the sting in his thigh. Surprised, he looked down to where a bullet had grazed him hours ago. He'd been in such survival mode that he'd hardly remembered it until now. When he looked back up, Kalakanya had quietly awoken and was watching him.

His face heated. "Hey." He grinned stupidly. "You're back."

Is everyone okay? Her gaze drifted to his bloodied pant leg. *Are you?*

"Everyone's alive. You and Kahali got hurt pretty badly. This"—he waved toward his leg—"isn't serious. I'll get it taken care of after the others. A few of Ferenk's men—"

At her confused look, he said, "Sorry. We found the Western Haveners. They're led by Ferenk, who's now buddy-buddy with Savas."

She raised an eyebrow in exhausted amusement.

He laughed with relief, overjoyed to see her awake and well enough to be amused. "Just my opinion, but Savas and Ferenk seem very similar. As if we need two of them."

He chuckled, much lighter now that he could talk to her again. Things were insane, but with her awake, the world seemed brighter. Together, they had survived entering Northern Haven and the giant bugs. Together, they could do this.

He said, "They attacked us because they thought you star beings were these dangerous creatures they call the Ruined."

Her face darkened.

"They say they look like you and killed most everyone from Western Haven. I didn't believe them, but then we were attacked by the Ruined, who killed a bunch of Ferenk's men. They shift and take on other shapes. Sometimes they looked like star beings."

These new humans sound like you all did when we first met. There must be a misunderstanding. Star beings are not violent.

"That's what I told them. But..." He had to ask, even if it seemed ridiculous. "*Can* star being shift to look like other things?"

I do not understand. Shift how?

"Could you make yourself look like a cave digger or an eagle?"

She laughed, and then grimaced as her laughter shook her shoulder. *I could growl like Digga? Is that what you mean?*

"No, these creatures literally change. Like, one turned into a giant eagle and flew. It tried to carry off Kahali."

She scrunched up her brow in thought and laughed as if she had finally gotten a joke. *That seems highly unlikely.*

"I'm serious." He paused to let that sink in. "So, they can't be star beings, then?"

Star beings would never attack and kill. If they did that, they are something else. Though I have never heard of anything else.

"You'd never met humans until a month ago."

She gave him an odd look, then assumed the same, walled-off Crowned One exterior she had worn when she warned him that he wasn't ready for the truth.

"What?" He narrowed his gaze, but she only gave a weak smile and shook her head.

He sighed in defeat, knowing that with her unusual abilities she often had to use this I-can't-tell-you bit. Kahali had said it was a Crowned One thing, so if he wanted to be close to her, he'd have to accept it. But what was the truth about these Ruined that she wasn't sharing?

Her expression grew concerned. *We got separated. I didn't know what happened to you.*

Oh. That. Guilt washed over him. "I'm sorry. They shot you and then attacked me..." He stared into the shadows beneath her cot.

He'd failed her during the attack. He knew nothing about battles except what he'd experienced in holograph games. He merely played at being a warrior. "I couldn't get a shot off fast enough. I messed up."

She placed her hand on his wrist, making his whole arm tingle. *That's not what I meant.*

He raised his gaze to meet hers, not knowing what to expect. Certainly not the intense wave of concern and caring that hit him. Lost in her jade-green gaze, Bleu couldn't fathom what she *had* meant.

Her grip on his arm tightened, pulling him slightly closer. *I was afraid I'd lost you.*

"I couldn't make them stop electrocuting you. I thought you were..." He gulped, having trouble breathing. "I know I'm just a stupid human, but the idea of living without you...I mean, I know you don't feel the same, but think I've fallen—"

Stop.

She smiled, probably relieved that she'd interrupted his foolish declaration.

He closed his eyes, shaking his head at his own naiveté. Of course, she wouldn't be interested. She was a star being. Even more, a Crowned One.

Bleu, look at me. Please.

Fighting his shame, he risked her alluring jade eyes. Her gaze was full of warmth. And humor. *Declaring your love means nothing unless we're equals.*

"Sorry. I didn't mean to be disrespectful."

You're only disrespecting yourself. I don't consider you a stupid human. Her eyes sparkled with mischief. *Well, maybe asking me if I can turn into a cave digger is a bit daft. Then you'd really have trouble declaring your love.*

He chuckled at the image of declaring his love to a cave digger. Wait. Did she mean she didn't see him as stupid? He opened his mouth to object, but she put her fingers to his lips. He tried to ignore their soft heat.

I didn't want to say anything because I didn't want to mess this up. We are very different—

"I know," he mumbled through her fingers, his face heating. "We're probably too different."

Maybe, maybe not. Like a star being, you seek to understand things on a deeper level. You naturally explore both the inner and outer landscapes. Like a star being, you want this mission to succeed with as little violence as possible. We both want peace.

Did she just put forth their commonalities? "But I'm *not* a star being."

For the umpteenth time since he met her, he was acutely aware of the constraints that came with being human. It pressed in on him, like the locked door to the Surface had constrained him in Northern Haven. He had made it to the open Surface, and he still felt trapped. Not by a locked door, but by his humanness. "No matter what I do, I'll always be human."

She grinned. *It's not a bad thing to be human. And we weren't always different.*

Chapter 54

Back Section of the Helicopter: Bleu Reinier

Kalakanya's statement confused Bleu, but before asking for clarification, he glanced at Kahali to make sure he wasn't eavesdropping. The poor guy still slept deeply, recovering from his head wound. His small snores sounded almost Digga-like.

Reassured of their continued privacy, Bleu whispered to Kalakanya, "What did you mean when you said you and I weren't always different?"

Her expression grew concerned. _You've been remembering more, haven't you? Visions of two humans?_

"Yes. Whenever I have a moment to relax, stuff from the past pours through my mind." His cheeks warmed at their past connection.

Somehow, he was the beaten man, and she was his wife being led away, though that logically made no sense. Those memories existed alongside his memories of Ayanna learning to walk and him and Stamf learning to play at the gaming arena.

Angry voices drifted in from the other room. Between Ferenk's men and the threat of the Ruined, he really shouldn't be swept up in a fantasy romance. He had to focus on the here and now.

Bleu? Her warm fingers touched the back of his hand. His gaze met hers, and another tidal wave of jumbled images hit him. He clasped her fingers in his hand, a drowning man grabbing for anything to pull him out of the deluge. But the memories poured forth, like videos paired with waves of intense emotions. The man and woman laughed at some monkeys in a tree above them—a wave of joy. Watching her teach before a crowded university auditorium—overwhelming pride. Running with young children in tow—heart-wrenching fear. The woman being torn from his arms by soldiers, kids screaming while other soldiers knocked him to the ground...

"No—" The man lunged for the woman...

Bleu opened his eyes, startled to see Kalakanya now sitting up facing him, her breath catching against his cheek.

"Sorry." He couldn't move. His heart still raced from the final images, and all he wanted to do was hold her so that nothing would ever separate them. "That all really happened, didn't it?"

Yes. We were them. We were both human.

Her words confirmed what he had believed was impossible, sending a shockwave of truth to his core. They had already been together. In another lifetime? It still seemed a question, too bizarre to be real.

She reached out her uninjured arm to brush his cheek. *I'm sorry you had to relive it. But part of me is relieved, too. It's one secret in time that I no longer have to bear alone. Selfish of me, right?* Her eyes searched his face.

He struggled to catch his breath. "I'd...I'd rather know than not know."

She laughed, leaning her face against his cheek. *See? You are like a star being.*

He yearned to hold her, to wrap his arms around her and never let her go. But he had no idea of protocol for this situation. As if there existed a human-star being intimacy protocol.

I'd like that. Her breath tickled his cheek.

He shook his head in silent laughter at how readable he was to her and wrapped his arms around her. "Your shoulder?"

Bleu, I'm fine. That mischievous tone again, as she smiled in a daring way.

"Okay, but you almost died a few hours ago." Was this really happening?

She nodded, so close that their faces brushed up against each other again.

His heart skipped a beat, possibly from joy, possibly from fear of making a fool of himself. This whole physical intimacy thing was Stamf's skill set, not his. Stamf was the womanizer. Bleu pretended, not because he didn't like women—he did—but because he was not driven by a need for sex like his friends seemed to be.

He inhaled the scent of her body pressed to his—pine, warmth, and the antiseptic Neviah had applied earlier. Eyes closing, he yearned to close the distance between them. This chasm—between human and star being, between their past and this present time—seemed uncrossable. But he would not allow her to be yanked from his arms again.

Is this okay? she said, her warm lips a hair's breadth from his, her breath feather-soft against his lips.

"Yes", he whispered, "this is *very* okay." A slight glow emanated around them. The boundary between his body and hers dissolved. They merged, and he lost all sense of his body and identity. They became a love so huge it wouldn't fit into a body. He gasped, wanting more of whatever this delicious energy was.

His lips met hers, and in a flare of light they became one: past and present, human and star being, Bleu and Kalakanya.

As the energy ebbed, her kiss shifted to a smile with her lips still against his. *Still okay?*

"Yes." He raised his hand and cupped the back of her head, pulling her closer. Her braids pressed against his palm. The white braids of a Crowned One.

What was he doing? He froze. *Shast*, what was wrong with him?

Bleu. Her warm fingers brushed his cheek. *Talk to me.*

"I don't want to mess this up."

Same.

"Really? But I'm so..." He pulled away. "I'm human. And I'm not like other human guys."

Thank you for clarifying that. She bit her lip, eyes sparkling with amusement.

"You know what I mean?" He was pretty sure he'd never exactly thought about being uninterested in sex around her, so if she really knew he was asexual, he was confused as to how.

Her smile faltered a little, and she tilted her head as if surprised. *Oh. Sorry.* She pulled back slightly to study his face better. *I didn't know. I thought you said kissing was okay.*

"It was, I said it was, and I'm honored that you wanted to." Heat pulsed in his face. "I just, well, I don't want to make assumptions, but I'm not into sex. You should know that. In case it's an issue."

But you like me?

"Yes." He moved closer until their breath mingled. "Yes, very much." He kissed her cheek, hoping she understood. Tears pricked his eyes. "But this is probably not what you want. I totally understand it if—"

She touched a finger to his lips again and smiled one of her devastating smiles. *Now you're the one assuming.*

She didn't reject him? An ember of hope flared in his heart. He'd never met a woman not hoping to go farther. One obstacle possibly solved... "But I thought Crowned Ones only dated other Crowned Ones?"

Stop putting me above you. Your soul and mine started out the same. We all did.

"Okay." He bit his lip, considering what she had said. "But our bodies are different this lifetime. Not horribly different..." He grinned. "But it's not like I'll wake up one morning as a star being. I'll always be this." He waved his hand dismissively at his body.

Yes, probably. Her face was unreadable. *What exactly are you saying?*

Was that fear in her voice? "Rana told me Crowned Ones only couple with other Crowned Ones. I'm not sure how coupling translates into human relationships, but it sounds like there's a law against us being together."

Delight lit her beautiful jade eyes. *You've been doing research?* She nodded in approval. *Coupling has two meanings. It's an agreement to be monogamous, and it also means physical intercourse. If I understand you, you aren't interested in sex right now anyways, correct?*

Blushing, he nodded. "Like, maybe never?"

Her one eyebrow lifted ever so slightly, but she didn't shove him away in horror. *Okay. Most of our intimacy in couples is energetic, like what just happened between us. But there's lots of techniques. Is that something you'd be interested in if this works out?*

"I'm very okay with that." He laughed at his own enthusiasm.

The joy in her face lit his heart. *Then we should be good. Just so you know, we don't normally do anything that could produce children until we are*

Crowned anyways. It's not a law like your laws. It's a guideline for the best of the community.

He frowned. "But I'm human and I'll never Crown. Will your community be upset if we're in a relationship?"

His brain needed this information, yet his heart didn't care. Holding her couldn't be wrong, could it? "I don't want to get you in trouble. Or put this team under any more stress. Rana has already expressed her concern about…us."

Kalakanya's eyebrow shot up. *You're not causing trouble.* She touched his arm, sadness flickering across her face. *And yet, I'm not quite sure how to make this work.* Her hand trailed down his arm to his hand.

Their fingers intertwined, but it was a grasping sort of hold. An unwillingness to let go of this fleeting moment hold. A this-won't-survive-in-the-world-outside sort of hold. Bleu held tight, unwilling to let go of this short-lived gift.

Her damp eyes met his. *When I realized who you were, I had hoped only I would remember. I am used to holding secrets and staying away from others because of them. But now that you know, I find it harder and harder to ignore how I feel. But still—*

"We live in different worlds." This truth spun like chaos inside him, creating an endless void of desperation. "So, that's it then? We leave this room and pretend nothing ever happened?" The aching void in his chest threatened to consume him. How could this have happened and ended all in a matter of minutes?

I choose Love. I always choose Love. But in this case, I am only half of the equation, and I don't know how to solve it, because you will have the more difficult part.

He paused, sensing something deeper than the obvious choice was at stake here, and wanting to prove his readiness to undertake such an unusual relationship. "I choose love, too, but I can't recreate human-to-star being evolution in my lifetime. I don't know how to do the impossible."

It's not a thinking sort of thing. It's not what you do, *but what you* be. *Only, sometimes you must do certain things so that you can be all of what you are destined to be.*

"I don't understand. When you switch into talking like that..." He shook his head in frustration. "What does that even mean?" His trembling hands took both of hers as he searched her face. "Please. Tell me, and I'll do it. I'll do anything."

She gave him a sad smile. *I know. But like I said back in my village, I can't read all the threads of time in regard to you. I can't tell you. But even if I could, I don't think it works that way. Some things you must discover on your own.*

"Shouldn't this be something we figure out together?"

She shook her head. *We face different challenges. And sometimes, we may need to keep those challenges private from each other.* She bit her lip. *I hope, no matter what happens, you trust me.*

He studied her odd expression and grinned. "Why do I get the feeling you're talking about something very specific that you're already keeping from me?"

Her eyes glistened, and she looked down at their clasped hands.

"What? Tell me."

Bleu, you know how this works. How I work. She smiled a sad, wistful sort of smile. *Your suspicion about me withholding something specific is right. I can't tell you now, and when it's time for you to know, you won't like it. But if I tell you now, it puts everyone, especially you, in danger.*

He sighed. "So, to be together, this is part of the deal? All these secrets?"

Yes. I'm sorry. She laughed. *I understand if you want to run.*

He gripped her hand tighter. "Nope. You're stuck with me."

Chapter 55

Surrounded by Enemies, Lost in a Sea of Humans: Kahali of Peleguin Rookery

Kahali's skull pounded as if it had been cracked open, and his body felt like an entire herd of salt deer had trampled him. He remained alive but not safe. That was clear by the strange human voices beyond the wall.

This betrayal by his supposed human friends—allowing those vile humans onto the ship he now resided in—pained him worse than any of his injuries. Every breath hurt, his stomach roiled, and part of his mind argued that it wasn't worth the pain anymore. The humans had infested their land, Rana had chosen Eka, all he had done to better the situation had only left him beaten and dead inside. And his new capability endangered others.

Kalakanya's gentle hands touched his head wound, but he kept his breath steady and his eyes closed. The last thing he wanted was to hear a Crowned One tell him that things would get better.

"Kahali, I know you're awake."

He could practically hear her smile, and it sickened him. He remained *asleep,* too stubborn and immature to care.

She carefully removed his head dressing and hissed out a long breath. "What did this?"

The image of Savas standing over him, rifle raised and ready to swing, was too much. He rolled to his side and vomited on the floor. Gagging and dizzy, he threw out his arm to balance himself, but there was no wall, and his sleeping furs weren't on the floor as he had expected.

Kalakanya grabbed his shoulders, grunting at the effort. The vile humans must have hurt her as well. "I've got you." Her hands held his shoulders as she breathed unsteadily herself.

He steadied himself against her hands and the waves of dizziness.

"Here." She handed him a cloth.

Wiping his face sent stabbing pains into his brain, and he fell back, gasping.

"Hold on." She leaned over him, one hand on his head, the other on his makeshift bed to balance herself. From her healing hand, soothing relief washed over him.

His breath normalized, but he couldn't thank her. His head hurt too much to mind speak. Attempting to move his jaw made his whole skull pound.

"Just rest while I do this. Don't worry. You'll feel better soon."

Not likely. No miracle could fix everything that had happened in the last sun, but he would gladly accept any pain relief offered. As she worked on his head and neck, he drifted off.

"Kahali, I'm sorry, but you need to wake up. I need to know you're okay before I rest. Can you open your eyes and let me know if things are in focus?"

His eyelids weighed heavy, but he opened them. In the dimly lit room, a blurry Kalakanya sat beside him, pale and leaning against the chairback as if it were all that held her up.

"Can you see?"

Yes. It hurt to focus, but he could again mind talk.

"Normally?"

No. Blurry and the light hurts.

"Okay, let me see what else I can do. Let your eyes rest." Her warm palm covered his one eye, a blessed relief from the light that still filtered through. Her other hand did something on the opposite side of his head.

His thoughts cleared, and he recalled the conversation he had heard while drifting in and out of consciousness. Bleu and Kalakanya.

Could that be, or was his head that messed up?

Was I dreaming, or were you talking to Bleu?

Kalakanya's hands stiffened, but she laughed. "You heard us?"

Some. He waited to see if she would volunteer anything.

She didn't.

He struggled to mind speak his fears. If what he'd heard between her and Bleu had been at all real... *What's wrong with you? Did you get your head smacked as well?*

"No, I got shot," she said, her tone flat.

Sorry, that was rude. I'm not very subtle at the moment.

"Pain will do that." She sounded sad. "Plus, you're still upset with me about when you first Called the humans and lost your arm. I know you've been trying to let the anger go, and you can't. Maybe if you understand where I was coming from—"

He snorted in anger. "Yeah. Because it's all about you."

"Of course not. I'm not making excuses for myself. And I can live with your not forgiving me, but I'm not sure you can live with it. I don't want you to think I'm making decisions against you." She grew silent.

He waited, fury swirling through him. How could she possibly defend having him get shot and lose his arm?

"Just like you never expected to move things with your mind to the degree you can, no one had ever read the threads of time like me. As soon as the Crowned Ones realized what I was doing, they wanted me to develop my capability. Imagine a kid trying to choose the best future among endless outcomes. Did I choose the right outcome for my friends? My family? My village? All star beings? Or all of life on the planet? The universe? There were endless complications."

"There still are complications."

Of course, there were complications. He knew that. But you don't set your cousin up to be maimed for life. Deep within him, the fury raised its head and came to life. Its power enthralled and terrified him. He sucked in a shaky breath. And another, willing himself to calm. After a moment, he risked looking at Kalakanya, hoping she had missed his slip into rage.

Her hands, still over his eyes, trembled. "I understand why you all get angry at me. But I swear I am trying my best to keep us all safe." She sighed. "And today, it appears I've failed you all again."

He'd never seen her like this. It was one thing to be furious at her. It was another thing entirely to see her fall apart. *I'm not blaming you for this. This head wound was completely Savas.*

"Savas did this? I thought he was coming around a bit." She lowered the ice back to the re-bandaged area.

No, don't trust him. He acted surprised and grateful that I saved his life and then beat me. Humans are unpredictable. He grasped her wrist. *I know you're Crowned and I'm not, but you're crazy if you think Bleu is any different.*

"You don't know him like I do." She gently removed his hand from her wrist. "Can you see okay now?" The chair creaked as she sat back again and waited.

Despite his roiling emotions, the pain in his head and jaw had lessened to a dull ache. He wasn't in any hurry to be up and about, to have to deal more directly with her and the others. He yearned only to return to his hut in Peleguin-Rookery-By-The-Lake and pretend none of this ever happened.

But the humans weren't going away. And this relationship possibility with Bleu was ludicrous. Slowly, to avoid a return of the dizziness, he turned his head toward her. His vision was clear enough to see she was not open to further discussion.

"Yes, I can see better now." He paused, fighting with himself to be polite. "Thank you."

"Was Savas trying to kill you?"

The monstrous look in the older man's eyes as he raised the butt of the rifle over Kahali haunted him—a twisted mix of calculated anger and cold resignation. Even worse was how completely incongruent the anger and resignation were with Savas' earlier gratitude toward Kahali for saving him. That sudden, unpredictable change gave him shivers every time his mind replayed it.

"Kahali, was he trying to kill you?"

Kahali blinked the images away. "He said what he was doing would hurt a lot less than letting the others kill me."

She grimaced. "I'm glad Bleu got us sequestered back here until this is sorted out."

"Look, this whole trip is out of control. I can't imagine why you Crowned Ones thought I should come along. This isn't helping me forgive. It's only messing me up more."

"I'm sorry." She looked sincere. "It seemed you and Atsushi were bonding."

"He's an innocent kid, but he'll grow up to be a monster like the rest of them."

Now that he had admitted this fear out loud, it seemed more likely than ever. Not only did Atsushi have his human nature working against him, but he had an awful mentor as well.

"He's only two summers younger than you. He avoids violence. And I wouldn't underestimate the impact you're having on him. He hasn't used the gun yet."

Kahali sat up, his heart racing. "He has one?"

"I believe Savas snuck him one. But he has not killed."

Kahali buried his head in his palm. Savas would be the death of him one way or another.

She put her hand on his. "You underestimate your power. They've only known us a short time. We'll teach them that it's possible to live without violence."

She clearly hadn't met the new humans. "No, now they'll think we're like the Ruined."

"Bleu mentioned them. That's a horrid name. No one is ever *ruined*."

"Some of us are." Tears pricked his eyes as he remembered how one of his stones, circling in defense only, had struck down one of Ferenk's stubbornly still approaching men.

She sat in silence.

The hairs on the back of his neck stood up. Great. He had expected her to argue with him, to tell him all would be well in a typical Crowned One manner. Instead, she was doing a transtemporal scan to see how long they had before he was totally a danger to them all. It was too much.

Terrifying images from earlier in the day played out against his closed eyelids—his inability to protect Rana and Atsushi, the rock as it probably killed Ferenk's man, Savas' face as he swung the gun. Next, he saw the possibility of Atsushi firing a gun. Sobs racked his body.

The door opened, and Kalakanya knocked the chair backward as she jumped to her feet.

"Bad timing? I can come back," Savas' horrid voice said.

Kahali wanted to scream, but he couldn't stop the tears. He couldn't even bear looking at him. Couldn't bear the hatred anymore.

Let him just shoot me and end this.

What do you want, Savas? Kalakanya's tone lacked warmth.

He couldn't see Savas, but he must have been taken back by her tone. She never spoke like that.

"I came to check on Kahali."

To see if you had succeeded in killing him?

Savas snorted in disgust. "He saved me, and I tried to repay the favor. But if you're too angry to see that, forget it." He stormed out, slamming the door behind him.

Shock washed over Kahali. Savas came to check on him? What did that mean?

"The idea that violence can be a show of love is the sickest idea I've ever heard." She picked up the chair from the floor and paced unsteady circles around the small room. In her blood-stained leathers, she made an eerie sight.

"You don't look so good," Kahali said. "Maybe you should sit."

She laughed a human laugh, bereft of joy and warmth.

"What did you see when you scanned me? How long until I kill someone?"

She froze and then slowly turned toward him, her face pale. "Until you kill?"

He nodded.

"You know I don't tell people what I see, but it was nothing like that."

"But that was what you were checking for."

"No."

They stared at each other, two exhausted and unnaturally stressed star beings pushed to their limits by events beyond their control.

Beyond the door, the men's voices had become less strained, and the sounds of spoons clinking on bowls filled the air. He waited. What had she been searching for? Was there anything he could salvage of his self?

She just stared back at him as if too tired to move or look away.

Finally, he could no longer stand the not knowing. "I'm still ruined, though, right?"

"I'm not supposed to share."

"Please? Do I have a chance?"

She sighed. "You and the so-called Ruined have similar paths. Keep your heart open. Only that will save you, Kahali." Spent, she leaned back in her chair and did whatever Crowned Ones do when they heal themselves.

Her words haunted him. *Keep your heart open. Only that will save you.*

Falling stars, he was done for. Collapsing back onto his cot, he sank into the knowledge that it was too late to save himself. He was drowning, already ruined. He couldn't even break the surface to catch a final glimpse of sunlight. Because after losing Rana to Eka, watching a flying rock he was controlling injure Ferenk's man, and then being beaten by his own teammate, his heart was done for.

Chapter 56

Campsite, Eastern Coast of North America:
Commander Kern Savas

Savas spun on his heels, slamming the door shut between him and Kalakanya. He had been actually concerned about Kahali. As he turned to stride down the aisle, he ran smack into Girak coming towards him. "Get the hell out of my way!" he growled.

Girak held his hands up in surrender but stayed put.

Savas shoved him out of the way, done with all of them, especially Kalakanya. She had kept him from learning how badly he had hurt Kahali. He'd been trying to save the guy's life and had never intended to seriously damage the kid, but the crack of the rifle against Kahali's temple still rang in his ears.

Girak resisted his attempt to shove him aside. "Savas, stop, please."

The damn fool was stronger than Savas expected, a veritable boulder in the narrow aisle.

"I'm sorry Kalakanya didn't understand. I know what you did on the mountainside. The others told me." Girak's blue-eyed gaze pinned him with something he couldn't even comprehend. Admiration? Pity? "I don't know what I would have done in your position, but I appreciate that you kept us all, including Kahali, alive."

Girak's gratitude was like a slap to the face—startling and infuriating. "Girak, you're the last person whose opinion matters, and I have a lot to do. Get the hell out of my way."

The bastard had the nerve to laugh. "I know, that's exactly why I needed to talk to you." Girak lowered his voice. "I know you hate me, but we have an issue that is going to take both of us to solve."

"You mean the fact that you're stuck in the aisle, blocking me from protecting us from those monsters out there?" He motioned to the window as a screech echoed in the night air outside his helicopter. Last night, he had wanted to know what would make such sounds, but now he almost wished he didn't know.

"Rana and Eka are keeping us safe for now. I meant the danger *inside*," Girak whispered, motioning with his chin to the cluster of Ferenk's men near the front of the helicopter.

Savas sighed. As much as he despised Girak for murdering Josefina, the guy didn't miss much.

He had the same concern. It just wasn't the top of his list this second. "I'm on it, Girak."

"Yeah, I figured. Look, I know Bleu is commander, but you and I are the two adults here."

Savas raised an eyebrow. *That* was unexpected. "What's your point?"

"I'm asking for a truce between us. I want us to work together. I don't trust these Western Haveners, and we need to keep the kids safe."

"I don't need a sidekick, Girak."

Girak sighed and then laughed. "Look, I'm trying to do what you just tried to do with Kalakanya. I know you never wanted to work with the star beings, but I think you're starting to see the benefit of it. I don't really want to work with you, either, but my wife always believed in you."

Savas froze. Josefina. She'd been the first person to support him in exploring the Surface. She *had* believed in him, but he thought he'd lost that, and her, when she'd foolishly fallen for Girak. Had Girak just confessed that Josefina believed in him until the end?

He opened his mouth to retort, but then closed it, unsure of himself.

"She believed in you enough to risk going to the Surface under your command when she was pregnant. She made the choice, Savas. I supported it, but *she* made the choice. She knew the whole mission would be compromised if she reported her pregnancy. You would have been short a person."

"She'd be alive if she had gotten an obstetrician to examine her."

"Don't you think I know that? She was my wife." Girak swallowed and looked away. When he looked back, his blue eyes burned with passion. "I know you hate me, Savas, but she'd want us to work together on this. She'd want us to do whatever it takes to keep the younger ones safe. I don't know what's going to happen, but I want our team united. Please? For Josefina?"

He glared at Girak. This day was an endless hell, and the last thing he wanted was to work with Girak.

Damn it, he needed all the help he could get. "Fine. But don't think this means you're not still a Deplorable."

Girak chuckled. "Believe me, I'm well aware of your feelings." His smile faded. "I know you're planning something. What do you need?"

He smirked. "For you to get out of my way. And when I need more from you—*if* I ever need more from you—I'll let you know." He waited for Girak to step aside and moved closer to pass him. As they brushed against each other, Savas hurriedly whispered, "Keep an eye on Neviah. They're more desperate than they're letting on, and if they steal our helicopters, they'll need Neviah or me to fly them."

Chapter 57

Campsite, Eastern Coast of North America: Bleu Reinier

When Bleu opened the door to the main cabin, both teams were wolfing down the stew that Girak and Atsushi had somehow concocted. Whispered conversations, wary glances, and the hurried scrapping of spoons in bowls permeated the room. Ferenk's men sat clustered by the door, some with their guns on their laps, others touching them every time another wailing shriek or guttural growl sounded outside. Now that Bleu knew what threatened them, the growls and screams were more terrifying.

Savas sat among the Western Haveners, carrying on a hushed conversation with Ferenk. As Bleu entered the room, Savas looked up, and the two exchanged weary nods acknowledging the other's existence but also making it clear neither desired a real interaction.

Between Ferenk's men and Bleu's team lay a wall of hastily thrown gear and medical supplies. Neviah, Atsushi, and Girak sat in hushed conversation with Obi. Zach stood, awkwardly moving between waiting on Savas and checking in with the rest of his team.

Another gurgling scream rolled down the mountain. Conversation stopped, and all eyes shifted to the windows or to check weapons. Tension hung in the air like a combustible gas. The smallest friction would spark an explosion.

Something had to shift, or someone was going to snap and do something stupid.

The idea of Rana and Eka, exhausted as they were, holding the shield outside by themselves gave Bleu shivers. He couldn't shield, but he could at least not leave the two of them out there alone as the animalistic screams of the Ruined rained down upon them. Shuffling down the aisle to Girak, Bleu tapped him on the arm and motioned for his ambassador to follow him outside.

In the darkness, Rana and Eka took turns shielding the helicopter and campfire while eating stew. Eka's face looked gaunt with his now widened white stripe of hair.

Almost like he's going for the Digga look, Bleu mused, dopey with exhaustion.

"I'm hoping you three could share your wisdom?" Bleu asked as he searched for the stack of clean bowls.

"Assuming we have some," Girak laughed.

Rana, her mouth full of stew, nodded in amusement. Eka only inclined his head, too tired to speak.

"Thanks," Bleu said, then noticed Eka's empty bowl. "Want some more?"

Please.

Rana shoveled in her last mouthful, and with a grin handed him her empty bowl as well. *Thanks. Digga ate most of my first bowl.*

She waved over to where the cave digger pup lay by the fire, head on her paws, black eyes watching them sleepily. She had torn off the bandages Rana had tied on her leg the previous night and seemed unusually quiet. Usually, by this time of the night she had raced off for her evening romp.

Digga's ears perked as another horrid keening echoed around them.

Shuddering despite the warmth of his bulky parka, Bleu turned back to Rana. "She's not going to go hunting tonight, is she?"

I asked her to stay, but she's her own being. However, I think she learned her lesson last night.

"Good girl, Digga." Bleu reached down to pat her, but the curve of her long canines around her black gums made him instead settle for giving her a friendly nod.

He straightened and watched Ferenk's men through the open door. Two of them had turned to keep an eye on their group outside. As if Bleu and Girak were plotting against them. "The tension in there is reaching critical levels. Any ideas?"

Eka let out an exasperated sigh. *We're both exhausted and still shielding them, but they don't even notice that we're protecting them. They look at us and only see monsters.*

Rana nodded. *When you humans first met us, you thought we were the enemy. What changed your minds?*

A blush crept up Bleu's face, part shame at his past acts of violence and part because he knew clearly what—or who—had changed his mind. "Kalakanya and I had a long talk." He brought back the two full bowls from the fire.

Girak shrugged. "I never experienced a reason *not* to trust you. Besides, my gut trusted you more than Savas and the doctors, all of whom were awful to me after Josefina died. Also, maybe because you're about the same age as my students and I naturally wanted to protect you. And I noticed you hadn't really attacked us on the Surface but were maybe only acting defensively?" He shrugged again.

Maybe because you are not only pleasantly surprising, but also surprisingly insightful? Some private joke that Bleu missed passed between them. *What if*—she turned to Bleu—*instead of trying to earn trust, we do something fun?*

Like getting some sleep? Eka laughed.

No, like music.

Bleu chuckled. She had to be joking.

"I'm not sure a campfire singing session will work." Girak stood and refilled his own bowl from the pot still hanging over the fire. He set it in front of Digga. Her short tail waggled in appreciation as she sniffed the steam and licked the air in anticipation.

Rana studied Ferenk's uneasy men through the open door. *Everyone is cranky, stressed, and tired. Everyone fears those with them inside the helicopter almost as much as those creatures out there.* She motioned to the dark mountainside. *Could music make things worse? I mean, music might even get Kahali out here.*

"He's not coming out of that room," Bleu said. "He's a mess. I mean, he has every right to be, but the guy needs a break from all this stress."

Rana and Eka exchanged a knowing, almost guilty look that baffled Bleu. He glanced at Girak, but the educator seemed nonplussed, as if he totally got what bothered them.

Bleu scowled. Had he said something wrong, or had he missed something? "What?"

Rana took Eka's hand. "I think we are also part of his problem."

"Oh." Bleu looked at Girak, who tapped his marriage ink on his palm and inclined his head toward Rana and Eka. Suddenly, it clicked. "Oh, I never realized...." He snapped his mouth shut.

Shast. He sucked at this relationship stuff. How was he ever going to make things work with Kalakanya without Stamf's coaching?

Maybe he could observe Rana and Eka's relationship to gain some context for what was normal for star beings? They were holding hands... *Shast.* They could read his mind. He attempted to look about nonchalantly, but everyone was watching him.

Rana grimaced.

"That didn't go through my head right." As if that would help.

Girak chuckled silently, looking embarrassed on Bleu's behalf. Bleu wanted to crawl in a hole.

Eka widened his eyes in surprise. *You and Kalakanya? For real?*

Bleu nodded, unsure whether or not he should be offended.

But... Eka shook his head, clearly baffled. *She's...I mean...* He squinted at Bleu as if seeing him for the first time.

Bleu snorted. "Thanks for the vote of confidence, man."

It's just... Eka was clearly speechless.

Rana cast Bleu a skeptical gaze. The tension from inside the helicopter appeared to be seeping out and swallowing them as well.

"Well, now that we're all on the same page,"—Girak grinned—"maybe we should refocus on Ferenk's men?"

"How come you know all this?" Bleu asked Girak.

"I work with teens. It's as obvious as the sky to me."

"Fine." He needed to change the subject before he made an even bigger fool of himself. He turned to Rana. "Music? How would that work if Kahali isn't going to start it."

Rana grinned. *Help me carry out the drums.*

✸ ✸ ✸ ✸ ✸ ✸

When Rana and Bleu entered the star being room to update Kalakanya and Kahali, their idea of making music was met with incredulity. Kalakanya snorted in amusement.

Kahali, now sitting and looking less pale, smirked. *Have fun with that.*

"We were hoping you'd join us." Bleu shot Kahali what he hoped was a winsome smile. Such grins had always worked for Stamf, but Bleu's attempts to replicate his best friend's winning grins had yet to work. The star being's frown made him even more skeptical. "If you're up to it. You're a great dancer."

Kahali's eyes widened. "Not with this headache." His lips curled upward in mischief. "But it's nice to know you noticed. Maybe sometime, if it's okay with Kalakanya, I'll teach you a few dance moves." He waggled his eyebrows suggestively.

Bleu's face froze in its ridiculous grin. Was Kahali making fun of Kalakanya and him, or was he not only into girls but also into guys? Or was everyone dancing with everyone normal among star beings? "O-kaay..."

Kahali, probably having just read his mind and enjoying watching a human squirm in confusion, grinned wider.

Bleu cleared his throat. "Well, maybe you could just sit outside? It might be better for you to join us than to sit in here by yourself."

Kahali's grin evaporated, and he glanced in Kalakanya's direction. "You were shot. Don't you need to rest?"

"Someone has to teach Bleu to dance, right?" She laughed and then winced at the resulting pain in her shoulder. "Though I'd do better to sit on the sidelines and hold the shield."

I'm not going out there. They wanted to kill me.

"We've had a talk. They agreed to behave. And if they don't,"—Bleu patted his gun on his hip—"I'm armed."

And I'm not. Kahali waved his stump sarcastically.

Bleu sighed. "It might be safer to stay with us, but if you're not up to it, one of us will stay in here with you."

Kahali stared at the door between their peaceful little group and the crowd outside. Now that everyone was done eating, the conversation had grown boisterous. At one of the new men's loud laugh, he began trembling.

"I'll go first," Bleu suggested. "And Rana and Kalakanya will both be with you, alright?" He cast a questioning look toward Rana, who shifted the heavy drum she held and nodded.

Kahali remained where he was, unmoving.

Kalakanya caught Bleu's gaze and shook her head slightly. She didn't think Kahali would go, or she didn't think he should. Bleu had always followed her lead, but he had lived longer with humans. If Kahali stayed in here alone, Ferenk and his men would be more likely to see him as different. As dangerous. He had to get Kahali to participate.

"Come on." Bleu offered his arm, grinning. "I'll help you in exchange for that promise of dancing lessons when you feel better."

Kahali stared at Bleu's proffered arm.

"Come on," Bleu cajoled him. "I bet those guys haven't had fun in forever. Let's remind them there's more to life than fighting."

It's not just them that's the problem. Kahali's gaze dropped to the floor. *What if I'm the one to get out of control?*

"Can you feel it coming?"

Kahali continued to stare at the floor but gave a slight nod.

"I'll sit right next to you. If you feel it building, let me know, and we'll get you out of there. We're a team. We all take care of each other."

Kahali furrowed his brow in skepticism.

"You protected our team on the hillside, right? With your rocks?"

Kahali winced at the mention. *I also made things worse by acting like a Ruined.*

"So?" Bleu shrugged. "You share some skills with those things. That doesn't make you one of them."

Those men won't hurt me? They'll leave me alone?

"Yes." Bleu held out his arm again. "Now, if you start dancing as well as the other night," Bleu laughed, "we might have to keep them away for other reasons."

Kahali rolled his eyes. Bleu had never seen any of the star beings do that before. But Kahali allowed Bleu to help him up and hobbled toward the door. No way he would dance tonight.

As they reached the door, Bleu stopped. With the drum in one hand and Kahali on his other arm, he had no way to open the door. Kalakanya passed him and opened it, giving him a subtle nod as if impressed that he'd gotten Kahali to leave.

He'd just surprised the Daughter of Time? Very pleased with himself, he returned her nod.

As Kalakanya opened the door, Neviah's eyes widened in delight as she jumped up. "You're better!" She rushed to Kalakanya and threw her arms around her, nearly knocking her over.

Atsushi rose, beaming at the sight of Kahali up and about. "Man, I was worried about you."

Kahali's hypervigilant gaze softened at Atsushi's concern. *Might want to remain on guard. I can feel their hatred from here.* He glanced toward the suspicious woodsmen at the front of the compartment near the door.

Atsushi stepped closer and frowned at Kahali's shoulder. "Your arm? May I?"

Bleu opened his mouth to warn Atsushi to keep his hands to himself, but before he got the words out, Kahali nodded.

I think the leather strap is twisted in the back. Kahali took a step closer to Atsushi, making Bleu move that way as well. *Sorry again that I was so rude with you this morning. I know you were only offering to help.*

Atsushi nodded, though he now stood behind Kahali, adjusting the strap. "Did I get it right?" He stepped around so the two were facing.

My arm—yes. Kahali locked his gaze on Atsushi's. *But regarding what's in your pocket,* that *you got wrong. If you value anything I taught you, you will get rid of what's hidden there.*

Bleu stared at the bulge in Atsushi's coat pocket. He had already taken a gun from Atsushi. But if Kahali was this unhappy, it was probably a weapon.

Atsushi paled. "How did you...?"

When you ask one of us star beings to teach you, you get us all. We're like birds in a flock, communicating midflight. Word travels. No more secrets from me, okay?

Atsushi nodded, then whispered, "I just wanted everyone to be safe..."

I will not train a killer. No guns. Kahali softened his gaze. *I'll keep you safe. I promise.*

Atsushi bit his lip as another yowl vibrated the metal walls around them. But instead of glancing out the window, Atsushi furrowed his brow and his gaze flickered to the Western Haveners. "It's not just me I'm worried about. I might need to keep you safe."

Atsushi, I would rather die than have you become a killer. The look Kahali gave Atsushi nearly broke Bleu's heart.

The room had grown silent. Eavesdroppingly silent. Ferenk and his men glared at the star beings. As Kalakanya led Bleu and Kahali down the gear-strewn aisles, Atsushi protectively followed his mentor.

"You all heal remarkably quickly." There was no warmth in Ferenk's statement. Only suspicion.

The power of the One In All, Kalakanya said, smiling warmly. *You are all well?*

"Well enough." Ferenk grunted, stiffening as she crossed the room toward him and the exit door.

Savas leaned closer to Ferenk and muttered something in his ear, laughing as he did so. Ferenk narrowed his eyes at Kalakanya in a way that made Bleu want to smack him.

But he had to make this work. These were the first new humans anyone from Northern Haven had seen in centuries. And they clearly had critical information about Western Haven's fate, the Ruined, and surviving on the Surface.

"Now that we've eaten, it's time to celebrate." Bleu forced a grin and held up the drum. "Humanity has grown today, and we have new allies. Despite those screeches, nothing harmful will get through the star beings' shields. It's quite safe. We're going to have some fun. Join us?"

Ferenk's jaw dropped. He leaned back on his makeshift seat, eyeing Bleu. "Have you lost your mind? You want to celebrate with the Ruined screeching and growling in the background?"

"Yup." Bleu grinned. "We'll show them we're not afraid."

Ferenk raised an eyebrow. His men remained watchful, ready to defend themselves.

It'll be fun, Kalakanya added.

As she strode into the midst of them to reach the door, several drew their weapons. Bleu's heart stammered, but she only paused long enough to make sure Bleu hopped down and assisted Kahali out without difficulty. Once she had hopped down onto the frozen ground, he noticed her slight glow. She had done her calming energy thing on them.

Kalakanya turned and waited. Rana, Neviah, and Zach stopped alongside the men.

Come on, Rana tried. *Dancing is always more fun if there's a crowd.*

The men all eyed Rana as if she were a wild animal that might turn on them in an instant. All of them except Obi, who stepped closer to Neviah.

"I guess you're the only fun one." Neviah bumped Obi with her shoulder and took his hand. "Come on." She jumped down.

Obi hesitated on the threshold as a guttural howl rang through the air. "Um..." He stared out into the firelight.

I'm shielding, Eka called. *See the shimmer around the helicopter and the fire? They couldn't get through it, remember?*

If Obi wouldn't join them, none of them would. "Come on," Bleu urged. Beside him, Kahali swayed, clearly exhausted by the short walk. "Follow Kahali and me."

He led Kahali over to the nearest folding stool, but Kahali whipped out a fur from under his cloak and plopped onto it, facing both the fire and the open helicopter door.

Bleu sat on the stool beside him and turned to see Obi following, his gun drawn.

"You can't fire that inside a shield," Neviah warned him. The four of them formed a small circle to the side of the fire. Kalakanya had remained standing by the door, putting herself between Ferenk's men and them.

"Why?" Obi asked, brow furrowed. "Will it ricochet back at me?"

"I don't think so. But Bleu did it once, and it knocked us out."

Obi's expression darkened. "But I thought their shields were safe?"

"Well, at that point, we didn't know the star beings. We had a misunderstanding and attacked them. They put a shield around Bleu and me so we couldn't shoot them, but we didn't know what the shields were. Bleu kept firing—"

"Neviah," Bleu interrupted, wincing at the shameful memory. "Is this really helpful?"

"He asked," she defended herself. "And yeah, maybe it does help to know we were fearful at one point, too." She raised a hopeful eyebrow at Obi.

"The misunderstanding...?" Obi cast a worried look at Kahali, the closest star being.

Kahali grunted something in his own language, probably a curse word.

"We were fools," Bleu blurted. "And I was the biggest one. They did nothing wrong, Obi, but we saw everything they did as a threat." He looked Obi in the eye. "Similar to how you now see everything about them as a threat."

Obi, still standing beside Neviah, chewed his lip, considering this. Then he took a tentative step toward Kahali. "It's Kahali, right?" Obi asked, holding out his hand in greeting.

Kahali nodded, an unreadable expression in his eyes. He ignored Obi's extended arm.

That wasn't good. Bleu wished he could send calming peace to Kahali like Kalakanya could.

"Oh, sorry. Human thing." Obi yanked back his hand and stepped backward as if Kahali had put up a wall. Maybe he had. "Can I ask you a question?"

Is it quick? I'm a bit tired after being attacked by your friends.

Bleu gave Kahali the side-eye.

"Um, I guess?" Obi looked from Kahali to Neviah. "It's just, like, I've always heard that some of the strongest warriors of the Ruined are missing an arm. I think it's why the others fear you so much. Maybe if you explained how—"

Kahali's glare silenced him. He reached up and gripped Bleu's arm. *I need to leave.*

Bleu knew that message was sent just to him. "Okay," he responded, disappointed. "Would it help if I told him what happened?"

I need to get away, Bleu. Tears formed in Kahali's eyes. *Now. Please.*

Bleu handed the drum to Neviah and pulled Kahali into a standing position, one arm protectively around him. He was definitely trembling now. "Obi, Kahali isn't feeling as well as he thought he was. I'm taking him back in."

Obi blinked. "I'm sorry. I was trying to help. I just wanted to explain the others' fear."

"Not now, Obi." Bleu shot him a stern look to silence him. Kahali's tremors grew into full body shakes. "Come on, Kahali. We're going." Bleu took a step toward the helicopter.

Something fluttered down onto Kahali's head. He cringed, but it was only a large feather, golden-brown in the firelight. As the feather swept over his shoulders and fell at his feet, Kahali's tremors faded.

Obi yanked Neviah back toward the helicopter. "It's them. The bird one. They must be flying over us, watching."

Everyone looked up. A massive bird passed overhead, temporarily blocking the stars beyond the shimmering shield. Bleu shivered. Yes, they were safe inside the shield, but knowing the Ruined surrounded them from above too made it extra creepy.

"The feather got through," Obi yelped. "It's made of feathers. It's going to get through the shield!"

Neviah gave him an exasperated look and picked up the feather, studying it. "It's just a feather, Obi."

Obi shrank back from her.

Kalakanya hurried over. *There was no ill intent in dropping the feather if it passed through the shield. Can I see it?*

Neviah handed it to her. Kalakanya turned it over, running her fingers over it. *It's an eagle feather. Beautiful.* She examined it, her hand glowing slightly as she scanned the feather. *Odd.*

"It's from them," Obi insisted. "It's dangerous." He pointed his gun at it. "Get it out of here."

Kalakanya looked up. *That's not necessary, Obi. It's harmless. Where exactly did it fall?*

Obi lowered his gun, but his wild look remained.

It fell on me. Kahali stared at the feather as if mesmerized by it.

Kalakanya and he exchanged a long, intense look. Probably more than a look, but whatever mind talk or transtemporal scan passed between them remained off limits to Bleu. It seemed to drag on forever.

"We need to get back inside." Obi attempted to pull Neviah and Bleu with him, but they both stood their ground.

"What does it mean?" Bleu asked.

It's yours, Kahali. Kalakanya handed him the feather. *Do you want it?*

She'd ignored Bleu's questions. It irked him when she got like this.

Kahali looked up, and Bleu followed his gaze. The bird or whatever it had been was gone. Giving a small nod to the empty sky, Kahali accepted the feather and tucked it into the leather strap holding his wooden arm to his shoulder.

"Kahali? Are you sure it's safe to wear that?" It was only a feather, yet fear of its probable connection to the Ruined curdled Bleu's stomach.

Kahali nodded, looking more sure of himself than he had for a long time. *It's an eagle feather. Eagles fly high and see a different perspective than we do on the land. The One In All connects all life, and this feather is a gift that connects me with a higher perspective. It's a reminder that I'm safe.*

Obi's eyes widened. "Inside, you said you were like a bird. I heard you. You *are* one of them."

No. Kahali said. *But I'm also not human, and I see things differently than you do.* He sat back down on his fur, now seeming completely at ease. *Neviah, hand me the drum.*

He was going to play music now? Confused, Bleu glanced about to see the others' reactions. With a sinking heart, he realized Ferenk hadn't missed any of the action. He stood on the threshold of the door, his eyes narrowed at Kahali.

Rana, who had been standing with Kalakanya between them and Ferenk's men, said something Bleu couldn't hear to Kalakanya and then carried her drum over to their fireside group and sat.

As Kahali and Rana began to play, Bleu decided to carry on as if nothing had happened. "Come on, Ferenk. Join us."

Ferenk snorted. "I'm not sure if you have the stupidest team I've ever seen or the bravest. But you're definitely the strangest team."

Bleu laughed. "We *are* a pretty strange team." He looked their odd group over. "We may be odd, but we work well together. Feel free to call us Team Strange."

Ferenk grunted something over his shoulder to the others and then jumped down to the ground. "Whatever you are, Team Strange or Team Stupid, you have impressive helicopters."

Chapter 58

Campsite, Eastern Coast of North America: Bleu Reinier

Bleu stifled his laughter as Ferenk's men hopped out of the helicopter and bobbed stiffly to the drums, hands never straying from their guns. They fanned out, not trusting the shield. They spaced themselves so some guarded outward while others drifted closer to the fire.

As he'd promised Kahali before he'd agreed to come outside, Bleu stayed close to him. But with his newfound feather giving him strength, Kahali sat erect and alert with a newfound ease in his bearing. Odd that a cast-off feather created such a dramatic effect. Kalakanya had declared it safe, but if it was dropped from one of the Ruined, didn't that make it a body part? For all Bleu's studies, he understood so little of nature.

Incredible rhythms erupted from the drums between Rana's and Kahali's knees. Even Bleu's exhausted and sore body itched to dance.

Kahali and Rana grinned at each other with joy. More than just friendship blossomed in Kahali's expression. How had he missed that until Rana and Eka had pointed it out to him? Did Kalakanya ever look at him with anything close to that expression?

After half an hour of restrained dancing, everyone settled around the fire's glow, basking in the music and starlight. Kahali sang a series of playful-sounding songs that rhymed. When Rana began mind talking the meaning of the lyrics, laughter broke out. Words of misplaced lovers, trickster animals, and the like filled the air.

Even Ferenk's men in the inner circle laughed along with the others, guns relaxed on their knees. Laughing with Kahali, of all things. Rana had been right. Music worked wonders.

As Kahali ended his latest about a fish falling in love with a sea bear, the older man, Jeb, turned from where he guarded against the Ruined and called out, "Kahali, how can you be so physically like the Ruined but so mentally...not?"

Everyone grew quiet, waiting for Kahali's answer. Bleu watched him closely for signs of anger, but his star being friend only chuckled softly and remained relaxed.

I'm probably not mentally like anyone. He stuck out his tongue and made a silly face.

Jeb slapped his knee and guffawed, while the other Western Haveners looked toward Ferenk to see how to react. Couldn't they think for themselves?

"No," Jeb cackled, "you're nothing like any Ruined I've come across."

Makes sense since I'm not one. Kahali grinned back at him and continued drumming. *Since they shift their form, do you know they truly look like us?* He shook his long ponytail as if he were some magnificent creature for all to admire. *Perhaps they just desperately admire us and yearn to imitate us.*

Ferenk snorted. "We know because they revert to a form identical to yours when unconscious or electrocuted." He patted his lightning stick with sickening affection.

His disgusting words smothered the brief flare of camaraderie between the two groups.

Bleu's stomach churned. He could only imagine the repulsion the star beings must hold for this vile man. Beside him, Kahali's face darkened. His soft drumming faltered, then stopped.

Bleu leaned over and whispered to Kahali, "You okay?"

He's sickening.

"Yup," Bleu whispered, then sat up. He needed to steer the conversation away from Kahali. "Have any of you ever tried communicating with the Ruined?"

"You can't talk with a monster that only seeks to rip your head from your torso," Ferenk said.

"Right." This wasn't working quite the way he'd hoped. He was considering how to shift the conversation when he noticed the howls and screeches had stopped. As if the Ruined were listening. He shivered.

May I ask you a question, Jeb? Rana said before Bleu could recover.

"I suppose."

Before we left the area where we were attacked, I noticed you doing something to the faces of your dead. Were you burning their faces?

Somehow, the silence grew even deeper. "Yes. It probably seems a gruesome tradition, but it's necessary to prevent the Ruined from luring the grieving family members into the woods by imitating the faces of their dead loved ones."

Rana gasped. *That's...beyond horrid.*

"Yup. They'll stop at nothing to destroy us. Makes it impossible to look at you star beings and not see monsters."

I am beginning to better understand why, she said. *But we are nothing like that.*

Again, no one spoke. Bleu wondered how close the Ruined were, and if they really were eavesdropping or it was just his fear. He still hadn't heard a threatening noise since the conversation started.

"It seems odd that the Ruined would hate humans with no reason," Bleu commented. This had been bothering him all day. Maybe it was a misunderstanding? "How did you first meet them?"

"If I didn't know better," Ferenk muttered through his clenched jaw, "I'd think you were defending their actions. When we surfaced, they attacked our mining machines, then us."

"So, you had time to begin mining on the Surface before you met them?" Girak asked.

"Yes. We were minding our own business and replenishing resources. Nothing that should have started a war."

Girak frowned. "That sort of thing started wars in the distant past."

"We didn't even know they existed. I mean, where did they come from? Just because humanity went underground for a few centuries doesn't mean they can claim the planet."

Maybe it's their planet as well. Kalakanya had been relieving Eka from shielding, but she now handed it over to Rana and stepped forward. *If it's also our planet, it may also be theirs.*

The Western Haveners bristled. But as usual, she walked toward the danger, not away from it. She could take care of herself, but did she always have to put herself in the middle of conflict? Every muscle in Bleu's body tightened like a spring ready to explode into action, but she stood, completely at ease, amidst their glares.

She glowed softly, but with the sparkling fire, it was probably missed by the new humans. *Many humans mistakenly believe they are owners of the planet, not guardians of it. And they're not the only guardians.*

"This planet wasn't vacated." Obi said. "It belongs to humans and native species of animals."

You went into your Havens as the ice age hit. The billions of humans left on the Surface had little food and had to fight over it. What do you think happened to them?

"They fought each other to death," Obi said, "or died in the cold."

Kalakanya gave a sad nod. *Yes, most of them did die. But a few banded together and tried something completely novel. They acted as one. And they survived. And evolved into us.*

Ferenk snorted in derision. "Nice try." He rolled his eyes. "Evolution can't occur that quickly."

Have you not noticed the animal species? The sea bears are much larger than the similar bears of the past. We, too, are taller. We have more rounded features, probably to prevent frostbite. But we still look quite human.

"And your powers?" he asked, his voice dripping sarcasm. "Those just conveniently appeared to save the day?"

Perhaps. She grinned. *Who knows how the One In All works? But humans with unusual gifts have always existed. To survive, the humans invested time in raising their consciousness to cultivate these gifts. They became normal, something passed on from Maha to child.*

"You're claiming you're the next step in evolution?" Ferenk asked, a dangerous edge creeping into his voice. "That humanity is outdated?"

Not at all. I'm stating simply that we're related and share the planet. I completely share your concern about these creatures' violence.

Ferenk opened his mouth to argue but then closed it. "You share our concern?"

Of course. I also am confused by these creatures' behavior. They cannot be star beings. We are never violent.

Ferenk laughed. "Just today your man there," he pointed to Kahali, "hit several of us with boulders."

I didn't witness that since I had been electrocuted by your men. She paused to let that sink in. *From what I understand, he swirled rocks in a circle to protect himself and Savas from being killed. Your men were injured by continuing to attack him.*

Ferenk uttered a begrudging grunt.

Surely you can see that there's a difference between creating a defensive wall of rocks to save lives versus attacking others to take lives? He was protecting Savas and himself.

"Yes. But I always put my own people's safety first. That's how we've survived this long."

Bleu tensed. Good to know that his first priority was Western Haven and not humanity.

Across the fire, Savas' narrowed gaze met Bleu's. Yup, Savas had caught that, too. Ferenk would do what he needed to protect his own. Maybe Northern Haven had been on to something when they designed the helicopters to require interaction with the pilot's implants to fly. Otherwise, they might wake up to two missing helicopters. Or never wake up at all.

He'd had his hands full trying to get Savas and Zach to accept the star beings, but what the *shast* was he supposed to do with these crude Western Haveners? They wouldn't hesitate to kill the star beings, and he wasn't so sure the Northern Haveners were safe, either. For now, Savas seemed to share his concerns, but trusting Savas was a leap of faith.

"We're not all as bad as you're making us out to be," Jeb added. "You don't survive by inviting everyone to tea and discussing it, because by then, you're dead." He laughed, holding up his steaming mug. "Not that I don't appreciate the tea."

Bleu tensed, ready to respond to the threat. He and Savas exchanged another glance.

"I'm assuming that's sarcasm?" Savas countered. He, like Bleu, looked ready to spring.

"What?" Jeb's smile tightened. "Of course." He awkwardly lowered his raised mug, sloshing tea all over himself in the process.

"Good." Savas smiled. "Because as I recall, we already passed your test."

If Bleu hadn't spent so much time studying Savas for danger signs, he would have missed the smile that came a bit too quick, the eyes tighter. His smiles always had a veiled quality, but this one was downright masked. His hand brushed something off the front of his parka and drifted down toward his sidearm.

"Was it really sarcasm?" Bleu whispered to Kalakanya.

Kalakanya didn't turn to acknowledge Bleu's question, but her gaze narrowed as it rested on Ferenk's men. *Yes. And no. I believe it's Jeb's way of warning you.*

Beside him, Kahali's grip on the drum had tightened until his knuckles were white. Had she sent that to all of their team, or had Kahali picked up the same warning?

Kalakanya faced Ferenk but addressed them all. *There are always options other than violence. One can be alert for potential danger and still be open to new experiences and people. Because some of the Northern Haveners were open to such experiences, they have now gained the star beings as allies. I would like to think that, someday, the same could be said for Western Haven. Until then, we will shield you and hope to gain your trust.*

Ferenk sniffed in disdain. "It's not my trust you need. You'll need to convince our Women's Counsel. And at this point, there's no way I'm taking you to them."

The women were in charge? How many other cultural differences had developed between the isolated Havens over the centuries? "But if you're not going to introduce us to them, how can we bring them on our helicopters to Northern Haven?" Bleu asked.

Ferenk narrowed his black eyes. "If they approve, you'll meet them."

The guy was impossible. "I thought we had an agreement that you were coming back with us. Are you allowed to make decisions or not?"

"I make decisions in the field."

"Since we've met, have you been in communication with the Women's Counsel?" Bleu pressed.

"I prefer to keep our procedures private, young man."

Young man? Bleu's blood boiled. Ferenk was probably over twice his age, but that didn't mean the jerk had to talk down to him. He took a deep, calming breath. "I simply want to know if I'm negotiating with the proper authority. Perhaps I should speak directly with your counsel?"

"Savas and I have already spoken. We are here tonight. I wanted to check your helicopters myself if I'm to propose to the Women's Council that we travel the world in them."

The world? They had only offered them a ride to Northern Haven. "I'm glad you and Savas have discussed this. But did Savas inform you that I have full authority here?"

"No, I didn't," Savas said.

Bleu's glare shifted from Ferenk to Savas. Savas was making his move now?

"I informed him that you are in charge of this particular mission," Savas said, "but that I am the lead commander of Northern Haven. Therefore, I'm the proper channel for overarching negotiations. Do you have full authority from Northern Haven, Bleu?"

Shast. Everyone knew he didn't. "I have full authority for this mission."

Bleu not only has full authority for this mission, but also speaks on behalf of the star beings. That was agreed to fully by Northern Haven, Kalakanya sent.

She was trying to help, but her assertion of his authority probably had the opposite effect with humans that mistook star beings for Ruined. He'd been almost holding his own up until now despite never having wanted to be named commander. Now, it shone clear that he was only an imposter propped up by the star beings.

He had to hold it together. "I have the authority to make decisions for this mission, which involves finding Western Haven and bringing people back. After we return, you can make further decisions with our Council."

He raised an eyebrow to Savas. "Or whoever the Northern Haven Prime Minister then grants authority to."

Savas smirked and gave him an acquiescing nod as if humoring a toddler.

Bleu wanted to both smack him and pull him aside to ask what he was playing at. Things were tense enough without this crap. They had been finally working together on the mountainside, both concerned about Ferenk's men, and now the jerk was attempting mutiny? He'd always known Savas would mess with him, but the betrayal still tasted bitter.

Ferenk sighed and waved dismissively at Bleu. "Whatever."

As if it could be decided later. But if Bleu were taking Ferenk's people back to Northern Haven, he'd expect some help in whatever lay in wait near Western Haven. He wasn't foregoing that part of the mission. Yes, they'd found people from Western Haven, but more survivors could be waiting for a miracle to save them from the Ruined. Their helicopters could be that miracle.

"This decision can't wait. We're still going to Western Haven to check for other survivors. Who among you will assist us?"

"Have you heard nothing I've said?" Ferenk shouted. "That would be suicide. The Ruined control that whole part of the continent."

Control? Kalakanya asked.

Ferenk furrowed his brow. "Yes. If we return, they'll kill us. Our only means of surviving has been to outrun them."

But why would they need that huge an area? Are there that many of them?

How odd the idea of owning a territory must seem to star beings. "I think he means they see it as their own land," Bleu explained. "They don't want humans around."

Beside him, Kahali chuckled. *Makes sense to me.*

"Stop it," Bleu hissed, amused despite himself. "I hope no one else heard that."

Kahali bit back a guilty grin.

"They want us extinct," Ferenk said. "They'll chase us to the ends of the Earth. I'm not willing to risk any men on your wild goose chase."

Ferenk's men murmured agreement.

"But surely there are other Western Haveners that survived?" Girak asked. "This can't be all? In the chaos of being attacked, isn't it possible that people got split up? Ran in different directions? We should find them as well."

The Western Haveners withered at his words. Some stared at the ground, others shifted uncomfortably. No one replied.

"I didn't mean that as an insult," Girak clarified. "It's just...well..." He furrowed his brow. "We had hoped you had fared better than us and that there would be thousands of you."

"Not anymore," Obi responded sadly.

Neviah, sitting beside Obi, reached over and squeezed his hand.

Ferenk nodded with a distant look in his eyes. A heavy silence fell over all of them.

The fire snapped and popped, and Ferenk seemed to rouse himself from the smothering loss of their haven. He turned toward the grizzled, older man with unexpected tenderness, "Jeb, would you honor us with your telling?"

Jeb gave a solemn nod, rose, and strode closer to the center of the circle. His gaze met Girak's. "Your question isn't an insult. It just reminds us of how lethal our enemy is." He let out a slow sigh. "I believe I'm the last human alive that was born in Western Haven. My family lived there until I was seven. When we first fled—"

"Hold on," Zach interrupted. "Why did you leave? The Havens were designed to be impenetrable."

"Yes. Impenetrable to Undescended human terrorists. But our early expeditions unknowingly brought back Ruined. At first, we found 'em and eliminated 'em. But as our knowledge of 'em increased, so did their knowledge of us. They became better at impersonating human looks and speech patterns.

"We were trapped below with imposter creatures that hunted us in our sleep. When they learned of our ventilation shafts that came down from the Surface, we were done for. They could enter at will, and we had no way to tell 'em from us."

Bleu shivered. His father was the engineer tasked with maintaining the ventilation shafts.

"Rather than being trapped in tunnels and slaughtered, we left in vehicles with weapons, scanners, lab equipment, food, and radios. We hoped they saw it as a territorial dispute, and that if we left, they'd be satisfied and leave us in peace. But up on the Surface in this constant cold with limited resources, our tech didn't last. In the first year, every single vehicle died. If we wanted to save anything, we had to carry it and stay ahead of 'em.

"The Ruined didn't care that we left the area. They tracked us. They somehow sensed our main camps as if drawn by our scent. I've seen 'em scent the air like wolves, but most of our scientists believe they sensed us another way, like through mind reading." He shrugged. "We dissected a few but never figured out how they ticked. We only learned that when they are unconscious or dead, they always return to their true form." He motioned toward the star beings. "They look like you all."

He held up his hands as if to ward off their argument. "I'm not saying you *are* the same. But you sure do look alike." He gave them an apologetic smile. "Sometimes, they fade into the forest, but no one has ever actually seen them shift into anything that's not an animal." He shuddered.

"Over the years, we figured out they could find our largest camps easier than our smaller ones. We split into smaller groups. My father coordinated our group's communication with the other groups. For a few years, that seemed to work.

"Then, they wiped out a group of sixty by imitating hunters returning with game. Even the hunters' family members didn't realize the ruse until it was too late. They killed everyone, including the kids." He shook his head in horror.

"We later discovered that when they are mimicking specific humans, they sometimes keep the humans they are mimicking alive. We think they do this to tap into their memories and better mimic their captive. That's probably how they acted so much like hunters to trick their loved ones. That's when we realized we had to use electric shocks to protect ourselves. We were desperate, willing to do anything to survive." Jeb rubbed his gray-bearded chin until his palm absently settled over his mouth, as if to stop his own words. He stared into the fire.

Bleu sat frozen in horror, imagining the nightmare of fleeing his home to be hunted down by terrifying shapeshifting creatures.

"When I was nineteen"—his voice quavered—"I found my dad sitting under a tree, hugging our radio and sobbing. The last of the other groups had been ambushed. He'd waited all night for an update. We never heard from them again." He sighed and pulled off his pack, tapping it with love. "I still carry that radio. I never heard a thing on it until you all showed up."

As if to underscore the daily terror of their existence, a throaty scream vibrated the hillside around them. Bleu flinched and stared at the barely visible shield, the only thing keeping them safe.

The shield will hold, Kalakanya reassured them. *I now understand why you are so fearful of us, but star beings would never behave like these creatures. And I'm terribly sorry for all the lives you have lost.*

Bleu had no words. What did one say after that? Sorry seemed trite. But he had to say something. "I'm glad you no longer face them alone. We'll all go back to Northern Haven, where you can live in safety."

They stared back with skeptical expressions as if they no longer believed in safety. Another howl flooded the camp. Was it possible the Ruined were listening and timing their horrifying sounds for the most dramatic effect? They must understand Standard if they could impersonate Western Haveners.

Bleu shivered again. He knew what he had to do. What he had to say. But, really, he wanted to flee this haunted wood. How had these men lived their whole lives with the Ruined hunting them? And without shields? How had they ever slept? "We have plenty of room for all of you. But first, I still want to fly over Western Haven and search for others."

Ferenk scoffed.

"Don't go," Obi begged. "It's not worth it."

"You realize you'd never be able to tell from the air if you were landing near survivors or Ruined, right?" Jeb asked. "My father was sure any survivors would have contacted us over the radio. They're all dead."

Bleu was treading on shaky ground. He needed Jeb's help, and insulting his father's conclusions wouldn't get him that help. "What if the radios were destroyed but the people survived? I couldn't live with myself if we didn't at least try."

Jeb gave him a forlorn look. "Even if it broke, they would have made another. Do you think we didn't try every possible way to contact 'em?"

"Sorry. That didn't come out right. I don't mean you gave up too easily. I just mean..." *Shast. Had* he meant they had given up too easily?

No. They'd been through hell. Bleu sighed in frustration and looked out across the field. The far helicopter's silhouette stood black against the starry night. "What I meant is, we have helicopters and advanced warning. We have your experience if you'll help us. And if no survivors exist, we might at least find the research equipment you or the other teams lost. We might be able to salvage something valuable."

"Like I said before, you're the stupidest, strangest team I've ever met," Ferenk said. "Either way, I'm not sending any of my men."

"I wouldn't want you to order anyone." Bleu said. "But we're going in two days, with or without you. I'm asking for volunteers."

He looked around the circle of men, attempting eye contact, but they all looked away. So much for the friendly request. "Remember, we'll need to survive and successfully return if we are going to fly you to Northern Haven."

Ferenk muttered something under his breath. It jogged Bleu's memory of Jeb's cryptic warning. Bleu had to make it clear that they needed each other.

"I can understand how desperate you all are to survive, so I want to make something clear. Our helicopters were engineered so that they can only be flown by us." He purposely left out the details. No need giving them info they might use against him. "We leave in two days. We have food and extra weapons for any who join us. Let's teach these Ruined what humanity is capable of."

Ferenk's men studied him and the star beings with new interest.

Men muttered, "Maybe we should..."

"There's nowhere else for us to run..."

He'd never considered himself much of a public speaker, but somehow he'd gotten the Western Haveners to consider going with them. Grinning to himself, he turned back to his star being friends. They too were looking at him differently. And not in a good way.

"Wow," Kahali exclaimed, his disgust clear.

Bleu stiffened. What had he done?

Kahali narrowed his gaze to glare at him. *Teach the Ruined what humanity is capable of? Nice.*

Kahali snorted and struggled to his feet, turning his back to Bleu. With Rana's help, he clambered back on board the helicopter.

Bleu watched them, shocked by their rejection. He'd been trying to help everyone stay safe. Even when Kahali and Rana were out of sight and probably back in their room, the sting of Kahali's anger still vibrated through him. The gathering had broken into small groups discussing the return to Western Haven. Bleu searched for Kalakanya, hoping she had understood what he had really meant.

She and Eka stood together near the nose of the helicopter, motioning at the shield. Their turned backs and urgent whispers made Bleu's stomach flip-flop. Was she avoiding him? All he'd done was say humans should stand up for themselves. Did they really think it was okay to allow themselves to be slaughtered and do nothing?

"Nice speech." Savas walked by and patted his arm. "Didn't think you had it in you." He stopped and snickered at where Kalakanya and Eka still whispered. "Looks like you're not getting any tonight."

Bleu dropped his jaw in incredulity. "Is that all you think of?"

Savas grinned. "Much more fun than those nasty morning chants she drags you off to."

Bleu sighed. "I have to go talk to them."

"Her. You have to talk to her." Savas shook his head. "Have fun with that." Sniggering, he sauntered off toward the far helicopter.

Bleu stood there, adrift, while everyone passed him to re-enter the helicopter and get some sleep.

As Girak passed by, he whispered, "Fix that." He nodded toward Kalakanya. But if his past educator had any lessons on how, he wasn't sharing.

Great. He'd impressed the Western Haveners and pissed off the star beings. And he wasn't even convinced he was wrong. They would have to stop the Ruined or share Western Haven's fate.

Chapter 59

Campsite, Eastern Coast of North America:
Commander Savas

Savas stood up from the meeting, grinning to himself. What a day. He'd found Western Haveners, connected with their leader, survived an attack by the Ruined, and watched Bleu piss off Kalakanya and probably lose the star beings' support. He didn't even have to undermine Bleu because the kid had done it all on his own. And if Savas was correct about the righteous star beings, they would still shield them simply because it was the *right thing to do.*

As he headed toward the helicopter, someone tapped his back. He turned.

Atsushi gave him a pained look. "Sorry, but can you come here?" He motioned to the edge of the helicopter, still within Eka's shield. Savas shrugged and followed him.

When they had moved beyond the line waiting to board the helicopter, Atsushi leaned forward. "Sir, I know I'm only fifteen, but..." He glanced toward the others and fiddled with his coat's zipper.

"Never apologize for yourself, Atsushi. What's going on? Ready to learn more about the gun? I see the extra one I got for you is in your pocket, right?"

Atsushi patted his pocket as he looked down and nodded, keeping his gaze on the ground. "It's not that. It's the new people."

"Oh?"

Atsushi looked up. "Can I say something that might get you angry?"

"I suppose." He grinned at him, amused at the unlikely idea of Atsushi pissing him off. He only got angry when Atsushi listened to Girak, and that oaf was nowhere in sight.

"I know you probably are still mad at how I lied to you to rescue Rana from the lab, but I was trying to prevent a war that might have gotten us all killed. And I know I probably seemed too willing to stay on the Surface, and I know my parents were probably upset that all I wanted from home was my music and research on Japan. But I also hope you know that no matter what I do, I still consider myself a Northern Havener." Having finished his confession, or whatever it was, Atsushi gasped for breath.

"I would hope so, because you are a Northern Havener." Savas furrowed his brow. "What is this about?"

Atsushi glanced over Savas' shoulder at the crowd again. "I can be Japanese and also be a Northern Havener, right?"

"Atsushi, are you trying to keep me talking over here so I miss something Bleu is up to? Of course, you can be both things. What's your point?"

Atsushi glared at him. "I'm trying to help you."

"Me? How?" Savas snapped. "Your personal identity is not my main concern. Not with the Ruined howling around us."

Atsushi groaned in exasperation. "Everyone is so excited to find the new humans. I mean, I am, too, but they're kind of jerks. I think we need to consider Northern Haven's safety. Just because they're human and from a SHAST Haven doesn't mean they're good. I don't trust Ferenk. He's horrid to the star beings, and well, I just think you need to be careful."

Savas stepped back. "You're worried about me?"

"Yes."

"You're adorable." Savas laughed and ruffled Atsushi's hair. "I'm quite capable of taking care of myself."

Atsushi stepped back and gaped at him. "I'm not being cute. Northern Haven is depending on us. We don't owe these others anything. I want to help them, but in less than twenty-four hours they've shot us and made us new enemies."

"I'm not going to put Northern Haven at risk." Wait, was he? His training was humanity first. Always, with no personal ties. Had he gotten so swept up in his success of finding other humans that he had neglected his allegiance to Northern Haven? If Ferenk tried to steal the helicopters, he could end up destroying valuable lives and equipment that Northern Haven couldn't survive without. He touched his chest where his mother's compass lay hidden. His secret oath was to SHAST to protect humanity. What did that mean for Northern Haven now that he'd found other humans? The kid had a point. "I'll keep what you said in mind. Sorry I got angry."

Atsushi widened his eyes, then gave a tense smile. "Okay, thanks." He hurried away.

With his intelligence and respect for authority, that teen would make an amazing soldier one day. Savas just needed to convince him to ditch Kahali and learn from him instead. Kahali's ridiculous protective chanting lessons wasted time Atsushi could be learning real skills. Snorting to himself, Savas remembered he still needed to attend to one more thing before he could rest.

As a Ruined roared from somewhere way too close, Savas checked the presence of Eka's shield and strolled to the helicopter.

"Ferenk," he called to the man who had just climbed up onto the helicopter, "can I have a word with you?" Savas jogged up the steps and waited in the open door.

Ferenk finished whatever he was saying in hushed tones to Miguel and Cheeks and turned back to him. "Of course." Ferenk narrowed his gaze out the helicopter door at something in the distance. "Your star being friends seem annoyed. Think they'll betray us tonight?"

"No, I meant it when I said they're not like those monstrous Ruined. I'm not sure what they're gaining by helping us, but they really can't tolerate violence."

Ferenk scowled.

He sighed and held up his hands. "I know it doesn't make sense, but traveling with them has been quite the experience." He snickered. "Kalakanya once told me I should get the *permission* of animals to hunt them. Can you imagine?" Savas laughed and stepped out of the way between two seats as Zach showed the Western Haveners how to convert the nearby chairs to beds.

"Could be an act," Ferenk said. "If the Ruined can imitate humans and live among us, maybe this is their way of tricking you. I still don't like it."

Ferenk sniffed and glanced outside at Eka's thin shield that domed the campsite. "Then again, if the star beings are different, we need to keep them on our side. They seem to want to talk to the Ruined. If they form an alliance with them, our people are done for."

"Hmm." Savas had already thought of that, which was why he'd told Bleu to talk to Kalakanya. He wanted the star beings on Northern Haven's side. For whatever crazy reason, they usually approved of that naïve eighteen-year-old.

Savas stepped backward, and one of Ferenk's men bumped him with their elbow while shifting packs to other seats—the excuse he'd hoped to create. "It's too crowded to talk here."

He motioned for Ferenk to follow him and led the way to a small, unoccupied room where they stored their provisions. As soon as Ferenk entered, he shut the door behind them.

"Now we can talk." Savas lowered his voice. "I noticed our star beings didn't seem to pick up your presence when you were hiding. Do you have tech to block that sort of thing?"

Ferenk grinned and patted his chest. "Yes. You?"

Savas raised his wrist. "You got yours activated?"

"I do. It's always activated. When it was clear I needed to speak to them, I switched it to the level where they can understand what we're saying, but still not read our thoughts."

"Hmm, impressive." He tilted his head. "Why did you make levels?"

"There's stealth mode, which we used when your allies couldn't sense us stalking you. And then there's the mode we developed for when we capture and question them. They need to understand us then."

Interesting. Their tech for this sort of thing went beyond Northern Haven's. It made sense, since they had known about the Ruined way longer than Northern Haven had known about the star beings, but he'd need to watch for how advanced they were in other ways. Savas snorted. "So, for the last few hours you've all been in torture mode?"

Ferenk smiled. "Basically, yes."

"Whatever works. We should still whisper because, from my tests, their hearing is better than ours. They've also started to learn Standard."

"I noticed," Ferenk said, frowning. "I'm glad you've got enough sense to still take precautions."

"I do. Unfortunately, Bleu doesn't. So, what we say here is between us, got it?"

Ferenk nodded and scratched his beard. "He's too smitten to think straight about them. How old is he?"

"Eighteen."

Ferenk scoffed and shook his head. "Barely out of his diapers."

Savas chuckled. "He is smart, though, and good with a gun. Don't underestimate him."

"Noted. Look, I've dealt with the Ruined all my life. Going back to Western Haven is beyond daft. You need to convince him to change his mind."

Savas just stared at him. He wanted Ferenk a bit unnerved but wasn't sure what it took to unnerve someone who lived with Ruined hunting him daily.

Ferenk ignored his stare as he settled onto a crate of dried goods, drew his knife, and began sharpening it with a tool from his hip pack. "I'm not risking my men's lives. What if he takes back a few of your people in one helicopter and the rest of us leave in the other?"

That was what he was waiting for. To see how long it took him to bring up the helicopters. He liked Ferenk, but the guy was so damn stuck on only thinking about his own people that he forgot about humanity as a whole. Everyone always did.

That's why SHAST had created protectors like his mother. Like him.

Atsushi had no idea how correct he had been. This was going to be a fine line to walk. Savas needed to save the remaining Western Haveners, keep the shaky alliance with the star beings, and figure out how to protect Northern Haven from the Ruined. The Ruined could blow all SHAST's planning to pieces. Humanity could be wiped from the Surface.

"Bleu told you our helicopters won't work for you. He told the truth. I appreciate your survival instincts, Ferenk, but you can't steal them."

Ferenk continued sharpening his knife. "Didn't say I was going to."

"I don't need to be a star being to know that's probably the first thing you thought of." Savas kept up his stare, impressed that Ferenk couldn't care less.

Ferenk chuckled and shook his finger at him. "I knew I liked you. That's the kind of thinking that might save Northern Haven. But you don't know the Ruined like I do. Going back there is suicide."

"Possibly."

Savas watched Ferenk closely. He may have already set things in motion for his men to try something tonight. Maybe they'd try to kill a few team members in hopes of scaring Neviah and him into flying the helicopters for them? They were clearly more trained and better at hand-to-hand combat that his own team. They didn't stand a chance if Ferenk turned on them.

Savas suspected that the confirmation about the helicopters might make Ferenk abort any plans to overthrow them. What other tech could Ferenk have to communicate with his team?

"I'm not going to die on an impossible mission that won't benefit my people," Ferenk said. He slid his hand into his pocket, and Savas assumed he might be signaling his men to stand down. The guy was too smart to shoot one of the only two pilots. "Why did you really come looking for us? What is it *you* need?"

SHAST protocol had always assumed the four Havens would eventually come together and rebuild on the Surface, so he'd been able to avoid this conversation earlier. He didn't want to mention the Sickness or how few of them were left, just in case Ferenk was planning something.

"Despite our best planning, we have developed too limited a gene pool. We were hoping to recruit some new residents. We also wanted to check on the other Havens since we'd lost contact with them. Do you know if any others survived?" Did they know about Eastern Haven?

"We heard Eastern Haven had problems, but that's all. I suspect we were a bit *preoccupied* to concern ourselves with the other Havens."

Ferenk's wording left too much to interpretation, but for tonight, Savas had to ensure the Western Haveners wouldn't attack. He'd solve the mysteries later. "We need to start thinking like one group of humans, not two groups fighting over resources. Your people have suffered too much. I want to get all of you to safety."

Ferenk sighed. "I've learned there's no such thing as safety. There's just living as long as you can."

"Stay hopelessly hopeful until you draw your last breath." *Damn.* That phrase, famously his mother's, had popped out. If anyone his age or older had heard that, they'd know he remembered her. Thank goodness Ferenk wasn't from Northern Haven.

To collect himself, Savas turned and found a seat across from Ferenk on the crates that secretly stashed their weapons. Guns calmed him.

Ferenk shook his head. "That works from the safety of an undiscovered Haven. None of us ever had the luxury of being hopelessly hopeful."

At his last two words, Savas' breath froze. Ferenk had repeated the phrase. Not a problem here, but if he returned to Northern Haven and said it, the ones who'd killed his mother would know Savas remembered. No one else on the expedition was old enough to have known his mother's famous phrase before she was erased. "I can't imagine the horrors you've all lived through. Hopefully, our combined resources and information will eradicate these Ruined."

Ferenk gave a noncommittal nod.

Damn. What would it take to get the guy's full commitment? Why wasn't the SHAST connection enough? He needed more information on the Western Haveners' beliefs. "How do your people feel about SHAST? Do they blame SHAST for leaving billions to die unprotected in the new ice age, or are they grateful that they got the world to cooperate for human survival?"

His mother had died when Northern Haven zealots had turned the populace against its founders. They had ferreted out and murdered her and the other last SHAST protector, positions so secret that, to this day, he didn't know who the other one was.

No one talked about what happened, and he had been only seven when they busted into his module. And after the mind control they did on him before declaring him deprogrammed and safe, he certainly wasn't going to risk asking around.

But SHAST had protectors in every Haven. Maybe he wasn't the last. "Do they blame SHAST?"

"Why would we blame SHAST? They did everything in their power to set us up for success."

Savas nodded and tried to hide his relief. "Agreed, though people in Northern Haven feel guilty about those left to die on the Surface. Instead of accepting their own survivor guilt, they blame SHAST. SHAST has become a curse word."

"Really?" Ferenk raised his eyebrows in surprise. "That's fascinating. They saved as many as they could."

Savas nodded and bit back the risky questions he yearned to ask regarding whether or not any SHAST agents from Western Haven had survived. It would be such a relief to not be the last one. Especially now that his safety depended on Luminary Vadin keeping his secret to himself.

SHAST had done what they could, and he'd tried to do what he could. If only he hadn't shot at Kalakanya that day, Stamf may have lived. Stamf should have received all of Savas' knowledge, but now, unless he had another suitable child, the SHAST protectorate would end with him. The memory of Stamf's crumpled body at the bottom of the cliff sucker punched him. He shoved it away and cleared his throat.

"Yes, SHAST saved as many as they could. And now it's down to guys like us," Savas said, filling the eerie silence.

Ferenk had stopped sharpening his blade to stare at him. After nearly a minute of silence, Ferenk sat back. "I won't steal your helicopters, Savas. I don't want war with the first humans we've found. It's far from my top concern, but I'd like our people to get along. After living on the run for so long, we've become a bit rough around the edges." Ferenk chuckled and rubbed his bristled chin. "Hell, with a shave and shower, my wife wouldn't recognize me."

Savas gave a dry chuckle. He could work with that. "We have lots of empty modules with showers big enough for you both to shower at the same time."

Ferenk smirked suggestively. "Ooh, *that* would be heaven."

Savas chuckled. Good. The helicopters were safe for tonight. Now back to his plan to secure their assistance. "In your travels across North America, did you ever find any Undescended survivors?"

"No, but without our tech, I doubt they would have survived against the Ruined."

"Right." He paused, hoping the risk he was about to take had the payoff he expected. "We were never attacked by the Undescended or Ruined, and our ancestors became sloppy about maintaining our arsenal of weapons." He wasn't about to admit Kalakanya had destroyed the last of them. "If the Ruined find us, we are not prepared."

He was also not going to admit that if he'd successfully blown up the star beings' village, his team likely would have all died today at the hands of the Ruined.

"It will still be safer than being endlessly pursued and hunted down here, though I need the Women's Council to agree. However, if your defenses are weak..." Ferenk chewed on his lip, deep in thought. "Argh. Maybe there is a reason for returning to Western Haven." He sighed with resignation and nodded as if convincing himself.

Savas waited, his victory within sight.

Ferenk looked Savas in the eye. "I *really* don't want to go back there. You have no idea what we'll be getting ourselves into."

"But?" Savas encouraged.

Ferenk's shoulders sagged. "We did a lot of research on the Ruined. When we left Western Haven, we brought what we thought would be most helpful, but there might be something of use left. You know, stuff that we couldn't develop without our full labs."

Now they were getting somewhere. These were the moments he lived for. "This is why I brought you back here," Savas said, motioning to the isolated room. He rose and sat closer to Ferenk so his next words could be barely audible. "Talk to me. Let's make a plan to protect all the humans..."

Chapter 60

***Campsite, Eastern Coast of North America: Bleu
Reinier***

Bleu was the only human to remain outside the helicopter. Kalakanya and Eka continued to ignore him while they spoke in their lyrical language. He shifted from foot to foot in the cold, waiting for them to finish, and then settled onto the rock by the fire.

Finally, Kalakanya said something to Eka that he thought meant goodnight in her native tongue and turned in Bleu's direction.

She was hesitating. *Shast*, she didn't even want to speak to him?

Bleu rose, heart racing. "Can we talk?"

She narrowed her eyes, not in anger but as if seeing him caused her pain.

A dull ache formed in his solar plexus. It grew, becoming a tearing sensation. "Please?"

I don't know. Can we? You seem pretty decided about what must be done. She sounded broken. Far away.

"I'm sorry. I'm not good at leading. I never wanted this."

Don't you dare blame us for supporting your leadership. This is about what you said. You chose those words.

He nodded. "Yes. I did."

He paused, staring at his feet. "I don't know how to fight—I mean, how to *defend*—against such powerful creatures." His gaze met hers. "I can't even *imagine* how we can get through this without violence." Frowning, he said, "I guess that makes me a failure at this"—he motioned between them—"before it even gets started."

Her cold gaze cut right through him. That day by the lake, Kahali had warned that Crowned Ones were not to be messed with. But as hopeless as it felt, he couldn't give up. He had to keep everyone alive—with violence if necessary—but he also couldn't lose Kalakanya.

Unless he already had.

He waited in desperation for some sign that she hadn't already rejected him. That she wouldn't find his inability to lead in a nonviolent manner disappointing. That his humanness wasn't disappointing.

She remained silent, watching him. What was she expecting? He'd been totally honest about what a failure he felt like.

A half-smile formed on her lips. *Okay, Failure. Apparently, we need to work on your imagination. You need to nurture your imagination to see the nonviolent possibilities.*

He grinned, relief rushing through his weary limbs. "Fine. I'm completely open to any imagination boosts you can give me."

Not me, it's your imagination. Start with this. She grinned. *What if the Ruined aren't the enemy?*

His grin evaporated. "They dismembered Ferenk's men with their bare hands."

Her face wrinkled in distaste. *Right. But what if the real danger is your fear of them? Think about it. They haven't killed any of our team yet. Have you noticed? It's almost like they only go after Ferenk's men. The one you saw in the woods could have killed both of us, but it didn't. Why not?*

"I have no idea. It might have, though, if Eka hadn't shown up and shielded us."

Then that's where you start. Figure it out. Because when the giant eagle grabbed Kahali, it could have shredded him, but it didn't. Something else is going on.

Bleu gaped in disbelief. "So, you don't think they're a danger?"

Oh, they're extremely dangerous. They're full of hatred and revulsion, two of the most dangerous emotions in the universe.

Bleu laughed. "You say that like you've travelled the galaxy."

No, not me, but the other Crowned Ones. They can star beam to other places.

"You're joking, right?"

No.

His mind spun. "They've met aliens. For real?" He laughed. It was so unreal.

But she looked anything but amused. *I've asked them not to tell me much, and I avoid going myself.*

"Why? It sounds amazing."

Every place has its issues. Her shoulders sagged, and she plopped down beside him on the boulder, so close that their shoulders touched.

"This has to do with you seeing time threads, doesn't it?"

She looked up, her jade eyes regarding him with surprised wonder. *Yes. It's hard enough choosing the best option when I'm taking into consideration the star beings, the planet, and all its plants and furred ones. Now, I've also got to consider the humans and the Ruined. Can you imagine if I started adding in the rest of the universe?*

"Sounds like enough responsibility to make your head explode."

She laughed into his shoulder. *Exactly.* She sighed and grew quiet. *Anyway, my point is, the Ruined are extremely dangerous. If we go to Western Haven, we may lose as many as half of us.*

"Half?" He jumped up. "No way." He began pacing back and forth in front of the rock. "Forget it. We're not going."

Some possibilities show half of us dying. Some show both you and me dying. She gave him a pained look. *The threads are an utter mess from this point on. I've never seen anything like it. Threads appear out of nowhere. They fray. Or there's knots. It's like nothing I've ever dealt with before.*

But despite the danger, we need to discover the truth about the Ruined. Because if they chased these Western Haveners across the continent, I'm guessing they could make boats and reach Northern Haven and our villages.

A shiver coursed down Bleu's spine. He'd had the same thought, but hearing her verbalize it shifted the horror from the realm of nightmares into reality. He tried to speak, but the words caught in his throat.

He swallowed his fear and managed a whispered, "Am I making a mistake to take us there? I don't know how I'd live with losing people."

She shook her head. *I think it'd be a mistake not to go, because we will need to deal with them sooner or later. This way, I see threads that allow us to make valuable connections with information and possibly even with them. But it may be a hard decision to live with because every thread I've found has deaths involved. I know how hard it is to choose for others. I had hoped you would not face this sort of dilemma when we asked you to lead.*

As he paced past her, she grabbed his hand and gently pulled him to her. Her jade eyes, full of infinite sadness, met his. *As bad as the odds are, all the threads for not going are worse in the long run. Now that they know Northern Haven exists, I don't think they'll stop looking for us.* She bit her lip. *Also, if people die, I hope you won't blame me.*

"I would never do that." He stepped closer until their faces were nearly touching and squeezed her hands back in reassurance. "But it sounds like horrible odds."

"Bleu, I need to be clear. Not all of us are coming back." A tear slid down her cheek.

He raised his palm to cup her cheek, and his thumb gently brushed the tear away. If only he could send her comfort like she always did for others. "Then we need other options."

She nodded, remaining silent.

He'd never seen her this upset. It undid him. Gently, he brushed his lips against her forehead and then met her gaze. "Would you like company while you shield? I'm wide awake, and maybe if we sit here long enough, a solution will come to one of us."

She gave him a sad smile. *That would be nice.*

He sat back down beside her and slid his arm around her shoulders.

She nestled closer. *I've already checked every time thread I can think of.* She gazed thoughtfully at the dome of stars above them. *Maybe you can help me?*

The idea of him somehow helping her seemed both ridiculous and the most wonderful thing he'd heard. "Okay. How does it work? What can I do?"

She gave a sad laugh. *I don't know, really. No one has ever helped me before. Maybe you can use that unique human brain of yours and see if you can think of any possibilities I haven't run through?*

No one had ever helped her before? His heart warmed at her allowing him into her world like that. "Well, according to Ayanna, my brain is too wildly imaginative and dreamy. We might be here a while."

She chuckled. *I'm good with that.*

"I always thought you magically asked a question and then picked the right answer from the threads—like a multiple-choice test. But if creativity is involved, I'm guessing it's not like that?"

She furrowed her brow. *A multiple choice test?*

He explained, and she gave a soft laugh. *I wish. Every small decision we make has repercussions and creates branches of possibilities. I could never read every one of those.*

Instead, I look at the major decision points and keep the successful outcomes to follow to the next set of major decision points. I can see the threads if I look for them, but I need to know what to check. That's where creativity helps. The more I check, the more accurate the picture.

Bleu stared at her, shocked. Her mind ran a computer program from hell to figure it all out. "I had no idea it was that complicated."

She grimaced. *Complicated is a good word. Are you still willing to help, or is it too much?*

Bleu grinned. "You can't scare me off that easily. What possibilities have you already run?"

She explained to him what she'd already considered. They sat on the boulder for hours, brainstorming possible threads and clinging to each other's warmth as throaty growls and screeches echoed around them. They stopped only when Eka needed her to take the shield so he could sleep. However, they came up with no plan that was fool safe.

Hours later, as Bleu climbed into the helicopter and tumbled onto a cot, his last thoughts centered around the deaths that would result from his decision. He'd already lost so many friends up here. The possibility of more deaths haunted the corridors of his dreams and tasted bitter on his tongue as he awoke.

He'd led the team in finding humans, but they'd also found new enemies. And in a few days' time, he'd lead them to Western Haven, where some of them would die.

The Adventure Continues...

If you enjoyed The Chasm, please leave a review on Goodreads or wherever you purchased the book. Reviews help us authors find new readers and pay our bills. Thanks!

The adventure continues in The Ruined, Book 3.0 of the Finding Humanity series. Coming soon!

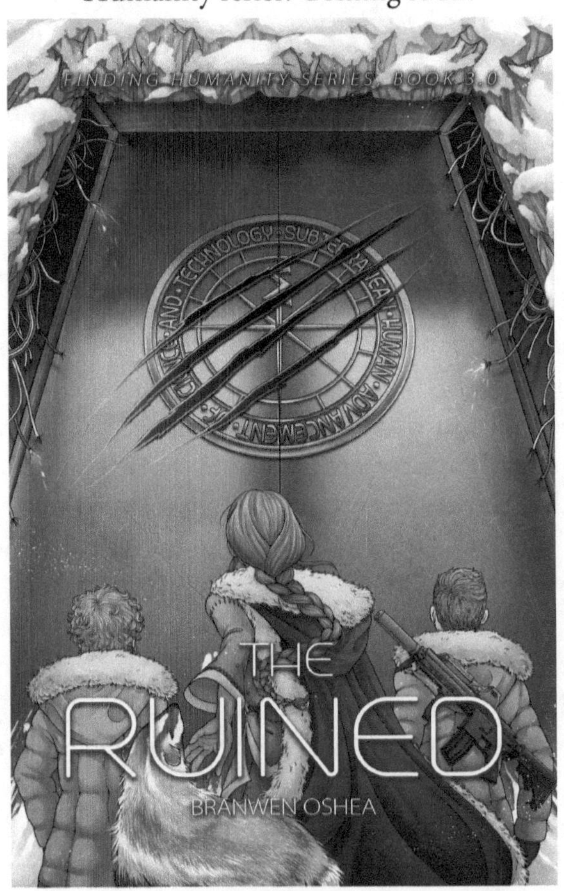

Also By Branwen OShea

Finding Humanity Series:
The Calling, Book 1.0
The Cords That Bind, Book 1.1
The Chasm, Book 2.0
The Ruined, Book 3.0 (Coming Soon)

Other Books:
Silence of the Song Trees

Acknowledgments

Just as characters need their friends to finish the mission, authors rely on many others to create their books. This is my clumsy but heartfelt ode to all those who have, over the last seven years, helped me produce the book you now hold in your hands.

First and foremost, I must thank my lovely co-conspirators— my children, Nur and Samina—who have known these characters most of their lives and shared in their adventures. Nur reads every version, always makes me laugh, gives excellent world-building feedback, and has written me a short symphony inspired by the books. Samina shares her excellent insight into each character, often draws them for me, and cracks me up with her theoretical 'shippings' of various characters (such as, Atsushi and Kahali, lol.) While I wrote the words, this book has both of you two in it, and it would be very different without your support and assistance.

Another special shoutout to my beta readers, Jean, Lisa, Emily, and Dawn. You've listened to and read the earliest versions and your feedback, enthusiasm, and support are priceless.

I also want to thank my amazing editors Teresa, Trish, and Ioanna. Your patience, expertise, and friendship is deeply appreciated.

The amazing cover on The Chasm was drawn and designed by Rai Fiondella, who once again exceeded my expectations. They also drew Savas' compass, the series logo, capturing all the symbolism it needed, and patiently shift the needle when needed. Without their artistic support, I'd be lost.

A special shoutout to my friends Jean and Lisa who both go above and beyond in their support of me and my writing. I don't know what I'd do without you two.

A big thanks to my writing group: Rebecca, Niamh, Tyler and Sabrina. You all are amazing and bring such joy to this process.

This book needed a lot of sensitivity readers. Though I'm not supposed to mention you by name, you know who you are and I thank you from the bottom of my heart for your feedback.

Gratitude to the furred ones who are my constant writing companions, and to all my amazing online writer friends, especially the writing community on Twitter. Your constant support, humor and advice is truly appreciated.

And finally, a huge thank you to all you readers who take the time to get to know Rana, Bleu, Atsushi, Kahali, and Savas. Without you, writing wouldn't be nearly as much fun. I truly appreciate you and your emails and reviews. Thank you.

About the Author

As a young girl, Branwen wanted to become an ambassador for aliens. Since the aliens never hired her, she now writes about them.

Branwen OShea has a Bachelors in Biology from Colgate University, a Bachelors in Psychology, and a Masters in Social Work. She lives in Connecticut with her family and a menagerie of pets, and enjoys hiking, meditating, and star-gazing. Her published works include Silence of the Song Trees, The Calling, The Cords That Bind, and The Chasm.

You can connect with me on:
https://www.branwenoshea.com
https://twitter.com/branwenoshea
https://www.facebook.com/branwenoshea
https://www.instagram.com/branwenoshea